BROKEN
Perfect
LIES

KATIE WISMER

for the kids who sang into hairbrushes in their bedrooms

ALSO BY KATIE WISMER

SIGN UP FOR MY AUTHOR NEWSLETTER

Sign up for Katie Wismer's newsletter to receive exclusive content and be the first to learn about new releases, book sales, events, and other news! Signed books can also be found on her website.

www.katiewismer.com

PLAYLIST

Listen on Spotify: shorturl.at/dxP34

Lowkey As Hell — Waterparks
oops! — Yung Gravy
acting like that —YUNGBLUD, Machine Gun Kelly
High — Miley Cyrus
long story short — Taylor Swift
Dress — Charlotte Sands
i think too much — Christian French
Are We a Thing — Leidi
Pretty Great — Fickle Friends
nevermind — Valley
decide to be happy — MisterWives
you should probably just hang up — Nightly
I Don't Miss You at All — FINNEAS
Karma — MOD SUN
Let's Fall in Love for the Night — FINNEAS
Roses — The Band CAMINO
Infinitely Ordinary — The Wrecks
parking lot view — almost monday
sucks to see you doing better — Valley
Talk to Me — Phoebe Ryan
Slow Dancing — Aly & AJ
Gone — Blake Rose
going out — ROLE MODEL
Pretty Lips — WINEHOUSE
The Ice is Getting Thinner — Death Cab for Cutie

Strawberry Sunscreen — Lostboycrow

Baby Blue Shades — Bad Suns

Potential Breakup Song — Aly & AJ

Try it Sober — Phoebe Ryan

A Thousand Ways — Phoebe Ryan

peace — Taylor Swift

Ain't It Fun — Parmore

Nothing New — Taylor Swift, Phoebe Bridgers

Turn You On — Cherry Pools

die in california — Machine Gun Kelly

This Love (Taylor's Version) — Taylor Swift

Overnight — Parachute

Die For Me — Post Malone

Sober/Hungover — Sueco, Arizona Zervas

Bad Behavior — The Maine

Heading Home — Griffin, Josef Salvat

You're On Your Own, Kid — Taylor Swift

Sweet Nothing — Taylor Swift

Keeping Your Head Up — Birdy

You'll Always Find Your Way Back Home — Hannah
Montana

Good and Broken — Miley Cyrus

Circus — Britney Spears

If U Seek Amy — Britney Spears

Piece of Me — Britney Spears

LoveGame — Lady Gaga

Learn to Let Go — Kesha

Fighter — Christina Aguilera

The Getaway — Hilary Duff

One Original Thing — Cheyenne Kimball

Rumors — Lindsay Lohan

Masquerade — Ashley Tisdale

CHAPTER 1
HEATH

How hard would I need to bash this guy's skull against the wall to kill him? Or maybe I should wait until we're outside the hospital so doctors can't intervene. If anyone deserves to bleed out alone on the street, it's him. His shoulder brushes mine as he passes, and it takes every ounce of self-control to hold myself back. My skin burns, and my jaw aches from clenching it so tightly.

But I don't move. I keep my gaze trained straight ahead, my hands balled into fists at my sides, and I let him go. If only so ending up in a police station won't take me away from Dani's side.

I just can't.

Bullshit isn't even a strong enough word.

Mom folds over the side of Dani's bed like her body is suddenly too heavy to hold up. She clutches Dani's hand in both of hers, silent sobs racking her shoulders. That fucking engagement ring glints under the fluorescent lights, and I turn as Dani's fiancé steps into the elevator, eyes trained on the floor.

Aside from a bruise on his cheekbone that's nearly healed, he looks perfectly fine. Ready to go on with the rest of his life as if none of this ever happened.

The doors slide shut behind him.

He lasted less than a month. She's been in this bed a *few weeks*, and he already can't take it anymore?

He'd been driving the fucking car.

Sharp breaths come in and out of my nose, and I leave the room before Mom can notice. I need to hit something.

The hospital is quiet this early, as Mom and I have learned from stopping by each day before work—on the days I don't sleep here, that is. A nurse with a high ponytail types away at the desk outside Dani's room—not the one who's usually here. She looks up as I approach.

"If you have any other questions about the billing," I say, lowering my voice, "can you make sure it comes to me? Not her."

The nurse glances from me to Mom, her eyes softening, and she nods.

I rub a hand along my jaw, sighing as my gaze falls on the clock behind the desk. The first of my two interviews today is in just over an hour. One of these better turn out, or I'm losing pay for no reason.

The elevator is empty as I step inside and quickly smooth my hair in the reflection. The suit might be a bit much, but I'm not taking any chances. I need this job.

We need this money.

And if nothing else, at least for today, it'll distract me from my need to murder John.

ᚻᚱᛚᚱᚱᛁᛏᛁᚤᛁ

THE SUIT WAS NOT OVERKILL. Three guys sit in the waiting room with me, and I'm willing to bet each of their shoes are more expensive than everything on my body combined, including the cash in my wallet.

Not like that's saying much. I probably don't even have enough for cab fare.

The bean pole of a guy on my left side-eyes me, gaze darting from the tattoos peeking out on the backs of my hands to my face. He looks like I could snap him in half. Who does he think he'll be guarding?

I mean, all the security history on my résumé is a lie, but at least I look the part. Maybe if the rest of my competition is like this guy, I stand a better chance than I thought.

They call Twiggly in first, and he shuffles to the door like his shoes are too big for him. I tug on my sleeves and shirt collar again, not sure if hiding the ink will make a difference or not, but I'm not taking any chances. I comb through my memory of the hundred applications I've submitted since Dani's accident, but all the details blur together.

This is some activist speaker...I think. Save the bees, that kind of thing. Apparently, some of her rallies have gotten rowdy in the past. I slide my phone out of my pocket to find the email, but it's nearly impossible to read anything with all the cracks in my screen. I've been needing to get a new phone for a while, but that's definitely not happening now.

Hopefully pretending to care about her cause isn't a prerequisite.

Twiggly steps out of the room a few minutes later, not even spending a quarter of an hour in there. I can't tell if that's a good or bad thing. He juts his chin at me as he heads for the door. "You Heath?"

I nod.

"They're ready for you."

The other guys turn to watch as I stand and straighten the sleeves of my jacket. Fuck, my palms are sweaty. I discreetly rub them on my pants before stepping into the room. I'm not usually this nervous for interviews, but I guess I've never needed it to work out this badly before.

"Heath Bridgers."

I freeze a pace into the room as the door clicks shut behind me.

Amelia Thompson watches me from behind the oak desk at the end of the room, hands on her hips, lips flattened into a thin smile.

Jesus fucking Christ.

I force what she used to call a charming smile onto my face. "Amy. What a surprise."

Her smile grows, the coldness of it somehow amplifying with each extra inch it takes up on her face. "Amelia is fine."

Right.

She gestures to the chair across from her desk. "Please, have a seat."

Straightening my tie, I do as she says, though I have a feeling I'd be better off heading out now.

These two interviews are the only ones I've been able to secure since the accident. I don't have another lined up if neither work out. If a girl I didn't call back freshman year of college—my only year, but semantics—ends up being the reason I don't land this job, I swear to God—

"I'm Gina's assistant, so she has me conducting the interviews," says Amelia.

I force myself not to fidget as she plucks a piece of paper from the desk with two fingers, holding it up like it's something filthy. My résumé, presumably. She tosses it onto the desk, and it slides toward me.

"So we both know every word on here is a lie, but I guess that should be expected of you."

I sigh inwardly. Definitely not over it then. It's not like we'd even dated. We hung out a few times and slept together once nearly a decade ago. Could I have been less of an asshole? Absolutely. But she stalked me for weeks after getting my class schedule from the registrar, then showed up unannounced at my apartment—an address I'd never given her.

Not that I would've called her again if she hadn't, but still.

The sex had been bad for both of us. She used a lot of teeth, and it was hard to stay in the mood after the first drop of "*Give it to me, Daddy.*"

I don't know why she wanted to see me again in the first place.

I loosen the tie around my neck. "Look, Amy—"

"Amelia."

"Right. Amelia. I apologize—"

She snorts. "That's a new one."

I hold her gaze. "Can we keep our personal history out of this?"

She lifts her eyebrows, her expression perfectly innocent. "I hadn't realized it was in it. I'm trying to find the best fit for my boss. She deserves someone trustworthy, reliable, honest."

"I can do this job," I say, fighting to keep my voice even. "And I can work as many hours as she needs—"

"I think I have all I need here, Mr. Bridgers." She folds her hands on the desk and leans forward, a genuine smile on her face now. "We'll let you know. Thanks so much for coming in today."

Dismissed, I rise from my chair. That hadn't taken five minutes. As I turn for the door, I hear her tear my résumé in half.

CHAPTER 2
PARKER

I pull my sweatshirt hood up and tug the neck gaiter over my nose. It's not *quite* cold enough to warrant it, but I don't dare leave it behind. Just in case, I throw on an old brunette wig and sunglasses for good measure.

Like the last one, today's bodyguard is rather incompetent. It doesn't take much at all to sneak past him and slip out of the apartment. I'm not sure how much time it will buy me —however long it takes him to get up and check the bedroom—but I'll take what I can get.

"Hey!"

I freeze at the elevators, the blood in my veins turning to ice. The door across from mine is propped open, and a girl who looks around my age—maybe a bit younger, but definitely in her twenties—is standing there in a bright red tracksuit with a trash bag in her hand.

"You moved in this month, right?" she asks, popping her gum.

I give her a tight smile and nod, glancing at my apartment out of the corner of my eye. If the guard in there overhears and comes to investigate, I'm done for, and I haven't even made it outside the building yet.

"Me too!" She flips her blond hair over her shoulder. "I'm Aly, by the way."

"Greta," I lie, having no idea why that was the first name that came to mind.

She waves, then turns for the trash room at the opposite end of the hall. "Guess I'll be seeing you around!"

"Yeah," I echo and offer a lame wave.

My heart doesn't stop pounding even once I'm in the elevator. She didn't seem to recognize me, but that was far too close of a call for comfort.

The sun beats down on my many layers as I walk, and I keep one hand in my purse, the Taser and pepper spray bumping against me in a comforting rhythm.

I'm perfectly capable of walking down the street alone, see? I used to do this all the time. It's fine. Everything's fine. Besides, vitamin D is supposed to be good for you, and I haven't been outside in days. So this is good. Yeah, this is good. Vital, even.

I make the order ahead of time on my phone to limit interacting with people, timing it so hopefully the coffee will be there waiting for me. Which is for the best, since the line is spilling out the door when I arrive, the shop buzzing with the morning rush as people pick up something on their way to work.

My chest contracts at the familiar bright red sign above the door. Bean There, Done That. The walls are covered in maps and chalkboards where people can add pins or write their names, showing all the places they've been. My gaze skirts away before anything can come into focus. Before I can seek out the places I know *his* name is.

I've made it this far. I'm not turning back now.

Swallowing the lump in my throat, I shoulder my way inside. The air is warm with the aroma of house-made pastries and freshly brewed coffee, so thick I can taste it on my tongue. The barista smiles as I head for the single to-go cup and paper bag waiting on the counter.

A man in a suit reaches for the coffee at the same time, and our hands collide. Adrenaline erupts in my veins as his eyes roam my face.

This is it.

But then he smiles apologetically when he notices the name on the cup, takes a step back, and nods for me to take it. I do, hoping he can't see my hand shaking, and hurry out of the shop.

I didn't even have a chance to pause inside and appreciate being here, not that I would've had much peace and quiet to think about Elijah with that crowd. Sipping his favorite coffee will have to do.

Can he see me now? People say they feel loved ones after they pass all the time, but how do they know? I tighten my fist around the cup, willing myself to feel his presence, for him to know that I'm thinking of him, that no one has forgotten about him. I glance one last time at our favorite table in the back—and run straight into something hard.

"Jesus!"

The coffee slips from my hand as I stumble, spilling right on the boulder of a man I just crashed into. He lurches back, holding the white shirt away from his chest as hot coffee mars his suit.

A tan suit, I might add. The stain travels all the way from his throat to his belt, a few splatters decorating his pant legs.

"I'm so sorry," I gasp.

"Are you *kidding* me?"

9

I don't know if it's his raised voice or the sight of Elijah's memorial coffee all over the dirty pavement, but tears spring to my eyes.

"I—I'm really sorry," I say again, my voice trembling. "I didn't see you there—"

"Obviously."

I swallow hard, the tears fading. I mean, yeah, I should've been watching where I was going, but it wasn't like I'd done it on purpose. And honestly, his chest is so hard, I feel like I ran into a wall. I might even bruise. "It was an accident. I—" I pull the napkin out of my food bag. "Here."

He glances at my outstretched hand but doesn't take the offering. "Like that'll do anything." He swipes at his shirt with his hands, then shoves the dark strands of hair from his face.

I take another step back, registering his towering height. I'm not a short person, but he's at least a full foot taller than I am. My hand twitches toward my purse, but despite the irritation rolling off him in waves, it doesn't feel threatening. I try to think of anything else to say, but if he doesn't want my napkin, I don't have much else to offer. And even if I did, he'd probably be an asshole about that too.

I sigh, glancing at the coffee on the pavement again. There's no way I'm getting in the back of that line for a replacement.

The guy must notice my attention, because he scoffs, then takes off down the street. I stare after him, shaking my head.

"Dick," I mutter, then start my long, coffee-less walk home.

CHAPTER 3
HEATH

I don't think this day could possibly get any worse. I have half a mind to apologize to that girl for being a dick, but when I turn, she's already disappeared into the crowd.

I huff out a breath as I take in the time on my watch, then the coffee splattered all over my suit. The second interview is in a little over an hour, but I can't show up like this. Especially after the disastrous turn of the first one.

Even if I had money for a cab, I wouldn't have enough time to make it to my apartment and back, not with this traffic. I guess I could try to snag the subway…

I glance at the street signs, an idea forming. I veer left, squeezing through a few cars stopped in traffic and hitting the opposite sidewalk at a run. And here I was disappointed I didn't have time for my morning jog today. Careful what you wish for, I guess.

"Hey, watch it!" someone calls as I pull out my phone and bring it to my ear. Thankfully, Greg picks up on the second ring.

"Bridgers! I—"

"Are you at your office?"

"Uh, yeah?" A coffee maker roars to life in the background as I weave through the crowd waiting for the light to turn. "Dude, are you panting?"

Car horns blare around me as I dart across the next street, ignoring the dirty looks people shoot my way. "I'll be there in five."

"Is everything—"

I hang up and shove the phone in my pocket. By the time I reach Greg's building a few blocks away, a fine layer of sweat has joined the coffee clinging to my skin. The lobby is full of people heading in for the morning, a large crowd already waiting for the elevators. I shoulder my way through them and head for the stairs on the other side. Luckily, Greg is on the second floor.

Heads pop over the tops of the cubicles as I hurry through the door, slightly out of breath and looking for Greg's mop of curly red hair. He steps out of the kitchen with a paper coffee cup, his eyes widening as I jog toward him.

"Heath! What's going on?" He looks at my ruined suit. "What the hell happened to you?"

"Remember that favor you owe me?"

A hint of wariness creeps into his expression. "Yeah...?"

Favor is putting it lightly. We were roommates that year in college. Even though he stuck through to graduation and I didn't, we've stayed in touch.

But three years later, despite him having that fancy piece of paper, he's hundreds of thousands in debt...and I built up enough savings from construction to get my own place.

Which he crashed in, rent-free, for over a year.

I take the coffee cup out of his hand and set it on the empty desk beside us. Greg is a good few sizes smaller than I am, but it'll have to do.

"The clothes off your back. Now."

CHAPTER 4
PARKER

The apartment is a circus when I get back. My mother is pacing in the kitchen, my father following behind with his hands held out like he's ready to catch her if she collapses. The temporary bodyguard is standing in the corner with his arms crossed while Faye, my manager, screams at him at the top of her lungs, pointing her black acrylic nail like a weapon. And Annie, my publicist, is bent over like a child crying on the couch with her head in her hands.

When I open the door, they all whip around to face me.

I clutch my scone to my chest.

"Parker!" Mom barrels forward and throws her arms around my neck.

"Where the hell have you been?" Faye exclaims at the same time.

"We thought you'd been abducted," wails Annie as she whips out a tissue to blow her nose.

The bodyguard mumbles something under his breath as Dad pries Mom off my body.

Faye stares me down from the living room, hands on her hips. They're already dressed for the funeral, all derivatives of the same black attire, despite us not actually attending the service today.

I hold up the scone. "I thought I could get there and back before you noticed. I'm sorry."

Faye throws her hands up and turns away as she yanks her black curls into a bun. "You're almost killed and your first response is to go traipsing down the streets of New York all alone. Brilliant."

The paper bag crinkles beneath my fist. "I just wanted to do something to remember Elijah, especially if I can't even say goodbye to him today."

"We're doing the best we can!" Annie yells, then shrinks back as if she scared herself with her own volume.

"You can't do this, Parker," Faye says.

"I know, I know—"

"No, you don't," she snaps, then swipes a scrap of paper off the kitchen island and thrusts it in my face. "You're acting like this is over, and it's not."

It takes a moment for my eyes to focus on the words.

You cannot hide.

I snatch the paper from her, my thumb running over the angry indentations left behind from the pen. "Where did you get this?"

"There's no need to scare her," Dad says, his hands cupping my shoulders from behind.

"Maybe she should be scared!" Faye continues. "Maybe that's the only thing that will get through to her. If trying to keep her safe makes me the bad guy, then so be it."

"It was taped to the front door of the building," Dad explains.

I look from the paper to each of them, my mouth opening and closing a few times before I can find words. Suddenly there's not enough air in the room. "But...who...he's..."

He's locked up. He's gone. He can't hurt me anymore.

"It's probably some copycat looking for attention," Annie jumps in before Faye can, back to her usual soft tone. "But it *is* troubling that they found this address so quickly."

"They could've put a similar note on dozens of other buildings," offers the security guard from the corner. "They might not know anything at all."

He has a point. The note was on the building, not my door specifically. It could be a guess, a joke—hell, it might not even be meant for me.

"Maybe it's best that you haven't unpacked yet..." Faye starts, her eyes lingering on the boxes lined against the walls.

"You want to move me again?"

"You should go get dressed," Mom offers, though her attention is completely on Faye, a warning in her eyes. "We brought you something to wear. We can talk about this later."

Dad gives my shoulders a reassuring squeeze as I silently slip into the room.

The dress is almost identical to Faye's—knee-length and sleeveless—and she's included a cardigan to layer on top. After wedging my feet into the black pumps laid out by the bed, I throw some dry shampoo in my hair and slather on makeup until I feel presentable.

I brace both hands on the bathroom sink and hang my head between my shoulders, pressing my lips together until I don't feel like crying anymore. I can't help but think if Elijah were here, he wouldn't be out there with the rest of the bickering team. He'd be in here, sitting on the toilet seat, watching me do my makeup. It was always under the guise of *keeping an eye on the room*, but I think he just liked our chats.

He was lonely sometimes too.

You cannot hide.

A shiver runs up my spine.

This building is full of security cameras. They'll catch whoever left the note. Probably some stupid kid playing a prank. Probably nothing to worry about.

Probably.

The conversations in the living room cut off when I open the door, and Dad gives me a pained smile.

"Ready to head out?" The forced-chipper tone of his voice falls flat.

A chauffeur and two extra security guards meet us as we head to the garage. No one speaks as we cut across town, the cemetery being all the way in Queens, where Elijah's family is from. If Elijah were here, he'd have horrible eighties music blasting through the radio until I forced him to change it.

It's sunny today, with the smallest hint of rain left in the air. The trees of the cemetery are lush and green, and a crowd has already accumulated as we idle on the other side of the street. A woman is standing at the front and speaking, Elijah's wife. His son is clinging to the dress of an older woman—probably his grandmother—and wiping his face.

"I could crack the window so you could hear," offers the driver.

"No." I shake my head once, then again. "No," I add, quieter this time.

Whatever she's saying isn't for me to hear.

I shouldn't have come.

These people are in so much pain, struggling with so much grief. Seeing me would only make that worse.

My mother grasps my hand. My first instinct is to pull away, but she holds on tightly, tears shining on her cheeks.

"He was a good man," she murmurs. "And you have every right to grieve him too. This was a horrible accident. And that man will pay for what he did. But this wasn't your fault."

I squeeze her hand because I know she needs it, but then turn back to the window and watch as a different man steps up to speak, Elijah's brother.

"We should talk about the appearance," mumbles Faye from the front seat.

"*Faye*," snaps Annie. "Not right now."

Faye shrugs. "We need to make arrangements, and it's best to get in front of this."

"This is a conversation for another time," says Annie, her voice surprisingly firm.

My gaze slides between the two of them, but I don't ask, because I don't want the answer right now. My phone buzzes in my purse, and I pull it out, tears springing to my eyes at the name on the screen.

ERICA

> I heard the funeral was today. I'm not ready to talk yet, but I'm really sorry for your loss and I hope you're doing okay. xx

The relief that she's talking to me again, even if just this once, is tangible. I check the rest of my messages, but still nothing from Rick. Not that I particularly want to hear from him right now, but somehow, him not even trying to reach out is worse.

The service wraps up quickly, and people filter back to

their cars. Elijah's wife, son, and parents linger longer than the rest, but eventually, they, too, turn and walk away.

Once everyone is gone, I throw open the car door.

"Parker," hisses Mom, but I avoid her hands, jump out, and hurry across the street.

Two of the security guards jog after me, like I knew they would. I hear more car doors slam, but I don't turn. My gaze is fixed on the fresh dirt, the bright red roses scattered on the ground.

Mom catches up to me first, but instead of pulling me back, she wraps her arms around my shoulders and stands there with me. Dad finds us next, adding his arms on top of Mom's, and he sniffles close to my ear.

I stiffen at the sound of a camera shutter. I squint and scan the surrounding area—there. In the trees, a little off to the right, a man is crouched with a camera, the lens long and wide. The shutter goes off again, the lens pointing directly at us. Mom notices him too, then steps in front of me.

"Come on," Dad says quietly and starts leading me back to the car.

"Don't you have any shame!" Annie surges toward the man, fist in the air. The branches rustle, and he disappears.

"Great," mutters Faye. "Now *that's* going to be the first sighting of you all over the internet."

Mom sends her a withering glare.

"What! If you don't want me to do my job, then why am I even here?"

"Technically"—Annie elbows her out of the way and joins my other side—"you're trying to do *my* job right now."

Faye mutters something else I can't hear as we head back to the car. No one says anything as we take off down the street, and when I search the trees for the photographer again, no one's there.

Mom squeezes my arm. "How are you feeling? If you're not up for the interviews today, I'm sure we can reschedule."

Faye makes a noise in the back of her throat at that but says nothing.

I lean my head against the cold glass of the window. I'd completely forgotten about the interviews, to be honest. I'd known the hourly security guards couldn't be a permanent solution, but the idea of replacing Elijah already, of having a new face I'll have to see every day...

But the agency guys can only do so much. And in light of what was left on the door today...it's something better done sooner rather than later. Just in case.

"I'm fine," I say.

"Good," chirps Faye from the front seat. "Because we're heading there now."

CHAPTER 5

PARKER

The office space they rented is a few blocks from the cemetery. Faye wasn't kidding when she said we were heading straight there.

"Here's some clothes if you want to change out of...well... yeah." Faye grabs a duffel bag from the trunk and hands it to me. The harsh lights of the parking garage cast shadows over her eyes, but that doesn't hide the moisture there.

She knew Elijah longer than any of us. She's the one who suggested him in the first place since they'd worked with a different client together before me. So if she needs to put up this attitude front to get through today, I'm not going to comment on it.

I learned a long time ago to not take it personally whenever she shifts into Business Faye. We're lucky to have her. She's one of the most knowledgeable managers in this space, seeing as her entire family has worked in the industry for generations.

Me being the first client she signed on her own after she broke away from the family business, she's always treated me more like a younger sister than a client. But when shit hits the fan? It's like an entirely different person possesses her body.

I follow her into the building, Annie and the security guards right behind me. We head to the twentieth floor, where I duck into a bathroom and pull on the faded skinny jeans and oversize sweater.

The office space is even plainer than the apartment. All the walls are bare except for a whiteboard, and the large conference table in the center is the only furniture in the room. The back wall is covered in wide windows, where trickles of rain have started to run down the panes.

"How many applicants did we get?" I ask as Annie, Faye, and I take seats at the far end of the table. One of the security guys comes to stand behind us while the other lingers by the door.

My parents and I came to an agreement a long time ago that they wouldn't be involved in the business side of my career so it wouldn't alter our relationship, so they're waiting down the street at a coffee shop instead.

No one answers my question. Faye and Annie exchange a look.

"Just tell me."

"None," sighs Annie. "At first. Given…the way the previous person in the position left it and the scandal in the news, it's considered an extremely risky and volatile position, so that wasn't unexpected."

"None?" I demand. "Then what are we even doing here?"

"We raised the salary quite significantly, with the caveat being getting locked into a yearlong contract."

"Okay. So how many applicants did you get after that?"

Annie sits up taller and smooths her hands over her skirt.

She stares straight ahead, like she's expecting someone to walk in any second. "One."

"Oh," I say softly and sink back in my seat.

Faye lays her hand on my arm. I jump at the unexpected contact—she's definitely not the touchy-feely type—but she gives my arm a reassuring squeeze, then pulls a folder out of her bag.

"His name is Heath Bridgers," reads Faye. "Twenty-eight years old, six-five, four years of experience working in security." Her eyes flick to mine. "Mostly within the prison system. He's agreed to the one-year contract and salary offered—"

"Just how much money are you offering him?"

Annie and Faye exchange another look. "One hundred and fifty thousand dollars."

Offering that much and we *still* only got one applicant?

The elevator across the hall rattles. My heart picks up like *I'm* the one being interviewed as the doors slide open and a man steps out in a crisp gray suit, the shoulders dark with rain. Neither Faye nor Annie have looked up from their notes on the table—apparently I'm the only one with a vantage point of the hallway. The man pushes his dark hair back from his face and straightens his suit jacket, pausing to take a deep breath.

"No fucking way," I mutter.

Faye turns to me as the man steps into the room.

"Heath Bridgers?" asks Annie.

The man gives a curt nod and stops behind a chair on the far side of the table.

"Feel free to have a seat," says Faye.

As he pulls out a chair and sits down, his suit strains over the muscles in his arms like it's too small for him, and he looks at each of us in turn. As he finds my face, I stiffen, but there's no hint of recognition. He offers a small smile and nods.

Oh, that's rich.

He doesn't even recognize me. Granted, I'd been trying to be in disguise at the coffee shop, so I guess I should be happy it worked.

But there is no way, absolutely *no way*, I am spending every hour of every day with *him* glued to my side.

Absolutely not.

Replacing Elijah with him would be like spitting on Elijah's grave.

I cross my arms over my chest and lean back in my chair, narrowing my eyes as Faye and Annie fire off their questions that will be of no consequence in the long run because there is *no way* we are hiring him.

He answers the questions with ease, his eyes flickering to mine when he's done. He doesn't bristle under the scrutiny. He stares back, a single eyebrow lifting an inch.

Not in question, but a challenge.

Smug bastard.

"Thank you for coming in today," says Annie.

"You're hi—"

"No," I cut Faye off. She whirls around to face me, but I shake my head and stand. "Thank you for your time. But it won't be a good fit," I say, then head for the door.

Heath looks at me, then at Annie and Faye scrambling to collect their things.

"Hold on," one of them says, but I'm already in the hallway.

Whether it's from confusion or incompetence, I'm not sure, but neither of the hourly guys follows me as I slip into the elevator and hit the bottom floor for the garage. Faye and Annie clamber into the hall as the door slides shut.

I stare at my reflection in the mirror and let out a shaky breath. I'm acting childish and reckless, I know. But just because he was the only applicant *this* time doesn't mean I should be stuck with him for the next year. We'll find someone else. We will.

But then I think about that note. What if it's more than a stupid prank? Is my pride really worth more than my safety?

The elevator slows and pauses at the eighteenth floor. I sigh and move away from the doors as they screech open and—

Heath Bridgers steps inside.

He's panting slightly, a few locks of hair sticking out of place, like he just ran down the stairs.

Which, I realize, must be exactly what he did.

He crosses to the control panel and hits the emergency button. An alarm shrieks overhead, and the elevator jerks to a stop.

"What the hell are you doing?" Instead of reaching for the button—that he's still standing in front of—I back up until I hit the wall, my breaths coming in hard and fast.

I'm trapped in here with him. Maybe this was all an elaborate scheme—the coffee shop, the interview. He's been following me. *Stalking* me. What if he was the one who left the note? And I ran right into his trap.

He takes in my defensive stance, raises his palms, and backs up. "Jesus. I'm not going to hurt you. I just wanted to talk to you, but you didn't give me the chance."

I eye him warily, then the emergency button. "By trapping me in an elevator?"

He sighs and steps away from the panel. "Go ahead. Just,

what was it that disqualified me for you? Was it something on my résumé?"

"God, you really don't recognize me, do you?"

He stills. After a moment, he slowly shakes his head. "Should I?"

I gesture at his suit. "Glad you had time to go home and change."

He glances down at himself, then slowly up to me. "Oh, *oh.*"

I give him a tight smile. "Yeah, *oh.*"

He grimaces and rubs a hand along the back of his neck. "Quite the first impression."

"Yeah. So excuse me if I don't want to be around *that* twenty-four seven."

"Look, I'm sorry. I'm not usually like that."

I roll my eyes.

"Which doesn't sound genuine at all, I know. You..." He presses his lips together in a hard line. "You caught me at a bad moment. For what it's worth, which I realize isn't very much, I am sorry." He straightens, an entirely different, formal demeanor snapping into place. "I understand if you can't look past it. But I think my résumé and experience speak for themselves. It's not your problem, but I need this job. I know the contract is for a year, but if you'd be willing to give me a two-week trial period, I can prove to you I'm the man for the job. And if you still hate me after that, I'll be on my way."

I cross my arms, but something stops me from immediately saying no. Maybe it's because I don't have another choice. Maybe it's because his experience *does* speak for itself. Or maybe it's that pitiful look in his eyes, evident despite him trying to cover it.

"Why'd you leave your last job?" I finally ask.

"I'm still there. I'm looking for a replacement because I need the extra pay."

I narrow my eyes, but he stands tall, meeting my gaze.

Fuck.

"One week," I say.

He nods.

A beat of silence passes between us. I sigh and jut my chin at the buttons. "Fine. Let's go."

The buzzing overhead cuts off as the doors glide open. Annie, Faye, and the two security guards are waiting on the other side. I hold up a hand before they can say anything. "He's hired, okay?"

CHAPTER 6
HEATH

Parker Beck and her temporary security guards climb into a black car outside the office building, but one of the other women from the interview— her manager, I think—grabs my arm and pulls me to a stop before I can get very far.

"I need to be absolutely certain that you understand the risk of this job," she says.

Her hand is still on my arm, nails digging in, but she doesn't let go. Rain hammers on the sidewalk around us, quickly soaking through the shoulders of Greg's jacket. It was already too small to begin with, but it's quickly becoming suffocating as the water suctions it to my arms. "I understand—"

"I'm not finished. It's not just what you've probably seen in the news."

I don't bother telling her I've spent the last few weeks inside the walls of a hospital and haven't seen whatever she's talking about. Hell, I'd never heard of this Parker person before today. But if they're going to this much trouble for her, she must be some big shot.

"It's not just that bastard who showed up at the wedding. Especially not now that she's all over the news. Parker doesn't know the full extent of it, and it's going to stay that way. But there have been death threats in the mail, more than I can count. Someone broke into her old apartment to jerk off in her bed after we moved her out. Someone shoved pictures they'd taken of her through her window under the door. There are entire forums online dedicated to her full of creeps who... Just, this isn't a job to be taken lightly. Now, I'll ask you again, do you understand what you're agreeing to?"

I meet her gaze. Behind the stern expression, the fear is evident. She cares for this girl, more than as a client. And if something happens to her on my watch, I have no doubt I'll be answering to her.

"I understand."

"Good." She releases my arm and steps toward the car, the other woman I hadn't even noticed standing there following silently behind. "You start on Monday."

AN INTERNET SEARCH on the name Parker Beck brings up a few thousand results. After getting her stage name from the first article, I try again with Ryker Rae, and *millions* appear. I rub my hand over my mouth at the picture of her on the front page of a gossip website. She's in a long dress—from whatever wedding her manager was talking about, I guess— and she's covered in blood. Her eyes are focused off to the side, clearly not seeing the camera. There are angry, red marks around her neck, vaguely resembling handprints.

Jesus Christ.

There's another hit from a few hours ago, paparazzi pictures taken of her standing in a cemetery with a few other people. An older woman with the same blond hair—her mother, maybe—has an arm wrapped protectively around her shoulders. She looks even younger in this picture.

How old is she?

I search again, this time flooding the page with videos of her onstage or doing interviews.

She's twenty-four.

Just a year older than Dani.

I pull up a video from a show in Paris, and she's barely recognizable as the girl who glared at me across the conference table earlier. Dark wig, dark makeup, dark clothes. The crowd screams along to her lyrics as she moves across the stage, confident and sure. She jumps and dances as she sings into the microphone, her voice loud and clear despite being a bit out of breath.

She's a good performer, I'll give her that. Someone throws flowers onto the stage as she falls to her knees and flips her hair, and the song comes to an end.

The video autoplays a TV interview from a few years ago. She's decked out in a similar all-black outfit, this time in a corset and knee-high boots. Even her voice sounds different as Ryker. Lower, raspier. She keeps her eyebrows high as she talks, her teeth flashing each time she smiles. Someone clearly used to the spotlight. Someone who loves the attention.

Someone used to getting whatever she wants.

There's another video about the five-million-dollar mansion she bought for her parents a few years ago, in cash. Another on the millions she donates annually to different charities—one she started herself to fund school art programs in low-income areas—how she sponsors a few of her fans each year and sends them to college... How much money does this girl have?

It feels weird having your donations splashed across every news site. Like she wants a pat on the back for something she probably only did for the tax write-off.

I grit my teeth, thinking about Dani in that hospital bed. They might not throw her out on the streets if she can't pay, but they'll send her into the kind of debt that'll end her life just the same.

Ryker Rae Lie Goes Deeper than a Stage Name

I skim the next article, which cites every detail about Ryker's life the press has released over the past six years— where she's from, where she grew up, what her parents' names are, her birthday.

All fake details, apparently.

She'd created an entirely different life for this character both on and off the stage. With that many lies, how did she even keep track of them all?

I close the laptop and stare at my dark apartment. *You don't have to like her to make sure she doesn't die*, I remind myself. I just need to get through a year of this to help with Dani's bills.

Even if she is as entitled and insufferable as she seems, I've been through worse.

I get up from the couch and head for the kitchen. After rooting through the cabinets for a minute, I come up with a bottle of scotch, nearly empty, and pour the rest of it in a glass. My phone flashes on the counter, a notification revealing a missed voice mail. I haven't saved the number, but I recognize it by now.

The hospital.

I down the scotch and jab the speaker button.

"Hi, Mr. Bridgers, this is Jamie calling from Heartstone General Hospital. We wanted to follow up about that payment plan you inquired about last time you were here..."

I turn it off and let out a slow breath through my nose. Honestly, you'd think they'd at least wait until *after* they were finished giving care to a patient before harassing the family about money.

Hey, we know your sister may never wake up, but do you have those hundreds of thousands of dollars we want lying around somewhere?

I have some savings, but dipping into those will barely make a dent. Even this new salary won't cover all of it, but it'll buy us some time or make me look like a better candidate for a loan.

I set the empty glass in the sink and shove my phone in my pocket. I should head back to the hospital and try to see Dani since I won't get a chance tomorrow. Faye—Parker's manager—left me a voice mail telling me to arrive at an address across town by seven tomorrow morning so they can go over some protocols with me. And I need to stop by the job site and break the news to Iz that I'm leaving before that.

It's after visiting hours, but the nurses like me, and I might be able to convince them to look the other way. Maybe I'll stay the night and head straight to work from there tomorrow. The cot I've been using is still in her room, I think.

After quickly throwing together a duffel bag, I head out into the rain. Maybe by some miracle she'll be awake by the time I get there.

AN EXCERPT FROM PARKER'S JOURNAL

it's almost funny
the way some people
take the mention of grief
as in invitation
to dig out
a measuring stick

which grief
is more valid?

what emotions
are you allowed to feel
if you were supposed
to see it coming?

why do you want
to have a contest
to see who is more miserable?

why does my pain
have anything to do with you?

CHAPTER 7

PARKER

TWO WEEKS EARLIER

There is no better drug than this. Thousands of voices vibrate through my bones, the flickering lights blurring my vision, but the dizziness is more welcoming than disorienting. For those few hours, I'm in another dimension. Another world.

Another life.

It isn't until I'm offstage that it all comes crashing back.

"That was amazing, Ryker." Faye, my manager, appears in a flurry of curly black hair, and the bangles on her wrists clang together as she tosses me a towel. I wipe the sweat from my forehead as she turns a smile to the people milling around us.

It probably looks genuine to anyone who doesn't know her. But I recognize the tightness in the corners of her mouth, the way her eyes keep shifting. Sure enough, as the backup singers wave me down, Faye hooks her arm through mine and pulls me away. I grimace, her message clear.

You're going to be late.

Her high heels make determined little clicks against the concrete as she leads me to my dressing room.

"Great work, guys!" I call over my shoulder, but we'll have to skip our post-show rituals tonight. I don't even have time for an encore, though I can hear the crowd chanting for one.

"We have ten minutes." Elijah's towering form materializes on my other side so he and Faye bracket me as we walk through the halls. The second Faye turns away, Elijah winks.

My heart is still pounding from the last dance number, and sweat drips down my neck, but his presence is immediately calming. He extends a fist, and I bump it with my own, then we interlace our fingers and wiggle them apart.

"Really, guys?" Faye huffs, though she's smiling.

Elijah smirks and drops his hand. It's not the full handshake, but I'm sure the affection in Faye's eyes would fade if we stopped to do the rest.

The rest of my security team isn't in the hall as Elijah urges me forward with a hand on my back, and neither is my boyfriend. Hadn't we agreed to leave together after the show? I *told* him not to be late. The timing is going to be tight as it is.

There's no way I missed him either. Some lighting guys are lingering in the wings, and a stagehand is passed out on a cart against the wall, but other than that, it's quieter back here than usual.

I frown as I survey our surroundings again. "Where's Rick?"

"He's meeting us there," says Elijah. His expression is entirely calm, which eases the apprehension threatening to build in my chest. If he's not worried, then I shouldn't be either.

He waits outside as Faye and I slip into the dressing

35

room, and I get to work peeling off the layers, starting with the wig. Despite being shorter than my natural hair—the midnight black strands barely skim my jaw—it manages to make my head feel like it's a million degrees. I run my fingers through my sweaty blond curls, then yank them into a ponytail while Faye pulls on the dress's zipper. It always gets stuck on the damn sequins, made even more complicated when you throw in untangling the wires attached to the ear monitors still hanging around my neck.

I blink at the harsh lights coming from the vanity, my makeup somehow still in place despite how much I sweat tonight. That last dance number is always a killer. I suppose the grunge look has its perks. It's supposed to look messy, so you can't tell if it's unintentional. I lick my finger and smudge away some stray black eyeshadow on my temple.

"There," Faye announces, taking a step back as the dress finally releases me. She eyes the Ryker wig lying on the makeup counter and raises an eyebrow.

"I know, I know." I tug it on again but leave the cap on the vanity as I quickly pin the wig back into place. It's a shoddy job, but I just need it to last me to the car. Sweat drips down my cleavage as I shimmy the rest of the way out of my dress, glitter sprinkling to the floor around me, and pull on the leggings and sweatshirt Faye hands me.

Once I've collected the rest of my things, Faye steps between me and the door, her expression dangerously close to the one she makes before she jumps into a lecture.

"Faye," I say, exasperated. We're already running late. I don't have time for this.

"Don't make me regret letting you do this."

"Faye, we've talked about this. She's my best friend. I have to *go*."

Her lips thin, that warning clear in her eyes, but finally, she steps aside, and then Elijah and I are running down the hall. He cocks his head as a voice comes through his headset. Hopefully, it's the chauffeur telling him they're already out back.

"You did great tonight, kid," he says as we round a corner.

"Did you see that transition between the first two songs? I wasn't sure how I was going to feel about the fire, but the crowd went *nuts*."

He holds out a hand to stop me as we come to the back door, then presses a finger to his earpiece. "There's a crowd out there." He glances at his watch.

Inconvenient, but not unexpected.

"Is the car here?"

"Yes, but—"

"Can you cover me?"

"Parker," he warns.

"What? We both know you're like four bodyguards rolled into one, and I am *not* missing our flight window because of this."

He scowls, and I smile and bat my eyelashes.

"Stay behind me," he finally growls, then shoves open the door.

The cool night air feels glorious as we hurry outside. A metal barrier cuts along the path from the building to the street, the crowd vibrating with energy behind it, but it's only a few dozen people. Two security guards are standing on our side of the barrier, arms spread wide as if physically holding them back, though it doesn't look like anyone is trying to break through. Thankfully they're fans wanting an autograph instead of a herd of paparazzi. I shoot a quick smile and wave to everyone before beelining for the black car a few yards away.

"Ryker!" A flash of blond hair catches my eye, and I turn, my face breaking into a grin.

"Addison!"

Elijah steps to the side to let the little girl sneak through. Not that she couldn't have easily slipped under his arm anyway, being like four feet tall.

She bites her lip, and I notice she's wearing the same sparkly pink Ryker Rae shirt she had on the last time I saw her, which was at a concert in a completely different state. Her mom smiles at me over her head as I crouch to get on her level.

"Can I have a hug?" she asks.

"Of course." I pull her in, then smile as her mom holds up a phone for a picture. "We're actually in a really big hurry tonight, so I'm sorry, but we have to go. But I have a feeling we'll see each other again soon, right?"

Addison gives a determined little nod.

"Thank you," her mom says, gently pulling her back.

"Can *I* have a hug?" teases a much deeper voice. One that's far too close for comfort.

The sound of it has my mouth dry as dust in an instant, but Elijah is already stepping between us and jutting his chin for me to get in the car.

I recognize the man, though I don't know his name. He's been to quite a few concerts, more than half the ones on this tour alone. Which wouldn't be nearly as troubling if he hadn't broken into my dressing room in LA a few months ago. Clearly the arrest wasn't much of a deterrent.

He's as tall as Elijah is and probably just as old—at least his midforties. His suit is obviously the wrong size and hangs awkwardly off his shoulders. He smiles at me like we have some inside joke, and it makes my skin crawl.

"Take a step back, sir," says Elijah.

"I'm a fan, just like everyone else here. Why does she get special treatment?" He nods at Addison, whose mother is actively pulling her away.

I grab the car door and tug it open.

"I'll see you again soon, Ryker," he calls.

Pointedly avoiding eye contact with the man, I force a smile and wave at the rest of the crowd, then slip into the car and lock the door behind me. Elijah ducks in a moment later, and it isn't until the driver takes off that I feel like I can breathe again.

Elijah sighs and rubs his eyes. "That's the sixth concert in two months."

"What does he *do* for a living? How can he afford to just follow me everywhere?"

Elijah frowns and watches out the back window as we pull onto the road. I glance back too, but the man is already gone.

ERICA HAMBY IS the most hungover bride I've ever seen. And knowing her, she wouldn't have it any other way. Her face is retaining twice as much water as usual from the night before, and if I get too close, I can smell vodka seeping out her pores. But being the dutiful maid of honor I am, I say nothing, my focus solely on trying to cover up the monstrous dark circles. Despite the layers of concealer and powder, they don't look like they're going anywhere.

Erica's eyes flick up and meet mine in the vanity's mirror.

I keep my expression perfectly neutral as Amber, the brides-maid pinning Erica's curls into an intricate bun, pointedly avoids looking at both of us.

"What?" Erica asks, her voice edging toward panic.

I snap the powder lid shut and take a step back so she has the mirror to herself. "Nothing. You look perfect."

She rolls her eyes at the blatant lie but smiles as she leans forward to touch up her lip gloss. Even with the bloodshot eyes and puffy face, she's stunning. The lace of her gown's sleeves drapes delicately across her collarbones, her dark hair pulled back to show off the sharp angles of her cheeks.

She's gone all out for the wedding's venue—a vineyard in the middle of nowhere—stretching her budget nearly to its limit with this alone, but she'd been confident with all her experience as a wedding planner herself she could cut the costs elsewhere to make up for it.

Honestly, even a professional makeup artist wouldn't have been able to pull off the miracle needed here, so maybe it was for the best.

My phone buzzes against the vanity, and Rick's name flashes on the screen. Erica zeroes in on it.

"Parker."

She'd made her *no cell phone* policy clear on her invita-tions, leaving the photos and videos to the dozen or so professionals she hired so all her pictures aren't ruined by people holding up their phones.

"Already turning it off," I assure her as I slide the phone from the table and shove it into my purse without reading Rick's text. He's probably just complaining again about being stuck downstairs without me.

"What were you doing last night?" asks Bonnie as she adjusts her boobs in the mirror by the front door, maximizing her cleavage in the dress's low-cut neckline. We all have the same olive green floor-length gowns that cross over our chests in a thick X.

I meet Bonnie's gaze, the concealer not covering the circles beneath her eyes either. They must have had quite the night. I've avoided asking exactly what they were up to so they wouldn't ask me the same question.

But alas.

"Oh, just this...family thing." I head for the bathroom, hoping she'll let the question drop if I leave the room.

"It better have been something important if you bailed on us," calls Erica as I slip inside. I close the door, pretending I didn't hear her, and stare at the porcelain toilet seat. I don't need to go, but surely it must almost be time for us to head down. I just need to kill a few minutes.

Even if I didn't have the tour commitments, I wouldn't have wanted to be a part of whatever the hell they got into. The bachelorette party was bad enough. Erica and I have been friends since we were kids, and that means something to me. But drunk Erica...the only way to deal with that is to also be drunk.

I check my reflection above the sink and adjust my bangs, swooping them to the side so they blend in with the loose blond curls around my shoulders. As least with whatever they had going on last night, the lack of sleep weighing down my features won't stick out as much. It being the result of a red-eye flight on a private jet instead of some late night at the club, well, no one needs to know that.

A knock echoes through the suite, and voices surge on the other side of the bathroom door. Steeling myself with a breath, I rejoin the others and plaster a smile on my face as a bouquet of flowers is thrust in my hands, and then we're moving.

Erica's dad waits with her as the wedding party heads into the hall. We pass white flowers along the bannisters and flickering candles, but my eyes shoot to the floor-length windows on the back wall. Dozens upon dozens of white chairs are facing the vineyard. There's an overhang of branches where small green leaves and twinkle lights dangle over the heads of the guests.

Erica lets out a low breath behind me as we descend the stairs, and her father murmurs something to her in a low voice.

My eyes skate across the sea of guests, finding Rick first. His head is turned away, though I can see the tension in his shoulders from here. When the doors open and the air fills with orchestra music, he takes a few seconds longer than everyone else to turn around.

A groomsman appears on my side and takes my arm, but I hardly look at him. Rick runs a hand through his dark hair as I approach, a small smile lifting the corners of his lips, but it doesn't meet his eyes. Elijah is beside him, his back perfectly straight, dark sunglasses covering his eyes. Even without seeing them, I know he's on high alert and sweeping the area.

Thankfully, since Rick and Soren are old high school friends, he'd gotten an invite of his own so I could bring Elijah as my plus-one. Bringing a man other than my boyfriend raised some questions, and I'm not sure if they bought he's a family friend, but I don't really care. I'm not sure how I'd get through today without the calmness his presence brings. He gives me a slight nod as I pass.

The sun is setting as we all find our places. The groom is

already crying, which would be sweet, I suppose, if it weren't for the snot bubble. I try not to let how much I want this to be over show on my face, but it's hard. The sun is in my eyes, this reverend talks slower than anyone I've ever heard, and my head is throbbing with a lack-of-sleep headache.

And yet, as kids, the one game Erica would make me play over and over was fake wedding. She pretty much always got to be the bride, and it would turn into an all-day planning extravaganza with handmade decorations and flowers we weren't supposed to pick from her mother's garden. We'd even bake a cake if her older sister was home to help us.

Erica has been counting down the minutes until this day since she learned the word *wedding.* The very least I can do is plaster on a smile.

But another unexpected feeling takes root in my chest as Erica and Soren gaze lovingly at each other. It's quieter, but there. I can't identify it, not at first, not until Soren winks and Erica lets out a small giggle.

It's so perfectly, beautifully *normal.*

I startle at the presence of tears on my cheeks.

As they exchange vows, I seek out Rick in the crowd again. He's still frowning, arms crossed over his chest. What is his *problem?* Surely he can't be that annoyed that we haven't spent any time together today. It's not like me being in the wedding party was a surprise. And it's not like he doesn't know *anyone.* There are a few other people from his high school here.

He could at least try to pretend like he's not miserable for Erica's sake. She might be a handful, especially with this tornado of a wedding, but we've been best friends since we were three. He knows how important she is to me. Hell, she's the one who introduced us. And this day is important to her. This day is *everything* to her.

Elijah frowns beside Rick and presses a finger to his earpiece. He tilts his head as he listens to something, then he's up. He ducks as he edges out of his row and disappears toward the winery building. He's so silent and smooth, barely anyone notices his departure, especially now that Erica and Soren are kissing and the guests have erupted in applause.

My heart hammers in my chest, and I scan the yard around us for whatever made Elijah get up.

If the problem was out here, he wouldn't have left, I remind myself, and that eases the panic, at least a little.

My entire body is numb as we file back down the aisle, the faces on either side blurring together. Bonnie nudges me from behind.

"You okay?" she murmurs. "You're white as a sheet."

I hum noncommittally. The sun is nearly behind the hills in the distance now, covering the vineyard in shadows. There's a second area on the west side of the property where the reception will be, the string lights already glowing in the distance. Maybe that's where Elijah went, to scope it out before we all head over there.

I'm being ridiculous. Paranoid.

The newlyweds disappear into the vineyard with a photographer to grab some shots before the reception while the rest of the wedding party is supposed to wait inside. I watch through the windows as the guests venture to the reception area but can't find Rick or Elijah. Maybe one of them texted me. I curse under my breath, realizing my phone is upstairs, and turn around to two very confused bridesmaids. I don't know either of them well—

Erica met them both in college—and based on the few interactions we've had so far, they must think I'm absolutely nuts.

"I'll be right back," I say, heading for the stairs.

"We have to make our entrances—" Bonnie starts, but I keep moving.

A wave of hairspray hits me as I open the door and cross the glitter-covered carpet, my purse where I left it on the vanity. I pull the phone out and nearly drop it when I find countless messages waiting for me. I scroll down, but it's never-ending. Some of the names aren't unusual—my publicist, my mom—but some are names I haven't seen in more than five years, like everyone in my contacts suddenly decided to text me today.

I don't read any of them, still searching for one name in particular, my heart rate steadily climbing in my chest as a nameless sense of unease collects like a cold sweat on my skin.

A new text comes in, Elijah's name flashing on the screen.

We need to leave. Now. Meet me out front.

I stop breathing.

I don't even have time to think about how odd it is for him to ask me to meet him somewhere instead of coming to get me. I don't ask questions. I just move. Laughter rises up from the bar as the rest of the wedding party lounges on the stools and throws back a round of shots. My phone buzzes in my purse over and over again as new messages come in.

I scroll through them, trying to find Rick's name. But Elijah wouldn't leave him behind if there was an emergency. He's probably waiting out front for me too.

I'm on the last step when one of the messages sharpens into focus and my brain finally processes what I'm seeing.

What the hell, Parker? Is this true?

It's from an old high school friend, and she sent along an article.

Pop Sensation Ryker Rae Isn't Who You Think She Is...She Might Be a Different Person Entirely.

My heart comes to a complete stop at the name in the first paragraph.

Parker Beck.

No. *No.* This can't be happening.

I head for the side entrance, hoping to slip out unnoticed. Erica is going to be pissed either way, but her maid of honor disappearing sounds better than causing a scene and ruining her wedding. The last remnants of the sunset are bleeding across the sky as my heels hit the gravel drive, the music from the party humming lowly behind me. I yank the long skirts of my dress into my hands so it won't slow me down, head whipping back and forth to search for Elijah.

But there's no one else out here.

The wind whistles through the trees, and the windchimes along the front of the winery harmonize in swift, metallic trills. I hug my arms to myself, every nerve in my body prickling. The news breaking wouldn't be enough for Elijah to pull the plug. There must be something else. But where is he?

Where is Rick?

I pull my phone out again, the screen covered in a dozen new texts.

"Parker?"

I gasp, my phone slipping through my fingers and landing in the rocks.

Erica, her new husband, and the photographer squint at me.

"What are you doing out here?" Erica asks.

"I—um—" I crouch and retrieve my phone. Of course she hasn't seen the news yet. I look around for Elijah. "I have to go. I'm so sorry—"

"*Go?*" Her voice spikes up an octave.

"It's an emergency. I'm so sorry."

"I'll go get set up for the entrances," the photographer murmurs and ducks around the back of the building.

"I'll wait for you inside," her husband adds before giving her a quick kiss on the top of the head and hurrying off in the same direction. Erica doesn't pay either of them any mind, her attention solely on me.

"What do you mean *go*? You're my maid of honor. What kind of emergency?"

"Erica." I look around at the dark trees, a pit forming in my stomach.

Someone starts slow clapping behind Erica, and we both jump. At first, it's too dark to make out the figure, just his towering height and thin frame. He steps into the moonlight, revealing khaki pants and a white button-down shirt, both sleeves stained with red. I swallow hard, recognizing him instantly.

Did he...follow me here from the show? But *how*? How could he possibly have known where we were going?

"Imagine my surprise when I followed Ryker Rae's personal bodyguard to the middle-of-nowhere New York right in the middle of her tour," he says. "Seems odd, doesn't it?"

Erica's eyes shoot between the two of us. "This wedding is invitation only," she says.

He doesn't even look at her. His gaze is locked on me, unblinking. I notice the stains on his shirt again, realizing there's a splatter of the same red substance across his chest. Logically, I know what it is, but my brain refuses to acknowledge it. Refuses to believe it, to think about where it could have come from...

"You look awfully different now," he continues. "But I guess a wig will do that for you." His features harden. "I guess lies will do that for you."

Erica stumbles back a step. "I'll call security," she says, her voice shaking.

I grab her elbow and pull her behind me.

"Parker," she whimpers.

"Parker!" the man scoffs, like the name tastes bitter in his mouth. "That's right. *Parker Beck.*"

My spine straightens, the fear collecting over my skin like a layer of ice. If Elijah isn't here yet to intervene, he's not coming. And I have a sinking feeling it has to do with what's all over this man's shirt.

"Go back to the party," I say under my breath. "And call the police."

"I wouldn't do that if I were you," he singsongs and flips out a knife in his right hand. His face shifts into something contemplative, wistful. "I loved you." His eyes dart from me and Erica to our intertwined hands. "But it was all a lie, wasn't it? *You* were all a lie."

I swallow hard, desperately trying to think of a way to distract him. I have a phone in my hand. All I'd have to do is unlock it and dial three numbers without him noticing. But then who knows how long it would take the police to get all the way out here?

"You're the one who leaked the story," I conclude.

He shakes his head and glances toward the winery—long enough for me to unlock the phone—then his gaze snaps back to me, a half smile on his face. "Ironic timing, though, I'll admit. Did you even read the article?" He cocks his head, like something just occurred to him. "Hey. Where's your boyfriend?"

My eyes shoot to the red stains on his shirt.

He runs a hand over his chest. "Oh, this? Don't worry. Taking down the bodyguard was enough for one day. Your boyfriend split all on his own."

I refuse to give him the satisfaction of looking at the parking lot to check for Rick's car. "What do you want from me?"

He twirls the knife around in his fingers, the dried blood catching the moonlight.

"Go!" I shove Erica toward the building. "Run!"

She shoots one last frantic look between us, then takes off, gravel spitting up beneath her heels.

I barely have time to turn before he fists his hand in the back of my hair, and I scream.

CHAPTER 8
PARKER

"And then I wake up, just like I always do." I rub my head like I can still feel him yanking me back, the bite of the rocks as I fell to my knees, his hot breath on my neck, the way my lungs ached as I gasped for air. Can remember the looks on the guests' faces as the red and blue lights cut across the party. The way they all looked at *me*.

I shiver and finally meet Dr. Martin's eyes in the leather chair across from me, and she smiles sympathetically. "Have you spoken to Erica yet?"

I shake my head and tuck my feet under myself on the couch, then grab one of the throw pillows to clutch to my chest for good measure. "She hasn't returned any of my calls still." Not one of the two dozen times I've tried in the past few weeks. I'm not sure what she's angrier about, the wedding itself or finding out the way she did.

It had always been the plan to tell her. We've been friends our whole lives. Keeping a secret of that magnitude had been no easy feat. But the fewer people who knew, the safer it was. It had never seemed like the right time.

And I think a small part of me was worried. Things changed when I became Ryker. The way people treated me. The way people looked at me. Half the time, I don't even feel like a person. I'm a character, an idea, a paycheck, a rung to propel yourself higher on the social ladder, a headline for a journalist's big break. And if you call it what it is—dehumanizing—you're ungrateful. Entitled. Undeserving.

With Erica, I never stopped feeling like Parker. Our relationship was one of the few ties I had back to the way things were.

I know she won't see it like that though.

But I mean, look where trusting other people with the secret got me. I haven't seen or heard from Rick since the wedding. And after reading the article all the way through, and seeing it wasn't some *anonymous source*, but his real, full name in print...

I guess whatever they paid him was worth a hell of a lot more to him than two years with me.

I hadn't even wanted to tell him in the first place. But the more serious we got, the more he could sense I was keeping secrets. And all it took was one stupid mistake—a night he stayed over and I hadn't properly put away my Ryker stuff. When I tried to convince him the wig and the clothes were for role play—something I was definitely not into—yeah, he didn't buy it.

I was so sure that would be the end of things. Not necessarily because he'd want to break up, but because he'd see me differently after he knew the truth.

But to Rick's credit, nothing changed. Not a damn thing about the way he treated me. He hadn't even been mad.

I curse under my breath and yank a tissue off the table beside me. I want to be angry. I want to be *furious.* But I'm too stunned to do much else than cry.

Of all ways the secret could've gotten out, Rick being the mole was the last thing I expected. We hadn't been perfect, but I trusted him. And now for him to disappear? No explanation, no apology. Just leaving me to deal with the hellfire consuming every inch of my life alone.

One hell of an exit, I suppose.

"The funeral was yesterday, wasn't it?"

I blink back to the office, focusing on Dr. Martin's kind eyes. They always crinkle in the corners like she's smiling, even when she's not.

I sniffle and nod. "I didn't go though. I just sat in the car across the street to pay my respects without bothering anyone. I didn't think—I didn't think his family would want to see me."

Not only am I the reason he's gone, but with this whole investigation, his family hasn't even been able to put him to rest for weeks.

Dr. Martin nods slowly. "How was that for you?"

I crumple the tissue in my hands, and my bottom lip trembles. With everything else going on—my face plastered across the magazines, the paparazzi stationed outside my apartment twenty-four seven, the constant cycle of new temporary bodyguards—I've tried not to let myself think about Elijah on top of it all. The only thing keeping me from falling off the ledge completely has been the blockade I've built in my mind.

I haven't let myself think about him being gone, because then I'd have to admit I'll never hear him snort when he laughs again or see the winks he shoots me when no one else can see, the rare crack in his steel exterior. I'd have to admit he won't play cards with me in the middle of the night when I can't sleep on tour or sneak me out to local coffee shops on the road even when the rest of the team advises against it.

I clamp my lips together and nod a few times before managing to squeeze out, "He was a really good man."

"How long had he been working for you?"

A small smile brushes my lips. "Almost six years. Since the start of my career. Back before I even needed a bodyguard. He...he saw it all with me."

I've met his family, a few times, actually. We had them over for Thanksgiving. And they probably wouldn't have said anything if I showed up to the funeral. They would have welcomed me with open arms. They understood the dangers of his job. How seriously he took it.

But I couldn't look any of them in the eye. I couldn't get down on my knees and hug his three-year-old son, mourning alongside them, knowing I'm the reason he's dead.

"What about your music? Have you started writing again?"

I crack my knuckles and sigh. "Not since the wedding."

"How about we call that homework for this week? No need to force anything, but sit down at the piano or grab your guitar. Just for ten minutes. See where it takes you."

I hum noncommittally, not bothering to tell her I don't have access to either of them right now. They're still holed up in the old apartment.

But something feels different about the music now. It used to be the first place I turned. Whenever I had a bad day, getting lost in a song, finding just the right notes, tweaking the lyrics until they were perfect, it was the only thing that brought me peace.

But now the idea of picking up my guitar or sitting at my piano has all my muscles tensing. This is the longest I've gone without practicing since I was a kid. Or if I wasn't practicing, at least I was scribbling poems and lyrics in my journal. But the only thing I'd be able to write about right now is *him*.

And I can't. I *can't*.

I can't think about him. I can't put it into words. I can't do him enough justice. Nothing I write would ever be good enough.

But the idea of writing about something else is worse, somehow. Like I'd be sweeping his memory under the rug, rushing to move on and get back to normal. Like he was just a blip on my radar. A speed bump. A minor setback.

"Or what about picking up some old interests? You used to scrapbook, didn't you?"

I hum again. I did, in high school. And the first year I'd been on tour as Ryker to document it all, but it's not exactly an easy hobby to travel with, and it's time-consuming if you want it to look decent. Besides, this year is turning out to be full of things I don't want to remember.

"Do you want to talk about the arraignment?"

I finally look up from my hands. The man who'd showed up at the wedding, Jasper Young, had been arrested that night. Apparently in his grand scheme to stalk me across six different states, Elijah hadn't been his only victim. He'd also killed the man at the front gates to the vineyard and a cashier at a gas station a dozen miles from the property. To avoid having any witnesses, the police suspected.

The hitch, of course, being me.

Because if everything had gone according to plan, he would've killed me last, and there would've been no witnesses. Just a lot of blood and a string of bodies in the middle-of-nowhere New York.

So I guess I have the blood of those two people on my hands too.

As for the arraignment, I don't see what difference it makes. He can plead guilty or not guilty. I know what he did. And it'll be months until the trial, at least. So it's not like this is going away any time soon.

I glance at the clock behind Dr. Martin's head, then sling my bag over my shoulder. "It looks like we're out of time."

She presses her lips together and lets out a small sigh through her nose. "Parker—"

"Thank you."

I can't even look at the man in the waiting room, but I know he'll follow as I duck into the hallway and head for the parking garage on the lowest level.

He's dressed in the same all black Elijah always wore, but his footsteps are louder, his movements less graceful. I can't remember his name, and it doesn't matter because he'll be replaced tomorrow.

I try not to think about Elijah as the car pulls onto the street and heads to the temporary apartment I've been staying at since this all went down. Even the driver is some new guy—Abe, my old one, quit a few days after the wedding. Not that I blame him for it. He's got two young kids at home and a third on the way.

I can't remember the new guy's name either. He's quieter than Abe ever was, seemingly content sitting in silence, though it's difficult to tell behind the dark sunglasses, beard, and hat.

Elijah always used to take me to Bean There, Done That

after therapy, and we'd order one of every pastry they had to take back and eat throughout the day.

The car passes the coffee shop without preamble, and I squeeze my eyes shut. Even the clothes I'm wearing are unfamiliar. With the ever-present crowd waiting outside my old apartment, no one has dared go in and retrieve my things in case they're followed back to the new place.

The new apartment looks more like a hotel than anything —all white furniture and no personal touches. The bodyguard does a quick sweep, then lets me shuffle to the bedroom, where I promptly close the door behind me, yank the curtains shut, and bury under the covers, where I plan to spend the rest of the day.

Just like I have every day this week.

An Excerpt from Parker's Journal

it's one of those nights
when I don't mind
being alone

the sadness is loud
but familiar

like a sweater worn
a few too many times

I think:

perhaps this is a lesson
a preparation
to brace
for greater losses to come

but then:

the possibility
is too cruel to consider
for more than a breath

both at the notion
that this hurt
is not the extent
of what my heart
is capable of feeling

but also:

could another life
really be expendable
for my sake?

I don't have room
left in my baggage
for the extra guilt

how conceited I'd have to be
to make it about me
in the first place

CHAPTER 9

HEATH

I don't know who's going to be on my ass more, the guys or Iz. I should've emailed or called to give notice, but I didn't want to say anything unless I knew I found something else. I hadn't thought ahead enough to expect the new job to want me to start right away.

I keep the run short this morning, just a quick three miles, and despite the welcome sting of the cold rain on my skin, it doesn't ease my mind the way it usually does. I'm just as tense and amped up as I climb into the shower as I was before I left.

I get to the site before sunrise, but unsurprisingly, Iz is already there. Car horns blare as I jog across the street through a cloud of vehicle exhaust and sawdust, mentally preparing my speech, but every word disappears from my mind the moment Isabella turns around.

She shouldn't be an intimidating woman. She can't be more than five feet tall, and after some of the guys gave her a hard time on the first day about being too weak or whatever, she started showing up in a hot pink hardhat and matching eyeshadow. As a daily *fuck you* reminder, probably.

And yet, as those calculating eyes fall on me and she props her clipboard on her hip, an icy sense of dread trickles through my veins.

"What are you doing here so early?" she calls, then her gaze flicks to my attire, and her eyebrows nearly disappear into her hairline as she realizes I'm not dressed to be on-site today. "And what the hell are you wearing?"

"You have a minute?"

She considers me then nods at the hotel's lobby. I duck through the sheet of plastic covering the entrance and follow her toward the back.

"How's Dani?" she asks without looking at me.

I flinch as I skirt around a stack of PVC pipes. That had been my excuse for calling out last minute yesterday. An emergency at the hospital. Definitely picked up some bad karma for that one.

"She's stable."

"Hey!" Iz shouts and snaps her fingers a few times. Wyatt's head appears through a tarp on our right, the hood of his sweatshirt so matted with dirt you can barely tell it's orange.

"Oh hey, Bridgers," he says.

Iz snaps again, bringing his attention back to her. She points at the ladder propped beneath the scaffolding, a rope draped over one of the rungs. "That's a disaster waiting to happen. Fix it."

"Yes, sir." Wyatt salutes her, then winks at me before disappearing toward the methodic thudding of a nail gun.

"Look, Bridgers," Iz sighs, finally facing me, "if you're quitting on me, can you spit it out already?"

"I—how did you know?"

She rolls her eyes as if the answer's obvious, but she doesn't look as angry as I'd expected.

"Look who finally decided to show up!"

Heavy boot clomps grow louder, and a hand claps between my shoulders as Duncan's bulky form appears on my right. "Am I interrupting a scolding?" He raises his palms and takes a step back. "Don't go easy on him, Iz!" With that, he heads off after Wyatt.

Iz gives me a pointed look as if saying, *Do you see who you're leaving me with?* "Is everything okay, really?" she asks, the hard edge to her voice gone.

"How much will you hate me if I tell you I found another job?"

She frowns as a metallic crash reverberates somewhere behind us. "Hate? No. Jealous? Maybe. But it will be a loss. You're one of the best we've got around here."

"I'm blushing."

She bangs her clipboard against my shoulder. "Shut up and get out of here then." She hesitates before passing me and adds, "And good luck to you. We won't judge you too much if you end up crawling back to us."

There's another clang of metal on metal, louder this time, and she lets out a small huff and hurries toward it.

From anyone else, the comment would feel more like a dig. But I know she's trying to be supportive, letting me know they'd welcome me back here if I needed them.

Shoving my hands in my pockets, I take in the surrounding chaos, the air heavy with cigarette smoke, dust, and the chalky aftertaste of plasterboard. Music drifts from a radio overheard as heavy footsteps stomp against the wooden scaffold platforms, and an odd feeling rises in my chest. Something almost…sentimental. Which is dumb, because it's not like I've particularly enjoyed sweating my balls off here with these idiots, but I've worked with a lot of the same guys for the past few years. Some I've known since high school. In a lot of ways, it feels like a large, dysfunctional family. And the work isn't terrible. The pay is decent. And it's familiar. I always know what to expect.

"Bridgers, what the hell are you doing? Give me a hand!"

I grab the other end of a piece of drywall as Duncan steps into the room. After a moment, my attire registers.

He scowls. "Ah, shit."

"I didn't get fired."

He smirks, unconvinced.

"I found a new job."

"Doing what?"

I hesitate but settle on: "Security."

"Traitor," he says, but he's smiling. "All right then, hotshot. Let us a buy you a beer tonight. Eight? Usual?"

I nod and help him carry the drywall to prop against the steel framing. "Sure."

"Bridgers!" he calls before I can head out, a small grimace crossing his face. "And Dani…is she?"

"Still the same."

"I suppose no news is better than bad news, right?"

"Yeah." I run my hand along the back of my neck and clear my throat. "See you tonight?"

"You know what'll happen if you're late!"

I wave my hand over my shoulder as I jog for the exit. "Yeah, yeah."

UP AND UP is probably the worst bar in town. It has to be in the top ten, at least. But it has its regulars, and unfortunately, I'm one of them.

Rachel waves at me from behind the bar as I step inside. She pointedly ignores the man at the far end, who is practically unconscious, his beard submerged in what's left of his beer. His mouth is moving, so he must be asking for another drink.

Each step feels like I'm peeling my boots off the floor, but there's something oddly comforting about the sensation. If the floor in here were clean, I'd be concerned.

The other guys aren't here yet, so I grab a seat at the bar, scanning the modest crowd. There are a few people in the back playing pool and darts, but it's relatively quiet.

Rachel slides the beer I like across the bar without me asking, and I nod my thanks. It's only been a week or so since I was in here last, but it looks like she added yet another piercing to her face. I lost count after ten.

The man at the other end of the bar lets out a wailing sound, and she sighs and heads his way. My gaze flicks to the TV overhead, hoping for a game, but it's set on some newscast.

"How the hell did you get here before me?" Duncan slides onto the stool on my right and taps the bar with two fingers when Rachel looks at us.

I don't bother responding and take a sip of my beer instead. Duncan's apartment is right around the corner, but so is the hospital. And after sitting in Dani's room for most of the day and seeing no signs of improvement, I was more than ready to get out of there.

"A few of the other guys said they'd stop by," he adds as

Rachel hands him a beer. "It's gonna be weird not seeing you around the site."

"It'll be weird for me too."

"You ever even worked in security before?"

I smirk. "No."

He barks out a laugh. "What poor sucker did you con into hiring ya then?"

A flash from the TV catches the corner of my eye, and Parker's picture fills the screen. The volume's muted so I can't hear what they're saying, but it's the same picture I've seen from the night of the wedding, followed by the mug shot of the guy who did it.

The look he gives the camera is undeniably smug. He has to be at least a decade older than Parker, if not more. But there's nothing deranged or crazed about the look in his eyes. Just cold, hard cruelty. He'd known exactly what he was doing.

Duncan makes a noise in the back of his throat. "You been following this? So fucked up."

"*You've* been following this?" He's hardly one to watch the news.

He shrugs. "Chelsea's a Ryker Rae fan."

I blink and sit back in my stool. It's easy to forget with Duncan that he's a good ten years older than I am—and that he has a thirteen-year-old daughter.

A daughter who, apparently, is a fan of my new boss.

"How'd she take the, uh...*reveal?*" I ask.

He shrugs again. "Likes her even more now."

"Huh." I swallow another mouthful of beer, watching as the screen shifts to some woman talking, though a picture of Parker onstage in her full Ryker look lingers off to the side. "That's actually it."

"That's what?" grunts Duncan.

I point at the TV. "That's the job."

"You're Ryker Rae's new bodyguard?"

I smirk at the way he says her name. "You sound like a fan."

He takes a long drink of his beer and shakes his head. "I don't know, Heath."

The use of my first name stops whatever smart comment I could spew out next.

"Did you see her last one? I heard there are still pieces of him missing. That lunatic didn't just kill him to get to her. He butchered him. Brutal," he says, shaking his head. "I'd hate to see anything happen to you, kid."

I roll my eyes at the word *kid*, but I know what he means. The construction jobs didn't come without risks, but nothing at this scale. But it doesn't matter. Because this is what's happening. It isn't an option.

There is no other option.

I clear my throat. "I haven't even had my first day yet and you already think I'm going to be that bad?"

"This isn't a joke," he snaps, his voice surprisingly hard.

I raise my palms. "I never said it was. The pay is good," I add, quieter. "Which we're going to need."

His mouth sets in a grim line. I don't need to elaborate. He drums his fingers against his glass. "That fucker ever show his face again?"

I scowl, my molars grinding together. "No. I think he knows I'd kill him if he did."

"What the hell are you two looking so serious about over here?"

I jump as Wyatt materializes behind us, throwing his arms around our shoulders and crushing us together.

"Rachel, my dearest! Another round, please!" he calls.

She rolls her eyes, smirking as Wyatt, Finn, and Banks fill the remaining stools.

"I don't know why we're celebrating you when I should be kicking your ass for leaving," says Finn as he takes the beer from Rachel and holds it up as if preparing to make a toast. "Bridgers, you son of a bitch, moving on to bigger and better things and leaving the rest of us in the dust."

"Looks like *you* might have a career in theater," I mumble into my beer.

"I hate to say it, I really do," he continues, "but we're all proud of you."

He claps me hard on the back as everyone takes a drink.

"You know, Finn," I say. "In the ten years I've known you, I think that's the nicest thing you've ever said to me."

He snorts. "Don't get used to it."

CHAPTER 10
HEATH

Maybe I got too carried away with images of James Bond in my head, but this is definitely not what I'd been expecting from the job. Something at least a *little* exciting. Maybe a few overzealous fans lunging at us on the streets. I didn't realize I'd signed up to be a goddamn babysitter.

I show up the first day expecting a fast pace and steep learning curve...only to find her team basically has her under house arrest. After getting acquainted with the surrounding area, the outside of the building, and the entrances, Faye leads me upstairs to her apartment.

The only way I can think to describe Parker's manager is she looks like an elementary school art teacher...but goth... and slightly terrifying. I can't tell if she's wearing layers or if all those scraps of patterned fabric belong to one piece of clothing. As if she weren't visually assaulting enough, she also makes noise. Lots of it. Her thick high heels pound against the ground, and she wears a million and one bracelets that bang together with her every move.

I can already feel a headache coming on.

"Don't take it personally," Faye says as we near the door.

I quirk an eyebrow.

She opens and closes her mouth as if debating what to say. "Things have taken a toll on her, as you can imagine. She's not usually...like this."

My eyebrow lifts another inch. Whatever the hell *like this* means can't be good. Not that she'd been especially personable at the interview.

Faye pats me on the back and grimaces, though I think she meant for it to be a smile, then opens the door.

Parker doesn't look up as we step inside. She's hunched on the couch, a blanket wrapped around her and some black-and-white movie playing on the TV. Every surface is littered with takeout food containers—the coffee table, the kitchen counter, even the stools. But they mostly seem untouched. Crumpled pieces of paper are scattered across the floor, blots of ink and angry pen strokes bleeding through the pages.

"Parker," Faye calls, the forced-chipper tone of her voice grinding against my nerves. "Heath's here."

She doesn't respond.

"I'll be in a meeting across town today, but you can reach me on my cell at any time, okay?"

I'm not sure if that's directed at me or Parker, but either way, Faye slips out the door without waiting for a response, and then it's just the two of us.

I stand in the entryway, hands in my pockets, and rock back on my heels. Aside from the takeout containers, there's not much else in here. Faye had mentioned this being a temporary apartment they'd moved her to after all the media attention, and it's clear no one bothered with anything other than the essentials. The walls are bare, the furniture minimal. Hell, even my dump of a place is homier than this.

Parker sits forward to grab something off the coffee table, her back still to me. The blanket is bunched up around her shoulders, shielding most of her face, and it looks like her hair's been in that knot on the top of her head for days now.

She grabs a small white container, pops it open, then digs out a spoonful and stuffs it into her mouth.

Is that...cake frosting?

"This isn't a nightclub," she says flatly, but even the quiet tone of her voice makes me jump as it shatters the quiet of the room. When I don't respond, she glances over her shoulder. "You don't have to stand at the door like some kind of bouncer." She turns back to the TV and shoves another spoonful into her mouth.

Right.

I drift forward, taking in the rest of the apartment. Seems like a pretty standard two bed two bath. I take the chair across from the couch, glancing at Parker sideways. She's not looking at me. She's not even looking at the TV. Her gaze is focused somewhere out the window.

Amid the chaos on the coffee table, there's a newspaper spread wide. The picture of her is huge—the one I saw online of her in the cemetery.

I can't help but wonder if that was a calculated move on her publicist's part. Try to gain some public sympathy. I have no idea how well Parker knew the guy who had this job before me. If today's any indication, she didn't even acknowledge when he was in the room. She's probably mad all this is cutting into her social calendar.

I push up from the chair, my jaw hard, and head for the

kitchen. Maybe some of these orders are still decent enough to eat since she's clearly going to waste them.

My phone buzzes in my pocket as I fish some French fries from a container.

> Saw Dani this morning. No change. The doctor said it might be time to start thinking about unplugging the machines.

My hand clenches so tightly around the phone I'm surprised it doesn't break. The one fucking day I'm not there and they spring that on her? I'm about to call her when my eyes flick to Parker on the couch.

Fuck.

I open the text instead.

> I'm sorry I wasn't there. Can we talk when I get off work?

> I just can't believe they think we're already at that point.

I rub my eyes with my hand hard enough that stars burst behind my eyelids. She's probably sitting alone in that room and crying. Dani hasn't even been in the hospital for a month and they're already trying to get rid of her? They just want to clear the bed so they can drain some other poor sucker's bank account. And they keep saying the tests look good—she has brain activity. Why would we unplug her and give up already?

My hands shake as I punch out my next text.

> We're not. It'll be okay.

I let out a frustrated breath through my nose, restless energy filling my body. At least at the construction site, I had ways to work some of it out. But here? Am I supposed to sit around with her all day? I'll go out of my fucking mind.

I pick through the different containers on the counter, finding ones recent enough to put in the fridge and throwing out things that have clearly been here awhile just to have something to do with my hands. At this rate, Parker's apartment will be spotless by the end of my shift today.

She glances up at the noise as I toss a few more containers in the trash. Wordlessly, she heads toward me.

I stiffen, wondering if she's about to yell at me for touching her stuff, but she picks up a container, sniffs it, makes a face, then tosses it in the trash.

The toll on her face is undeniable. I've grown far too familiar with the same signs all over my reflection the past few weeks. It isn't just the bags under her eyes, the unwashed hair, the puffiness in her face.

It's that distant look. The detachment. The kind you can't fake.

Some kind of understanding passes between us, and we turn and get back to work in silence.

WHEN IT'S FINALLY time to head out for the day, I don't even make it to the end of the hall before I'm ambushed by a very small woman in a very large dress. Annie, Parker's publicist.

Where Faye looks on the verge of instigating a séance, Annie looks ready to drop everything for a picnic. Maybe it's just noticeable since we're in New York. The weather here isn't terrible, but it certainly doesn't warrant the endless sundresses, sandals, braids, and freckles—which I'm pretty sure are fake.

She shuffles her weight back and forth and tugs me toward the stairs, shooting a glance over my shoulder at Parker's apartment. There will still be security overnight, her team has informed me—both the kind employed by the building and some hourly guys they've brought on. They said they might want me to stay overnight sometimes, but I'm really hoping that's not starting now.

All things considered, it wasn't a bad day. Neither of us said much, but she had groceries delivered so there was actual food, and we managed to clean the takeout chaos.

Her team supplied me with blueprints of her apartment and the building, all the exits highlighted. I'd spent some time studying those, wandering around the apartment to see everything for myself, and watching whatever Parker had on TV at the time. She'd disappeared into her room before noon for a nap, and I didn't see her for hours. Long enough that I'd nudged the door to check on her, but sure enough, she had the curtains drawn and slept most of the day away with the covers over her head.

It gave me the opportunity to call Mom, go through emails, pay some bills. But something twists in my stomach for being at all grateful for the time to myself.

"So how'd it go?" Annie says, her voice hushed as if Parker will hear us even though we're in the stairwell now.

I shrug. "Fine."

"Did she...say anything?" Annie wrings her hands together.

"Not much."

She deflates and takes a step back. "I don't know how else to help her," she murmurs, almost to herself. "I'm sorry. I don't mean to hold you up. I know you probably need to get home."

As anxious as I'd been to get out of here before, her words make me pause. "I'm sure the news will die down," I say slowly, hoping my response comes off as comforting, but it also sounds like a question by the end of it.

"Oh, it's not that." She waves her hand, eyes trained somewhere over my shoulder as if she can see Parker through the walls. "Losing Elijah... I don't know if she'll ever get over it."

"I—I didn't realize they were that close."

She gets a funny look on her face, followed by a small, sad smile. "We all loved him, but Parker especially. You should've seen the two of them. I think she saw him as a second father figure, at the very least. But they were also so buddy-buddy, sometimes it was infuriating. They were always getting into trouble."

I don't know why the words surprise me, but they do. Parker's grief is obvious. Anyone can see it. But I guess I didn't expect for it to run that deep. For it to go beyond how traumatic the attack was, how thoroughly her life got flipped upside down. But she'd also lost someone close to her. I've lost a lot of things in my life, but thankfully nothing at that scale.

My mind drifts back to Dani in that hospital bed, and my jaw tightens. The pain is immeasurable, and that's for someone who's still here.

And...I am a complete dick for assuming the worst.

"Anyway. We're all just worried about her. I know keeping her locked in that apartment all day isn't helping, but we don't know what else to do. I don't know if it's worth the risk, but then..."

"You and Faye are staying in the building with her, right?"

She nods.

"Do you...do that for all of your clients?" Crisis or not, uprooting your entire life seems a little much. Don't either of them have homes? Families? Hell, other clients to manage?

She lets out a small, humorless laugh. "No. I know it seems silly. And Faye has her own reasons. But for me, it wasn't even a question." She shrugs. "Parker's family."

"You guys are that close, huh?"

"Well, yes, but she's also my goddaughter." She smirks at whatever she sees on my face. Surprise, probably. Not that she's her godmother, per se—just that she's old enough for that. "Her mother and I went to high school together, then we were roommates through college. And I took a step back in the company a few years ago. Parker's the only client I manage myself anymore. I leave the rest to the youngsters." She steps aside to let me pass and gives my arm a gentle pat as she moves to the stair above me. "Have a good night, Heath."

"Have a good night," I murmur, though she's already slipped through the door.

CHAPTER II
PARKER

Heath Bridgers moves like a ghost. For such a large man, you'd think he'd make a sound, but no, his footsteps are silent. I never hear him enter the room. Sometimes I turn around and he's just *there*. I never hear him breathe or laugh or sigh—he's like a robot. And I can't tell if his face always looks like that or if he's scowling at me.

After the team set him up with a schedule, he's started appearing at the apartment first thing in the morning, though we haven't gone anywhere in the past few days.

Until today.

"Your wardrobe is already at the studio," says Annie, checking something off on her clipboard. "And they'll do your hair and makeup there. You're expected to go on for the evening show at seven, so we'll need to get there before five."

Heath is still waiting in the doorway. He cut his hair since the interview, leaving it short enough that he doesn't have to push it out of his eyes anymore. He's kept the all-black attire, though it's not like I enforce a uniform. His jaw flexes as he catches me looking at him. Even behind the scowl, he looks exhausted.

We've barely exchanged a few words since he started, but I feel his attention on me all the time. Which is his job, I suppose, but sometimes it feels like there's more to it. Like he's...studying me.

"Parker," says Annie. "Are you listening to me?"

I blink back to her. "I'm going on at seven."

She sighs and tucks the clipboard under her arm. "The car is downstairs. Faye is meeting us there. We can do practice questions on the way and while you're getting ready."

Practice questions, as if she's my lawyer preparing me for a trial. I didn't even want to do the damn interview in the first place, but she and Faye had insisted, saying it was best for the public to hear my story sooner rather than later—both for the upcoming arraignment's sake and my career's. To make it clear that I'm not hiding.

Even though that's exactly what I'm doing.

Heath sits beside me in the car as we head to the studio, and I stare at my hands in my lap. With each passing minute, the anxiety crawling over my skin digs in deeper, and my heart pumps out a frantic rhythm against my ribs.

I've never dealt with stage fright before. Being the center of attention has never been an issue for me. But maybe that was because *I* was never the actual center of attention. Behind the wig and the makeup and the fake name, it was all a performance, and one I could walk away from at the end of the night.

But tonight, I won't be stepping in front of that camera as Ryker Rae. I'll just be Parker.

Faye and Annie swarm around me as some woman I don't know does my makeup. A man appears about halfway through to do my hair. They try to make conversation but give up fairly quickly. Not that I'd be able to make out their words enough to respond even if I'd wanted to. The entire room is buzzing, everything a blur of movement. The air is too warm and full of hairspray, the lights of the vanity leaving behind spots in my vision. I stare at my reflection, the eye makeup natural and understated.

Usually when I go onstage as Ryker, I'm decked out in smoky eyes, the black wig, and nose piercings. Today, the man sets my blond hair in loose waves, and the woman finishes me off with a light pink lip.

I see what they're doing—trying to make me look young and innocent. Probably to elicit some sympathy, maybe help the intensity of the anger directed toward me die down.

I blink up at Annie leaning against the makeup counter, looking at me like she asked me a question.

"She's fine." Faye slips into view and wraps an arm around Annie. "The camera loves you. Just go out there and be yourself."

Myself being Parker, not Ryker. Do I even know how to be her in front of a crowd?

A man with a clipboard and headset pokes his head through the black curtains behind me. "They're ready for you."

Annie gives my shoulder a reassuring squeeze as I blow the air out of my cheeks and stand. Heath lingers by the curtains and gives me a curt nod as I pass.

The three of them follow me out and find their places behind the camera crew. Annie stays within my sight in case there's a disaster and she needs to signal me.

Miranda Meadows sits on a circular platform with bloodred velvet couches, lights pointing at her from every angle. She rises to her towering height, further accentuated by her dizzyingly tall heels, and grins as I approach.

"Parker Beck! We're so thrilled to have you on the show."

I shake her hand and sink into the couch she indicates, where another woman quickly scurries over to check my mic.

"I must say, I am incredibly sorry for your loss. These past few weeks must have been a real whirlwind for you."

I can't tell if she's being sincere or not but manage to force a smile. "Thank you. Yes. It's been...difficult."

"Well, the world is dying to hear your story. I can guarantee that."

I open my mouth to respond, but the conversation is apparently over because she turns so a man can dust more powder on her face. Immediately after, she jumps into some vocal warm-up exercises. I fidget in my chair and force out another calming breath. The lights are so hot I can already feel the sweat collecting on my lower back. Annie shoots me a thumbs-up from the sidelines.

You've done this a thousand times before, I remind myself.

"We're live in three...two..."

"Our next guest is someone you've probably seen all over the internet the past few days. Formerly known as Ryker Rae, the MTV Choice Awards Pop Singer of the Year, just weeks ago, it was revealed Ryker is not her real name. In fact, she's a different person entirely. Today I'm here with Parker Beck, the woman behind the wig. Tell me, Parker, has it been difficult to keep this up all this time? Your first album came out nearly six years ago. Seems like a long time to keep such a huge secret."

The camera swivels to me, and my cheeks cramp around my smile. "I guess I never thought of it that way. I just wanted what everyone else wants, to be able to go to work during the day but leave it behind when you go home. And if you're in the spotlight, you don't really have the luxury of doing that. So I decided early on that to keep those two parts of my life separate, I'd need something like a stage persona. So that's where Ryker Rae came from."

Miranda nods seriously. "Do you understand why some fans may be upset now though, hearing of this news?"

Upset or psychopathic?

I nod slowly. "I can definitely understand that if people felt like they could identify with Ryker or looked up to her, to find out she's not exactly what they thought could be confusing. Maybe even disappointing. But I hope they can understand why I did it."

"What would you say to the people who think you're a liar now? Fake?"

I shrug. "I may have used a wig and a different name, but I still wrote the music. Those words came from me. I meant everything I said when I was Ryker. I was trying to protect myself and the privacy of my family."

"There are certainly some people who don't see it that way."

There's a shift in Miranda's expression, the friendliness in her eyes sharpening into something else. "I'd like to talk about Jasper Young, if that's all right with you, Parker."

There is clearly no choice in the matter, so I nod.

"For any of you who don't know, Jasper Young was arrested a few weeks ago for the alleged murder of three people and the attempted murder of Parker Beck. He followed her to a wedding in upstate New York, where Young killed Parker's bodyguard and attacked her."

I bite the inside of my cheek so hard I taste blood. *His name was Elijah. Not Parker's bodyguard.*

Miranda turns away from the camera and faces me again. "His arraignment is coming up fairly soon now. Are you ready for that?"

"I'm ready for him to be locked away for good. There were countless witnesses and evidence. There's not much else to say."

"I'd argue there's plenty else to say!" Miranda laughs like somehow this situation is funny, and my spine stiffens. "Jasper Young reported that he'd been in contact with you over many years—sending fan mail, notes, coming to your shows. Can you tell us what that night was like? What he was like when you saw him?"

"You mean when he was covered in blood and came at me with a knife?"

A few people gasp, and I catch movement out of the corner of my eye—Annie making desperate hand movements, though I have no idea what they mean.

"It was terrifying," I add. "I was standing there with my best friend who had just gotten married. Elijah, my bodyguard, was dead, and my boyfriend was missing, so I had no idea if he was dead. All I could think about was how to get my friend away so he wouldn't hurt her too."

Miranda's eyes flash. "Ah yes. Let's talk about your boyfriend, Rick Aldine."

I silently curse myself. I set her right up for that one.

"The story that leaked about your name identified him as the source. Was this something the two of you had discussed?"

"No, we had not discussed it."

"So why—"

I cut her off because suddenly hearing the actual question feels unbearable. "I'm assuming he did it for the money. We're no longer together or in contact with one another."

Miranda lets an awkwardly long stretch of silence grow between us. "You seem angry," she finally says.

It takes every ounce of my remaining willpower not to laugh. "It's been a lot to process. Clearly traumatic. I'm just trying to deal with the aftermath and move forward."

"And what does that look like for you? Moving forward? Will you continue to put out music as Ryker Rae or as Parker Beck now?"

I shift in my seat, almost not wanting to say my next words just so she doesn't get the satisfaction of airing it on her show first. I glance at Annie, hoping she can read the apology in my eyes. Heath stands behind her, his usually stoic expression pinched together. For the briefest moment, I meet his eyes, then turn back to Miranda.

"Actually, I'm thinking I might take a step back and not continue with this career at all anymore."

AN EXCERPT FROM PARKER'S JOURNAL

a love letter to the girl who wrote love letters to other people:

it was your pretty words
so delicately chosen
that made him glow
from the inside out

without your filter
without your sight
he was just another face
in the crowd

CHAPTER 12

PARKER

"Parker Beck has *murdered* Ryker Rae! That's what the headline says!"

"How could you not run something like this by us first—"

"Are you insane—"

"You have outstanding contracts—"

"I realize this is an emotional time, and a break is completely understandable, but *quitting*—"

I sigh and pinch the bridge of my nose with two fingers as Annie and Faye talk over each other, their voices blending until I can't differentiate who is saying what.

Heath sits silently beside me as the car pulls away from the studio, the blinding lights burned into the backs of my eyelids.

"Can we talk about this later?" I mumble.

Faye sucks in a sharp breath. "Oh, you can *bet* we're going to talk about this."

I put up a hand before Annie can jump in. "I just—need tonight, okay? Just."

Faye humphs but relents.

There's a crowd accumulated at the front door of the new apartment building, several of them holding signs with red hearts and cutouts of my face.

"We love you, Parker!" they chorus.

I force a smile and wave through the window, then sigh inwardly as the car pulls into the parking garage. Keeping this address a secret clearly didn't last long.

Faye and Annie head for their own temporary apartment a few floors lower than mine, but Heath follows me upstairs. I head straight for the kitchen and dig a bottle of wine out of the fridge. I'd grab something stronger if I had it.

I pause at the cabinet, eyeing the glasses. "Do you want one?"

He doesn't respond at first. "I'm still on duty."

I eye him over my shoulder. "Shouldn't you be done for the night?"

"I've got the night shift."

"Night shift," I mumble, eyes darting to the guest room behind him as I realize he's intending to *stay* here. I sigh and uncork the bottle with a satisfying pop. "So they have you babysitting me full-time now."

"They're just being extra careful until after the news dies down."

I snort and pour myself a generous glass, knowing full well it's *until the news dies down* for now, but then it will be *until after the trial*, and then it will be something else. Now that the secret's out, there's no going back to the way things were. I'm sure my *errand* before the funeral didn't help calm their nerves either.

"You dropped quite the bomb tonight," he offers as I slide onto a barstool.

I swirl the wine, surprised he's actually trying to have a conversation with me. He hasn't been much of a talker so far. Though, to be fair, neither have I. "Forget Jasper Young. I think Faye wanted to murder me herself."

"Did you know you were going to say that before you went on there?"

I swallow half the glass in a single gulp, then stare at the smudge of lipstick left on the glass. "No."

It hadn't felt impulsive though. More like the thought had existed in the back of my mind for a long time, buried deep in my subconscious, far before the wedding.

Ryker Rae was all I ever wanted at eighteen. And the momentum she took off at, it was the kind of current that swept you up and didn't let you go, didn't let you stop to *breathe*. And who was I to question it? Who was I to be anything but thankful that all of my wildest dreams had come true? A million girls would've killed to be in my shoes.

It's not that I don't love it, the music, the performing.

But I'm not eighteen anymore. And this hasn't felt like a dream come true in a long time.

I glance from the stool beside me to where he's awkwardly standing by the door. "If you're going to be here all night, you might as well sit down."

Half a smirk sneaks onto his face at that, and he pulls out the seat beside me. He drums his fingers on the counter as I pour myself a second glass, and strangely, the first thought that pops into my head is *His hands don't look like bodyguard hands.* I suppose I should know, considering how many I've gone through. His fingers are long and thin like they're more equipped for a piano than the gun I know he has strapped to his belt.

The veins stand out and dance along the backs of his

hands as they move. Two thick silver bands sit on his pointer and middle fingers, tapping lightly against the granite. I noticed the tattoos at his interview but hadn't gotten a good look at them. They must be on the backs of his arms and wrists, the edges barely sneaking out of his sleeves.

"I talked to Annie," he says.

My eyes snap back to his face.

"About Elijah. I didn't realize the two of you were so close." He pauses. "I'm sorry."

My throat tightens at the sound of his name. I don't know if I'll ever be able to hear it without feeling like I got punched in the stomach.

"He was like that cool uncle, you know?" I murmur. I don't even know why I'm saying it, why I'm suddenly able to talk about him. Maybe it's easier with someone who never knew him. "He acted like my father half the time, but the other half, we just had fun. It drove Faye nuts. She always felt like the two of us were ganging up on her."

The smile falls from my face as my mind drifts back to the wedding. It had taken the police hours to find his body once they'd started searching the vineyard.

"I can't even remember the last thing I said to him," I whisper. "I barely spoke to him that day at all. I was so busy with the wedding. And I *saw* him get up in the middle of the ceremony. I *knew* something was wrong, but I—"

"If you'd followed him, you'd be dead too," Heath says quietly. "And there's no way he would've wanted that."

"Well." I cough a little and run the back of my hand across my nose. "I'm sure he didn't want his son to have to grow up without a father either." I down the rest of my wine and set the glass on the counter, wavering on whether my empty stomach could handle a third. "Can we talk about something else? Like why you needed this job so badly?"

A shadow falls over his face, and he pushes his chair back. At first I think I've offended him and he's going to disappear into the guest room like some sulking teenager, but he ventures into the kitchen, pulls down a glass, and fills it with water from the sink.

"My little sister," he says, then slides the glass across the counter to me. He raises his eyebrows and waits until I take it. "She's in the hospital right now. Bad car accident with her fiancé. She doesn't have insurance, and the bills are piling up. My mom can't take them on, so..." He gestures to me.

"Oh." I sip the water. "I'm sorry. But she's okay?"

"She's been in a coma for the past few weeks."

"Oh my God," I breathe. That would explain why he's looked on the brink of death himself. The worry. "Heath, I'm —I'm so sorry."

He nods stiffly.

"And her fiancé? Was he okay?"

That sparks a bitter laugh out of him. "He was the one driving. He was the one at fault. And he got away without a scratch. And you know what he did when the doctors said there might be a possibility of brain damage? He left her. He left her in that hospital bed, and we haven't seen him since."

"And I thought my ex was shitty," I mutter.

He rubs a hand over his face. "He was the one who leaked all of this to the press, right?"

I nod. "We were together two years. He was the only person outside of my team or family who knew. I guess whatever paycheck they offered him this time was too big to refuse."

"Wow, fuck that guy."

I laugh and cover my face with my hands. "Fuck *all* guys, honestly. No offense."

"None taken." He braces his arms on the counter and leans toward me. "Maybe I will have that glass after all."

IT'S COLDER in the dream than I remember it being that night. I stand barefoot in the gravel in front of the winery, my toes numb. The wind picks up, and my dress blows around my legs. But there's no one else here. I try to call for Elijah, but no sound comes out.

A branch cracks in the vineyard behind me. I turn, my body stuck in slow motion, and try to run toward it, but my legs move like they're in wet cement.

The wind roars and stings as it lashes my eyes, but I push forward until I break through the tree line. It's darker over here, and I squint, trying to make out the path. My toes brush something wet and warm, and I crouch to get a better look. Thick red blood is pooled among the dead leaves.

Elijah! I try to scream again.

Then, up ahead, I see it.

He's on his back, his arms bent the wrong way and laid out around him. Blood has already soaked through the front of his white shirt. I fall to my knees, pushing the sunglasses from his eyes, and they stare up at me, unseeing.

This time when I scream, the sound rings loud and clear. Birds jump into flight from the trees as I clutch Elijah's chest and sob.

Light momentarily blinds me, then I jerk into a seated position. I blink a few times, and slowly, my bedroom swims into focus. The sheets are damp with sweat, and I pull in a shaky breath as I take in Heath standing in the doorway.

His hair is tousled, his eyes half-open. He's changed out of the many layers he'd had on earlier today, now in a black T-shirt and dark gray sweatpants.

"You all right? I heard screaming."

I swallow and nod. My hands shake as I push the sweaty hair out of my face.

He eyes me for another moment, then nods toward the kitchen. "Come on, I'll make you some tea."

I don't argue and wrap myself in a blanket before I follow. Even though the apartment is perfectly warm, my body feels chilled to the bone like I'm still in the dream.

He sets the kettle on the stove as I slide onto a barstool and wrap the blanket tighter around my shoulders.

"You have the nightmares a lot?" he asks.

"Since the night it happened."

He nods slowly, a weird look on his face, like he's debating his next words. "You ever try imagery rehearsal?"

"Imagery rehearsal?"

He scratches the back of his neck. "You, uh, basically practice how you want the nightmares to end, so you have more control. Some people write it out. Or you can just repeat it in your head a lot. Change the narrative, basically."

It sounds like he's speaking from personal experience. Hell, it sounds like something my therapist would suggest. And there's far more behind his eyes that he's not saying.

Heath Bridgers has nightmares.

"And which do you do?" I whisper.

He gives me a grim smile. "Writing it out has been better for me."

I tighten my fingers around the blanket, resisting the urge

to ask what his are about. It feels like too personal a question for a near stranger. But still...I find myself studying his profile, like I'll find the answer on his face.

We watch the kettle in silence until the tea's ready. He pours two cups and slides one across the counter. I mumble a thanks and wrap my hands around the mug, hoping the warmth will soak into me.

He doesn't say anything else, and neither do I. But the silence feels less empty, less suffocating than it does when I'm alone. We sit together until we finish our cups, then head to our respective rooms. And this time when I sleep, I don't dream at all.

CHAPTER 13
PARKER

I wake to banging on the front door. My heart lurches into my throat, my body immediately awake, and I roll off the bed. Only a handful of people know about this apartment. The building is all over the internet now, sure, but the actual unit... And even if they were in a bad mood, I can't picture Faye or Annie knocking like that. But someone who wanted to cause harm wouldn't be knocking, right? They'd just break in?

Heath's door creaks open across the hall, and I hesitate in the doorway, watching as he goes to look through the peephole.

Whoever is outside knocks again, louder this time. Heath doesn't look particularly worried, so I venture out of my room to squint through next.

"You've got to be fucking kidding me."

"Who is—"

I swing the door open, revealing a very disheveled Rick in the hall. He's been drinking, that much is clear from the musty whiskey tang emanating from him, and his jeans and wrinkled T-shirt look like they're yesterday's clothes.

Despite the hot anger flooding my system, the sight of him makes my stomach drop. After being together for over two years, of course we've had disagreements and fights. I've been angry with him before. But I've never felt this...hurt. Betrayed. Entirely and completely blindsided.

And then I never got an apology. An explanation. An effort to fix things. He just disappeared. Like I never meant anything to him at all and he didn't care about the damage he left behind.

He takes in Heath standing behind me, then looks to my face, a question in his eyes, something like hurt flashing across them. I know the wrong assumption he's made, but I'm not going to correct him.

"What are you doing here?" I demand instead, hardening my jaw. "How'd you even know where I was?"

"Who's that?" he asks.

An incredulous laugh gets stuck in my throat. "Is that *really* the first thing you want to say to me right now?"

He narrows his eyes at Heath, like *Yes, this* is *the most pressing matter*, before focusing back on me. "Can I come in?"

My hand tightens around the door. "No."

"Parker—"

"What do you want, Rick? You're not welcome here."

Under different circumstances, the pitiful slump of his shoulders might spark some sympathy in me. Concern, even. But for all I know, he's faking it. I don't trust myself to read him anymore, since I clearly didn't know him at all the way I thought I did.

"Can we just talk—"

"Talking would have been a good idea *before* you decided

to blow up my life then disappear and leave me to deal with the aftermath."

Heath retreats into the apartment, and Rick's eyes track the movement. When he finds my face again, he swallows hard and drops his gaze to the floor.

"Look, I saw your interview. I've felt so awful this whole time, but didn't know how to... I'm so sorry about how everything went down, Parker. I am."

I want nothing more than to slam the door in his face, but something makes me hesitate. If not for his sake, then for mine. Because as much as I haven't wanted to, I've spent nights going through the possibilities in my head. Dissecting every moment between us, every touch, every glance. Trying to pinpoint when things went wrong. When he decided to do this.

"Then why?" I ask quietly.

He looks at me through his lashes and spread his hands, the look in his eyes desperate because we both know there isn't an acceptable answer.

"I was going to lose my job," he says, his voice hoarse. "And I've worked so hard to get here. And I couldn't imagine all those years and student loans and late nights being for nothing. I just...I panicked."

A small jolt of surprise goes through my chest. Rick *has* worked harder than anyone I know. I lost count of how many times I'd wake up in the middle of the night and find him hunched over his laptop, desperately trying to meet a deadline. How many times we had to reschedule our dates because he was working late—but I never faulted him for it, not with how crazy my schedule is.

I helped him practice his pitches, proofread his proposals, gave him pep talks before every meeting. But he never complained about it, not once. He loved his job with a passion I admired—it was one of the first things we bonded over.

The stress and pressure he was under would have been impossible to miss...but everything at work always seemed to be going well for him. The magazine has been growing, he had great relationships with his coworkers. I'd even had dinner with his boss a few times with him.

I shake my head. "What does that have to do with me?"

He lets out a slow breath and closes his eyes. "Angie Redford—a writer at our biggest competitor—she knew. I don't know how, but she knew I was walking on thin ice. And if she printed that...if what little staff I had left that believed in my vision smelled blood..."

My muscles stiffen at the name, the same one in the byline of the article that burned my life to the ground.

"She already had the story on you written. She had all the details," he says quietly. "She already had the pictures. The ones of the two of us together when you were dressed like Ryker, and they connected it to the one of us kissing on New Year's last year when you looked like you. She basically blackmailed me. I just had to nod if it was true, and that's all I did. I nodded."

"All you did?" I demand, my voice spiking up an octave. Any softening my heart may have been doing for him hardens into ice. "All you *did*? So you came all this way with this—I wouldn't even call it an apology—to tell me you'd rather—"

"I was in a horrible position. I was scared. And I will regret it for the rest of my life."

"Then where have you been?" I grit my teeth, hating the

tears threatening to rise. "Elijah is *dead*. And I—" My voice breaks, and I shake my head and look away.

He opens and closes his mouth with an audible snap.

"You didn't think to come to me with this?" I whisper. "To ask me for help? You didn't think to *warn* me, at the very least? You didn't think I deserved that much?"

I don't care that there are tears in his eyes now. That he actually looks like he's sorry. That for some goddamn reason my heart still aches seeing him in pain.

"You're a lot of things, Rick. But I never realized you were a coward."

He swallows hard but says nothing. And it's this, more than anything else he's said or done, that makes something snap inside me. Because he's not here to beg for *my* forgiveness. To make things right. To see if I'm okay. To fix the mess he's made. He's hurting and feeling guilty, and he wants *me* to feel sorry for *him.* To make *him* feel better.

I shake my head and take a step back. "I hope it was worth it."

"Parker," he starts, his voice cracking, but the door slams in his face before any more words can come out.

I allow myself one moment—a single moment—to stare at the surface of the door and pull in a deep breath. To let the emotions warring inside me have free rein. But then as I exhale and turn, I force myself to let it all go.

"Is that coffee?" I ask.

Heath watches me from the kitchen with wide eyes. "Yeah, I just started a pot."

"Great." I edge past him and pull down a mug as Rick starts knocking again. Ignoring it, I grab the coffeepot. The knocking continues. My molars grind together, my skin feeling hot. Hasn't he done enough? What does he possibly think he can say to—

Heath throws the door open and slips into the hallway. I freeze. Maybe I should go after him, but instead, I drum my fingers against my mug and wait. When a minute passes and I can't hear anything, I make my way to the hall. The door opens before I can reach for the handle.

Slowly, I look from the hallway behind Heath—now noticeably empty—to his face. "What did you say to him?"

He avoids my eyes as he heads past me to the kitchen. "He won't be bothering you anymore." He pauses with the coffeepot in his hand, a hint of uncertainty creasing his fore-head, like maybe I hadn't wanted him to scare Rick off.

Curiosity buzzes in the back of my brain, but I don't push it. God, I just don't want to keep talking about this. The longer we do, the more I'll think about it, and the harder it will be to keep the emotions at bay.

So instead, I nod, slide onto the barstool, and take a sip of my coffee.

I know Heath heard all of that. And maybe I should be embarrassed about him being an audience to my personal life going up in flames, but I can't muster the energy to care. The whole fucking world is in my business now.

"Was the—uh—guest room okay?"

"Oh, yeah." He leans back against the cabinets. "It was fine."

"Cool."

"Cool."

We stare at each other, the awkwardness settling in the air like humidity.

"So are you ever planning on actually moving in here?" he asks.

"I—what?"

He smirks, sets his coffee on the counter, and raises his eyebrows. "This place is covered in boxes. You have barely any furniture. Nothing on the walls."

"Oh." I grimace. Decorating my last apartment had been one of my favorite things to do. It was the first place that was entirely mine. I could do whatever I wanted with it.

Which doesn't mean it looked good, but it was a combination of all my favorite things. I painted the walls different colors—some black, some olive green. I had shelves everywhere. Plants. A million different light fixtures. My collection of instruments. The comic books my brother got me into. It felt unequivocally me.

But then I had to leave it all behind.

I took some things with me, of course, but most of my stuff is back in that apartment. And now that the address has leaked and people have broken in, it all feels contaminated. Violated. Like something that was completely mine somehow no longer belongs to me at all.

And this new space is empty and blank and white, and the idea of trying to decorate it, of trying to make it feel like me, is exhausting. Because trying to make it look the way the old one had doesn't feel right. But if not that, then I don't know what to do. I don't know what would look like me now.

I guess starting over from scratch is always daunting.

Stupidly, something I can't help but think about is Rick. I've never been super handy. So any time I'd wanted to try a new project, he'd really been the one to do everything, and I supervised. He hung the shelves, he bought all the hardware. If I couldn't find a piece of furniture that was exactly what I wanted, he built it for me.

My throat tightens. I look down at my coffee, trying to

hold on to the cold indifference I'd had a few moments ago. Hell, even the anger would be better. I don't know what to do with the good memories.

Because clearly they didn't mean as much to him as they did to me.

I glance up to see Heath watching me and cringe internally. My thoughts probably just played out on my face. He crosses his arms as he takes in the space around us.

"I've never been much for decorating," he admits, "but how hard can it be?"

I raise an eyebrow. "You want to help me decorate the apartment?"

"Well, it seems like I'm going to be here as much as you are, and I would rather not look at four empty walls all day. So really, I'm doing this for me, not you." He smiles as he says it, and I can't help but smile back.

"I wouldn't even know where to start."

He shrugs. "I have a few ideas."

CHAPTER 14
HEATH

Faye's instructions were clear—keep her out of public. But I'm not a warden, and how long can they expect her to stay locked in that apartment before she loses it? Hell, I've only been there a few days and I'm already getting antsy.

And I definitely wasn't going to let her sit around with that miserable look on her face all day. Besides, I doubt the kind of people who would recognize her frequent Home Depot.

Though, if anything's going to give her away, it's how damn obvious she's being about it. She's wearing a similar outfit as the one she wore to the coffee shop the day we met —brown wig, black baseball hat, hoodie. But she keeps looking around like she's expecting to someone to jump out and scream *Gotcha!* When she goes to tug the hat lower for the *fifth* time, I swat her hand aside instead.

"Quit fidgeting."

She scowls as I grab one of the orange carts and head through the door, the familiar scents putting my mind at ease. It's something about the combination of sawdust, paint, metal, cement, and lumber that feels homey—maybe because it smells like a lot of the sites did. There are worse things than getting paid to walk around here. Certainly better than the apartment that's starting to feel like one of those solitary confinement cells in a high-security prison.

"What are we even looking for here?" she asks.

I shrug. "Whatever catches your eye."

It's fairly quiet since it's the middle of the day, and the majority of the customers are men my age or older—none of whom give us a second glance. She somehow manages to look even *more* miserable than she did in the apartment, her feet shuffling more than walking.

Maybe I should've taken her to one of those stores that sells overpriced canvases with stupid quotes on them.

We walk in silence through a few of the aisles before she throws her hands up. "I don't know, Heath."

I brace my forearms on the cart and lean toward her. "We're not leaving until we find something. So either you choose or I'm going to. And you're not going to like what I pick."

I was hoping for a smile, but apparently pursing her lips is the best I'm going to get. At least, that's what it looks like. I can barely see her face beneath the hat. She must have tugged it down again when I wasn't looking. She sighs and tucks the fake hair behind her ears.

Well, considering her net worth, it's probably real hair.

"There must be something here you like. A plant. A shelf. *Something.*"

She lets out an impatient noise in the back of her throat that she probably doesn't mean to be cute, but it is.

"I don't know. I don't even know how long I'm going to be in this place, so what's the point?"

"Ah, but that's the beauty of it." She's clearly not going to take the reins here, so I pivot and wave for her to follow me as I head for the opposite side of the store. "If it's temporary, there are no stakes."

There's no way she's supposed to paint the walls since it's a rental, but we can either cover it up after or I'm sure the fee would be pocket change to her.

She lets out another little exasperated noise as I stop at the paint section and search through the palette cards, handing them to her one by one as I pick them off the wall.

She flicks one around in her fingers. "Bubblegum pink, really?"

Once I've picked out a little over a dozen, I nod for her to follow me to the counter.

"I—which one are you getting?"

I smile and take the rest of the cards from her. "All of them, obviously."

I THINK it's the first genuine—if a little devious—smile I've seen from her as she looks at me over her shoulder. "Faye is going to *kill* us."

The room is covered in plastic sheets, though we tried to move most of the furniture out of the way. I rip the blue tape with my teeth as I finish covering the molding.

Parker pops open the last of the paint cans, then stands and tugs her hair into a bun. She already changed into an old pair of gray sweats and a white T-shirt.

I really don't want to ruin the clothes I'm in—I'm not in a

KATIE WISMER

position to replace them right now—but I'm also not sure she'd take well to me stripping down to my boxers. And if I don't do this with her, I know she won't follow through. So I leave the pants and undershirt, but toss my button-down into her room and out of the way.

"Maybe we shouldn't..." she starts as I step beside her.

"No turning back now, superstar." I reach down, covering my hand in the blue paint, and raise my eyebrows at her. "Come on. You're first pitch."

She makes another of those little sounds of hers—this one something like a squeak—as she looks from me to the wall to the paint. "Heath..."

"Five. Four. Three."

"Okay, fine!" She reaches into the black paint and quickly flings her hand like she's trying to get a bug off.

The paint mostly lands on the plastic covering the floor, but a solid splatter hits the wall. She lets out a laugh—a real, genuine, *deep* laugh—then sidesteps to the pink paint. She looks at me as she throws it, the pink crisscrossing the black. "You're not going to make me do this all by myself, are you?"

The air quickly fills with the chalky scent, the paint cold as it drips down my fingers. Grinning, I throw a handful of the blue, and it lands as a large splash beside hers.

I'd tried to pick out colors that wouldn't look too awful together, so they're mostly varying shades of the same few. We add more blues and pinks and grays until the paint is dripping down the wall, the hesitation in her throws fading more and more each time.

Parker laughs and brushes a piece of hair out of her face with the back of her hand, smearing blue and pink along her cheek. She catches me staring at her a moment later. "What?"

I motion to my face. "You've got a little..." I trail off, not at all liking the look in her eye as she steps closer. "I know what you're thinking, and don't you dare."

"What?" she asks innocently. I think she even bats her eyelashes.

I hold a hand between us, and black paint drips from my fingers to the floor.

"What am I, five? You think I'm going to try to get paint on you?"

I slowly lower my hand, and her eyes track the movement like a deadly predator. We lurch forward at the same time, but I'm faster, and I wrap my arms around her waist and haul her against my chest.

She squeals and struggles as I smear the paint on her arms, her chest, her face, covering myself in the process as her hands tug on my arms.

I release her, laughing, and her hair comes loose from the tie. I reach to grab it for her but realize my mistake a second too late as she lunges for the blue paint. She crashes against me, her blue hands smearing against my face, my neck, my hair.

"Oh God. You got it in my mouth."

"Oh, I'm sorry!" She stumbles back, enough for me to grab the pink and dive for her legs. "You little liar!" she cries as we tumble to the floor, landing in the splatters already covering the plastic.

She's all too easy to pin, her body fitting perfectly under mine. I jerk back an inch, the thought coming out of nowhere, but Parker doesn't seem to notice.

"Truce! Truce!" she squeals. "I surrender!"

I roll onto my back beside her, grateful for the space as my skin tingles, and both of us laugh breathlessly. But even with the distance between us, the ghost of the feel of her body against mine lingers.

So much for trying to keep the paint off my clothes. But as I tilt my head to look at Parker—smiling with her eyes closed, paint in her hair and spread across her face—I can't bring myself to care.

"Thanks, Heath," she says, then squints an eye open. "That wall is fucking ugly, but I needed this."

I snort. We must've bumped into it as some point while we were struggling because there's a smear that looks a lot like a body in the center.

There's a softness to her profile, a peacefulness, that I haven't seen before. Had she been like this all the time before the attack happened? That seems the most tragic of all, for her to lose this...*light* in her. My gaze trails to the smudge of pink across her lips, her jaw, carving through the delicate angles of her face.

I quickly look back at the ceiling and clear my throat. "Can I ask you something?"

She hums.

"How did you pull off the Ryker secret? To strangers, sure, but everyone in your life? What the hell did they think you did for a living?" I tense as soon as the words leave my lips, thinking she's going to shut down. But she tilts her head, a thoughtful look falling over her face.

"It was easier than you'd think for the first few years, to be honest. I was eighteen, all my friends were going off to college and busy with their own lives. We told people I was a flight attendant to explain the traveling and why I was gone all the time."

"Makes sense," I murmur.

"Can I ask *you* something?"

I can't imagine anything about my life would be remotely interesting to her, but I nod.

"It's personal and none of my business," she adds.

I cough out a laugh. "Can't wait to hear this then."

"What are your nightmares about?"

Sighing, I fold my hands over my chest and focus on the stray splatters of paint on the ceiling. Opened myself right up for that one. I don't know why I'd said anything in the first place. It's not something I've ever felt the need to talk about before. But I don't feel any of the...resistance to tell her that I'd been expecting.

"Lately, they've been about Dani's accident. Only I'm the one driving the car, and it's my fault." I swallow, the image materializing. The shattered windshield, the blood, Dani hanging out of her missing door, held back only by her seat belt. I shake my head to clear it. "But when we were kids, our mom worked late, and we'd stay home alone a lot younger than we should have. I'd have these dreams about someone breaking in, Mom never coming home, waking up and Dani being gone, stuff like that."

She doesn't respond for long enough that I peer at her sideways, bracing myself for the Sympathetic Look Dani and I have gotten our entire lives. But as Parker stares back, there's a harsh line between her eyebrows, a firmness to the set of her mouth. After what feels like a very long time, she says, "I'm sure you don't want my pity. But thank you for telling me that."

"What. The. *Hell*. Happened. In here?"

We jerk up to find Annie standing in the doorway in a bright yellow sundress, eyes wide enough they look dangerously close to popping out of her head.

"We—um—" Parker starts.

"Home improvement project?" I offer.

"I'm sorry, Annie," Parker says. "We just—uh—got a little carried away. I promise, I can paint over it—"

"It's my fault." Surely they wouldn't fire me over something like this, right? "It was my idea."

Annie looks around the room, taking in the wall, the paint cans, the plastic tarps, *us*, and her expression twists into something that looks like a...pout?

"Why did no one invite *me*?"

AN EXCERPT FROM PARKER'S JOURNAL

it was a simple day
but one where being alive
felt more natural

CHAPTER 15

PARKER

The wall looks even worse in the morning, but that makes me love it more. Having all the furniture back in place helps, and maybe if I hung some pictures or something...okay, it would still be ugly, but it makes me smile when I look at it, and that's good enough for me. Certainly an improvement from before.

Heath has today off, and my body is having an annoyingly conflicted reaction to that. I mean, of course he deserves it. I can't honestly expect him to be here twenty-four seven. But it's also just...empty without him. The apartment is quiet, still. Hourly guards are taking shifts—either outside the building or my door, I don't know. I haven't bothered to check.

He's been here barely a week...but I've gotten used to having him around. Maybe that's heightened by him being the *only* person around.

I stand in the middle of the living room, my pulse in my ears the only sound, and hug my arms around myself. Before now, my life was always moving a million miles a minute. I was either at rehearsals practicing choreography, at the studio recording, at home writing songs, on tour, attending events, doing press interviews, at wardrobe fittings...I never had enough time to pause and really think.

But now, if I put all of that behind me, the days are this never-ending expanse of time. Seconds and minutes and hours that I don't know how to fill. Don't even know where to start.

I've toyed with the idea of going back to school more times than I can count, but it always seemed impossible. At first because of my schedule, but now...even if I managed to convince the team to let security follow me from class to class, I'd feel like more of a spectacle than I already am.

If I'm stuck in here anyway, maybe online classes wouldn't be too bad. It would give me something to do, at the very least. A distraction.

I consider the maze of boxes scattered across the apartment that's been collecting dust since I moved in, then grab the scissors from the kitchen to rip into one before I can talk myself out of it.

There's nothing particularly interesting inside—some books, a makeup bag, a jewelry case. None of the boxes are labeled, and seeing as I wasn't the person to pack them in the first place, I have no idea what to expect. I cut into the one beside it, this one much heavier, and my stomach immediately flips at the contents.

They're packed neatly with wadded-up towels on each side for padding as if they're something breakable, valuable.

So Mom must have packed these then.

My fingers tremble as I dig the first notebook out. There's a small metal closure on the side with a heart-shaped keyhole, the cover decorated with purple flowers and butterflies. The key hangs off the side by a chain, and it makes a tiny click as it opens.

The handwriting is horrible—gigantic and looping, each *i* dotted with a heart. Based on the dates scribbled at the top of each entry, this one's from sixth grade, maybe fifth. Below that is a thicker neon pink one—seventh grade. One that looks like it's covered in newspapers—eighth. By high school, I'd moved on to plain leather-bound ones, probably thinking it made me sophisticated or something. There's barely any gap in the entries, a day or two at most. I flip through the pages, the smell of old paper and ink filling the room. I'd probably need to be drunk to actually read through the songs now, especially the earlier ones.

Some old spiral-bound notebooks are at the bottom too, crunched lyrics in the margins around my Chemistry and AP Lit notes. It used to be such an unyielding impulse. The *need* to write. The lyrics would pop into my head whether I wanted them to or not, and I knew if I didn't write them down right away, I'd lose them.

But now...I can't even remember the last time I had that urge, that frantic *need* to find a pen.

The rest of the box is filled with VHS tapes, and I don't have to hunt for a player to know what's on them. My mom was all about the home movies growing up. She always had that damn camcorder out, filming everything from birthday parties to family game night to walks around the block.

Based on the other contents of the box, these tapes are probably from all the *concerts* I'd performed for them as a kid, a sheet hung on the wall behind me as a makeshift stage. Sometimes I managed to rope in Nick as a backup dancer, and there were more than a few occasions when Erica and I tried a duet.

My phone buzzes on the counter, and I jerk back, a tear escaping onto my cheek. I wipe it away as I push to my feet, my mother's picture flashing onto the screen to inform me of an incoming call.

"Hey, Mom," I say but immediately pull the phone back from my ear as a car horn blares on the other side of it. "Mom? Where are you?"

"Why on *earth* are we not on the approved guests list?"

"I—approved...are you *here?"*

My mother huffs. "We're *downstairs.* They won't even let us into the elevator."

I frown, surprised. Maybe Heath had them tighten their restrictions after Rick showed up here.

"Here," my mother says, then the line fills with crackling until her voice is replaced by one much lower—the man at the front desk, I'm assuming. "Um, hello?"

I sigh. "This is Parker Beck in 713. Those are my parents. You can go ahead and send them up."

"Right away, ma'am."

I glance down at my sweats, the same ones I've been wearing for days. At least the takeout containers are gone. They definitely didn't tell me they were planning on coming today, but they've always been a fan of surprises.

I quickly grab the dirty dishes off the counter and toss them in the sink, cleaning up as much as I can as I go.

"Parkerrrrr," my mother sings as a fist pounds on the door.

I barely manage to get the door open before she charges and throws her arms around my neck. I grunt and stumble back a step, but instead of *helping* me and prying her off, Dad attacks from the other side, sandwiching me between them.

"I can't breathe," I mutter.

111

"Yes you can," Mom says cheerily.

"Are you...interested in painting now?" Dad asks as they finally release me. Mom follows his attention to the wall, but her eyes widening is the only indication of her actual thoughts about it. Otherwise, surprisingly, she keeps her mouth shut.

I shrug. "Thought it could use some color in here."

Mom's head bobs a few too many times. "It's certainly...colorful."

"What are you guys doing here? I didn't realize you were coming by today."

Dad brings his hand to his chest and theatrically stumbles back a step. "We need a reason to come see our one and only child?"

"You have two children, Dad," I deadpan.

He lifts his eyebrows and glances sideways at Mom. "Oh, that's right."

My eyes flick between the two of them, both sporting cartoonish smiles. "Annie called you."

My mom opens and closes her mouth like she's considering denying it, but settles on: "She was worried about you spending so much time alone. And we wanted to come visit again anyway."

"We thought it would be nice for you to get out, get some fresh air, you know," says Dad.

I perk up at that. "We're going somewhere?"

My mom laughs at the blatant eagerness in my voice. "Not looking like that." She gestures to my sweats and unwashed hair. "Go get ready first, then we'll talk."

112

WHEN NICK and I were kids, every once in a while—maybe once or twice a month—we'd have special snack dinner nights. Our parents would set up a picnic in Central Park to make it feel special, and it wasn't until I was a teenager that it occurred to me the reason we were eating peanut butter and jelly on crackers for dinner wasn't because it was fun—it was because they couldn't afford much else that week.

But I guess that was the point. They never wanted us to worry. They made the best out of everything they could.

The hourly guard gives us space, though I can see him leaning against a tree in my peripheral vision. I keep tugging on my hat and sunglasses, the paranoia tightening my shoulders up to my ears, but no one pays us much attention as Dad smooths out the blanket and starts pulling our lunch from the basket.

"You're not too old for these, are you?" he asks as I sit next to him and take the cracker he hands me.

I grin and take a bite, the taste somehow so much *more* than any other food. It's full of memories and laughter and years from another lifetime. "Of course not."

"I wish Nick could be here," says Mom, taking a seat on my other side. "But he has midterms coming up. He said he'd give you a call later though."

Translation: you will not hear from him for months unless *you* call *him*. Which is fine. Nick and I get along well, but we've never been the check-in-with-each-other-daily kind of siblings.

A bright orange frisbee flies in front of us, followed by a golden retriever who leaps into the air after it. The dog's owner claps and coos as it trots back to return the toy, kicking up grass as it goes.

"How are you doing, honey?"

Mom's voice snaps me back and I look over at her. I could tell her *I'm fine* or any of the other lies I've been feeding everyone else lately, but she'd know.

"Better than before." Before she can read too much into that, I take another cracker. "This was a good idea. Thank you."

We chew in silence for several seconds before Mom hedges, "Have you spoken to Erica?"

Her name hits me like a punch to the chest. This is the longest we've gone without speaking in...well, since we met as kids. We've fought before, plenty of times. There were even a few occasions in middle school where we swore we'd never be friends again—what the unforgivable offenses were, I can't even remember now—but we always were back to texting and sleepovers by the end of the week.

I shake my head. "I've reached out a few times, but I don't think she's ready to talk yet."

"She will be," Mom insists. "This was a big shock to her, in more ways than one. But a lifetime of friendship means more than that. She'll see that."

I nod, my mouth dry, and it has nothing to do with the peanut butter.

"Well, what about the other girls?" she asks.

"Other girls?"

"You know!" She flaps her hands around as if I'm being difficult on purpose. "Kayla, Regan, Viv—"

"Okay, I get it." I take my time chewing my next cracker before answering. Some of them did reach out once the news broke, but I didn't get back to anyone. I didn't have the emotional capacity to deal with it.

It's not that I don't like them, but friends I've made in the industry after Ryker happened have always felt different from the ones I had before. And I don't think it has anything to do with them. It's my fault, not theirs. None of them knew Parker. They only knew Ryker. And how close can you really get to someone if you're never able to take off the mask?

"They'd understand what you're going through more than anyone else," Dad offers. "At least to some degree."

"You should give them a call," Mom adds.

I lean back on my hands, savoring the feel of the sun on my face. "Ah, so this *isn't* a friendly family lunch. This is an intervention."

"It can be both!" says Dad. "We know you tend to hibernate when things go sideways...but I don't think that's gonna work this time, bug. You need people. Everyone needs people."

"I have people!" I insist. "I have...Annie. And Faye. And you guys..." I almost say *and I have Heath,* and the thought stops me cold, but that's nothing compared to the ice that fills me when I think *Elijah.* Because I don't have him. Not anymore. And he used to be the first one I'd turn to. He always had the best advice.

"We're just saying..." starts Dad.

I clear my throat to stop the ache starting to rise that feels a little too close to tears for comfort. "I'll call Kayla if you both agree to stop meddling and just eat your damn snack lunch. Deal?"

"Deal!" they say at the same time.

CHAPTER 16

PARKER

L ittle do my parents know—or hell, maybe they do— but Kayla Whitlock is a total cokehead. She got her start on reality TV, and there's something about that pipeline, going from completely obscure and ordinary to famous for just being yourself overnight, that seems to have the same effect on people. At least with all the reality TV stars I've met.

And yet, compared to all my other friends in the industry, she's the tamest. She'd never agree to having a night in, but I'm also not worried I'll get arrested when I'm around her... which is not something I can say for some of the others.

"I am *so* glad you called," Kayla singsongs as we weave through the dark hallway. One of the club's security guards walks in front, and Heath takes up the rear, a presence my body is very aware of, for some reason.

It's been a long time since I've come to the Fleur Lounge, years maybe. This kind of scene was a lot more fun when I was younger, when the fame was new. But, of course, I'd always come in full Ryker armor.

Tonight, my blond hair is loose and wavy over my shoulders, and I'm in a simple little black dress and matching heels, hoping the plain outfit won't draw any more attention than necessary.

I'm starting to think that was a stupid, naïve hope though.

The VIP section here is the only reason my team agreed to let me out for the night. There's a branch of the club completely separated from the rest for the more *affluent* clientele, as the owner likes to describe it.

The hall is dimly lit and soaked in an amalgamation of a million different perfumes from whoever got here before us. Based on the laughter and voices buzzing against the deep bass vibrating the walls, it's a decent crowd.

The back room is sectioned off by velvet red curtains, and the muscles in my shoulders harden as we near.

"Everyone has been asking about you," Kayla continues.

I tug on the hem of my dress, making sure it doesn't ride too high up my thighs. But it's shorter than I remember it being the last time I wore it, and no matter how much I adjust it, it still feels too high.

Maybe I've gotten a little too used to only wearing sweatpants these days.

Mercifully, the room isn't too packed when we step inside, and aside from a few curious glances as I follow Kayla to the bar in the back, our entrance goes unnoticed. I recognize a few faces, but not enough to remember any names—a girl who won that singing show, a few models, that guy in the latest alien action movie.

This is supposed to be fun, I remind myself as I force my shoulders to relax.

Kayla hasn't asked about the news leak or the fact that I look completely different now than any other time we've hung out. And I'm not sure if I'm grateful or dreading when it'll eventually come up.

"If there was a contest to see who looked the most miserable in the room, you're really gunning for first place, huh?" She smirks as she props an elbow on the bar. Her outfit is tame tonight, tame for her, at least. The dress is simple and sleek—bright red and easily the most eye-catching in the room, but still. It has a single slit up the thigh and a neckline made of mesh. Her hair, as always, is slicked back in a bun. On me, I'd look like a child, but it always makes her look classic, sophisticated.

"Is it that obvious?" I mutter.

"That girl," she says, pointing to a redhead sitting on a beast of a man's lap in the corner booth, "just had a sex tape leak. That guy"—she moves on to a tall, thin man snorting something off a table in the back—"was arrested the other day and there are pictures of him in handcuffs *everywhere.* Oh, and her"—she points to a little blonde girl who pushes through the curtain entrance—"she just got a DUI. So I promise, no one is paying attention to you. We've all got our own shit."

The bartender appears with two mojitos. Kayla flashes him a bright smile as she takes one then slides the other to me. I didn't even see her order.

She holds her glass up, then raises her eyebrows expectantly until I clank mine against hers.

The amused twinkle in her eyes dims, and for a moment I think this will be it—she's going to get sentimental and serious and everything is about to get awkward—but then she winks and says, "Welcome back, bitch."

ʳΙʳΙʳʳΙʳΙʳΙ

AFTER THE FIRST DRINK, and still, no one comes up to me or makes a big deal out of me being here, my body finally relaxes. A few of the other girls show up—some I'm friendly with, some I've never met. I think they're mostly from the same show as Kayla.

Aside from some drunken hugs and *"sooooo good to see you out again"*s, everything feels pretty normal. Dare I say…fun?

The music is so loud I can barely think about anything else. Kayla grabs my hand and twirls me in a circle, laughing. They must be having a theme night because they've pretty much only played throwbacks so far.

I freeze as the song shifts.

Kayla lets out a scream and jumps up and down. "That's your song! That's her song!" She points at me, still jumping, as one of my first songs, "Lie for Me," fills the room.

The irony is not lost on me.

It's always been one of my favorites to perform though, probably because it's a fan favorite. If I close my eyes, I can see them screaming along to the lyrics and jumping to the beat. It's one of those songs that basically wrote itself. We'd been messing around in the studio, and by the end of the hour, we had the full lyrics done.

Kayla's laughter stretches thin like it's farther away now, and hands grip my hips from behind. I open my eyes, the room blurry, and the strobe lights and constantly moving bodies around me don't help.

Hot breath skates across the small section of skin between my neck and shoulder. Whoever it is says something, though I can't make out the words over the music. But the voice sounds deep, masculine.

I try to take a step away, and the hands on my hips tighten, his fingers digging into my skin now. His chest presses against my back, vibrating as he says something else. It takes a moment for my brain to finally process the words. *It's just a dance.*

I try to seek out Kayla to at least get confirmation if he's cute or not, but the floor is a lot more crowded than it had been a few minutes ago.

The stranger is far more into this than I am, but I dance along, bobbing my head to the familiar beat, feeling like I'm onstage. Like nothing has changed. It's me and the music and the lights and the crowd...

But then I open my eyes, and that image shatters.

My gaze lands on Heath standing next to the bar. His eyes are locked on me, unblinking, his arms tightly crossed and jaw flexed. He's supposed to be watching me, obviously. That's his job. But the heat in his gaze feels like *more.* The closer the guy behind me gets, the more he touches my waist and leans his lips near my ear, the tenser Heath's shoulders get.

Suddenly, his touch makes my skin crawl. I take a step away, but he hauls me back none too gently, one hand on my hip, the other on my ass.

"Get off me," I slur.

The room spins, and I search the crowd for Kayla or the others. I'd thought they were right next to me...

The stranger's weight disappears from my back, and I stumble forward, finally turning and getting a good look at him. The man isn't much taller than I am, and not someone I recognize. Heath stands behind him, his hand clasped around the back of the man's collar like he's disciplining a child. He must have pulled him off me.

The man's lips move, but I can't hear what he's saying. Whatever it was, it makes Heath's glare turn harder, colder, and he roughly shoves the man away.

The guy stumbles and swats at his shirt like he's trying to smooth out the wrinkles. I send a little prayer up to whoever is listening that this doesn't turn into some cliché fist fight on the dance floor. The tabloids would have a field day with that one.

Thankfully, the man takes one more look at Heath's towering height and turns away, shaking his head. Kayla and the others are nowhere to be found—off in the bathroom doing lines, if I had to guess. I sigh, the good mood I'd managed to find earlier quickly slipping through my fingers.

I blink as Heath grabs the cup out of my hand, a good half of my drink still in there.

"I—"

He shakes his head as he pours it out in a nearby plant.

Realization dawns and quickly sours in the pit of my stomach. I definitely hadn't noticed. I would've continued drinking that without a second thought.

Oh God. I don't want to think about what could've happened if Heath wasn't here. I got too comfortable. Sloppy. I'm usually more careful than this.

Whatever rose tint had been over the club a moment ago vanishes, and all that's left is the nausea in my stomach.

I nod at the curtains behind him. "Let's just go."

He shakes his head. "We can stay—"

"No, really." I grab his arm and pull him toward the exit. "I am more than ready to leave."

AN EXCERPT FROM PARKER'S JOURNAL

*I hope the next person
who calls you beautiful
says it because they mean it
not because they're trying
to get something out of it*

CHAPTER 17
HEATH

For a moment there, I could've sworn she was actually having fun. Her smile was contagious as she spun in circles and laughed with her friends. I've seen a few videos of her dancing onstage—the moves all precise and choreographed. This was nothing like that. She was clumsy and kind of bad at it on her own. I have no idea how a musician is even capable of having no rhythm, but she managed it. She swung her hips and threw her hands over her head, half the time not even singing the right lyrics, though she screamed them with the utmost confidence just the same.

It was...adorable.

Until that asshole. Watching him grope her was bad enough. I mean, I'd been expecting to have to rip someone off her at some point the moment I saw that dress, but then I saw him slip something into her drink...

I pointed him out to the bartender before we left, trying to ignore the voice in my head screaming at me to go back in there and take care of it myself.

Parker says nothing as I lead her to the car, but her body language is entirely different now, her shoulders slumped and head low like she's trying to disappear. Like this is somehow her fault.

My fists clench at my sides. The one time she finally got out to do something normal for her...I can't let her go back to the apartment and end the night like this.

I lean between the front seats and mumble a different address to the driver.

Parker's head pops up, and the driver meets my eyes in the rearview mirror as I lean back in my seat. Finally, he nods and pulls away from the curb.

"Heath," she sighs. "I just want to go home."

"I know."

"This isn't the way to my apartment."

"I know." I turn and smile at her, but that makes her frown deepen. "Hey." I lift my hands. "You wanted a night out. I'm giving you what you asked for, superstar."

"Did my parents put you up to this?"

I crane my neck as we near the right street. I'd sent out the text before we left the previous club, but there's no telling how long it'll take everyone to get here.

And I was, indeed, roped into this night by her parents, not that it took much convincing. I've been telling Parker's team since the day I started that keeping her locked inside wasn't going to solve anything. But I'm not going to tell her that.

"I promise the only conversation I had with your parents was when I asked for your hand in marriage."

"You're hilarious. Really." She tries to keep her voice flat, but the curl at the corner of her lips is unmistakable.

I smile innocently and hop out as the car pulls up to the

curb, then jog around to the other side to open her door. I don't give her time to protest, or maybe I don't hear her over the music pouring out of Up and Up's door.

As we cross the threshold through the reek of greasy food and cloying perfume, I glance at her sideways, half expecting a look of disgust on her face as she no doubt feels the floor sticking to her shoes, but she furrows her brow as she meets my gaze.

"Why did you bring me here?"

I nod toward the bar, and she follows without question.

"Figured this would be a safe bet." I gesture to the half dozen other patrons—all at least twice her age and far more interested in the pool table than they are our entrance. "Doubt anyone will recognize you here."

She tucks a smile between her teeth as she slides onto the stool beside me.

Rachel nods at me from the other side of the bar as she places some beers in front of a couple of guys in suits. I'm about to ask Parker what she wants when Rachel appears in front of us.

"Well, look what the cat dragged in. Haven't seen you in a while."

I frown—I was just here the other day—but then I realize Rachel is looking at Parker.

Parker shrugs. "I assume not much has changed in the meantime."

"You're damn right about that. You still a mojito snob?"

Parker laughs and nods. She looks completely at odds with everything in this place—her hair too put together and shiny, her outfit too expensive, her voice too light and airy. And yet, the way she leans forward and props her elbows on the bar, she looks completely at ease. More comfortable than she ever did at the last place.

"Hey. You." Fingers snap in front of my face, and Rachel raises an expectant brow. "Usual?"

I clear my throat and nod.

Parker drums her fingers against the bar as Rachel turns away, and I find myself staring at her again, her profile drenched in the green and purple glow of the neon sign out front.

"What?" she asks without looking at me.

"You...I..."

A small smirk appears. "Did my parents tell you to bring me here?"

I blink, momentarily thrown. "No. Why would they?"

She faces me, curiosity punching her brow now. "Before Ryker and everything, this was where we always went. They're lenient with fakes," she adds with a wink. "And the drinks are cheap. It was my first bar, actually. Erica and I were so obvious. I don't know how we got away with it." She laughs, but there's a noticeable shift in her voice when she says her friend's name—the one from the wedding, if I'm remembering correctly. "I was...sixteen? They still do that darts tournament for free beer?"

I know my jaw is hanging open, but I've forgotten how to shut it.

She thanks Rachel as our drinks arrive, then nudges me under the bar with her knee. "What?"

I shake my head to clear it. "I'm just surprised that you've been here before. I...this was my first bar too. Some of the guys and I stop by pretty often."

I try to imagine a younger version of her, who she was before the fame. For her to come to a place like this by choice…well, it goes against pretty much every picture I've built of her in my head.

We could've been in the same room before, could've crossed paths, maybe even exchanged words, and just never known it.

Her jaw drops open in mock surprise. "So you're saying we actually have something in common?" Her smile fades, and she takes a sip of her drink. "Things were…different before Ryker, to put it lightly. I'm guessing you thought I was some spoiled trust fund kid." I grimace, but she shrugs. "I get it."

Her knee bumps mine under the bar again, but she doesn't pull away. Every nerve in my body zeros in on the contact as I drink my beer. God, it's really warm in here. When she leans over the bar and says something to Rachel, I let out a slow exhale and subtly adjust my pants. I don't know what the fuck is going on with me tonight. Probably some leftover adrenaline or something from earlier. Seeing that guy all over her, even before he tried to drug her, the last time I felt anger like that…

Well, it was the day John walked out on Dani.

Rachel laughs at something Parker says—her real one, not the fake giggle she uses when she's trying to get a good tip. "How do you two know each other?"

"Work," I say slowly, trying to gauge Parker's expression out of the corner of my eye. She's clearly familiar with Rachel, friendly. But Rachel's not the kind to keep up with pop culture stuff. Does she even know about Ryker?

Rachel's eyebrows shoot up. "What the hell are you doing on construction sites?" she asks Parker.

I wince as Parker looks back to me, a question churning

behind her eyes. Construction work definitely hadn't been on my résumé.

"Hey, Rach?" I tap my beer even though it's half-full. "Can I get another one of these?"

She narrows her eyes, clearly not pleased at the dismissal, but turns away.

Parker's still watching me as she sips her drink. "So how much of your past work experience was a lie?"

"All of it," I admit.

"You were convincing though."

"Are you...mad?"

She shrugs again and finishes the last of her drink. "Beggars can't be choosers."

I don't know what I'd wanted her to say or why the words make my chest deflate. I should be grateful I'm not getting fired.

"Maybe we've crossed paths before," she muses. "I'm trying to picture a younger you. Why do I get the feeling you were a late bloomer? Have you ever worn a cowboy hat?"

I choke on my beer, but that just makes her smile widen, her cheeks flushed from how much she's had to drink.

"I wasn't a late bloomer," I mutter. "And definitely no to the hat."

"Sure." She pats my knee comfortingly, at least, I think that's how she intends it. My body is a little too aware of her hand on my thigh to tell. *It's just the drinks.* She's not usually this casually touchy.

But something about her smirk, the way she leans toward me, it *feels* like more. And I'm not fucking oblivious. I know when someone's flirting with me. We've been giving each other shit since we met, but the lines here feel blurry.

I should back off, let this cool back into friendly territory.

Instead, I close the gap between us by a few more inches. "Late bloomer means someone got hot later in life, right? Is this your way of saying you're attracted to me?"

She sputters, the blush in her cheeks deepening. "It doesn't *have* to refer to appearances."

She wets her lips, and my eyes track the movement, the heat in my blood rising.

"But that's how you meant it," I murmur, my voice low as I drag my eyes back up to hers. "If you were trying to picture me."

She opens her mouth then slams it shut again, her nose scrunching as she scowls. "I think *you* think you're hot."

I chuckle, and despite how visibly hard she fights her smile, it creeps out just the same. For a moment, it steals my breath. It's the genuine kind, crinkling her eyes and reddening her cheeks. She blushes so easily, the color pretty and delicate on her features. The lightness I'd started to see come through at the club before everything went sideways filters through again, and I find myself smiling back.

There are only a few inches between us, our legs still pressed together beneath the bar. My fists ache from clenching them so tightly, resisting the urge to touch her, to—

"And here we all thought you were too good for us now."

I jerk back from Parker, feeling...*caught*...as Duncan strides through the door, his shoulders damp with rain that must've started after we got here. Banks and Wyatt aren't far behind, all looking like they came off a site, their clothes covered in dirt and dust.

"You must be Parker." Duncan removes his red baseball cap and bows. "A pleasure."

She laughs, glancing from him to me.

"We're friends of Heath's," Banks explains.

"*Friends* is a generous word," I mumble, and Wyatt whacks me in the back of the head. I jut my chin toward Duncan. "He's a fan of yours."

Her eyebrows fly up, and if I didn't know Duncan better, I'd swear his smile turned a little shy. "My daughter," he explains. "She's thirteen. Her entire room is Ryker Rae themed."

"Oh my God." Parker beams and sets her drink on the bar. "What's her name? Do you want to take a picture or something for her?"

"Chelsea. You wouldn't mind?"

"Of course not."

"I'll take it," I offer.

Duncan hands me his phone and hesitates awkwardly beside Parker. She pushes herself off the stool, throws her arm around his shoulders, and hauls him against her side, clearly at ease and used to the routine. He lets out a surprised grunt, and I snap a few pictures. He's still stunned in the first —hell, he looks *starstruck*—but he manages a smile in the second. By the third, Parker's gaze has drifted behind my head, and the color drains from her face.

An icy gust of air fills the bar as the front door opens and a couple steps inside. They talk among themselves as they near the bar, and when the woman finally looks up, she stops cold in the middle of the floor. It takes a few seconds before the man beside her catches on, and his expression devolves into one of panic as if he's facing down a gunman and not a five-foot-three and slightly drunk woman.

"Hi, Erica," Parker says softly.

CHAPTER 18
PARKER

At first, I think she's going to ignore me and leave. But instead, she gives her new husband a reassuring nod and waits for him to head to the other side of the bar. Heath stands next, picking up on the silent hint, and gestures for his friends to follow him, saying something about a game of pool.

Seeing her in this place transports me back to when we were teenagers. It hits me how long it's been since I've seen her. Not that I wasn't aware of it before, but the distance between us feels so much greater now that she's standing in front of me and she's looking at me in a way that she never has before. There's uncertainty there. Wariness. And something else I can't quite place. Maybe remorse, or maybe I'm seeing what I want to see.

"You look good," she finally says.

I swallow hard, wishing I hadn't already finished my drink, but I'm too afraid to turn and ask Rachel for another, as if Erica is going to disappear if I take my eyes off her. "So do you," I manage.

She got a haircut. Her curls are chopped below her chin now, and her skin is tan and glowy, further accentuated by her white silk dress. It's probably leftover from their Hawaii honeymoon. I'm seized with the urge to ask how it went. Before everything happened, I would have been the first person she called to share every detail with. She would have asked me which pictures to post. I would have helped her pick outfits. And now, for the first time, it doesn't feel like my place.

"Do you want to sit down?" I gesture to the stool beside me.

Slowly, she nods, leaving a full foot of space between us as she takes the seat.

Nerves flood my stomach like I'm going on a first date instead of sitting next to my best friend. When I glance up, I catch Heath's eyes across the room. He's standing beside the pool tables with his friends, a stick in hand, though his gaze is intent on me and Erica.

"How are you?" she asks. "With everything."

"Fine," I lie, attention snapping back to her face. "You?"

"Fine," she echoes, a small smirk on her lips because we both know that's not true.

"It's really good to see you."

She brings her hands together on top of the bar, playing with her rings. "It's good to see you too, Parker. I'm sorry I haven't..." She scratches the back of her neck. "I'm sorry for the way things are between us right now. And I'm sorry that I don't know how to fix it."

All the air leaves my lungs. "You don't have to apologize. You don't have anything to apologize for. It's my fault. I'm the reason for all of this."

She glances at me sideways. "You are," she agrees. "But I

also know you didn't mean to, and I get why you did it. And I know you're going through a lot right now too."

I nod a few too many times, too afraid to let the seed of hope in my chest grow into anything stronger. "Do you think..." I sigh and twist the empty glass in front of me, the condensation wetting the palms of my hands. "Do you think we're ever going to get past this?"

She considers me, and her hesitation makes my throat close up and my heart feel like it's dropping into my stomach. Because I can't imagine an alternative. Can't imagine her disappearing from my life completely, as gone as Elijah is.

"I want to," she says finally.

Tears prick my eyes, and I press my lips together. "So do I."

She exhales loudly and waves Rachel down at the other side of the bar, holding up two fingers and gesturing to my empty glass. "Right. So. Who is that delicious man in the corner and why has he been watching us this entire time?"

I choke out a surprised laugh. "I see married life hasn't changed you."

"I'm married, not blind." She quirks an eyebrow. "Another *family friend?*"

Maybe it could've sounded like a joke if her voice didn't have an edge to it. The words cut deep just the same. *Family friend* used to be the explanation for having Elijah around people who didn't know about Ryker.

"I'm sorry," she says after a beat.

I nod and give Rachel a small smile as she sets the drinks in front of us. "His name is Heath. He's part of my security."

I can see her arguing with herself, debating what to say. At this point, I'll take whatever jabs and bitchy comments she wants to throw at me as long as she keeps talking. As long as she doesn't leave.

"I'm really sorry, Erica," I murmur, and her face tightens. "I just want you to know that. You're so important to me. And I'm really, really sorry."

The smile she gives me is pained, but she reaches over, takes my hand in hers, and squeezes. And for the first time since that night, the knot in my chest loosens, its grip on my lungs and my heart relenting, just enough for me to think that things will be okay after all. The pieces might not fit together the way they did before, but we can still glue them back together. Nothing is shattered beyond repair.

Her smile loses a bit of its edge, and she flips her hair over her shoulder, though it's too short to stay behind her back anymore. An old habit, I suppose. "Do you want to see some of the honeymoon pictures?"

I grin. "Yes."

"Okay, you're totally going to think I'm awful." She digs through her purse until she comes up with her phone and quickly flips through her camera roll. "But Soren got food poisoning on the second night."

I gasp.

"*Yes*, the *second* night. So what was I supposed to do? Just let all of our plans go to waste? We had so many things scheduled!" She sets the phone on the bar between us so I can flip through the pictures, which are all pretty much of her alone, at least for the first few dozen.

"Poor Soren," I mumble.

Erica shrugs. "He was feeling better by day four. Though he did puke after our zipline. He was a good sport about it."

"I like this one." I flip to one of her and Soren on the beach, the sunset behind them. Their arms are wrapped around each other, both of their heads thrown back in laughter. They look so genuinely happy that it makes my chest ache.

Her returning smile is soft, small, as she gazes at the screen. "That's one of my favorites."

A camera shutter goes off behind me. I know what it is immediately. I've heard more than my fair share in my life, and somehow always at inopportune times like this. My shoulders tense, and I let out a breath through my nose.

"What is..." Erica starts to turn, but I grab her shoulder. "Don't."

Her eyes widen in realization as bright flashes surround us. At least four cameras, if I had to guess.

How the hell did they even find me here?

"Is this the bridezilla?" calls one.

"Have you two patched things up?"

Jesus Christ.

Heath stands behind Erica, blocking her from view, then tugs gently on my arm. "Parker. We should go."

"Erica..." I start, knowing full well nothing I say right now will matter.

She wraps her arms around herself as she stands. The familiarity in her expression fades, like she no longer recognizes the person in front of her. "You should go." She cranes her neck, looking for Soren, then sidesteps toward him at the other end of the bar.

The wall slams between us again, whatever progress we'd made shattering like a sheet of ice.

"It was good to see you," I say weakly.

She nods but doesn't look at me again as we head for the door.

135

An Excerpt from Parker's Journal

I think one of the hardest parts
of becoming comfortable
just being myself
is looking back
and seeing
how many more people
liked me
when I wasn't

CHAPTER 19
PARKER

Our chauffeur jumps out to help Heath block the photographers as I duck into the car, finally able to breathe once I'm behind the darkened windows. Heath lets out a heavy sigh as he slides into the seat beside me. Six men with cameras stand on the sidewalk, one still turned toward Up and Up's windows like he might get a good shot yet.

My heart pounds against my ribs, and I put my head between my knees. Who tipped them off? Hell of a time for it. Erica and I were finally making progress, at least I'd thought we were. But the moment she saw those cameras, that they were pointed at me...

"She's never going to talk to me again," I mumble.

"This isn't your fault," says Heath.

I shake my head and pinch the bridge of my nose. "It doesn't matter. I can't even blame her. *I* don't want to be around all of this, so how can I expect her to?"

My phone buzzes in my pocket, and I toss it onto the seat

at the sight of Faye's name. I really can't listen to a lecture right now on top of everything else.

"Parker," says Heath.

I don't look up. It's my own fault. It was stupid and naïve to think things could get back to normal in a matter of weeks. That I could go back to life as usual as if my entire world didn't get flipped upside down.

"*Parker.*"

I sigh and roll my head to look at him. "What?"

He stares at me, his expression unreadable. I'm used to the hard looks, the scowls—I'm beginning to think that's his default expression. But this? This...concern? I don't know what the hell it makes me feel, but it isn't good.

"This will pass," he says quietly. "It'll blow over."

Easy for him to say. Easy for *everyone* to say. And say it they do, over and over and over again. But they aren't the ones who had their identity forcibly stripped off them, leaving them naked in front of the entire world.

I hold his gaze, my jaw hardening. "And what if it doesn't?"

We lapse into silence for the rest of the drive, broken up only by New York's soundtrack of blaring horns. Maybe that's the problem. Maybe I should leave New York. Surely there won't be as many paparazzi waiting around in some small town in the Midwest or up north. I could go wait it out at our family's lake house in Maine. The property's not even in my name, so maybe no one would think to look there.

"You look like you're scheming something."

I glance at Heath. "How would you know what my scheming face looks like?"

He presses his lips together like he's suppressing a smile.

"You have a very obvious one. If you were a cartoon villain, you'd be twisting your mustache right now."

"Are you saying I have a mustache?"

He barks out a laugh, the fullness of the sound surprising me. It comes out deep, genuine. "I just want to know if I'm going to be privy to the scheme beforehand or if I'm going to be roped into it later."

"Maybe you won't be included at all."

His amusement fades. "Parker, promise me you aren't going to do anything else stupid."

"Anything *else*?"

He gives me a pointed look. "Like sneaking out without a bodyguard before the man who tried to kill you even goes to trial."

I can't help the shiver that runs down my spine, a flash of that night appearing in my mind, perfectly crisp and clear, not blurry around the edges like some memories get. I have a feeling that one is never going to fade.

"You're not going to get fired," I mumble.

"It's not about—" He makes a noise in the back of his throat and stops, the silence stretching between us. When he speaks, the tone of his voice shifts back to his earlier amusement. "Just promise me the next time you want to do something you're not supposed to do, will you at least let me come along and give me the chance to complain?"

He's smiling again. He's trying to lighten the mood, I realize. He's trying to be...nice.

"You're still on a trial period," I remind him.

"Oh, I know."

And goddamn it, no matter how hard I try, I can't help but smile back.

"Ah, so she can smile."

I roll my eyes and turn to the window. "Shut up."

"You know, Parker Beck, I don't think you dislike me nearly as much as you're trying to."

"Probably about as much as you dislike me."

His face falls. "I never disliked you." He pauses, the smile returning as he leans his head to the side. "I dislike when you throw your coffee at me, but you seem to be getting better about that."

"I did not *throw* my—"

"And yet I was covered in it."

"Oh my God, you are *exhausting*."

He gets a mischievous glint in his eye. "So I've been told."

"Oh my *God*." I smack him on the arm, and he fills the car with that laugh again. And damn it, now I have a *very* different picture in my head, one that makes the roots of my hair sting with heat. I hope the blush doesn't show on my cheeks. That'll just encourage him. "This is your idea of professional?"

"Well, it's like you said." He winks. "I'm not getting fired."

CHAPTER 20

PARKER

Faye and Annie show up to the apartment early the next day, and if the energy in the air doesn't warn me of incoming bad news, the fake, forced smiles on their faces definitely do.

Heath had the night off again and showed up this morning less than an hour ago. He sits at one of the barstools now, downing his coffee like his life depends on it. He's also refusing to meet my eyes, so whatever Annie and Faye know, he's in on it too.

Faye nods toward the living room and waves around the stack of papers in her hand. "Come on. We have a lot to get through."

Annie sighs and disappears into the kitchen as I sink onto the couch.

"So we talked to the lawyers," starts Faye, "to examine all of our options. And what it comes down to is if your label was willing to be cooperative and the desire to void the contract was mutual, this wouldn't be that big of a deal."

Annie reappears with a mug and slumps into a chair.

"And they're...not?" I conclude.

Faye presses her lips together. "No. In fact, they were quite upset by *your little stunt* in the interview—their words, not mine. They have no intention of breaking the contract."

"So what does that mean? Whatever the fine is, I'll pay it—"

"Parker," Annie says gently. "They would take everything. Your assets, the rights to your masters...this would affect your life more than you realize. And the lives of others as well."

At first, I think she's talking about Faye and herself, but then I realize Mom and Dad's house is in my name. Their retirement fund would be nonexistent without me, since they sunk all their savings into trying to help me launch my career in the first place. And I'm paying for Nick's tuition and his apartment right now...

But then what? They can't force me to keep performing, can they?

"I can't just...I can't just put on a Ryker wig and get up onstage like everything is okay."

Annie and Faye exchange a look.

"Maybe you shouldn't," says Annie.

"What do you mean?"

"I mean, maybe you shouldn't try to go back as Ryker. Maybe you should get up there as Parker."

I push off from the couch and pace toward the kitchen. "I can't do that."

"There's good news though," says Faye in a forced-chipper voice.

I turn and lean against the counter.

"Your contract is just through this year. Which means you

only have a handful of obligations to fulfill, and then if you still want out, you can walk."

Her expression doesn't look like this is good news at all.

"What are the remaining obligations?"

She licks her fingers and flips one of the pages in her lap. "They want you to finish out the tour—the last three stops. And you have to attend that charity function this weekend and help promote that new single dropping in a few weeks. That includes an interview and a performance on the *Today Show* during release week."

"This is ridiculous," I mutter under my breath, brace my hands against the counter, and hang my head between my shoulders. I never should have signed that contract. I was *eighteen*. I'd barely understood what it meant, but I hadn't cared. I just wanted to make music.

But now I'm some puppet owned by a company that doesn't give a shit about me. And if it was just about the money, maybe I'd do it. Maybe I'd walk away and let them take it all.

But I can't do that to Nick. To Mom and Dad. To Annie or Faye. Or Heath, for that matter.

And it's a few more months. A few more concerts. A few more appearances. And then it would be done. I can hold my breath for a little while longer.

What the hell I'm going to do after that...well, that's a different story.

"Fine." I turn and head for my bedroom.

"Parker!" Annie calls.

"I really don't want to talk anymore. I said it's fine. I'll do it." The last thing I see is three pairs of wide eyes as I close the door between us, then collapse back into my bed.

I WAKE up fully dressed on top of the comforter, though someone must have come in and thrown a blanket over me. I have no idea what time it is and twist around, trying to find my phone in the covers, but it's not here. Pots and pans clang in the other room. It's dark outside the window, so I must have slept for most of the day.

After silently crying into my pillow for an hour straight, of course.

I wrap myself in a blanket and hesitantly poke my head into the hall. The living room is empty, though all the lights are on. Something smells like garlic, and I follow it toward the kitchen where Heath is standing with an oven mitt on each hand. The barest trace of stubble shadows his jaw, catching the light as he bobs his head back and forth. His dark hair falls to the side, revealing headphones in his ears. He hums along to what sounds like a rock song and plays the air drums, oven mitts and all.

I press my lips together and linger in the hall, just out of sight, as he spins around, eyes closed, lip syncing. His face looks entirely different without all the harsh lines cutting through it. He looks...younger.

The oven beeps, and he slides over to pull out a sheet pan. The scent of garlic in the air increases tenfold, and he picks up a small dish with sauce to drizzle over whatever he's made. I can't see what it is, not that I'm trying. My eyes are stuck on him.

He's still bobbing along to the music and accidentally splashes the red sauce on his white shirt.

"Shit," he mutters and stares down at himself for a few

seconds. Then all at once, he grabs the back of the T-shirt with one hand, tugs it over his head, and plops it in the kitchen sink.

My mouth goes dry. The muscles of his back ripple as he leans over, scrubbing at the stain. The tattoos I always see peeking out of his shirtsleeves travel higher than I realized, almost brushing his elbows. One side looks like a web of tree branches, or maybe vines, but they dissolve into smoke the farther they trail up his arm. The other side is just as intricate, but harder to make out from here. The design is made up of countless smaller pieces—birds, plants, insects. I can't help but wonder if there's a meaning to any of them, or if he just liked the way they look.

Now I *really* need to make my presence known. If he sees me now, he's going to think I was staring at him.

Which I am.

I stomp my feet a little louder than usual and make a big show of yawning and rubbing my eyes as I reach the kitchen. He turns, surprise flickering over his face.

"I didn't know you were up."

"I just woke up."

Look him in the eyes. Keep looking at his eyes. Do not *look at his abs. Damn, he has a lot of abs.*

I'm not even usually an abs person, not particularly. But he's the kind of muscular that it's clear it's functional, not aesthetic. Something built out of necessity instead of carefully crafted in the gym. Not that there's anything wrong with that, but it does make me wonder about his life outside of this job.

Not that it's any of my business.

Though I'd gotten a hint of it last night when Rachel mentioned he worked on construction sites.

The pan on the stove is covered in an assortment of vegetables, russet and sweet potatoes, and cubes of tofu. He tugs out his headphones and sets them on the counter, and I very pointedly do *not* look at his chest, which is perfectly at eye level now. His skin is tanned and freckled, so whatever gave him those muscles must have been outdoors.

But construction workers don't usually work *shirtless*, do they? That has to be a safety hazard or something.

Oh my God, why am I still thinking about this?

"Sorry, I made a mess." He gestures to himself, then jabs a finger over his shoulder. "I'll go grab another shirt."

I stare at his back as he goes, the wide set of his shoulders, the narrow taper of his waist—

Jesus fucking Christ, I need to get it together.

I turn around and scrub at my face. I hadn't even looked in the mirror before coming out here. I'm probably puffy and red and have mascara smudges all over me. I'm also definitely hungover from yesterday.

But somehow, I don't feel as hopeless as I had this morning. Sure, I'm locked into this contract, but at least there's an end in sight. Letting myself cry it out and have a pity party got at least some of it out of my system.

Heath returns in a black T-shirt and nods at the pan on the stove. "You hungry?"

My stomach growls in response. Heath raises his eyebrows but says nothing and pulls down two plates from the cabinet. We resume what I'm coming to think of as our usual stance, me on a barstool, him leaning against the counter across from me, and eat in silence for a few minutes.

The walls in this place are thin, so he probably heard all my crying earlier. My face burns at the thought.

Which is dumb. It's not like he hasn't seen worse. That

146

first week he was here I didn't shower once, barely made it out of bed, and my apartment looked like it was on the verge of being condemned for health concerns.

I chew slowly, trying to think of something to say, then pause, really tasting the food for the first time. It's *divine.* Perfectly seasoned, perfectly cooked, a perfect blend of different flavors…

"This is…amazing."

"Don't sound so surprised," he laughs.

"How'd you learn to cook like this?" I shove another bite into my mouth. If he saw my idea of a homecooked meal—a bag of ramen—he'd probably keel over.

He shrugs. "I've always liked cooking. No one else really did it at home growing up, so I had plenty of time to practice. Took culinary classes in college for a year until…well… just didn't work out." I peer at him, trying to gauge his expression, but then his head pops up. "Hey, you want a change of scenery?"

I slowly set the fork back down. "What do you mean?"

He's smiling now and heading back toward his room. "Go grab your coat."

"Heath—"

"*Coat.*"

For some reason, I listen. He meets me back in the kitchen in a black hoodie and nods at my plate on the counter. "Bring that."

"I—what?"

He grabs his own, then heads for the door without waiting for me, seemingly assuming I'll follow.

Which I do.

The elevator slides open, and I feel ridiculous standing here with my plate and puffy winter coat. Heath looks entirely at ease, like he does this all the time, then saunters out of the elevator when we reach the roof.

There's usually a bar and a pool up here, though they're both under construction. Judging by the caution tape and signs, we're not supposed to be up here. A few lounge chairs are stacked by the pool tarp, and Heath hands me his plate as he wrestles out two and turns them to face the edge of the roof.

"I don't think we're supposed to—"

"Oh, we're definitely not," he says cheerfully, taking the plate from me and sinking into one of the chairs. When I don't move, he glances from the chair beside him to me. "I mean, if you'd prefer to stand there all night, I suppose that's all right too."

Sighing, I take the seat and follow his gaze toward the city. It's a clear night, showing off the sea of glittering lights before us. I huddle into my coat against the wind and nibble on my food.

I've always loved New York from vantage points like this. I've spent far more money than anyone ever should at rooftop bars in this city just so I could enjoy the view for a while.

But even this feels tainted now. Looking out at New York, the only place I've ever called home, it's not just the city where all my dreams came true.

It's the place that tore my life apart. That made me lose my best friend, my boyfriend, and a man I'd come to see as my second father. No amount of good memories can outweigh that.

"For what it's worth," Heath says. "Your record label sounds like it's run by a bunch of raging assholes. I think it's absolute shit that you have to keep performing or whatever if you don't want to." He shrugs and takes another bite. "Can't believe that's legal."

"I keep thinking it's my own fault," I say without thinking. "For signing the contract. I didn't know what I was agreeing to back then, and I didn't care."

"How old were you when you signed it?"

I set the plate on the chair beside me, my appetite gone. "Eighteen. My parents didn't know any more about this industry than I did. It sounds stupid, but we just didn't know any better."

"It doesn't sound stupid." He shakes his head. "I know it's not worth much, but I'm sorry."

The words make my eyes burn, and I clear my throat so he can't hear it in my voice. "Well, you're the only person who's actually said that to me, so thanks."

I can feel him looking at me, but I keep my gaze trained ahead.

"The whole Ryker Rae thing, how did that happen? It's not just the name. I've seen interviews and everything—it's like you're an entirely different person when you're her. Was it the label's idea?"

I remember all too well the day we'd finally decided on the name. It was Nick's idea, actually. Named after some motorcycle he'd been trying to convince our parents to get despite him being thirteen—and us only having one shared car with three drivers in the family.

We weren't sharing a room anymore by then, but he still hung out in mine every day after school. Living that close to one another, he'd always heard me writing songs. He suffered through me learning the piano, the guitar, practicing when he was trying to sleep or do his homework. He was the only person who heard most of the early stuff. And despite his many complaints growing up, he was the one who insisted I give music a shot before settling with some stable job I hated.

"I guess I wanted Ryker to be the opposite of me," I murmur. "If she felt like a character, it was easier to be brave because it was like she wasn't really me." I glance at him sideways. "And kids are cruel, and I was still in high school when I started posting the videos, and I didn't want anyone to know it was me..."

"The videos?"

"Oh." I flick my wrist. "That's how Ryker started. She took off once some bigger artists invited me to join their tours, but those videos I think are part of the reason my fans feel so close to me, you know? They were casual, personal. It let people feel like they knew me. Like we were friends. My brother would record me working on my songs, and I had a few go viral when I was seventeen. We were just doing it for fun at first, but by the time I graduated high school, I had labels and managers reaching out to me—that's how I met Faye—and well...you know the rest. That is *not* an invitation to go dig up those old videos, by the way."

He snorts out a laugh. "How many are there?"

I grimace. Hundreds, probably. We used to make them pretty much every day. "A lot. The first dozen or two got basically no views. I think that's what was so shocking about it. One just took off overnight, and once we got swept up in the storm, it was like there was no turning back."

"Do you ever wish you had?" he asks quietly. "Stopped with the videos?"

The answer is immediate in the back of my mind. *No.* I shake my head. Despite this godawful mess, I wouldn't give up the countless priceless moments I've had. How I was able to help my family. How *alive* performing makes me feel. And the music—I don't know who I'd be without it.

I sit up straighter and force a smile. "What were you like in high school?"

He doesn't comment on my subject change. He just chews his food thoughtfully, then sets his plate aside. "Busy."

"That's all I get? *Busy?* I just gave you my whole life story."

A smirk tugs at his lips. "I mean it. I was so busy and sleep-deprived that I barely remember it. I had school, I worked two jobs, and I made sure my sister got everywhere she needed to be. My grades were pretty shit. Average, if you're being generous. But my mom, she—" He sighs. "She did the best she could. Raising us alone was an impossible job." He stares out at the city as he talks, the line of his jaw sharp.

"And your dad?"

"Split when I was in elementary school. Dani was still a baby. Haven't heard from him since. Wouldn't know where to look even if I wanted to."

"God, Heath, I'm sorry."

He shakes his head. "Don't be."

It makes sense then, him frequenting a dive like Up and Up. But where my parents tried their best to hide our financial situation from me and Nick, to make sure we never worried, it sounds like Heath has been in the heart of it since he was a kid. Trying to fill the space his dad left behind helping his mom and looking out for his sister.

If I wanted anything growing up—new clothes, music lessons—I had to pay for it. So I picked up jobs like babysitting, waitressing, and a short stint as a barista. But I'd never felt the weight of needing to contribute to the family to keep it afloat.

I retrieve my plate just to push the food around, the gentle ting of the fork against the ceramic the only noise between us for what feels like too long. I clear my throat.

"I liked your friends the other night. They seem...enthusiastic."

He rolls his eyes with equal parts disdain and affection. "They're idiots, but they're good guys. Your friend Erica... pre-Ryker days, I'm assuming?"

I nod. "We've been best friends since we were kids."

"When did she find out?"

I blow the air out of my cheeks. "On her wedding day. As her maid of honor was attempting to flee the property. Until a lunatic came at us with a knife."

"Jesus fuck," he mutters. "I'm sorry. I didn't know the whole story—"

I wave a hand. "It's all right."

"She'll forgive you," he says, his voice barely audible over the wind. "And I'm willing to bet she misses you just as much as you miss her."

The words settle into a lump in the back of my throat, but I just tilt my head to the side and bat my eyelashes. "Because I'm just *so* unforgettable?"

His smirk is barely there, but his eyes soften he says, "You are not the worst company in the world, Parker Beck. I will give you that."

I look away, the intensity of his gaze making my cheeks warm, and huddle further into my coat. "So what happened with culinary school?"

"I finished my first year. Decided it wasn't worth the price tag. I could cook anywhere. And Dani would be off to school a few years later, and she wanted to pursue nursing, and with her out of the house, there would be no one around to help Mom...anyway, construction's been good to me. And it's been good for me to stay close by."

I follow his gaze back to the lights, caught between wanting to know more—wanting to know *everything*, actually—and not wanting to cross a line by prying too much. I'm technically his employer. It's none of my business.

"*So*," I say, my voice light, though my teeth are starting to chatter. "If I wanted to rehire you as, say, a personal chef..."

He laughs. "I will be sure to leave you a business card... once I, uh, make some business cards. We can go back inside if you're cold."

"No," I say, then wince at the desperation behind it. It *is* cold out here, but I've been staring at the same four walls in that apartment for so long they've been permanently seared into my head. And now that I've gotten a taste of fresh air— of freedom, no matter how small—the thought of going back already makes me want to scream. "Just another minute."

He nods and leans back on his hands. "You can have as many minutes as you want."

CHAPTER 21

HEATH

"**M**om?"

The plastic grocery bags dig into my hands as I shove the front door open with my shoulder. It's usually dark when I swing by, with Mom working late nearly every night and Dani still in the hospital. But at least dropping off food every week gives me peace of mind she isn't shoving down microwave dinners, and it gives me a chance to make sure the house hasn't completely fallen apart. She's always been the kind who's too proud to ask for help, even when a pipe exploded in the bathroom or there's a literal hole in the ceiling.

I've tried explaining to her that waiting makes the problem worse sometimes, but then she gets those Worried Mom Eyes and says something along the lines of "You already do too much for me."

But tonight, the kitchen is bright, and a blue light flashes against the wall. She must be watching from the tiny TV in there.

"Mom?" I call again. "Are you home?"

A chair scrapes against the floor, but she doesn't respond. My steps slow. I've never considered myself to be a paranoid person, but after being around Parker and her team...what if someone followed me? Or was waiting here already? My hands are too full to go for the gun at my belt, and dropping a dozen plastic bags to the ground isn't exactly inconspicuous, but—

"Oh, hi, honey." Mom steps into the hall, backlit by the overhead light, and sniffles as she presses a tissue to her face. "Are you all right? You look like you've seen a ghost."

I let out a long exhale, though some of the tension in my shoulders remains as I edge around her to set the bags on the counter. "Are *you* okay? What are you doing home? I would've come over sooner if I'd known you had the night off."

She lets out a choked sob and falls onto a stool behind the counter. I freeze, hands spread wide over the bags.

"Mom?"

She sniffles and blows her nose, and that's when I notice the pile of envelopes spread out beneath the groceries, enough to cover the entire counter.

Final notice and *past due* glare up at me in accusing red letters.

Shoving the groceries aside, I pick a few up and sift through to look at the dates. Some are several months old.

Mom's finally stopped crying, and she winces as she looks up at me, the guilt clear on her face.

I would've helped you is on the tip of my tongue, but then she says, "I wanted to handle them on my own."

I sigh and shuffle the rest into my hands to create a neater pile. "Have you gone through and tallied them up yet?" I start unloading the groceries to have something to do with my hands.

Her swallow is audible, even from across the room. Judging by the dozens of unopened envelopes, I'm assuming not.

"Okay, so you and I will go through them once I'm done putting these away—"

"They cut my hours at the diner."

I set the loaf of bread on the counter with a sigh. She doesn't just mean tonight, that much is clear from the look on her face. "How long ago?"

She looks away. "Business has been slower these past few months. I—I thought I could find a second job before it got to be too bad. But my schedule at the diner is so unpredictable, and now with Dani..." Her chin wobbles like she's about to start crying again, and I gently nudge the door to the fridge shut and take a seat beside her.

"It's all right," I murmur, wrapping an arm around her shoulders.

"It's *not*," she insists. "I can barely keep this roof over our heads, and I have one kid already in the hospital and the other with a target on his back with his pictures all over the internet!" She jumps up from the stool to pace the length of the kitchen, her strides short and fast.

"Hey, hey." I hold up my palms and keep my voice gentle, but there's not much that can calm her down once she gets like this. "What are you talking about?"

"You *know* what I'm talking about." She points a finger at me, and suddenly I feel like a fifteen-year-old getting scolded about smoking weed again. This really isn't the turn I'd been expecting the conversation to take. She whips out her cell phone and drops it on the counter beside me.

I grit my teeth to keep from cursing under my breath. The photos are watermarked and splashed across some tabloid website—from the club the other night. They're mostly of Parker and her friends, though a few of the pictures managed to snag me with my hand on her waist, trying to get her to the car. There's also some blurry ones of me standing in front of her friend at Up and Up as she stares out the window.

"They're just pictures, Mom—"

"Her last bodyguard was *murdered*," she shrills, her voice so loud I flinch. "And now she's out clubbing like nothing happened!"

The edge to her voice catches me off guard, and her chest rises and falls rapidly with her breath.

"The money is good, Ma," I try, my voice as gentle as I can make it. "And this is temporary. Just until we can get out of this bind. I know you're worried, but I can handle this. I'm the careful one, remember?"

I consider my next words, but I can't help the itch in the back of my brain that wants to defend Parker. *Now she's out clubbing like nothing happened.* It hadn't been her idea. She'd never wanted to be there in the first place. That second set of pictures wouldn't even exist if I'd taken her home when she'd asked.

But Mom won't hear any of that right now, no matter how I say it. Not once she's wound up like this, and especially not with that empty wine bottle sitting behind her on the table.

She slumps into a chair, sighs, and puts her head in her hands. Every muscle in my body tenses, and I'm half wishing she'd start screaming because the silence is so, so much worse.

"I can't lose you too," she whispers, almost too low for me to hear. "I can't lose both of my babies. I can't. You're all I have left."

"Mom." I slide into the seat beside her and gently pry her hands away from her face. "You haven't lost Dani, and you're not going to lose me. Look at me." Tears stream down her cheeks as she lifts her head, and I pull her into a hug. "I promise you everything is going to be okay. We'll work it out like we always do."

"I'm scared for you," she whispers, then sets her phone on the table. She scrolls through her camera roll to a different screenshot. "One of the kids at work showed this to me." She offers nothing else, so I pick up the phone and zoom in.

It looks like a forum, all the posts from random usernames with no profile pictures. The sight of Parker's name turns my blood to ice.

> Anyone find her new address yet?

> The things I'll do to that whore when I find her...

> Find the name of the new guard, maybe? Might be easier to track, just like the last one.

> I'll make sure she wears the wig when I—

I lock the phone and turn it over, trying not to let my emotions show on my face. But that ice in my veins quickly turns to fire, burning and blistering through every cell of my body, and I clench my fists in my lap.

What the hell is *wrong* with people? And if there's one forum like this, there's probably dozens, if not hundreds, more. God, I hope Parker hasn't seen these.

Faye must have, I realize. This was what she was trying to warn me about before I agreed to take the job. These incels online are looking at Jasper Young like a hero, an inspiration. Him getting arrested wasn't the end. It blew open the door for others like him.

I run a hand under my jaw, lost for words. Mom leans her head against my shoulder, and I wrap my arm around her.

"I can't lose you," she whispers.

"You won't," I promise, and I hope to God I'm not lying.

CHAPTER 22
PARKER

I have nothing against charity, but I hate these motherfucking events. The thing is, it's not really about the charities. It's about the rich people. It's about silently one-upping everyone else in the room all night long with how expensive your outfit is, the car you showed up in, how much you donate at the auction. It's a bunch of people who've never had a care in the world patting each other on the back over a charity they don't know the first thing about. *Ah yes, save the children. End world hunger.* That's about as far as it goes.

The worst part is, I'm one of them. Or at least, I'm expected to be. Growing up, our house had been so small Nick and I had had to share a bedroom—which was especially bad once puberty hit. When Nick turned fourteen, my parents *finally* finished a room in the basement to let him move down there and give us our own space.

And then Ryker Rae happened. It changed my life, of course, but the money changed it for all of us.

Which is why I'm doing this, I remind myself. That's why I'm here.

"You might want to work on that," Heath murmurs beside me.

I blink back to the car. We're currently waiting with the other limousines queuing around the circular drive, since the photographers for the event want to catch each entrance into the building.

Heath sits next to me in a black tuxedo, his usually messy hair carefully slicked back. Although he's working tonight, he's also technically my plus-one. Not that I needed the reminder about my lack of a real date.

Heath let me go on a run with him this morning to blow off steam. I don't have anything against exercise—I have to stay in good shape to get through the Ryker routines and still have the breath to sing—but *running*? Torture. But when fueled by rage and irritation? Effective. Why Heath goes on a jog every morning for *fun* though is beyond me. On the loop back to the apartment, we'd passed a cart full of tabloids and magazines. Front and center was my face and a profile shot of Rick.

Targeted and Betrayed was the headline.

Seriously, who comes up with this stuff?

"Work on what?" I ask.

"Your face. You look like you want to kill someone." He realizes his word choice a beat too late and flinches. "Sorry."

I smooth my hands over the cream silk of my dress— Annie's choice, not mine—and catch a glimpse of my reflection in the car window. My blond hair is loosely tied back in a low bun with several strands left out to frame my face.

It'll be the first time I've ever shown up to one of these things without the Ryker wig. Without the Ryker...everything. I guess it wasn't until she was gone that I realized how often I'd hid behind her.

"Are you nervous?"

"Yes," I say immediately.

"We don't have to stay the entire time, right? As long as you make an appearance and talk to a few people, we can get out of here."

I nod, his words loosening the knot of dread in my chest. The car inches forward, and cameras flash in rapid succession as a woman in a feathery black dress steps out, her jewelry glittering beneath the lights. I suppose I should feel grateful Annie picked a classic silhouette. That room is bound to be packed with extravagant, eye-catching gowns. Nothing is that noticeable about mine, though the golden embroidered bodice is nice. She probably assumed I'd rather blend in as much as possible tonight.

All too soon, it's our turn. Heath jumps out and quickly circles the car to open my door. Camera flashes surround him, and I hesitate, my heart thudding in the base of my throat. He looks down, and his expression softens at whatever he sees on my face. Extending a hand, he gives me a small nod, and with trembling fingers, I take it.

The moment I'm out of the car, the space around me is filled with so many flashes, I can't see. Heath guides me forward with a hand on the small of my back, and I force myself to smile and wave.

"Is this the new boyfriend?" calls one of the photographers.

"May I say, quite the upgrade!"

Less than a minute in, and they already want to talk about Rick. I stare at them, lost for a response, and Heath steers me toward the front door. A man in a black suit hands a paper to Heath, then nods for us to pass.

The vast ballroom is dimly lit, the only light coming from the row of chandeliers overhead and candles flickering from the center of the dozens of tables neatly situated throughout. The elaborate center pieces are the most eye-catching, made of bright orange and pink feathers that are glowing so much, there must be some kind of light inside them.

The room is only about half-full so far as people drink and mingle, waitstaff in black and white whisking through the room with trays. My eyes narrow on a champagne flute in the hand of a woman on our right, and Heath follows my gaze.

"You want one of those?" he asks.

"I *need* one."

"Coming right up." He disappears toward the bar, and I hesitate awkwardly near a tall bar table covered in a white tablecloth, searching the crowd for a familiar face. Crisp white name cards dot each of the seats at the dining tables, so we'll need to figure out where we're supposed to be eventually.

Most people here seem a lot older than I am and are from the film industry instead of music. *Why* was the label so insistent I come to this anyway? I don't see any of Allen's other clients.

Right as the thought passes, a familiar head weaves around the enormous dove ice sculpture in the center of the room toward me.

I groan internally.

He grins and runs a hand through his unruly dark hair. He's in a fitted gray suit tonight with a black bow tie, a far cry from his usual punk ensemble.

"Ryker Rae," he calls, practically bouncing with each step until he reaches me. "Or do you prefer Parker now?"

I silently will Heath to reappear while I try not to choke to death on his cologne. "Parker's fine."

"Quite the publicity stunt. I have to admit, I was impressed. Jealous, even. Wish I'd thought of that."

I say nothing in the hope he'll walk away.

"Let me guess, Allen made you come tonight."

My eyes flick to his face. "You too?"

"Me? Oh no." He shakes his head, still grinning, and nods toward the stage at the other end of the room. "The band is performing tonight. But you look miserable."

"Thanks."

He laughs as Heath resurfaces with two glasses of champagne.

"Thank God." I down half the glass, not caring as the bubbles burn in my chest.

Heath looks questioningly between me and the man in front of us, but before I can introduce them, Grey gives a little salute and disappears into the crowd.

"That's Greyson Carter," I mutter under my breath. "Lead singer of United Fates. We're signed with the same label. Absolute jackass."

Heath barks out a laugh.

"Apparently they're performing tonight, so if we don't manage to slip out of here before then, I'll end up hurting someone."

"Duly noted."

"Thanks for this." I take another sip of my champagne, actually tasting it this time, and notice he hasn't touched his. "Is yours bad?"

"Oh, this is yours too. I figured you'd finish that one fast. I can't drink on the job."

I smile up at him. "Smart man."

He winks as someone starts playing the piano onstage. The music trickles softly through the room as people mill about, finding their place settings, grabbing drinks from the bar, and chatting among themselves. There's space between the tables and stage for a dance floor, and a few couples venture over.

Another band starts setting up as the pianist finishes and bows to a polite round of applause.

"Do you know them?" Heath juts his chin as the lead singer grabs the microphone from the stand and pushes her curly black hair over her shoulders. The spotlights swivel until they find the right place and set her dark skin aglow.

I shake my head, and the woman beams at the crowd.

"How's everybody doing tonight?"

The crowd gives her another round of applause, though it's too polite and quiet for the energy she's putting out. I set my champagne flute down and clap loudly, annoyed for her.

"This first song is called 'Don't Go Slow.'"

The song starts with a punch, and the entire band vibrates with energy, perfectly in sync. The older couples that were dancing to the pianist retreat to their tables, leaving the dance floor empty. I glance around to see if anyone from the younger crowd will join in, but there isn't much of a *younger crowd* here.

"You've got that look again," Heath murmurs under his breath, a smile in his voice.

"Come on." I grab his hand and yank him toward the dance floor hard enough that he lets out a surprised grunt.

I've never heard this song—or this band—but I go right up to the front of the stage and clap, my hips swaying. The lead singer beams down at me with that all-too-familiar glimmer in her eye—relief.

Heath stands awkwardly beside me until I grab his hand and rope him in. It doesn't take as much encouragement as I'm expecting until he's twirling me around and moving his feet to the beat. He picks me up with his next spin, then goes straight into a dip, and I cling to his shoulders and let out a breathless laugh.

I've danced with hundreds of men at this point from all the different tours, some of the best and most attractive male dancers in the country. But there's something distinctly different about the way Heath's hands feel on me as he clasps my palm in his, as he grips my waist, as his laughter stirs the hair at the back of my neck.

It's just the position. It's his job to protect me, so of course I trust him not to drop me. Of course I feel safe with him.

But the rest of it? The pride I feel when I finally get him to smile—a real, genuine smile. The warmth in my chest when he looks at me and I can tell he's really *seeing* me. He spins me out again, and his smile widens.

Despite how *good* it feels to have the music vibrating through my body again, a hint of sadness follows it. I can't help but think about how different this would look if Elijah were here. He'd shake his head and pretend like he didn't want to dance. He'd shuffle his feet awkwardly, scowling all the while, but it would be for show.

The first song bleeds into the second, and by the third, a few others join us on the dance floor. By the time the band is finished and the lead singer jumps down from the stage, I'm a little sweaty and out of breath.

"Parker Beck, right?" she asks.

"Yeah. You guys were amazing up there."

The rest of the band streams behind her, heading for the bar. "You saved the night," she says. "Thank you."

"Yeah, well, this crowd sucks, so someone had to do it."

She smirks and squeezes my shoulder before following the rest of the band.

When I turn, Heath is grinning at me.

"What?" I demand.

"Oh, nothing. Nothing at all." He does a little jolt as his phone buzzes, and he slides his hand into the inside pocket of his suit. He frowns at the screen, his eyebrows pulling together, and mutters a quick "sorry" before turning away and bringing the phone to his ear.

The room is buzzing too loudly to make out anything from the conversation, but the moment the speaker on the other end starts talking, Heath goes rigid. I follow as he drifts to the back corner of the room.

He doesn't turn after he hangs up. Not at first. When he does, all the color has drained from his face, and my heart drops into my stomach.

"What is it?"

"I—" He backs up a step, eyes slightly dazed. "That was the hospital. Calling about my sister."

I stop breathing. *Oh God. Oh no.*

But then he lets out a small, breathy laugh and shakes his head. "She's awake." He swallows hard and looks back at his phone like he's double-checking.

"She's awake?" I repeat.

He nods, still looking dazed, and I grab his arm. "Then let's *go*. Call the driver, and we'll go straight to the hospital."

He blinks, finally coming back to the room. "But the—" He gestures around, and I smack his arm.

"Heath. Of course we're not staying. Get the car."

CHAPTER 23
PARKER

My usual bravado escapes me as the car takes us to the hospital. Heath isn't saying anything, so I assume he doesn't want me to either. Maybe he's in shock. He must be. He's staring at the black screen of his phone as if trapped in the moment it rang. He might not want me here at all, I realize. But he's still on the clock, so he's forced to bring me along. Suddenly I feel like I'm intruding on a private moment, and I cast my gaze out the window.

Traffic is thick tonight, and the longer we sit in the car, the heavier the silence grows between us.

When we finally reach the hospital, Heath jumps out, and I hurry after him. He practically collapses against the front desk.

"I got a call about my sister. Dani. Danielle Bridgers. She woke up from a coma today."

The woman behind the desk taps away on her keyboard, and then we're moving again. Heath heads for the elevators, already familiar with where he's going. When we reach the right floor, the nurses nod at him as we pass as if they recognize him, and he hurries straight for a room toward the back. My heels click loudly against the floor, and I cringe, trying to disappear. At least no one's recognized me or made a big deal yet.

Heath freezes in the doorway, his chest rising and falling with his breath. I linger a few feet behind as a doctor checks the machines surrounding the bed.

Dani looks exactly like Heath. Like *exactly*. I know they're not twins, but *damn* could they pass for it. Her tangled hair is spread out over the pillow, nearly as dark as the bags beneath her eyes. She gives a weak smile when she spots her brother standing in the doorway and waves a hand for him to come inside.

He grabs a chair and pulls it beside her bed, reaching for her right hand. Her left is bound in a cast and so is her left leg.

"You're awake," he breathes, his voice softer than I've ever heard it.

"Well spotted."

He huffs out a breathy laugh. "Are you okay? How are you feeling? Do you need anything? Water? I can—"

"Heath."

He freezes with his mouth still forming the next word. "Yes?"

"Take a breath."

He laughs again and scrubs his face with one hand. "Right. I'm just—God, I'm so happy to see you."

Affection softens her eyes as she extracts her hand from his and pats his cheek. "Don't go all sappy on me now." Her eyes flick up to me, and a single eyebrow arches. "Um...?"

"Right. God, sorry. This is—" Heath turns, his brow

furrowing at the sight of me still in the hallway, and he waves a hand impatiently for me to come into the room. "This is my...friend, Parker."

Dani grins. She has the kind of smile that immediately puts you at ease, and the tension in my shoulders fades. "You look *gorgeous*," she says, then glances at her brother, noticing he, too, is all dressed up. "Where *were* you guys?"

"That's a story for another time," says Heath. "How are you feeling?"

"Well, the doctor said I've been asleep for *months* now, so I guess the answer should be well rested, right?"

"Dani," Heath warns.

"I'm *fine*." She rolls her eyes. "I feel fine, Heath." She looks up and does a quick sweep of the room again. "Mom? Or John?"

Heath's expression darkens, and he clears his throat. So John must be the fiancé who skipped out after the accident.

"You know what?" he says, his throat thick. "Let me call Mom really quick, okay? She's probably on her way." He stands and heads for the door, squeezing my shoulder as he passes.

Dani's eyes shoot to the contact. "So, Parker." She waits, and I venture a little farther into the room. "How long have you been seeing my brother?"

"Oh. *Oh*." I glance back at him as he paces in the hall, phone held to his ear. "No. He actually, uh, works for me."

Dani's eyebrows rise so high they nearly disappear into her hairline. I realize a beat too late she probably now thinks I've hired him as an escort or something.

"Mom will be here as soon as she can." Heath pokes his head into the room and nods for me to join him in the hallway.

"It was really nice to meet you," I say.

Dani still has that same knowing smile. "You too."

Heath rubs his eyes and pauses once we're out of hearing range. "I'm sorry about all of this. I'll call around and see if I can get you a temporary replacement for the night and get the chauffeur to take you home—"

"Heath. I don't mind sticking around."

He freezes midsentence. An annoying rush of heat goes straight to my cheeks, and I nod once. "Unless this is your nice way of trying to get rid of me."

"No, *no*. I just—I know this isn't what you had in mind for tonight. And I don't want you to feel like you're trapped here."

"I don't feel trapped," I say quietly.

"I'm looking for Danielle Bridgers."

Heath's head snaps up at the voice, and I turn. A blond man in dark jeans and a gray sweatshirt stands at the end of the hall. The nurse behind the counter points in our direction. When he looks up and sees Heath, he goes still. But then he thanks the nurse and continues toward us.

"You have a lot of nerve coming here," Heath says lowly.

The man—John, I'm assuming—looks from Heath to Dani's room behind us. "Look, they called since I'm her emergency contact. I just want to see her."

"Convenient now that she's awake," Heath practically growls.

"Look, man, this has nothing to do with you."

"Nothing to do with me?" Heath steps closer, and John immediately steps back. He's not a small man, but in comparison to Heath, there's no question who would get hurt in this scenario. "When she finds out what you did, she won't want anything to do with you."

171

John's expression actually brightens at that. "You haven't told her?"

"No, I didn't think the first thing my sister would want to hear after waking up from a coma was that her piece-of-shit fiancé nearly killed her and then walked away because it was too much for *him* to deal with."

"Look, you don't know the first thing about me or our relationship." John tries to move around us, but Heath steps to the side, blocking him.

"Heath," I say lowly.

"You're not seeing her."

"She asked for me, didn't she?" says John.

Heath doesn't even blink. "Because she doesn't *know*. Why don't you do what's best for everyone and leave?"

"I'm not leaving until I see her," John says calmly.

Heath's hands tighten into fists at his sides. A muscle jumps in his jaw.

"Okay!" I step between them, putting a hand on Heath's chest until he takes a step back. John's eyes flicker to me, an annoyed look pinching his eyebrows together. It's almost enough to make me step aside and let Heath throw the punch I know he's dying for. But instead, I say, "Here's what's going to happen. We're going downstairs to find some coffee. You're going in there and talking to Dani. If you haven't told her what happened by the time we get back up here, then we will. And trust me, this will go over *a lot* better if it comes from you. Okay? Okay."

I grab Heath's arm and yank him toward the elevators. He doesn't resist, thankfully—there's no way I'd be able to move him otherwise. The elevator doors slide shut, and I glance at his scowling reflection.

"You weren't going to stop him from getting in there," I say.

He says nothing.

"All that was going to do was cause a scene. Maybe even get you kicked out so you couldn't see your sister."

Still, nothing.

"*And* your sister would end up getting pissed at you if you didn't let her talk to him on her own."

He opens and closes a fist at his side.

I sigh and soften my voice. "I know you want to protect her, but you have to let people make their own choices. And sometimes that means letting them make mistakes."

The second the elevator dings open, Heath takes off. I don't follow. I just watch as he storms straight out the front door, and the doors slide shut behind him. Sighing, I head off in search of a cup of coffee.

IT DOESN'T TAKE LONG to find him. There's a bench outside the front doors, and he's sitting with both elbows braced on his knees, his head hanging between his shoulders. He doesn't move as I approach, even though he can definitely hear my heels clacking against the ground. So I slide onto the bench next to him and nudge his thigh with the Styrofoam cup.

"Peace offering."

He chuckles and takes the coffee. "Sorry about all of that. I just needed some air."

"It's okay." I wrap my hands around my own coffee, trying not to shiver as the breeze picks up against my bare arms.

He wordlessly shrugs off his suit jacket to place over my shoulders.

"Thanks," I murmur, huddling into it. "You should stay with her tonight because she's going to need you after that conversation."

He shakes his head. "No, no, I'll get you home—"

"Heath, we both know this around-the-clock security thing is ridiculous. I'm going to go home and lock my doors. There's a security man for the building. Faye already filled him in on the situation when I moved in. I'll be fine."

He stares at me silently for several seconds. "At least let me take you home and sweep the apartment. Then I'll come back."

"All right."

He sighs and rubs his eyes. "You know how to turn on those security cameras we installed? And how to monitor them—"

"Heath—"

"I'm just saying!"

I smack him lightly on the arm and push to my feet. "Just get us a car."

CHAPTER 24
HEATH

"Stop mother-henning me, for Christ's sake, Heath."

"I'm not mother-henning you," I mutter under my breath as I fluff the pillow a few more times before sliding it beneath Dani's leg.

She gives me a knowing smirk as I slump into my chair beside her bed, careful to avoid all the wires connecting her to the various machines around her. But I know it's a front. Her eyes are red and glassy. So at least the prick followed through and told her the truth while I took Parker home.

But there's no sense of satisfaction in that.

"You say the word, and I will go track him down and beat him to a pulp," I murmur.

I was hoping to get a laugh out of her, but instead, she bursts into tears.

Ah, fuck.

"Dani..." I start to rise from my chair again, but she holds out a hand to stop me.

"Please don't. I just—" She sucks in a deep breath. "I just want to talk about something else."

I glance at my phone, checking for a text from Mom. She was in the middle of a shift when we got the news, but hopefully she'll manage to get here soon. She'll be a lot better at comforting than I am.

My eyes linger on the screen, my fingers itching to text Parker and make sure she's okay. I triple-checked every corner of that apartment, and she's only been alone there for half an hour, but still... If something were to happen to her—

"Tell me about Parker."

My eyes snap to Dani's face, and she pushes her lower lip out and brings her hands under her chin.

"The puppy dog face has never worked on me."

"I think it's going to work now," she insists. "Your little sister is stuck in a hospital bed and just dumped the person who was supposed to be the love of her life and you won't even humor me?" She keeps her voice light, teasing, but the tears are reemerging, her chin wobbling around the words *love of her life.*

I raise my hands. "Okay. Okay."

She grins triumphantly.

"There's not much to say though." I lean back in my chair and cross my ankle over my knee. "I took the job a few weeks ago and joined her security—"

"Security?"

I wince. I guess all the press coverage has been after Dani's accident. Otherwise, it's definitely something she would be following. "Have you heard of Ryker Rae?"

"The singer?" She glances from me to the door, her eyes slowly widening. "No," she whispers. "You're shitting me. I *thought* she looked familiar."

I flick my wrist.

"Oh my *God*. She's like *famous*, famous. You know that, right?"

"Yeah, Dani, I know that."

"Holy shit." She grins and sits up a little straighter. "This is so cool. I'm out for, what? A couple weeks? And everything happens without me!"

I chuckle and shake my head.

"Well, how long have you had a crush on her then?"

"I—" I make a choking sound in the back of my throat. "What are we, in fourth grade?"

Her grin twists into something mischievous.

"I work for her," I insist.

"She's awfully pretty..."

"Dani."

"What!" She throws her hands up. "You might be able to lie to Mom or your buddies, or even Parker, but I *know* you. And I could tell the second she walked in here."

"I—" I shake my head. The nurses' station is empty, the halls quiet. No one nearby to potentially interrupt this conversation. I rub a hand across my mouth. All this talking about her has me picturing her alone in that apartment. The pictures of her after the attack—covered in blood and with bruises around her throat. Maybe this was a mistake. I shouldn't have let her stay back there alone. I could call Annie or Faye, but she specifically asked me not to. But if it's for her own safety...

"Heath?"

My eyes snap back to Dani, who's watching me with her eyebrows drawn, all the amusement gone from her features.

"I got here as soon as I could!" A wave of Mom's ambery vanilla perfume washes through the door as she beelines for

Dani. They both burst into tears as Mom throws her arms around Dani's shoulders and leans over the bed for a hug.

"Don't smother her, Mom."

"Right. Right." She sniffles and loosens her hold. "How are you feeling? How are you doing? Do you need anything?"

"I'm fine, Mom," says Dani.

She touches Dani's cheek, then her forehead, then smooths her hand over her hair. "Oh, I'm just so glad you're awake." Mom turns her attention to me next and throws her arms around my neck before I can react.

"I—*oh*." I grunt as she momentarily cuts off my air. Her tears soak through the collar of my shirt as I pat the back of her head, but instead of calming her, she sobs harder.

I meet Dani's eyes over her head, and she smirks. Our mom's always been the kind to burst into tears at the drop of a hat, so this is pretty par for the course. All you can do is let her ride it out. I rub my hand against her back until she finally calms down and releases me.

"Sorry, sorry." She sniffles.

"You don't have to apologize," I say, then guide her to the chair I'd been sitting in. "Why don't you two catch up? I'll go grab you some coffee."

Mom catches my hand before I can leave and gives it a squeeze. "You always take such good care of me."

"And you always make sure to make it as difficult as possible." I pat her hand and wink before stepping out of the room, well accustomed to this walk to the coffee machine at the end of the hall by now.

I yawn and crack my neck as I wait for the coffee to pour, the compounded lack of sleep from the last few weeks seeming to catch up with me all at once. It's like my body had been waiting until Dani woke up to process it all, and now that it thinks it can finally relax, it wants to sleep for the next week straight.

But they'll probably want to keep Dani here for another few days—weeks?—for recovery. And the longer she's here, the more it'll cost.

I sigh and sink into the chair beside the coffee machine. I can't think about that right now. I can't—

ꓩꓕꓲꓩꓲꓩꓕꓩꓩ

"HEY. ARE YOU ALL RIGHT?"

A light kick to my foot jolts me awake, and I sit up straight, cold coffee splashing all over my sleeve in the process. I blink, struggling to adjust to the harsh fluorescents. A male nurse with thin lips raises an eyebrow at me.

"I'm good." I cough, trying to clear my throat.

The nurse studies me for a minute more before heading down the hall.

"Shit," I mutter, glancing at my watch. It's already six in the morning.

Discarding the coffee I never took a sip from, I jog down the hall to Dani's room. A sigh of relief escapes me as I find her and Mom fast asleep. Mom's curled up in the chair beside the bed, her cheek resting on her fist. Dani's turned toward her, as if they fell asleep talking.

The red battery icon glares at me as I pull my phone from my pocket. It'll die any minute now.

I send Parker a quick text to make sure she's okay. My foot taps nervously against the floor as I wait for her response. Maybe I should call? But it's early. She might be asleep. Or I could take a quick trip over there—

I'm alive

I exhale as her response comes through. Barely a few seconds later, the phone screen goes black.

Shit. Someone around here has to have a charger.

"Cliff?"

My head jerks up. Dani's facing me now, a sleepy smile on her face. The old nickname makes my returning smile automatic. She went through a *Wuthering Heights* phase in high school and started calling me Cliff—as in Heathcliff—for *years*. I can't even remember the last time I heard it.

"How are you feeling?" I ask, pulling a chair up as quietly as possible. Mom's snoring on the other side.

She yawns. "Tired. Which is dumb, right? Since I've technically been doing nothing but sleeping for so long."

"Yeah. How dare your body want rest after nearly dying?"

She lightly punches me in the shoulder and tries to hide the wince the movement causes, but it's there.

"You should rest," I say quietly.

"Don't you have a job to get to?" she mumbles. "Someone else to micromanage?"

"I'm calling out today." I'm sure Faye won't be thrilled about replacing me last minute, but I also know she has about a dozen hourly guys on speed dial at this point. And as cold as she tries to make her exterior, something tells me she's a lot more understanding than she seems. "So it looks like you're stuck with me."

Dani beams.

CHAPTER 25
PARKER

I didn't think I'd notice Heath's absence in the apartment that night, but I do. After triple-checking I locked the front door before heading to bed, I shove a bookshelf in front of it for good measure. I'm not usually a paranoid person, but the surrounding silence sinks into my skin as I pull the blinds closed, then double back to the kitchen for a knife to keep on my bedside table. Just in case.

It takes forever to fall asleep, and when I do, I wake up every few hours until I finally give up around four in the morning and head to the living room instead. Getting drunk won't help matters, but I pour myself a glass of wine anyway, then tuck myself into a mountain of blankets on the couch.

There's nothing good on TV, so I leave on whatever pops up first—some crime documentary. Two minutes in I realize what a stupid idea that is and change the channel...to a rerun of the reality dating show Erica and I met up to watch together every week through our teen years. My fist tightens around the remote as I flip to a black-and-white movie instead.

Is this what it's going to be like for the rest of my life? Too afraid to be alone, always looking over my shoulder? Always on edge?

I must fall asleep at some point, because the next time I open my eyes, light is coming through the window. The TV has shifted to a news story, and I untangle myself from the blankets to swap my glass of wine for a cup of coffee.

My phone lights up on the counter with a text from Heath.

> Text me when you wake up so I know you're okay.

I send back a quick *I'm alive* text before starting the coffee, then frown when I realize I'm smiling. I kind of want to text him again to see how everything went with his sister last night, but if he wanted to talk about it with me, he'd bring it up first.

I stare at my phone until the coffee maker beeps, waiting to see if he texts again, but he doesn't.

Sighing, I dig in my coat closet until I find my old yoga mat, then roll it out in front of the TV so I can stretch while I drink my coffee and watch the news. Faye and Annie should be stopping by later today to go over the itinerary for the concert this week, so I just need to kill time until then.

I hold the mug under my nose, letting the warm and nutty aroma of the coffee sink into me. It feels different this morning, the empty apartment. No longer this looming, foreboding threat, the adrenaline in my blood sky-high as I wait for a crazed fan to break down the door and lunge at me in my sleep. Instead, just for a moment, it feels the way it did before.

Mornings have always been my favorite time of day. No

matter how late the nights, I'd get up with the sunrise, finding those quiet hours the best time for inspiration. More than half my songs were written on my balcony while I sipped my coffee before the rest of the city started to rise.

For the first time in a long time, my fingers itch to play. To write. That used to be a near-daily impulse, but not since the wedding. I haven't written a single lyric, a single note. I wasn't sure if I ever would again.

Back at my old apartment, I had every instrument I could get my hands on. But here, I don't even have a keyboard.

I tilt my head to the side, considering, then scroll through the app store on my phone until I find something that resembles a piano and set it on the floor. I close my eyes, trying to imagine a real one in front of me and let a soft G fill the apartment. An immediate calm washes over me, and a shadow of a smile curls my lips as I tap out a couple notes. After only a few seconds of this, I rush to the kitchen to find a notepad, humming under my breath a few lyric variations.

People say I love you
Then they leave
But only once they get
Between your sheets
It's just a type of social
Currency
But I believed him
So they'll say it's on me

I frown at the angry pen strokes as I return to my spot on the floor. I can already hear the comments.

Yet another breakup song.

Bitter...jaded...melodramatic...
Had it coming.
She's complaining about lies? The irony.
The definition of a one-hit wonder. Peaked years ago.
It's like she gets worse with every song.

The voices are like insects buzzing around in my skull. I crumple the paper in my hand, toss it aside, and start on a new one. I tap along the app again until I find the right key, squeezing my eyes shut, trying not to overthink it as I let the lyrics come.

Everyone's getting married and
having their ba-bies
and I never wanted that but
now I'm thinking may-be
I don't know if that's growing up or
maybe just feeling left out
wanting someone to choose me
and intend to stick around

"Parker?" Faye's voice startles me out of my thoughts, and I drop the pen as a knock sounds behind me. "Open up!"

"Shit." I grab the bookshelf blocking the door and shimmy it toward the wall. I wince, trying not to scratch the hardwood, and a few books thump against the ground. This felt a lot lighter in my fear-induced desperation last night. When it's finally out of the way, I put my hands on my knees, catching my breath, then open the door.

Faye and Annie stare at me, then the line of book casualties, in what can only be explained as looks of horror. They're both fully dressed and ready for the day, makeup and curled hair and all. And I'm slightly breathless, my makeup from the function last night probably smeared all over my face since I hadn't bothered to remove it before bed, and now that the coffee has hit my bloodstream, I'm practically bouncing on the balls of my feet. I swat away the stray piece of hair in my eyes and force a smile.

"Did you have a bookshelf in front of the door?" asks Annie.

Faye eyes the bottle of wine on the counter. "Are you drinking at eight in the morning?"

"We should really hang out more," I say, stepping aside so they can come in. "You guys are so *fun.*"

Annie carefully steps over the books, her hot pink kitten heels making delicate taps against the floor. "Where's Heath?"

"Oh." I scoop my coffee off the ground and head for the couch, my shoulders already creeping up in a defensive stance around my ears. "He's, um, at the hospital. Family emergency."

"*What?*" Faye closes the door behind her with more force than necessary.

"And you didn't *call?*" demands Annie.

"We could have gotten someone else!"

"Or we could have stayed with you!"

"Hey! I'm clearly alive. No harm done. And it was nice to not have a babysitter for once."

"Clearly." Faye motions to the bookshelf sticking out awkwardly from the wall.

Okay, so fair enough.

"Are you here to talk flight details, or what?" I say.

Annie and Faye exchange a look. I shrug and unmute the TV as the weather guy appears.

So yeah, maybe last night was pretty dumb. I can't even blame it on the amount of champagne I had because I wasn't that drunk and I would've asked for the same thing sober. Alone time has been so hard to come by these days, and it's fucking exhausting when everyone around you is screaming about how *the sky is falling* twenty-four seven.

And people need normalcy, right? It should be right up there with basic needs and human touch and connection.

Annie starts tidying up the kitchen as Faye digs something out of her bag and comes to join me on the couch.

"They rescheduled your Vegas show for Tuesday," she explains, setting some papers on the table that I don't bother looking at. "We'll be flying in day of and flying out that same night. They've assured me they'll have double the usual security and...Parker, are you even listening to me?"

My eyes flicker from the TV to her face. "I'm listening. But what does it matter? I don't have any say in it. Whatever you tell me to do, I'll end up doing. Isn't that how this works?"

She pulls back, a rare flash of hurt crossing her features, and she joins Annie in the kitchen.

"Faye," I sigh. "I'm sorry. I'm in a mood. I didn't sleep well last night." I grab the papers from the coffee table. "I'm listening, really..."

The TV flashes as a new story comes onto the screen. Specifically, *my* face. It's some shot taken by a paparazzi. I can't even tell when it was taken. I'm on a sidewalk in New York with my head down and a cup of coffee in my hand. The next picture that flashes on the screen makes my entire body go cold. It's his mugshot, a picture I've seen everywhere since the wedding. I stare into his eyes—one green, one brown—and it feels like he's looking back. He's looking right at me, and he's laughing.

"Now if you're not caught up on this case, it's quite the story. Driven by what he claims to be love—"

The TV goes black, and I glance up to see Annie with the remote.

"I'm surprised the lawyers don't want me to testify," I say quietly.

"There's no need," Faye says. "There's enough evidence and witnesses that they can win this case without it. There is absolutely no reason for us to put you in the same room as that man again if we don't have to."

Annie's forehead wrinkles. "Did you...*want* to, Parker?"

"No, of course not." I wrap the blanket a little tighter around my shoulders. "I want to be sure they lock him away, you know? I just don't want to take any chances."

"He's getting locked away," Faye says, her voice hard. "Guaranteed. You don't have to worry about that, or him, ever again."

Letting out a shaky breath, I nod and force myself to smile. Annie returns one that looks as fake as mine. "Want to go over the wardrobe for the show next?"

CHAPTER 26
PARKER

The first time I was on a private plane, I was eighteen years old. Back then, I'd been in awe, grinning the entire flight and snapping pictures on my phone to send to Nick, soaking up the food and champagne and comfy leather seats that reclined flat to sleep. Today, all I can think about is the only reason I'm on here is because it's not safe for me to fly with everyone else. I take a seat by the window and stare outside at the runway as I wait for us to take off.

The rest of my team files in, along with my parents. Seeming to sense I don't want to talk, they take the seats across the aisle from me without a word. I check my phone again, but the various apology texts I've sent to Erica stare back at me, all left on read.

There had, however, been a string of texts from Rick this morning. *I'm sorry, please call me, can we talk, Parker please.* Blah blah blah. They'd annoyed me enough to block his number.

Either oblivious to my mood or he doesn't care, Heath

takes the seat facing me and puts his hands on the table between us. There's a noticeable shift in his energy today, the shadows beneath his eyes less severe. But now with Dani awake, of course there's less stress weighing him down.

I wish I could say the same. It's not unusual for there to be no time for rehearsal before the show since we're in the middle of a tour, but with my unexpected break, I can't help but feel off my game. I'm not easing back into things—we're going full fucking speed ahead.

What if I can't fall back into everything as easily as everyone's expecting me to? All eyes are going to be on this show. It'll be the first time Ryker Rae is seen in public since the attack. One wrong step and every pop culture journalist in the world is going to gleefully plaster it all over the internet.

Faye and Annie chat quietly somewhere behind me as we take off. I close my eyes, my fingers tightening around the leather arm rests in a death grip, and I let out a slow breath through my nose. The flight to Las Vegas isn't that long, but I've never been able to sleep on airplanes, and the several hours of waiting before a show with nothing to do but overthink always makes me more nervous than I'd usually be. Elijah was the only one who ever helped.

"Wanna play?"

My eyes snap to Heath's face as he pulls a deck of cards out of his pocket. It's like he read my mind. There were so many times Elijah and I sat in these exact seats and Elijah asked me the same thing.

Heath's eyebrows pull together. "Or not. Bad idea. I just remembered you saying that you used to—"

"Yes," I say, my voice coming out scratchy and small. "I want to play."

He nods and shuffles the cards. I wait to see if he's going

to mention his sister and what happened that night, but maybe he has things he's trying not to think about too. Maybe this distraction is for him as much as it's for me.

"I have to admit," he says, "I don't know many games. You might have to teach me. What's your favorite?"

"You know how to play Speed?"

He shakes his head and hands over the cards.

"We each have five cards," I explain as I set it up. "And— you know what? It's kind of hard to explain. I'll show you. Hey, Dad?"

Dad's head pops up from his book across the aisle. I gesture for him to take the seat next to Heath and pass him five cards. "I'm trying to teach Heath how to play Speed."

"Ah." Dad slumps into the chair and sighs. "There's a reason she likes this game," he mumbles to Heath. "She always wins."

I finish setting up the cards and quirk an eyebrow. "Ready?"

Dad brings his shoulders to his ears like he's bracing himself, but nods.

We quickly start flipping the cards, and I bite my tongue as the table becomes a flurry of movement. Dad likes to pretend he's the victim in this situation, but the only reason I got any good at this game was practicing with *him*. We're both down to two cards, and I slam mine on the table before he gets the chance and let out a little "whoop!"

He mutters something under his breath and returns to his seat, where Mom pats his knee comfortingly.

"No one likes a sore loser," I say.

When I turn, I catch Heath watching me.

I gather the cards to shuffle. "What?"

He presses his lips together like he's fighting a smile and

shakes his head. "I already knew how to play. I just wanted to watch you."

I stop shuffling and kick him under the table. He laughs and takes the cards from me.

"I should warn you though," he says, setting them up in four piles. "I won't be as easy to beat as your dad."

I sniff and snatch my cards off the table. "I've never lost a game of Speed."

He raises an eyebrow. "Never?"

"Not a single game."

"Maybe we shouldn't play then." He arranges the cards in his hand. "Wouldn't want to throw you off your game before your show tonight."

I lay my hand over one of the cards in the middle. "Oh just flip them."

His hands move faster than anything I've ever seen, and I hold my breath as the decks on each side quickly disappear. I can hear my dad laughing, but my focus is narrowed in on the game. The plane grows quiet except for the slamming of cards on the table, and then we're both down to five.

Three.

One.

I slam my final card down less than a second before he does. We stare at each other, wide-eyed, both breathing a little heavily.

"Tell me you didn't let me win," I say.

"I take offense to that. I'm definitely not that chivalrous."

"Want a rematch?"

He grins and sweeps his hands across the table to collect the cards. My brain glitches, remembering Elijah doing the same thing, grinning the same crooked smile I see on Heath's face.

But for the first time since the wedding, I don't feel sadness when I think about him. I meet Heath's eyes and smile back.

LAS VEGAS USED to be one of my favorite places to perform. The energy of the crowds here feels different than most places, and it's easy to feed off that and energize yourself more onstage. That's what I repeat to myself over and over as I sit in my dressing room and my makeup artist does my face. I stare at my reflection in the mirror as she builds on my smoky eyes and adds fake lashes. The black wig skims my chin, and she darkens my eyebrows to match it.

I thank her quietly as she finishes and slips from the room, and then for one merciful moment, I'm alone. A lump forms in my throat, and I grit my teeth against it. The rest of the team is waiting for me—my dancers and backup singers and the band. And seeing them as I'd walked through the halls had been a comfort, but it also dug into my stomach like a knife.

Because among the sea of familiar faces, there was one noticeably absent. The one who would wait outside my dressing room and do our secret handshake with me for good luck right before I stepped onstage.

Nope. Nope. We're not thinking about that right now.

I go through another round of vocal warm-ups as I pace, then stretch my neck, my shoulders. It'll feel different once I'm onstage with the music, the lights, the people, the dancers. It'll feel natural again.

It will.

A soft knock on the door jolts me out of my trance. "Come in."

The door cracks open, and Heath pokes his head inside. His eyes land on me, and he pauses, no words coming out as he opens his mouth.

"What?" I glance at myself in the mirror to see if there's anything out of place. I'm already in the leather corset and black pants for the opening number, but I've been putting off the platform boots for as long as possible.

His eyes slowly trail from my feet back to my face. "I—sorry. They wanted me to check if you're ready."

With a sigh, I yank on the shoes and follow him into the hallway.

"How're you feeling?" he asks under his breath.

"I took a shot of tequila," I admit.

He lets out a surprised laugh as we reach the rest of the team, but the room is a blur around me. All too soon, one of the stagehands is helping me into the crawl space for the trap door as music reverberates through the venue. I squat in the small space, my breathing echoing around me as I wait for my entrance.

You've done this a thousand times, I remind myself. *You could do this in your sleep.*

Faye's face appears at the end of the long crawl space, and she shoots me a thumbs-up.

The panel beneath me buzzes and starts to rise. I adjust the headset in my ears and blow out a calming breath as the stage lights wash over me, and the crowd erupts in screams and applause. My body moves like it's on autopilot, and I grab the microphone from the stand and raise it in the air as the music shifts to the intro for the first song.

Falling into step with the other dancers is as easy as it

always was, and I let myself get lost in it. The music vibrates through my chest, warming me from the inside out. It's so demanding, it's enough to clear the rest of the thoughts. I grin, the muscle memory carrying me through the dance. *This* is why I do this. *This* is what I love. I could experience this feeling a million times and still never get enough, like floating on your back in the water and flying through the clouds at the same time.

But then I open my eyes, and my focus snags on someone in the pit. My vision blurs too much to see the details of his face. It can't be—

The room finally sharpens, revealing someone completely unfamiliar. Red hair, thick beard.

Not him. But of course it's not.

He's locked up.

I turn away to finish off the number. When the song ends, the applause returns, and I take a second to catch my breath, forcing a smile and wave. The voices roar and blend together like a wave crashing on the beach. A girl in the front row, maybe in her early teens, jumps up and down, gesturing frantically for me to touch her hand. Tears stream down her face, and I reach for her.

At first, I don't know what happens.

All I know is my head hurts, then I'm on my back on the stage. The lights blur, the surrounding noise muffled. The wind is knocked clear from my lungs, and I gasp for air, then reach a hand to my forehead. My fingers come away covered in blood.

Oh God. Pain explodes through my temples, and no matter how many times I blink, I can't get my vision to focus. I don't know how long I lie there, trying to catch my breath, trying to—

Hands slip under my shoulders, and then someone is dragging me offstage. My head spins, and I close my eyes against the dizziness as someone picks me up and the noise steadily trickles back in.

"We need a medic—"

"I'm calling Allen. I *knew* this was a bad idea—"

"You can put her over here—"

"Parker, honey, can you hear me?"

"Someone get a towel to stop the bleeding."

Something soft meets my back. My vision blurs around the light fixture above me as a towel presses against my temple.

"Ow," I breathe.

"Sorry," a deep voice mumbles beside my ear. It sounds like Heath. "They're going to get a medic." His words come out so fast they're nearly tripping over each other. "It's probably a concussion. You'll be all right."

"Heath," I gasp, urgent. "I need a—" I twist and hurl over the side of the couch.

"Okay, okay." Heath grabs my hair with one hand and rubs my back with the other.

I vomit again, my head pounding with each retch. I rip the wig off and throw it to the end of the couch.

Heath disappears for a second, then hands me a tissue to wipe my mouth. I stay bent over, my head hanging between my shoulders in case it happens again. The pain pounds so violently behind my eyes it feels like it's going to explode out of my head.

"What was it?" I murmur.

Heath gathers my hair again and pulls it behind my back. "What was what?" he asks quietly.

I cough and wince at the new stab of pain through my temples. "What did they throw?"

He hesitates, and his hand on my back tightens. "A steel-toed boot. Security took the guy who threw it."

"I feel like I might throw up again."

He traces small circles on my back. "That's okay."

"She's right over here!" my mother calls from somewhere behind us, but I don't look up.

A man kneels in front of me and gently puts his fingers under my chin to tilt my head up. I wince at the light he shines in my eyes, then he inspects the cut in my hairline.

"We'll need to get her to a hospital for some scans. She has a concussion, at least."

"Parker." Dad reaches for me, and he and Heath help me to my feet and away from the mess I've made on the floor.

"Where's Faye?" I murmur.

"Off yelling at Allen, I think," says Heath.

"You don't need to worry about any of that right now," says Dad. "Let's get you to the hospital, okay?"

I stumble in the stupid platform shoes, but Dad catches me and sweeps me into his arms. And suddenly I feel like a little kid again. So I bury my face in his neck and let myself cry.

An Excerpt from Parker's Journal

how does your heart feel
after all the lies you've told

does it weigh on you
building like tiny layers
beneath your skin

the change so slight
you may not notice it at first

or does it just roll over you
as simple as ducking your head
beneath the smoke

how is it possible
to put so much poison
into the universe
and feel none of its effects
in return

CHAPTER 27
PARKER

I feel like I have antiseptic burning the inside of my nose. Machines beep and whir on either side of me, and when I blink my eyes open, I wince as the light cuts through my head like a knife.

"Sorry, sorry."

The light switches off, though it's still bright in the hallway beside me. I cover my eyes with my hands, then hear someone lowering the blinds over the windows.

I open my eyes again, and the pain is still blatantly there, but less intense. Heath stands at the end of my bed, brow furrowed, arms crossed over his chest.

I lick my lips and glance around the rest of the room, but there's no one else here.

"Your parents went downstairs to get something to eat," he says quietly. "And last I saw Faye, she was on the phone with Allen."

I push myself into a seated position, and he drifts closer, hands extended like he's ready to catch me.

"Do you want some water?" he offers.

I nod, then wince, and he brings over a little plastic cup with a straw. I eagerly drink it all.

"The doctor should be back soon." He sets the cup on the table and wrings his hands together. "I think he said they're going to want to keep you overnight for observation, just in case."

My shoulders tense, my pulse picking up at the thought. At all the empty space behind the windows. All the entrances and exits and halls and rooms and people I don't know—

"Parker."

My gaze shoots to Heath's face, and I realize I'm panting.

"You'll be fine. They're going to bring in a cot, and I'll be in here with you the whole time, okay? I imagine they won't be able to get your parents to leave either."

I cover my face with my hands and blow out a slow breath. "I'm so tired."

"You want to lie back down?"

"That's not what I mean."

A chair scrapes lightly against the ground, and when I look up again, he's sitting beside the bed. The concern is all over his face, far too close to pity for comfort. He opens and closes his mouth like he's trying to decide what to say.

I wonder if it bothers him, being in a hospital again after everything that happened with Dani. From what he's told me, it sounds like he's basically been living there since the accident.

"How's your sister?" I ask quietly.

A bit of the weight seems to lift from his shoulders, and he smiles softly. "She's okay. She's with my mom. She's still pretty upset, but the doctors say her recovery is looking good."

I lie back against the pillows, a sudden wave of exhaustion weighing on my eyelids. "That's good news."

"Yeah." He hesitates with his hand in the air before finally lowering it onto mine. "It sounds like Faye is getting you out of the rest of your contract. Don't quote me on that, but it sounds like you may be done, Parker."

I close my eyes, but don't feel the relief I'd been hoping for.

"You really scared me today," he says, his gaze on our hands. "We all watched you go down backstage. And I—I don't know if I've ever felt anything like that. My heart just...dropped."

"I can't even remember it happening. One minute I was up, and then I was on my back, and I couldn't see anything."

He gives my hand a light squeeze, but the contact shoots up my arm like a jolt of electricity, setting every nerve alight. For a moment, his gaze trails to my mouth. "I'm glad you're okay."

"Oh good, you're awake."

Mom and Dad hurry into the room, closing the door softly behind them. Heath pushes back from the bed, getting out of their way as they pull up chairs beside me. Mom runs a hand over my forehead and leans down to plant a kiss on the top of my head.

"How are you feeling?" Dad asks.

"Like I got hit in the head with a steel-toed boot."

Of course neither of my parents laugh, but Heath presses his lips together like maybe he wants to. He nods at me over my parents' heads. "I'll be just outside," he says before slipping into the hallway.

"As soon as the doctor gives you the all clear, we'll head

straight home," says Dad. "Even Nick is going to fly in from school, and we're going to spend some good old-fashioned family time together."

Few things would be less appealing to me right now, but I don't have the energy to fight it.

Mom gently pushes the hair from my eyes, careful to avoid the bandage wrapped around my head, and kisses me on the forehead again. "We're so happy to see you awake."

"I know you probably don't want to talk about it," says Dad, "but you were *really* good up there. I was just telling your mother how proud I was."

"Dad." Tears spring to my eyes, and he wipes at his own.

"It's true," says Mom, her voice wobbling. "The two of us are hopelessly tone-deaf, so I don't know how in the world we ended up with a kid as talented as you."

They huddle in on both sides, wrapping their arms around me and pressing their cheeks against mine.

"Even if this is the end," Dad says quietly, "it was a good run, kid. You did real good."

The tears run down my cheeks in earnest now, and a tight fist squeezes in my chest. Because as much as I've grown to hate everything that comes with this life, for a moment there, when I was onstage and the crowd was roaring so loud I could feel it inside of my bones, when the music picked me up and I felt like I was floating above it all, I remembered why I do this in the first place. How addicting it can be. How it's hard to imagine ever wanting anything as badly as I wanted this. How badly, at times, I still do.

But then I think of Elijah. And Erica. And all the things I can't do and places I can't go. Of shoving furniture in front of my door at night or the terror I feel anytime I dare to go somewhere alone. The countless death threats I've gotten over the years. The pictures stalkers have taken through my windows and then shoved copies under my door, my face cut out and pasted on a naked model's body. And I can't help but wonder, even if I leave all this behind, if I'll ever be able to have any kind of normal again.

AN EXCERPT FROM PARKER'S JOURNAL

I'm young but I'm aging
the rules are always changing
and I'm holding on
to a life raft
like I'm lost at sea

or maybe I'm just afraid
of losing the person
I used to be

CHAPTER 28
HEATH

There's still dried blood in her hair. She's asleep on her side facing my cot in the corner, her hands tucked under her face. The moonlight from the window falls across the bed, highlighting the hollows of her cheeks. The rest of the hospital is quiet, a single nurse sitting at the desk in the hall.

I rub a hand across my face. I've spent too much fucking time in hospitals lately. Every time I blink, Parker's face morphs into Dani's, then back again.

I hadn't been there at Dani's accident, but I *had* been there for this. I was supposed to protect her. To keep her safe. I'd been so swept up in watching her perform, figuring the venue's security guys knew what they were doing. But I should've known better. I should've been watching the crowd. I should've seen this coming.

It could've been much worse than a mild concussion and a few gashes on her head. What if it had caused brain damage? If she hadn't woken up? If it had—

I pull in a deep breath through my nose, forcing myself to stop the line of thinking.

Her eyelids flutter as her head twitches. The clock behind her says it's just after three in the morning. She must be having a bad dream. Every time she moves, I keep thinking she's going to wake up, but then she flips over or tucks herself further into the pillow.

She twitches in the bed again, her hands flying out from under the blankets. She scrubs at her arms, her chest, desperate little sounds coming out of her throat, like she's trying to get something off her.

I jump up and pause beside the bed, wondering if I should wake her. Turns out I don't need to because her eyes fly open and she jerks upright.

"Hey, hey, you're all right."

She turns to me, then presses her lips together. "I'm going to—"

I lunge for the trash can beside the bed as she leans over, barely managing to position it beneath her before she empties the contents of her stomach. I grab her hair with one hand, trying to get it away from her face while also keeping the trash can under her.

After a moment, she stops heaving and hangs her head between her shoulders, her chest rising and falling with her small, rapid breaths. She pushes the remaining strands of hair from her face with shaking hands.

When it's clear she's not going to be sick again, I set the trash can on the floor.

"Are you all right?"

She sniffs and wipes the back of her hand under her nose. "I'm fine."

Her voice sounds anything but fine, and she hasn't lifted her head. It takes me a moment to realize it's because she's crying.

"Hey." I hesitate, then take a seat next to her and place a hand on her back. She doesn't react, but she doesn't pull away. "What do you need?"

She sniffs again and grabs the tissues from the bedside table to wipe her face. "Nothing. I'm fine, Heath. Sorry if I woke you."

"I'm on duty, remember? Not sleeping."

"Oh, right." Her voice comes out small, hollow. Not at all the way she usually sounds. Even those first few days when she was barely moving around her apartment, her words still had an edge to them. Not anger, just a little sass.

Now, I'd give just about anything to hear it.

She grabs the water cup and takes a small sip.

God, I wish I were better at comforting. I have no fucking idea what to say. All I know is the sight of the tears on her face sinks like a rock in my chest. It makes me want to drive to the police station holding the guy who did this and cut off the hand he used to throw the boot.

After all the shit they've put her through, she finally mustered the courage to get back up there. She even looked like she was enjoying it for that first song.

I've seen videos of her performing—I already knew she was good at her job. But seeing it live was an entirely different thing. The way she captured the attention of every eye in the room, the way she engaged with her fans, making them all feel noticed and appreciated.

Suddenly it all made sense. The craze. The undying devotion her fans have for her. She isn't just an artist to them. It's a community, a family. Her talent is undeniable, even if her genre isn't your thing. But it's *her* more than the music that makes them show up.

I don't know how well she can make out the signs in the crowd with the lights pointed at her, but nearly every one I saw had her face—Parker's, not Ryker's—and some variation of *we love you, we support you, you're my hero* on it.

She winces and massages between her eyes with her fingers.

"Your head hurt?" I immediately curse myself for the stupid question. She has a concussion. Of course her head fucking hurts.

"Yeah," she murmurs.

"Why don't you lie down? I'll do that."

She peers up at me like she doesn't understand, and I gesture to the pillow.

"Go on. Lie down."

She complies and tucks the sheets back under her chin. I pull a chair over as quietly as I can manage and lean forward, propping my elbows on the side of the bed.

"Close your eyes."

She does, and I press my thumbs against the bridge of her nose, then gently massage up toward her brow bone. She lets out a soft sigh, the muscles in her face relaxing. Her lips part as I work my way to her temples.

I don't think I've ever been this close to her before. I've definitely never noticed the freckles. They're light, faint. In certain lighting, it looks like she doesn't have them at all. Even this close, I can barely make them out.

I press a little harder, massaging by her ears, and she lets out a small, soft moan that I feel all the way in my bones. I pause.

"Is that too hard?"

"No," she whispers. "Please don't stop. It's helping."

I try very hard not to imagine any other situation where she would say those words to me.

She hums as I work my way back up to her nose.

"What were you dreaming about?" I murmur to distract myself.

A single eye squints open.

"It was a nightmare, right? That woke you up?"

Her eyes are so much greener than I realized. There's a trace of dark blue in there too, just on the outline.

"The night of the wedding."

"Is it the same one every time?"

That picture from the tabloid flashes into my mind again —a necklace of bruises, the rips in her dress.

"Kind of. It starts the same, but it plays out differently. Sometimes it's exactly like it happened. Sometimes security doesn't get there in time. Sometimes Erica doesn't get away. No matter what version, I always end up covered in blood." She swallows hard and lowers her gaze to the bed between us.

So that was what she'd been trying to get off before she woke up. The blood.

"Can I ask you something?"

She hums and closes her eyes again.

"If they get you out of your contracts, if you're done after this...then what next? What would you do instead?"

She gives me a soft, sad smile. "I don't know. This was all I ever wanted for so long, I'd never thought ahead to what would come after...if there ever was an after. I don't even think I know who I am without Ryker anymore. I feel like I should know what I want, but I don't."

"But you do."

Her eyes snap back to mine.

"You *want* to know what you want. That's step one."

"How did you figure it out?" she murmurs. "What you want?"

Her eyes fall shut as I massage toward the bridge of her nose again, her eyelashes fanning out against her cheeks. For some reason, it feels much easier to say without her looking back at me.

"After my dad left, I wanted to make sure my mom and sister were okay. The means of doing that didn't matter."

"They're lucky to have you. But if they were okay? Then what? What would you want for yourself?"

My fingers still, and she opens her eyes and searches my face.

"I guess I'd want to know what I want too."

She smiles, and I find myself smiling back.

"Thanks, Heath," she whispers. "I know this isn't exactly in your job description."

"Anything for you, superstar. Now try to get some sleep."

A small smile curls her lips as her eyes fall shut again. But even once her breathing evens out and I know she's fast asleep, I don't return to my cot against the wall, her question burying deeper in my mind.

But if they were okay? Then what? What would you want for yourself?

It's not that I'd never thought about it before. A million versions of my future have played out in my mind—if Dad never left, if I'd stayed in college, if I'd gotten some office job, if I'd moved away instead of staying close by to help Mom and Dani, if I'd settled down by now.

I've spent so many years swallowing what I want in favor of what needed to be done. Now it's been so long, do I even know what it feels like anymore? To want something?

My gaze drift back to Parker on the bed.

My stomach sinks as I realize yes, I do.

CHAPTER 29
PARKER

My parents' house isn't the one I grew up in. We found them a new place on Staten Island once the Ryker money started rolling in, one with a little more elbow room and functioning heat and air conditioning. It had been the first thing on my wish list if I ever made it big.

Even though they've only lived here for about five years, they've completely transformed the house into a home. The outside looks straight out of a storybook with its redbrick gothic style and sprawling front lawn. But despite the extra space, the interior is full of the same furniture from my childhood. I'd offered to upgrade the furniture too, but they'd been adamant it didn't need replacing.

Dad heads straight up the spiral staircase with my suitcases when we arrive, and I follow Mom to the kitchen.

"Nick's flight should land in a few hours," she tells me.

The fridge stands several feet taller than her, and she practically disappears inside as she pulls open the door. I prop myself on a stool behind the counter as she produces a few glasses from the cabinets. I quirk an eyebrow at the bottle of champagne she pulls out next.

"It's not even noon yet," I remind her.

She scoffs and adds orange juice to the counter. "It's never too early for a mimosa."

I guess there's no arguing with that.

"Bags are in your room, bug." Dad slides onto the stool beside me and drums his hands against the counter.

"Thanks, Dad." I plant an overly theatrical kiss on his cheek. He flails away, wiping at his face like I covered him in slobber.

Mom slides him a glass and raises hers in a toast. "To having the family back together."

"Shouldn't we wait for Nick for that?" I mutter.

"He doesn't count," Dad whispers back, then clinks his glass to mine.

Mom sighs and gazes out the floor-to-ceiling windows leading to the backyard. "It's so nice out. How about we all go out to the pool?"

"Sure. But do you mind if I head upstairs for a bit first?"

Dad squeezes my shoulder. "Take as long as you need."

The second floor is silent, and I wonder if the house is always quiet these days with me and Nick gone. They still have both of our rooms set up, not a thing out of place. I'd insisted Nick get the bigger one since he'd be living here longer with them. I was here less than a year before getting my own place, but mine has the best view.

The house isn't exactly on the waterfront, but it's close enough.

Dad left my bags at the foot of my bed, and I dig through them until I find my hairbrush. Though after I find it, I set it aside on the bed and start looking for something else. I didn't need to freshen up so much as catch my breath.

My phone buzzes in my pocket. I pull it out and stare at the screen a moment too long, specifically, at Heath's name.

> Just wanted to check on you and see how you're holding up.

My hand squeezes around the phone. I gave Heath the week off while I'm visiting my parents. He's been working practically nonstop since we hired him, and he has everything going on with his sister, so the time off was more than deserved.

Letting me come here alone, of course, was out of the question, so a few other temporary security guys are staying in the guest rooms, but Faye assured me they'd be outside and out of sight the entire time unless they were needed.

> Still in one piece

Three dots appear like he's typing, but they disappear just as fast. I wait for them to pop up again, but they don't.

Sighing, I toss the phone on the bed and search the dresser for a swimsuit. As I pull out an old black bikini, the phone buzzes.

> Try not to throw coffee on anyone while I'm gone

My lips twitch, and I shake my head.

> Why? Afraid I'll replace you?

I set the phone aside as I slip into the suit, my eyes never leaving the screen. The moment it lights up, I snatch it off the bed.

> You won't.

> > You're awfully confident for someone still on a trial period

> I'm beginning to think I'm just always going to be on a trial period

Cheers from outside draw my attention to the window in time to watch my dad do a cannonball into the deep end. Mom's lying out on one of the lounge chairs, shrieking with laughter and covering her hair from the splash.

When I make it downstairs, Dad's treading water and holding his mouth open while Mom waterfalls her mimosa to him. I smirk and fall into the chair beside Mom's, snapping a picture as Dad finishes off the glass.

"I'll get the bottles!" Mom announces, then hurries into the house.

I send the picture to Heath.

> > Looks like I've found my new calling: lifeguard.

"What are you smiling about over there?" Dad calls.

I set the phone on the table and come to the edge of the pool. "Just thinking about the look on your face when I beat you in a race." I dive headfirst into the pool and streamline toward the shallow end, popping up once I'm near the wall.

"Don't hurt your father!" Mom calls as she returns with the bottles and pours herself a refill.

I push my lower lip out as he dog-paddles toward me. "Do you need to sit this one out, old man?"

Dad points at me and whips around to Mom. "Did you hear that?"

"She gets the sass from you, Doug. You have no one but yourself to blame."

I grin at him as we get set against the wall.

Mom glances at us over her glass and waves an impatient hand. "Go."

I push off the wall and press myself into a perfect line beneath the water. When I break the surface, I gasp in as much air as possible and shoot forward. When I reach the opposite wall, I flip beneath the water and push off, my muscles burning with the familiar movements, until, finally, my hands land against the concrete again.

I stand and put my hands on my hips, waiting for Dad, who's half a pool's length away.

"That really wasn't fair," Mom tells me.

I wink and shove myself out of the pool, wrapping a towel around my chest as I go. By the time I pick my drink up, Dad reaches the end, then looks around, confused. When he spots me over with Mom, he frowns.

"She didn't cheat," Mom says. "You're just slow."

I stifle a laugh as he grumbles something under his breath and flips over to float on his back.

Mom taps her glass against mine. "Oh, uh, by the way," she says, leaning back in her chair, "your phone has been going off."

"Why don't you tell me whatever it said since you've clearly already read it?"

She shrugs innocently and sips her drink.

I snatch the phone up and see a picture and text from Heath. It's a selfie with his sister. They're still at the hospital.

> She keeps asking about you.

She looks better than the last time I saw her, more color in her cheeks. But my eyes keep drifting to Heath. His hair is tousled around his face, and he's in a plain gray hoodie, the bags under his eyes suggesting he slept there last night.

> You better not tell her anything bad. I like her.

> I don't have anything bad to say.

I sip my drink, not sure how to respond, when another message pops up.

> ...although I did tell her about the coffee. She loved that.

"*So.*" Mom clears her throat, and I shove the phone under my leg. "Heath's your new bodyguard, right?"

"Mm-hmm." I turn and watch Dad struggle to get the basketball out of the water. Every time he gets a hand on it, he accidentally pushes it farther away.

"He was awfully handsome."

"Mom."

"What?"

"Don't be weird."

"I'm not *being weird!*" she insists. "I promise I'm not the only one who noticed the way he looks at you."

I snort. "Yeah, like he's trying to make sure no one kills me. That's his job."

Mom shakes her head, a thoughtful look on her face. "Like he'd jump in front of a bullet for you, job or not."

BY THE TIME Nick gets home, it's already dark out. He shows up with a backpack, duffel bag, and wearing a matching sweatsuit he most definitely slept in. Dad takes his bags, and Nick pulls me into a hug.

"Good to see you, sis." He leans back, holding me by the shoulders, and inhales deeply. "You smell like alcohol. Where can I get some?"

I ruffle his curly blond hair that is somehow almost down to his shoulders now. "None for you, youngster."

"Oh, *come on.*"

Mom breezes into the hallway, arms outstretched for a hug. "I got some sparkling grape juice for you." Nick practically slumps against her, and she pats his back comfortingly.

"Glad to know you came home to get drunk, not to see me," I say.

He glares at me and shuffles toward the kitchen. "I turn twenty-one in two months," he calls.

"Which means I still get to tease you for two more whole months! You can't take that away from me!" I glance at Mom and lower my voice. "Did you actually buy grape juice?"

She presses her lips together to hold back her laugh and nods.

Nick keeps up his scowl until about ten minutes into dinner when Dad brings out a real glass of wine for him. Mom and I roll our eyes, but he's always been the first to cave. The fire crackles in the fireplace behind the table, and for the first time in a long time, I don't spend the evening eyeing all the windows or bracing my muscles.

"You've looked about five seconds away from falling asleep in your potatoes all night." Mom rubs a hand down my hair. "Why don't you go to bed early, and we can do something as a family tomorrow?"

"I'm sorry." I yawn into my hand. "I don't know why I'm so tired."

Actually, I know exactly why I'm so tired, and it has something to do with not sleeping for several weeks straight.

"Go on upstairs," Mom urges, taking the plate from in front of me.

Honestly, nothing sounds better than my bed right now, so I call out a quick goodnight and shuffle toward the stairs, equally weighed down by the exhaustion and the amount of alcohol in my system. I stumble into my room and pull the blinds closed before stripping down to my underwear and finding an oversize T-shirt to sleep in. I fumble with my phone as I try to connect it to the charger beside my bed, then accidentally knock my bag onto the floor.

"Shit." The phone falls next, and I squat to retrieve my things.

"Hello? Parker?"

I look down at my phone in horror. My messages with Heath must have been pulled up, and I somehow called him.

I quickly jab the end call button and shove the rest of my belongings into a little pile before climbing into bed. I'm about to plug my phone back in when Heath's name reappears. *Incoming call.*

"Hey, sorry, I accidentally hit your number."

"Oh." Something rustles on the other end, then his voice

comes through clearer. "Just wanted to make sure everything was all right."

"Oh yeah, everything's fine. Don't worry about me. I know you're probably busy with your sister."

"I'm actually home tonight. Figured I'd try to get some decent sleep for once."

I pull the covers up and roll onto my side. "Yeah, me too." I stifle a yawn. "Can't remember the last time I was in bed by nine on a Friday."

"Is it really only nine? Shit, it feels so much later than that."

His voice sounds deeper over the phone. I flip onto my back, now unable to get the picture of him lying in bed out of my head. Silence passes between us, and I wonder if he's thinking about the same thing.

"It's been weird not having you around all of a sudden," he says.

The gravelly texture of his voice sinks into my skin, and suddenly I'm warm all over. "Yeah, you too." I close my eyes. I shouldn't have had so much to drink today. It's making me—

"Parker?"

"Yeah?"

"There's something I want to talk to you about when you get back."

I swallow. "Why don't you talk to me about it now?"

"Because I don't know if this is a conversation you want to have while you're at your parents' house."

"Well, now I'm really curious," I say, my voice light, although now my heart is *definitely* racing, loud enough he can probably hear it through the phone.

Enough time passes that I check if the call ended, but

then lowly, he says, "I can't stop thinking about you. And in ways I know I shouldn't be thinking about you."

My breath catches, and I don't know if it's the darkness, the phone between us, or the alcohol blurring my senses that makes me say it, but the words roll off my tongue. "And what ways, exactly, would that be?"

"Parker," he says, the word coming out like a plea.

"I want you to tell me."

There's a moment of hesitation, long enough I think he won't respond at all, but then: "I think about touching you. I think about how soft you would feel in my hands and how you would taste."

I let my eyes fall closed again, and it's like I can feel him beside me. For some reason, the words don't surprise me. Maybe just because I've been thinking the same kinds of things, trying to shove them down, ignore them, clinging to the professional nature of our relationship like a safety net.

But now, there's no ignoring them. I can't picture anything but him. How the muscles in his back had moved that day in the kitchen, how his hand felt in mine in the hospital, how his arms had felt around me while we danced, how sure I'd been at the bar that he wanted to kiss me just as much as I wanted him to. And those were just glimpses, small tastes of the real thing.

And I want more. God, I want more.

"And what are you doing right now?" I whisper.

"Holding on to my self-control by a thread," he grits out.

"So why hold on at all?"

"*Parker.*"

"Do you want me to stop talking?" I ask, one hand coming between my legs. "Do you want me to stop thinking about you touching me?"

"No." A beat passes, then he adds, his voice dangerously low, "Are you thinking about me touching you now?"

My voice comes out like a gasp. "Yes."

"Are you thinking about my hand between your legs, and my mouth on your neck, so I can whisper in your ear all of the things I want to do to you?"

"And what, exactly, do you want to do?" I ask, my fingers moving in slow circles now, but the ache between my legs just spreads like fire, desperate, needing more. My sex drive has been nonexistent since everything happened—maybe that's all this is. It's been too long. Just once and I'll get it out of my system. Just once—

His breathing gets faster, and he lets out a husky laugh. "It would take all night to get through all the things I want to do to you. But I think first, I'd push you up against the wall and get down on my knees to make you come with my tongue until you can't stand anymore. When I finally get to taste you, I damn well plan on taking my time."

A shiver rolls through me, every nerve in my body raw and buzzing. "And then what?"

"I'd memorize every inch of your body with my mouth. I want to find every place you like to be touched, every way I can make you moan. Every way I can push you to the edge and ease you back. And when you can't take it anymore, I'll bend you over the counter so I can fuck you just the way you want it." He pants, and my heart throbs in my ears. "Would you like that?"

"Yes." My back arches at the thought of his mouth on my skin, his body moving against mine. The way his muscles would feel beneath my hands, to hear the sounds he'd make when he finally lost control.

"Are you wet for me, superstar?"

"Yes, Heath. Yes."

"God, I'm so hard right now," he breathes. "I wish I was inside you."

"I wish I could feel you." The fire builds in my stomach, and I feel it all the way down to the soles of my feet. I'm so wet it spreads to the insides of my thighs.

I want his hands on my skin, in my hair, intertwined with mine. It's almost unbearable, how much I want to feel him inside me, pressing down on me, his mouth on mine.

"I want to hear the sound you make when you come. I want to feel your body shake under mine as you beg me for more. I want to hear you scream my name over and over again."

I moan low in my throat, my hips twisting on the bed. His words paint too clear of a picture in my head. I can feel the way his body would shudder under my touch, how the heat from his skin would melt into mine.

"Yeah, just like that. You like it rough?"

"Yes," I gasp.

"You'd like it if I held you by the throat while I made you come?"

I lick my lips, panting now. "Yes."

"You'd like it if I held you down, your body still shaking, and I keep going until I make you come again? Because I'm not gonna stop. I'm not gonna stop until I've had enough."

I cry out as I come undone and turn my head into the pillow to muffle the sound. Distantly, I hear Heath finish too. My ears ring, and I lie there staring at the ceiling, trying to catch my breath as my hands tremble at my sides. I don't say anything, and neither does he, but we also don't hang up. I just lie there listening to his breathing slow until we both fall in sync and stay that way until I fall asleep.

CHAPTER 30
ĦEATH

I stare at the black screen of my phone on the bed beside me. If it hadn't died sometime during the night, it would probably still be on the call with Parker.

Parker.

I let out a slow breath through my nose. A weird tangle of emotions gets caught in my stomach. Panic, lust, frustration, guilt, and something else I haven't let myself feel in a long time.

But most importantly: how could I have been so selfish and reckless? She'd been drinking last night. What if she wakes up today horrified about what happened? I could lose this job.

I could lose her, says a small voice in the back of my head.

I shove it down. She's not even mine to lose. And that's not what's most important right now.

But then why can't I stop hearing those pretty little sounds she'd made in my head? The breathy moans...the way she'd said my name...how easily I could picture her on top of me with my hands digging into her full hips...

"Jesus fuck." I throw the covers off, plug my phone in, and head straight for the shower, cranking it as cold as it can go.

I brace a hand against the tiled wall and hang my head, letting the stream fall over my back, and despite the icy water raising every hair on my body, my blood is still red fucking hot.

She's your client.

You can't keep this up.

What about Dani? Mom?

I tilt my head back, letting the water run over my face.

I wish I could feel you.

I snatch the bar of soap off the shelf, but no amount of scrubbing my skin raw gets her voice out of my head.

And what, exactly, do you want to do?

I just need to get this out of my system. Then I'll be able to get my head on straight. Just one more time.

My hand fists my cock without my brain instructing it to do so. I grit my teeth, each pump of my hand amplifying her voice in my head. The breathy yes she gasped after each of my questions with no hesitation.

Do you want me to stop thinking about you touching me?

My head falls back against the shower wall, and it's like I'm fourteen all over again because I'm already fucking close just thinking about how soft she'd be. How her pussy would taste. How it would feel to pull her full lips between my teeth as I kissed her.

How she'd moan when I pinned her chest against this shower wall and took her hair in my fist, bringing her head back enough to trace my tongue along the side of her throat. How she'd open her thighs wider for me in invitation and whimper as she leaned back, her hips meeting each of my thrusts from behind, as desperate for it as I am.

Heat spreads in my stomach, my thighs, and my cock pulses. The muscles in my hand burn as I tighten my grip and jerk myself harder.

Yes.

Just hearing her breathe that one word had me coming out of my skin last night. I want her voice here, in my bed. Not just over the phone. I want to feel her hands on me, to watch her come undone, to feel her pussy clench around me. To see her lips swollen and red, her skin flushed. To have her look me in the eyes as I fill her for the first time. I'd like to think I'd be in control, but hell, I know I'd do anything she asked me to. I'd give her anything she wanted.

"Fuck. *Fuck*," I grunt, my hand slowing as my cock twitches and it all spills out of me.

Jesus Christ, that was pathetic.

I lean my forehead against the wall, panting.

What's worse is I don't even feel better.

Her goddamn voice is still in my head, and I want more.

This is my own fault. I should've hung up the phone after I knew she was okay last night. I shouldn't have let it get that far.

I slam my hand against the handle, shutting off the shower, then wrap a towel around my hips and head back into the room. I stare at the phone on my nightstand for a moment too long before tapping the screen to life. The charging icon appears, but even after it clears, there are no notifications. No calls. No texts.

I should be the one to reach out to her, right? To apologize. To try to salvage whatever is left of this professional relationship if I can.

Not talking to her would make things worse. Then she'll think I'm avoiding her.

It's still early. She could be asleep.

Or maybe I'm thinking too much into this and she's enjoying her week with her family. Maybe she was too drunk to remember last night at all.

For fuck's sake, now I really feel like I'm fourteen again. I scrub a hand against my face then turn for my closet to get dressed. I don't have time for this. I need to get to the hospital. Depending on the test results, Dani's doctor said they might let us take her home today. *That's* what I should be focusing on.

I HAVE TURNED into a complete doormat. Dani blinks up at me with that damn puppy dog face, complete with batting eyelashes and begging hands. Maybe in another location it wouldn't have the same effect, but with her in a hospital gown and surrounded by beeping machines, it's hard to say no without feeling like an utter dick.

"*Please,*" she pouts. "For *me?*"

I rub my eyes. "A family welcome home dinner isn't enough for you?"

"Of course it is! I just happen to also want Parker there."

I scowl, but that innocent smile doesn't miss a beat.

"You don't even know her."

"Exactly! But I want to. And this would be a great way for us to get to know each other. Plus, I'm a huge Ryker Rae fan."

"You're so full of shit," I mutter. That is definitely not Dani's genre. I should know, seeing as I grew up next to her blaring music through the walls. God only knows why she's always been drawn to country. The farthest south she's ever been is the Jersey Shore.

"Language," Mom scolds halfheartedly from her chair in the corner.

"I'm sure Mom would prefer to just have a family dinner too," I try.

"No, she's right," says Mom without looking up from her book. "You should bring Parker. You said herself she's been practically locked up with this media circus. I'm sure she'd appreciate a home-cooked meal, poor thing."

I glare at her. Traitor.

Also unexpected considering the last conversation we'd had about Parker. But maybe Dani waking up has put things into perspective for her, or at least helped her calm down a little. She'd just been worried, scared.

And drunk.

"Is there a reason you don't want her to come?" Dani asks.

"No," I say a little too quickly. *Last night.* I've already complicated things enough. I can't very well explain that to Dani. That'll make her want Parker to come more. "I'll ask her," I concede. "But I can't guarantee she'll want to come or can even make it. She's out of town visiting her family right now."

Or I'll never ask her and tell Dani I did.

Dani shrugs. "So we'll wait until she gets back."

The smile on her face tells me she knows exactly what she's doing, sees exactly how much her words are making me squirm, and she's loving every second of it.

There's a reason I haven't introduced anyone I've dated to my family since high school. Not that there have been many since then—nothing serious, at least—but still. Dani's made sticking her nose in the center of my business a full-time job since we were teenagers. And I haven't exactly had a bunch of free time lying around. The two women I already have in my life are enough of a handful.

Dani must see it in my face the moment she's won, because she beams and claps her hands. "I can't wait!"

CHAPTER 31
PARKER

"Sleep well?"

I glance at Mom across the breakfast table as I pull a pancake onto my plate. The question is innocent enough, but I feel like I'm sixteen again and the guilt is written all over my face.

"Better than I have in a while," I say, reaching for the syrup next.

Silverware clangs against the plates, but I can barely force down half a pancake before my lack of appetite wins. Dad shoots a questioning look at me as I set my knife and fork on the table.

"Is there something wrong with the pancakes?" he asks. "They're usually your favorite."

"Oh, they're fine. Just...a little nauseous. Too many mimosas yesterday." I am, in fact, nauseous, but it has nothing to do with a hangover.

Maybe I should be relieved that Heath has the week off so I don't have to face him. But instead, I keep checking my phone every five minutes to see if he's called.

229

What if I made him uncomfortable? I'm technically his boss, or something in that neighborhood. Hell, this is probably considered sexual harassment. The one person who was willing to take this job, and I—

My phone buzzes in my pocket.

Heath's name appears on the screen, and my breath catches in my throat. I consider letting it go to voice mail, but then he might think I'm avoiding him.

I shoot my parents an apologetic look before pushing back from the table and hurrying to the backyard. As soon as I slide the glass door shut behind me, I let out a shaky breath and bring the phone to my ear.

"Hello?"

"Hey, Parker."

My stomach flips at the simple words. His voice sounds so different now than it did last night. Lighter. Heat burns from the roots of my hair to the tips of my toes at the memory of his groans, the low, gravelly quality of his voice, how he'd practically growled my name.

I pace along the edge of the pool, the sharp morning breeze doing nothing to cool the burning of my skin. "Hey. Um, what's up?"

He clears his throat. "So, Dani is coming home today. And I know you won't be back in the city for a bit, but she's insisting she wants to have you over for dinner. My mom too."

I blink, freezing at the end of the pool. I don't know what I'd been expecting him to say, but it wasn't that. "Oh."

"Feel free to say no," he says quickly. "I know it's weird. She's nosey. And she likes you. But if you want to…"

I can see the kitchen table through the windows, and my mom's head is thrown back in a laugh as my dad reaches across the table to refill her cup. Nick shoots a questioning look at me, and I quickly turn away. "I…well…I'm glad to hear she's going home."

I wince, trying to shake off the awkwardness that's clinging to me like a second skin. But I can't tell from the tone of his voice if he wants me to say yes, or if he's asking because his sister is making him. How fucking awkward would it be to see him for the first time after last night with his mom and sister there? Or is this his way of trying to pretend it didn't happen?

"My mom's a horrible cook—don't tell her I said that—so I'm not going to lie and tell you it'll be good. But I'll be helping with some of the dishes, so I can promise at least a few things will be edible."

"You make it sound like it's a four-course meal."

"I take offense to that. There will be at least five."

I snort and squint at the sun reflecting off the water, my heart doing annoying little leaps in my chest.

"So…is that a yes? You're coming back next Saturday, right? Does Sunday work? I can pick you up at seven."

Why does it feel like he's asking me on a date? This is most definitely not a date. "Okay, yeah. Seven works."

He lets out a breath, and his voice lifts like he's smiling. "Okay. I'll see you then."

I shake my head, unable to stop myself from smiling back. "I will see you then."

An Excerpt from Parker's Journal

my confidence lives on a tightrope

CHAPTER 32
PARKER

I never met Rick's family. Despite being together for two years, and him meeting everyone in my life, he never introduced me to any of his relatives. It hadn't seemed that odd at the time. Both of our schedules were crazy, and I was in a different city every other week. He'd said they weren't very close, that he didn't talk to his parents for years at a time and pretty much never went home.

Then there was the secret. So if he had taken me home, we would've had to lie to his family for me, about what I did, who I was.

It was understandable, and it didn't bother me. At least, that's what I'd told myself for the past two years.

Same for the guy I'd lost my virginity to in high school. We'd never even dated. I couldn't remember his last name now if I tried.

Maybe that's why my brain is trying to twist this situation into something bigger than it is. Heath and I aren't together, and I've already met Dani. This isn't a big deal. It's basically their family taking pity on me.

Staring at my reflection in the mirror, I grip the edge of the sink hard enough that my joints turn white. I already changed my outfit an embarrassing number of times, and I refuse to do it again. The jeans and white sweater combo will have to do. I gather my hair in a low bun, leaving out a few pieces to frame my face. I kept my makeup simple, natural, and I eye the pink lip gloss on the counter, wondering if it'll be too much.

"What am I *doing?*" I mutter, then force myself to turn and head for the kitchen. I don't even spend this much time getting ready for dates.

My phone is lying facedown on the kitchen island, and I argue with myself about checking it again.

He said he'd pick me up at 7. It's still 6:58. I should just—

I freeze at a light knock on the door, and a weird buzz of nerves comes to life in my chest.

But it isn't Heath in the hall.

"I—oh! Did you dye your hair? I love it!"

Fuck.

Neighbor girl—I desperately search my brain for her name but come up with nothing—is standing there with a glass measuring cup. She's in sweatpants again, though this time her hair is curled, and she has a full face of makeup on.

"Aly," she says, pointing to herself, then at her door behind her. "We met—"

"Yes, of course! I remember."

She winces as she holds up the cup. "This is totally cliché, but do you have any milk? I'm making these cupcakes for my book club tonight and I. . ." Her gaze trails down to take in the rest of my appearance. "Oh shit. You look like you're going on a date. Is this a bad time?"

Shit, maybe the outfit is overkill.

"No, no, it's fine." I wave her in and head for the kitchen. She seems nice enough, and if things were different, I'd try harder to be her friend. It's not her fault she ended up with me as a neighbor. But it's not like I can explain even half the complications in my life right now. But if she recognizes me as someone other than her neighbor—I already can't remember the fake name I gave her—she doesn't show it. I dig in the fridge for a second before coming up with the carton. "Is oat milk okay?"

"That's perfect."

She fills the measuring cup, her eyes lingering on the splatter-paint wall, but she doesn't comment on it.

"Thank you!" That smile never leaves her face as she heads for the door, but she hesitates before slipping through her own. "I don't know if you're into that kind of thing, but my book club is always taking in new members. If you want to swing by sometime, just let me know."

She must think I'm a total bitch. She's trying so hard even though I'm willing to bet there's been nothing inviting about me in our interactions. "Thanks, Aly. I appreciate that. I'll let you know."

She offers a small wave before heading into her apartment, and I close my door and lean against it. I can't even fathom trying to nurture new relationships right now. The ones I already have are hanging on by a thread.

I jump as someone knocks on the door behind my back.

This time when I open it, Heath stands in the middle of the hall, hands in his pockets and head tilted down so I can't see his face. At least I don't have to worry about being over-dressed. He looks...nice. I don't know why the navy dress pants take me by surprise, but they do. That paired with his dark gray sweater, and what seems to be a fresh haircut...*this isn't a date.*

He smiles softly as he looks up, his gaze taking me in, starting from my black heels and slowly working up to my eyes. I swallow hard and jab my thumb over my shoulder. "I just need to grab my bag—"

"Ready to go?" he asks at the same time.

We both let out an awkward laugh, and I quickly gather my things before closing the door behind me.

"After you." He gestures to the elevators, and we walk together in silence.

I drum my fingers against the chain of my purse and press my lips together. Is the air between us as tense as it feels to me, or am I the one making this awkward? If we're going to address what happened last week, maybe we should do it *before* I'm sitting across the table from his mother. But if he's not going to bring it up, I'm sure as hell not going to.

The silence continues as the elevator arrives and we step inside. He hits the button for the parking garage then folds his hands in front of his body, his gaze trained on the glowing red numbers overhead.

I clear my throat. "So, how's Dani doing?"

I catch his smile in the reflection on the elevator doors. "She's good. She's staying with my mom for a few weeks so she can keep an eye on her while she's recovering."

"So...things with John..."

Heath's expression darkens. "He told her. She kicked him to the curb."

"Thank God," I mutter.

He grunts his agreement, and we lapse back into silence as the doors slide open, and I follow him to a black pickup truck waiting in one of the first spots. I try to hold back my laugh as he unlocks it, but he still catches it.

"What?"

I shake my head innocently as he opens the door for me. "Just...the truck. It makes sense. You look like you'd drive a pickup truck."

He narrows his eyes as I climb inside, though the hint of a smile plays at his lips. "I'm choosing to take that as a compliment," he says before closing the door. What *is* surprising is how *clean* everything is. What little odds and ends are in here are neatly organized, every surface glossy and giving off subtle notes of lemon cleaning supplies.

Is it always like this, or did he clean just for tonight?

I ignore the little flutter in my stomach the thought causes as he climbs into the seat beside me.

The AC hums faintly in the background as we pull out of the garage, the sun lingering on the horizon. "How's your head feeling?"

"Oh." I wave my hand. "It's fine. Only really bothered me for a few days after."

He bobs his head. "Glad to hear it. Concussions are the worst."

I hum my agreement, and the conversation filters off again as he takes the bridge out of the city. It occurs to me I don't even know where his mom lives.

"She's in Brooklyn," he says with a small smile as if reading my mind.

The rest of the drive doesn't take long, but it certainly feels like it as we struggle to fill the space with small talk— anything and everything other than what we probably should be talking about. How he spent his week off, how my time with my parents went—hell, we even end up talking about the weather.

I cringe internally as he pulls up outside of his mom's townhome and manages to squeeze into a spot on the same block. I've never struggled to make conversation. Even with people I have nothing in common with. Talking to people has always been one of my strong suits. But the awkwardness between us grows thicker as we head down the sidewalk and he rings the doorbell.

"Parker!" The door flies open, and suddenly a plump older woman is trapping me in a chokehold of a hug. "So, *so* glad you could join us tonight."

Heath's mom can't be taller than five feet. She smells like cinnamon as I squeeze her back and let out a breathless laugh.

"Mom, don't suffocate her," Heath says behind me.

"Sorry, sorry." She squeezes me one more time before taking a step back.

"Let her in, Mom!" Dani calls. "It's not fair to hog her when I can't even get up."

"Of course. Come in. Come in!" She steps to the side, and I exchange a quick glance with Heath, who gives me an amused nod before crossing the threshold.

The home is small, but warm, in every sense of the word. The heat is cranked high, and everything around me is bright and colorful—dark wooden furniture, red walls, woven blankets and rugs.

The scent of garlic hangs in the air as Heath's mom leads me to the kitchen, where Dani is already seated at the head of the table, her leg, still in a cast, propped on the seat next to her.

"I hope you're hungry!" Heath's mom grabs bright red

potholders from the kitchen island and heads for the oven.
"Have a seat! Heath, drinks?"

"On it."

I jump a little, not realizing he was right behind me, and
he presses a hand to my back before sliding behind me
toward the kitchen. The contact burns right through my
sweater, and I swallow hard as I take the seat on Dani's other
side.

She grins at me. "You look *gorgeous.*"

"Oh." I wave a hand in front of my face. "Thanks. So do
you."

And she does, in an effortless way. Her hair is tossed up
in a messy bun, and she's in a button-down shirt a few
shades darker than mine.

"Oh, I know." She gestures to the casts on her arm and
leg. "They're all the rage right now."

I snort and find Heath watching us from the kitchen.

Dani follows my gaze and snaps, "Stop eavesdropping!"

An actual blush creeps up his neck as he turns away to
grab some glasses from the cabinet.

"He needs a firm hand, that one," Dani murmurs to me
conspiratorially. "But he's good when you give him
directions."

"You make him sound like a trained dog."

She shrugs, a thoughtful look on her face. "Not a bad
comparison."

I laugh, and Heath sets glasses of water in front of us.

"I heard that," he growls.

"This is all we get?" Dani retorts, frowning at the water.

"I'm working on it," he sighs, heading back for the kitchen
and grabbing wineglasses this time.

I don't realize I'm staring at his back as he pops open a

bottle and starts pouring until I see Dani watching me watching him, and I shoot her a quick smile and take a sip of my water.

"Here you are, your highness," Heath says as he sets the wine in front of Dani and bows his head.

"Thank you," I murmur as he sets a glass in front of me too, and he winks before heading back for the kitchen.

"You have a brother too, right?" Dani asks.

I nod and sip the wine. I'm not as familiar with whites, but this one is light and sweet and deliciously cold. I hold back a moan as it slides down my throat. "Nick," I say. "He's in his junior year of undergrad."

"What's he studying?"

"That's a great question." I smirk. "It was engineering. Then it was biology. Then it was criminal justice. I'm pretty sure it's film right now...but ask me again in a week. At this rate, he'll graduate when he's thirty."

"Did you go to college, Parker?" Heath's mom asks from the kitchen.

"Uh, no." I shift a little in my seat. "I've always thought about going back to school eventually though. Maybe doing it online." I glance at Dani. "You're in nursing school, right?"

Her smile drops, just a few degrees. "On pause for now."

I nod, not knowing if asking for more details will make it more awkward, so I sip my wine instead.

Thankfully, Heath and his mom take that moment to reappear and set a couple of dishes along the center of the table—lasagna, garlic bread, a salad, and roasted vegetables.

I meet Heath's gaze as he takes the seat next to me. He wasn't kidding when he said there would be a lot of food.

My mouth waters as everyone passes the dishes around and fills their plates. I pile mine high—my eyes definitely bigger than my stomach—but I am more than happy to go into a food stupor after this if the smell is any indication of how good this will taste.

Heath's mom opens her palms toward both of her children, and they join hands. I realize what's happening a beat too late and quickly take the hand Dani offers to me. Heath meets my eyes as he gently takes my hand in his. I feel the contact down to every nerve in my body, and force down a steadying breath as I face forward again.

Thankfully, Heath's mom takes over saying grace—a concept I'm familiar with, though my family has never done it, so I'm glad I don't have to say anything.

Everyone bows their heads, and I quickly follow suit, though I can't help myself from peering at Heath out of the corner of my eye. A jolt goes through me as I catch him doing the same, and we both smile and look away.

"Dig in!" insists Heath's mom as we drop hands.

"Thank you so much for having me, Mrs. Bridgers. This looks amazing," I say as I spread my napkin on my lap.

"Oh, please. Call me Susan. Now, I won't tell you which dishes I made and which ones Heath did. So try them all, and tell me which is your favorite."

I laugh and inspect the food on my plate. "That doesn't seem fair."

"I'll tell you!" Dani says around a mouthful of the salad. "Tastes healthy," she concludes before moving onto the bread, then the lasagna, and finishes with the vegetables. "Lasagna wins."

I take a bite of the garlic bread, perfectly warm and crisp and buttery, and my eyes all but roll back in my head. "I don't need to taste the others," I decide. "This is it. This is the one."

Heath pumps his fist.

"She hasn't tried my dessert yet," Susan warns.

I take in the mountain of food still on the table between us. *"There's more?"*

"Of course!" says Dani. "You can't have dinner without dessert in this house. It's against the law."

I nod. "My kind of people."

"So, Parker, how are you holding up?" Susan asks. The look in her eyes is not unkind, but there's something different about the tone of her voice now.

I give her a tight smile. "As good as can be expected, I guess."

"That must have been very traumatic," Susan continues. "Not just being attacked like that, but seeing all of the other people who died because of it—"

"Mom," Heath cuts her off, his voice hard.

"What? The person who had this job before my son is dead. You don't think that makes me worry?"

I flinch. *The person who had this job before.* Everyone likes to throw around meaningless words and descriptors like that. No one ever just says his damn name.

I jump when Heath's hand rests on my thigh above my knee, his fingers pressing in lightly.

"Of course," I say, fighting to keep my voice even.

"This stalker," Susan continues, "how long has that been an issue? Have you...spoken to him before? I imagine you must have run into similar problems a few times with how well your career has been going."

"That's enough," Heath snaps, his hand tightening around my leg.

"What?" She throws her hands up. "It's an honest question. I don't know anything about being famous. I imagine that's shaped how a lot of her life looks. I'm just curious. If violent attacks are common—if she's lost other people on her team in a similar way before—of course I would want to know that. You're my only son, and I worry about you. That may be par for the course in that kind of life, but not in ours."

The garlic bread I inhaled threatens to come back up, and suddenly it's so *hot* in here. Sweat beads on my forehead, and I roll up the sleeves of my sweater, wishing I'd worn a layer under it so I could take it off.

"Excuse me," I say quietly, pushing back from the table. "I'm just going to..."

"Bathroom's down the hall," Dani says, nodding behind her. "Second door around the corner on the right."

I give her a grateful smile and all but flee the room.

I collapse against the door the moment I close it behind me, breathing hard. Is this what a panic attack feels like? I strip my sweater off, leaving me in nothing but my bra, and fill my hands with cold water in the sink.

I don't know why I'm surprised she asked me about it. Of course I should have expected it. I should've prepared ahead of time what I was going to say. I guess I hadn't expected to think of Elijah tonight, and now that I've started, all I see when I close my eyes is that night. The blood on the gravel. The rips in my dress and cuts along my arms as I'd tried to fight back.

I splash the water on my face and let it run down my chest, forcing deep breaths in and out of my nose.

People are bound to ask. I need to get used to it. I need to find a way to stop breaking down every time it gets brought up.

I haven't been to therapy in weeks. Maybe I should

schedule an emergency session, but they never seemed to help much anyway.

I close my eyes, sink onto the plush rug, and hang my head between my knees. I just need my nervous system to calm down. Once I get that back under control, I'll be fine. Everything will be fine.

CHAPTER 33
ᕼEATH

"What the hell are you doing?" I demand, trying to keep my voice low so Parker doesn't overhear.

"I was just asking her questions."

"You were interrogating her." My gaze swings from her to Dani. "Is that what this was about? You two planned this?"

Dani's face falls. "Of course not."

"I was worried that you were getting too attached," Mom says calmly, and I whirl around to face her. "And clearly I was right to worry." I sputter, but she holds up a hand to stop me before I manage to get anything out. "She's a very nice girl. No one is denying that. She seems genuine. She's very pretty. I get it. But you need to get out of this job. And you need to get away from her."

"Mom," Dani starts, but she keeps going.

"You know what her kind of people say? No press is bad press. Of course this time it went too far, but can you honestly tell me that for a man to go these lengths, there hadn't maybe been some encouragement there on her part? Just a little?"

I collapse against the back of my chair, staring at my mother. My brain short-circuits, trying to reconcile the woman I know her to be and this version in front of me. It takes me a few tries before I finally manage to get the words out.

"I can't believe you just said that." I shake my head once, twice. "You think—" I take a deep breath and force myself to lower my voice. "You honestly think she wanted to get brutally attacked and almost die for *publicity*?"

"She's more talked about now than ever, right? I hear her music is setting records with how much she's selling. Her face is everywhere. People will be talking about this for a long time, especially with that trial ongoing. I'm not saying it was her idea, but can you honestly tell me her team hadn't thought about it? That they played no hand in this? That no one tipped that man off as to where she'd be? Sure, she might be dealing with a few negative consequences of this right now, but in a few months, years, she'll walk away millions of dollars richer and unscathed. And her last bodyguard will still be dead. And for what?"

"I cannot believe you," I say through my teeth. "I cannot *believe* you. How dare you ask me to bring her here just so you could do this."

"Heath—" says Dani.

"No." I hold up a hand and push back from the table.

Mom stands too, anger pinching her features together. "I'm your mother, and I know you better than anyone. You've always had a savior complex, and in part, that's my fault. I let you take on too much burden and too much responsibility too young. So of course, you see this girl in crisis, and you feel like you need to save her—"

"That is not what's happening here," I growl.

"But I won't let you get yourself killed over it," she talks over me.

"You don't know a damn thing about her. And you couldn't be more wrong. We're done having this conversation."

I don't hear whatever she says next over the roaring blood in my ears as I head toward the bathroom to get Parker. I stumble to a halt when I find her already standing at the end of the hall, frozen. I can see all over her face that she overheard at least part of that.

My jaw flexes, and I slowly extend my hand to her. "Come on," I say, my voice coming out harder than I intended. "Let's go."

Uncertainty flits across her face. I take another step toward her and soften my voice. "Let me take you home."

She bobs her head once but doesn't take my hand as she follows me toward the door. And despite everything she heard, she still says a polite, "Thank you again for dinner, Mrs. Bridgers. It was nice to meet you. And it was nice to see you, Dani." before we leave.

My hand tightens around my car keys as I follow her to my truck, and I clench and unclench my jaw. *Encouragement on her part.* She'd actually said that. I shake my head, my face feeling hot as I watch Parker circle the car to the passenger side.

I brought her here. I talked her into this dinner.

Our living situation was never a secret as Dani and I were growing up. And kids are cruel. We weren't the poorest kids at school, but we were close. Close enough that teachers tried to intervene once or twice. Close enough for us to go to school early to use the showers in the locker room or for us to show up no matter how sick we were just to get our free lunch.

Close enough that Dani and I would lock ourselves in a closet every Thursday for two years in elementary school, too terrified to sleep as we waited for Mom to get home from the night shift.

But never, not once, have I felt ashamed of them before now.

The silence crowds in as we head toward Manhattan. Parker's looking out her window, her hands tightly knitted together in her lap.

"Parker."

"It's okay," she says quietly.

"It's *not* okay."

She doesn't turn, and she doesn't respond. Streetlights reflect off her face as they pass in quick succession.

"Parker," I say, my voice gentle.

Nothing.

"Parker," I try again, louder this time.

I curse under my breath and whip the wheel to the side at the last minute. She grabs the handle overhead in surprise as I pull into an empty gas station parking lot.

"What are you—?"

I cut the engine and throw my door open. I don't look back at the car as I pace from one end of the parking lot and back, trying to burn off the anger vibrating through my system. Gravel crunches under my feet, and I take a few calming breaths and open and close my fists before climbing back into the car.

"I'm sorry," I say. "I had no idea she was going to do that. I never would've brought you there if I did."

"I know," she says quietly.

"Are you all right?"

She nods unconvincingly, her gaze trained on her hands.

Impulsively, I take her chin in my hand and tilt her head up. A surprised breath escapes as her lips part, and I can't help the way my attention zeros in on them. I meet her eyes again.

"You know I don't think that about you at all, right?"

She wets her lips and hesitates longer than I'd like.

"Parker, you're...you're one of the most generous, humble, and talented people I've ever met. A lot of people are nice just because they want everyone to like them, but it's real with you. I don't know how you do it with all the shit life's thrown you, but you've stayed this genuine, caring person. You're also a fucking smartass, but it's part of your charm."

She narrows her eyes, a smirk tugging on her lips, and I tighten my fingers on her chin. "So I don't want you to think on what she said for another minute. Because she's wrong."

She shakes her head, forcing me to drop my hand. "I don't blame her. I'm sure plenty of people are thinking the same thing. And she's just trying to protect you."

"Parker..."

"It's okay." She sighs and glances at the dingy parking lot around us. "What are we doing here anyway?"

"Well, you were promised dessert. So I'm making sure you get some." I'm not sure if this night can be salvaged, but I'm damn well going to try.

She lets out a startled laugh as I round the car and open

her door. This time, she accepts the hand I offer to help her down and doesn't let go as I link my fingers with hers.

"Can't guarantee the quality here though," I mutter as we duck inside the convenience store. The guy behind the counter remains engrossed in his magazine as the bells ring overhead and I steer Parker toward the back. "But I will give you two options."

She raises her eyebrows. "Only two?"

"Don't get greedy on me now. Ice cream or donuts?"

She eyes the donut case on our right—all of which have probably been sitting there for several days, maybe more— then nods at the frozen section.

"Probably a safer bet," I agree.

A smile that actually looks genuine sneaks onto her face as she peruses her options, and a hint of a dimple appears as she chews on the inside of her cheek. "Are we sharing, or do you want your own?" she asks without looking at me.

"I trust whatever you pick."

She considers her options for another minute before finally settling on a carton of dairy-free cookie dough with peanut butter cup chunks.

A strand of hair falls loose from her bun as she closes the freezer door, and she blows it impatiently out of her face, and Jesus fuck, that was cute.

I don't know why I blurt it out. I've been meaning to since the moment I picked her up, but every time I tried to broach the subject, nothing came out. "Parker, about last week…"

She raises an incredulous eyebrow at me over her shoulder. "You want to have this conversation in a gas station convenience store?"

The scandalized tone of her voice makes me grin. "Bad timing?"

She laughs—a real, full, *deep* laugh—and I'm immediately glad I brought it up. I wave for her to hand over the ice cream so I can pay.

"You want anything else?"

She shakes her head as we head for the cashier. I drop a few bills on the counter, to which the clerk grunts his approval, then grab some plastic spoons.

Parker holds her hand out for one as we head for the door, and I laugh.

"You're very impatient."

A light flashes somewhere behind her head, and at first I think it's someone's headlights as they pull in. But then the air fills with an ear-splitting crack.

I yank Parker back. She hits my chest hard, and I throw us both to the side between two of the aisles, trying to simultaneously cover her head with my hands and break her fall. The window shatters, and I roll so she's under me, trying to shield as much of her as I can.

My ears ring, and I wait for another explosion to come, every muscle in my body tense. My hearing finally starts to trickle back in, and Parker whimpers beneath me, her hands fisted in my shirt.

I push back, eyes scanning every inch of her exposed skin, but she seems unharmed. Bags of candy and chips are scattered on the floor in the aisle around us.

"Are you okay?" I ask. "Are you hurt?"

She's trembling, and her eyes are wide like she doesn't understand the question. She glances down at herself, like she's not sure, then shakes her head.

I bring a hand to the side of her face. There's blood right

below her ear, but the scratch from the broken glass looks shallow.

"Are you sure?" I ask.

She gives me a shaky nod, and I help her sit up, but she doesn't release her death grip on my shirt.

"What happened?" she whispers.

"Stay behind me."

We stand, and I poke my head around the corner. The clerk has disappeared, the entire window behind his desk gone now. Shit, I hope he's okay.

"Stay here—" I start, but she shakes her head and tightens her grip on me. "Okay." We inch forward enough that I can see out the door. "Fuck."

"What is it?" She edges around me before I can stop her.

My truck is completely engulfed in flames. I don't have time to dwell on that because it is far too close to that gas pump for my liking. I do a quick glance beneath the clerk's desk to make sure he's not injured under there, but he's gone.

I reach for Parker. "Come on."

She follows and grabs my hand.

"We need to get out of here." I need to get her as far away from here as possible before it blows.

"Heath," she gasps, looking back at the truck as I yank her toward the street at a run.

"I know, come on." I usher her in front of me, keeping one hand firmly in hers. The fire rages high, black smoke billowing above it. Police sirens wail somewhere in the distance, and my mind spins, trying to figure out what the hell could've caused that.

A second explosion cuts through the air and rocks the ground beneath us. I throw my arms around Parker from behind and hunch over her. The heat from the fire reaches us, but we're far enough away to miss the worst of it.

The bright orange fire climbs toward the night sky, and the taste of smoke is thick in my mouth. I can't even tell which fire surrounds my car or the gas pump.

Tears stream down Parker's cheeks, and I grab the side of her head, inspecting the rest of her face for injuries.

"How the hell did that...?" she gasps.

"I don't know." I wrap my arms around her and pull her tightly against my chest, mesmerized by the flames, just now registering the flashes of pain from the broken glass in my arms. Red and blue lights join the glow of the fire on the pavement as police cars and a firetruck approach.

We hadn't even touched the gas. And I hadn't noticed anyone else out there.

But it wasn't the pump that went up in flames first. It was the truck. No matter how many scenarios my mind runs through, I know in my bones this wasn't an accident.

CHAPTER 34
PARKER

The rest of the night—morning?—is a blur. I think my brain stopped retaining information some-where around when they put the fire out and determined there had been a homemade bomb attached to the bottom of the truck.

The police take us back to Manhattan. I close my eyes once we're in the car, and Heath wraps an arm around my shoulders and pulls me against his chest.

There's so much activity—so many people and voices and lights and cars. I don't know what time it is when we finally make it to my apartment, and the police won't let me step inside until they do a thorough search for anything else suspicious looking.

I think Annie and Faye show up at some point. Heath ushers me into bed and closes the door to my room. Voices and footsteps sound on the other side for a while. But no matter how exhausted I am, I can't sleep.

There was a bomb on the car. Had someone put it there before Heath picked me up tonight? While it was in the parking garage here? While we were at his mom's? While we were in the store? Whoever did this, were they hoping to scare us or that we'd be inside when it went off?

A full-body shiver rolls through me, and I nearly jump out of my skin as my door cracks open.

"Hey, superstar. Can I come in?" asks Heath.

I nod, unable to muster a response. The lamp on my nightstand is on, casting an orange glow to his features as he crouches beside my head.

"The team wants to get together tomorrow to figure out next steps."

"Did anyone...my parents...?"

"We called them. And Nick. Everyone knows you're okay."

I bite my lip. I can't help but think about everything that could have happened. If that bomb had gone off while we'd been at Heath's mom's house...how many innocent people would've been caught in the middle of it?

Heath's mom was right. People get hurt around me. People die.

"Hey." Heath's fingers brush my cheek and tuck my hair behind my ear.

"I'm sorry about your truck," I whisper.

He blinks, surprise washing over his face. "Park—Parker, I don't care about the truck." His hand drifts forward, cupping the side of my face. "I don't care about the truck," he repeats, quieter now.

I tug the blankets up to my chin, unable to pull myself out of the endless blue of his eyes. They're so dark, I hadn't even realized they were blue until now. But there's a clear outline toward the center, the color bleeding into something darker the farther it gets from his pupils. There are specs of gold in them, like tiny stars.

His thumb rubs absently back and forth against my cheek. "I'll be here tonight if you need anything."

I nod, and he doesn't move, not at first. If it weren't for him, I don't know what I would've done. My entire body shut down. I thought I'd gone into shock before, but nothing to that degree, to truly not be able to function. How he's managed to stay so calm is beyond me. It was *his* car.

He lowers his hand and leans back.

"Heath?" I ask before he can leave.

He meets my eyes, a question in his, and I hold his gaze as I push myself back in the bed.

"Will you stay with me?"

At first, I think he's still going to leave. I wouldn't blame him if he did. But the idea of lying here alone in the dark with nothing but that fire waiting for me when I close my eyes has my throat closing up. I won't beg him to stay, but I'd be lying if I said the feeling bubbling in my chest wasn't eerily similar to desperation.

He lifts the blankets and sits on the edge of the bed as he leans down to remove his shoes, then his sweater. The white shirt beneath is spotted with small bloodstains, and my breath hitches.

"Are you okay?" I murmur.

He glances down as if noticing the injuries for the first time, then offers me a tired half smile. "Just a few scratches. Nothing to worry about."

I sit up anyway, my fingers tracing over his back.

"We should make sure you don't have glass in any of them." I climb out of bed before he responds and flick on the overhead light on my way to the bathroom. He says nothing, but his footsteps pad lightly on the floor behind me.

"Sit," I instruct, pointing at the toilet as I duck beneath the sink for the first aid kit. When I reemerge with it, he's done as I said, though he's not even trying to hide his amused smirk. "What?" I demand as I prop the kit on the sink and sift through it.

"I like it when you're bossy."

I make an unintelligible noise in the back of my throat and gesture for him to take the shirt off. But focusing on him and a tangible task I know how to handle—like patching up minor wounds—is the first thing that's made the static in my mind clear since the explosion.

His entire upper body is a patchwork of injuries, and I shoot him a disbelieving look. "You should have said something. Why didn't you let the paramedics do this?"

"Guess I was distracted. Didn't really feel it."

I shake my head, biting back my next words. *Fucking lunatic.*

A low laugh rocks his shoulders. "Heard that."

"I didn't say anything."

"It was in your eyes."

I ignore that and clean off some tweezers with rubbing alcohol. Probably best to get any glass out before trying to clean the wounds.

"A paramedic would've been a lot better at this than I am," I mutter as I kneel in front of him, squinting as I inspect each cut.

I hesitate, then brace a hand on his leg as I find a small shard near his hip. The tensing of his abs is the only sign he feels anything as I pull it out. I wet my lips as I move to another one farther up, right beneath his pec.

I am entirely focused on the blood and the glass, not at all distracted by how tan his skin is. How his defined muscles tighten as I brace my hand on the other side of his chest. Let alone the fact I'm on my knees with my face practically in his lap.

Dear God, I hope that's not giving him the same image I'm seeing in my head right now. My skin burns as I move on to a few smaller pieces in his forearms, finding it hard to swallow past the dryness in my mouth as a different heat winds its way through my body. The kind that coils itself low in my core.

"Do you have another?"

His voice jars me out of my thoughts, and I blink up at him. "What?"

His expression is off, uncertain, and I can't read whatever is in his eyes. He just looks...tense.

"Tweezers," he explains. "Do you have more? I can get these"—he gestures to his arm—"if you can get the ones I can't reach in my back."

"Oh." I swallow and lean back. "Let me look."

I feel his gaze on me as I head back to the sink and dig through the kit until I find a second pair of tweezers. His fingers brush mine as he takes them, and our eyes lock before he quickly turns so I can reach his back.

"Shit, Heath," I breathe.

The cuts on his back are a lot worse. *Because he'd been trying to protect me.* I had a few cuts the paramedics took care of at the scene, but it would have been a lot worse if Heath hadn't covered me during the explosion.

I start with the largest gashes near his shoulder blades, wincing at how deep the shards go. He stays silent as I pull them out, but his muscles tense and he hisses in a breath.

"You okay?"

"Never better," he says tightly.

Tossing the glass in the sink, I frown at the remaining pieces. "Maybe we should get you to the hospital..."

He adds to his own growing pile on top of the toilet as he continues working on his arms.

"Afraid of a little blood?"

I chew on my lip before leaning back in and pulling out some of the smaller pieces. "What if these hit something important or something?"

"I guess we'll know when you take them out."

"*Heath.*"

"I'm not paying for an emergency room visit," he says quietly. "It's not bad. I can tell. I promise."

I open and close my mouth a few times. "Jesus Christ, Heath. I will pay the bill—"

"No."

"I'm not doing it as a favor to you!" I throw my hands up and let them slap against my thighs. "It happened to you because you were doing your job and protecting me. I'd offer the same to anyone working for me."

"Parker," he says, his voice softer now. "I'm exhausted. It's been a long night."

I let out a frustrated breath through my nose but say nothing else as I pull the rest of the pieces out then get started on cleaning the wounds.

He flinches as the alcohol hits his skin, and the veins in the backs of his hands stand out as he clenches his fists.

"Do you...do you want to talk about the other night?" he asks through gritted teeth.

Heat fills my face, and I'm grateful he has his back to me and can't see the blush spreading. "Right now?"

"I'm looking for a distraction here, superstar," he says, his voice thin as I dab at the cuts on his back, adding bandages over the worst of them.

"Right. Um." I squeeze my eyes shut, every moment of that conversation perfectly vivid in my head despite how much I'd had to drink.

I'd memorize every inch of your body with my mouth.

I want to find every place you like to be touched, every way I can make you moan.

I'll bend you over the counter so I can fuck you just the way you want it.

Summoning that image is far too easy right now with him half-naked. And the thought of hearing his voice like that in my ear and not just over the phone has the heat in my face spreading to the rest of my body. I clear my throat. "Look, we can forget about it. I'm sorry if I made you uncomfortable. I was drunk and—"

"I'm not," he says, his voice stronger now. "I mean, I'm not uncomfortable. And I'm not sorry." He pauses. "Are you?"

A tension I hadn't realized was in my shoulders releases. I gently add the last of the bandages to his back and whisper, "No."

He rises to his feet, and I brace myself against the sink as he turns to face me. He meets my eyes, then inches closer, his knuckles lightly tracing from my wrist to my elbow and over the curve of my shoulder. His gaze follows the movement, and I stand completely still, every hair on my arm standing at attention.

I feel the heat rolling off his bare chest as he presses closer, our bodies almost touching, but not quite.

"Parker, I care about you," he murmurs. "And it's not

because this is my job. That's not—that's not all this is for me."

I swallow hard as his fingers trail across my collarbone, up my neck, my jaw, into my hair, and he tilts my head back to look at him. Goosebumps blossom in the wake of his touch, every nerve in my body vibrating at their highest setting.

"Your mom hates me," I whisper.

"Can you please not talk about my mom right before I kiss you?"

I smile a little, breathless.

His mouth connects with mine, his hands finding either side of my face, the kiss slow and searching. My eyes flutter shut, my fingers exploring the bare skin of his hips.

A shaky breath passes between us, and he weaves his fingers through my hair, his grip tightening as he deepens the kiss until his tongue brushes my lips, and then into my mouth. My body somehow simultaneously relaxes and tightens against him.

He leans back, and for a moment, I think that'll be it. But then he grabs me by the waist. He searches my eyes, and I slide my hands from the top of his pants up his abdomen, his chest, his muscles tightening beneath my touch. When my hands reach his face, his mouth lands back on mine.

All hesitation vanishes as the kiss turns hungry, desperate. His knee pushes between my legs, and my head spins, drunk on the taste of him, the feel of his hot skin as his hands slide beneath my shirt, the soft growl he makes when I rock my hips against him. His mouth finds the hollow of my throat, my chest, the stubble on his jaw scraping against my skin.

But then his lips slow, leaving soft, light kisses on my

cheek, my forehead, my lips. My eyes open as he frames my face with his hands.

He holds me there, his chest heaving slightly with his breath, until he finally says, "You should get some sleep."

I nod, unable to deny the utter exhaustion weighing me down, though my body aches at the loss of his touch when he lets me go. He follows me back to bed, but when I reach over to turn off the lamp, my hand freezes, hovering above the pull chain.

It was supposed to be over. Jasper Young is in custody. So he couldn't have done this, could he? But then that would mean there's *another* person who wants me dead. So even if the trial goes as we're hoping and they put him away for good, it could happen again.

What if they hadn't been targeting me at all? The bomb was on Heath's car. What if they were trying to hurt *him*?

The heat of Heath's chest presses against my back, his voice low and his breath dancing across my neck as he murmurs, "You can leave it on. It's okay."

I don't move, not sure why my eyes are now deciding to fill with tears. My hand shakes, my breaths sounding more like pants. All that glass in his back...Elijah bleeding out in the woods...the security guard who never even met me with his throat slashed...

"You're safe, Parker." His hand brushes my arm. I swallow hard and nod, but I don't turn. "We have two other guys out in the hallway and two downstairs, in addition to the building's security. I searched every inch of this place after the police left. You're safe here. I promise."

The tears break free, and Heath's arms wrap around me from behind.

"Come here," he says, pulling me into his chest. "Shh. It's

okay. I've got you." He laces his fingers through mine and squeezes, but I can't relax. "We're going to get to the bottom of this," he insists. "They're checking security footage from the parking garage here and at the gas station."

He still doesn't get it. He still doesn't understand. I might be the target, but it's not me who keeps getting hurt. It's not me who ends up bleeding. It's not me who doesn't survive these things. And those who do, they leave, and who could blame them?

"You could've died," I choke out on a whisper.

He doesn't say anything for what feels like a long time, but then he tightens his arms around me and rests his chin on the top of my head. "I'm right here."

"You shouldn't be. Your mom was right. You should get as far away from me as you can. You're in the middle of this now because of me—"

"It's not your fault bad things happened to you," he says, his voice hard. "And it's not your fault bad things happened around you. I'm here because I want to be here, Parker. I want to be here." His fingers caress my hand, the touch featherlight, as he presses a gentle kiss to the back of my neck. "And I'm not going anywhere."

AN EXCERPT FROM PARKER'S JOURNAL

it's magnetic
the grief
shifting faces
like Halloween masks

one moment
struck with the weight
of carrying the absence
for the rest of my days

the next
choking on guilt
for wanting to shed myself
of it in the first place

CHAPTER 35
PARKER

S omething happened overnight. I'm not sure what, exactly. Maybe it should've happened before. This shift in my brain, like something took a blade to all that fear and anxiety and shame and worry, sharpening it until it glistened and gleamed.

Until it looked more like rage.

Seeming to sense my change in mood, Heath says nothing that morning as I dress and eat some cereal without tasting it, other than to tell me Annie and Faye are expecting us in their apartment in a half hour to debrief.

My dreams, unsurprisingly, were full of Jasper Young. Him crouched in the bushes in an orange jumpsuit, planting the bomb on Heath's car, leaving the note on the building. Logically I know it couldn't have been him. If he'd escaped, someone would've alerted us, never mind it would be all over the news.

But that's not as reassuring as it should be. Because that means someone else is doing this—maybe several someone elses. To what end, I have no idea. For fun? To get off on it? Some other motive?

Whatever the reason may be, I am so fucking tired of it.

I'm tired of being scared and hiding and feeling sorry for myself. Of letting my entire life come to a screeching halt. It feels like letting them win.

"You know the preliminary hearing is coming up this week?"

Heath freezes in his spot against the kitchen cabinets, his eyes snapping to where I sit. "I heard, yeah."

I drum my fingers on the counter. I don't know if it would help anything or make matters worse, but at the very least, it would get the idea out of my head. Just to see him in those handcuffs, to confirm what I already know.

"I'd like to go."

Slowly, he sets the bowl of cereal on the counter. "Parker," he starts, and I hate the sympathetic voice he uses. Like he feels sorry for me.

"I just want to be there. I'll sit in the back. I just—" I don't know how to explain my reasoning to him because I don't understand it myself. "Please."

He spreads his hands. "I don't have a problem with it. I'll take you wherever you want to go. But I have a feeling I'm not the one you'll be needing to convince."

"You think it's stupid."

"I don't, actually. If it were me, I'd probably ask for the same thing."

I meet his eyes, the tension in my shoulders fading. "So you'll back me up with Faye and Annie then?"

"Oh, absolutely not." He grins and crosses his arms over his chest. "They terrify me."

"Ah yes, five-foot-two women are clearly the biggest

threat here—" I straighten in my stool, everything going quiet.

"Parker?"

"The note got here the day I left for the coffee shop. The day of your interview."

He furrows his brow. "Right..."

"And the bomb on your car went off the night we had dinner at your mom's, after you picked me up."

"Parker, I'm not following—"

I hadn't thought anything of it before. Hadn't seen any connections between those days at all.

"Parker, where are you—?"

But I'm already out the door and through the hall, my vision tunneling around me, my blood blazing through my veins like fire.

The day of the note—the day I met Aly.

The night of the bomb—the night she came over for milk.

She'd been there right before both things happened, knew where I was.

I pound my fist on the door, not stopping until it opens.

Aly stands on the other side, her hair mussed like she just rolled out of bed. "What's going on—?"

"Who the hell are you?" I demand, pushing my way into her apartment. "What do you want from me?"

She stumbles back a few steps, her eyes darting from me to something behind my head—Heath, probably. "Greta, I don't know what you're talking about."

"Greta?" asks Heath.

"You really thought I wouldn't figure it out?" I demand. "Did you think all of this was *funny*?"

My teeth grind together, my vision going red, my hands

balling into fists at my sides, but something stops me from taking another step toward her.

Heath's hands wrap around my arms, holding me back.

"Why did you do it?" I snap.

"Do what?" Aly shrills. "Look, I—I'm sorry if I overstepped, but—"

"Parker, come on," Heath says lowly, trying to pull me to the door.

"You put that note on the door," I seethe.

"What note?" She throws her hands up. Tears are shining on her cheeks now, and she's backed up against the wall.

"Parker," Heath murmurs, his grip on my arms tightening. "It wasn't her. Take a deep breath."

"But she—I—" My breaths come in hard and fast.

"I know." He tugs me until we're back in the hall and utters a quick "sorry" to Aly before closing the door, but he doesn't let me go.

Every muscle in my body is wound tight, my breathing rapid.

"I—she—"

"I know. I know." Heath's arms wrap around me, crushing me against his chest to an almost painful degree. "I know," he murmurs against my hair. "I know."

FAYE AND ANNIE have done a much better job filling their apartment than I have. I guess I heard the word *temporary* and decided that meant keeping everything I owned in boxes would be easier. I haven't even touched the storage unit. And other than the disaster of a wall Heath and I made, I haven't bothered to decorate. But Faye and Annie have built this place into a home. The walls are overflowing with art. Even though they have very different styles—Faye with her minimalism and Annie with the eccentric colors—somehow, it works.

The layout of their apartment is the same as mine, though, admittedly, mine feels a lot more spacious from the lack of furniture. They've crammed a long blue velvet couch against the back wall with two white leather chairs cattycornered off to the sides. A massive TV is mounted on the wall, framed by various hanging plants and floating shelves full of books and mini figurines.

"I can't believe this is the first time you've been in here." Annie scurries back from the kitchen and passes me some steaming tea, the cup delicate and painted with little red flowers that she probably did herself.

I take it mostly to warm my hands and hope they don't notice the way they're still shaking from the confrontation with Aly a few minutes ago. I've never had something happen like that before, the absolute haze that clouded my mind. I almost feel hungover from the adrenaline now. The logic had seemed so airtight, like it was so obvious I couldn't believe I'd missed it.

But no, I'm just losing my mind.

God, poor Aly. If she'd thought I was a bitch before...

I pretend like I'm still trying to take in my surroundings. "Very slumber parties vibes in here."

"We can get you a sleeping bag," teases Annie.

"But I'll warn you ahead of time," says Faye. "Annie snores. You can hear it through the walls."

Annie rolls her eyes, but they're both smiling. Not just smiling. I noticed it the moment I walked in the door. It's cartoonish. It's almost as bad as the way Heath's been watching me since we headed over here, the concern in his face all too clear. Even now as he leans against the wall behind me, I can feel his gaze burning against the back of my head. Shame tingles along my skin, but for some reason, he hasn't brought up what happened with Faye and Annie.

"Look, I'm fine. What's one more near-death experience to add to the tally?" No one laughs at that. I sigh. "You don't have to walk on eggshells around me like this." My gaze shoots to Faye. "Especially you. Nice from you freaks me out."

Faye scoffs. "I'm nice sometimes."

I take a sip of my tea, surprised when sweetness floods my mouth. "I was actually hoping to apologize to the two of you. I've been meaning to for a while."

"Apologize?" asks Faye.

"You have nothing to apologize for," Annie says at the same time.

"I do." Sighing, I set the tea on the coffee table. "The two of you have always been there for me. Not just with my career, but with everything else. You've been so good to me, and yet, neither of you even crossed my mind when I made that announcement on Miranda's show, even though I know that obviously affects both of you. It was selfish of me, and I'm sorry."

Annie rises from her chair and joins me on the couch. "Neither of us blame you one bit for wanting out after all of this." She squeezes my shoulder. "*We're* sorry we didn't try harder to get you out of your contract."

"Especially after what happened in Vegas." Faye shakes her head. "I'll never forgive myself for letting you get up there, Parker."

I force myself not to flinch, but I can remember staring

up at the ceiling, the room spinning, the roar of the crowd muffled like I was underground. I cough. "You couldn't have known that was going to happen, and you got me out of the contract in the end."

"We should've expected that someone would try something." Faye gets up from her chair and paces into the kitchen, then glances back at me with her teeth deep in her lower lip.

As much as they've tried to frame this as a social visit, we all know why we're here. I have no idea why the saying is an elephant in room, because it feels more like a black hole slowly sucking out all the oxygen. I flick my wrist. "Get on with it then. What do we know?"

"Well," Annie says slowly, "nothing came up on the cameras from the parking garage here. And same with the gas station. So the police think whenever the bomb was planted—whoever planted it—it must have happened elsewhere."

"Could they tell how it was triggered?"

I jump at Heath's low voice behind me, having almost forgotten he was here.

Faye shakes her head and braces her hands on the counter. "They're still trying to see if they can find any prints or DNA on the bomb or the car though."

"So we know nothing," I say. "Is that it?"

Annie grimaces. "The police are investigating, and we're increasing your security detail. So hopefully we'll know more soon."

I nod slowly. Whoever's behind this is either smart or exceptionally lucky.

"It's quite an escalation from a note to a bomb. You're saying you don't have any leads at all?" Heath demands.

Faye scowls at the tone of his voice. "You're the one who's with her practically twenty-four seven. Have *you* noticed anyone unusual?"

Heath mutters something unintelligible under his breath.

A vein pulses above Faye's eye, but I intervene before she can respond.

"I have a favor to ask."

All eyes turn to me.

"Anything you need," says Annie.

"There's someplace I want to go today. And thought maybe you two would want to come with me."

IT'S WARMER TODAY than it's been in a long time. The sun cascades through the trees, though despite the nice weather, the cemetery is empty. The three of us silently trudge through the rows of sun-bleached stone angels and memorials, stopping at a plot where the earth is freshly overturned.

Heath hangs back a few yards so he can keep an eye on our surroundings. The marble headstone is covered in candles, handwritten notes, and flowers, fresh enough to assume someone was here recently. My stomach tightens. I'd thought staying away from the funeral was the kinder, more responsible thing to do. But why haven't I tried to come back since then?

I set down the white flowers I brought, breathing in the smell of fresh dirt and hot stone. There's nothing comforting about the scent. Nothing familiar. Nothing that reminds me of Elijah.

Annie braces a hand on my back as a lawn mower sputters to life in the distance.

"Hold on," Faye murmurs, digging in her purse. She pulls out a lighter and leans forward to light each of the candles. The flames flicker gently in the breeze.

My eyes catch on a framed picture leaning against the base of the headstone—Elijah with his son on his shoulders. They're in matching Yankees jerseys, and he's grinning at the camera, the love in his eyes making me think his wife took the picture.

Annie tightens her hold on me, and Faye lays her hand on my shoulder.

"Do you want to say a few words, maybe?" she asks.

I suck in a shuddering breath, a lump forming in the back of my throat. "Could you?" I whisper.

"I've worked with a lot of men in my life," Annie says. "And especially in this industry, and in Elijah's line of work, I've found a lot of them to be cold. Distant. Struggling with the things they've had to see. And Elijah was so damn good at his job, and he'd been doing it for so long. But you never would have known. He was as gentle and kind and funny as he was diligent and focused and ruthless when it came to protecting those he cared about. And I've loved working with Parker. This has been my favorite job I've had. And seeing the way Elijah looked at her, seeing the sheer love and protectiveness he had for her, like she was his daughter, there was something so pure and fulfilling about being a part of that. I don't know why he was taken from us so soon, but I know he was meant to come into our lives. And I know, without a doubt, he wouldn't change a thing if it meant keeping Parker safe."

"Thank you, Annie," I whisper, the tears rolling down my cheeks in earnest now. She wraps me in a hug. "I miss him every day. Sometimes it's not until someone tells a joke he would have liked and I don't hear him laugh that I remember he's gone. I still feel him with me all the time."

A tree branch snaps behind us. I glance over my shoulder as the breeze picks up and shakes through the trees, but the rest of the cemetery is empty. I stare a moment too long at the bushes directly behind us as they sway back and forth.

"How about some lunch?" Faye says. "On me. I'll even let you pick out some gross vegetarian place."

"Faye, you're the vegetarian," I remind her.

She throws her arm over my shoulders and yanks me against her side. "Okay, okay, if you insist. We'll go to that new one around the corner."

She leads us in the opposite direction we parked, though I catch the chauffeur pulling away from the curb and following us out of the corner of my eye. It's a quiet neighborhood, the street relatively deserted. Brown and gold leaves crunch underfoot as we head down the sidewalk toward a cluster of businesses, all quiet but one.

The narrow front windows are crowded with vines and potted plants, and a thick line of people is already spilling out the door. I brace my shoulders as we step inside, the crowd eliciting a spike in my blood pressure. Heath's hand rests against the small of my back. A few people glance up at our entrance, but they all quickly turn back to their business, no hint of recognition in their eyes.

Faye shrugs at my look of surprise. "Vegetarians are chill."

"There's no way we're getting a table," mumbles Annie.

The hostess beams as we approach, and my body tenses again. But her eyes aren't on me. "Faye! Come on in. We've got a booth for you in the back."

She leads us through the maze of tables, her head of fire-red hair bobbing above the crowds, until we reach a four-top in the corner. Annie and I slide in on one side, Faye and Heath on the other.

All eyes turn to Faye.

"What?" She throws her hands up. "So I know the owner. Sue me for planning ahead."

Warmth blankets the table from the low-hanging lamps, casting everything in an orange glow. Vibrant paintings line the walls in all different styles, though they follow a similar color scheme—bright reds, oranges, yellows. Little tags sit below each with a price and the name of the local artist.

Elijah would've liked it here. He appreciated art in every form, always willing to learn, to listen. Annie's hand squeezes my knee under the table, and she gives me a sad smile like she's thinking the same thing.

Faye orders for the table, and I poke at the plate suspiciously once it arrives.

She rolls her eyes. "You'll like it."

After taking a bite, I realize I do, in fact, like it. Not that she'll need that boost to her ego.

"So how are you holding up?" Annie asks. "With the trial and everything. They're meeting again this week, aren't they?"

Heath meets my eyes across the table, a question in his. If there was a time to bring it up, I guess this is it.

"I was actually thinking about going," I say.

Faye frowns, though she's not yelling like I'd been preparing for. If anything, it looks like she'd been expecting this.

Annie pats my leg beneath the table. "I don't think it's the worst idea." Faye shoots her an incredulous look, but Annie barely spares her a glance. "Parker, if this is what you need for closure, we'll make it happen."

"Really?" I'd been preparing to plead my case. At least *some* arguing.

"There will be precautions," says Annie.

"*Lots* of precautions," chimes in Faye.

"But I don't think it's an unreasonable thing to ask."

I throw my arms around Annie's shoulders and pull her into a hug before she finishes the sentence.

CHAPTER 36
PARKER

It's difficult to untangle the emotions clogging my system. The very idea of being in the same room as Jasper Young makes my hands sweat, and flashes of that night appear in my head. But there's also this buzzing in my veins. This building adrenaline. A *need* to be in that room. To see it for myself.

It takes a few hours to get us upstate with traffic, and I pump my leg up and down, checking the time on my phone every few minutes. If we get there too late, I don't think they'll let us in. Then I would've dragged Heath out here for nothing.

The new driver pulls up to the front of the courthouse. Heath climbs out first, shielding his eyes from the sun and holding the door open for me. He's in slacks and a white button-down, a look I'm starting to find odd on him. It's not that he doesn't look good, but it doesn't suit him. I ended up borrowing a modest black dress from Mom and threw a simple matching jacket on top.

Heath's expression is somber as I join him on the curb,

but he gives me a small, reassuring smile. I let out a shuddering breath and turn to the courthouse behind him. His fingers brush my elbow as the car pulls away from the curb.

"You ready for this?"

"Not even a little bit," I admit, but hook my arm through his as we head inside.

The wooden benches creak beneath our weight as we slide into the last row, both because I don't want him to see me, but also because the room is packed. I suppose I shouldn't be surprised given how much of a spectacle this whole thing has been.

I tug on the collar of my dress, unsure if the room is as stuffy as it feels, or if the cocktail of varnish, pine cleaning supplies, and an overheating laptop on the defense's table is just too overwhelming in addition to all the noise. The heater thuds behind us as it kicks on, mingling with the buzz of hushed voices, rustling papers, and the echoes of the prosecutor's footsteps on the polished floor as he crosses to his table.

My heart stops in my chest as my attention lands on the head at the defense's table. He's in normal clothes today—I don't know why I'd been expecting an orange jumpsuit—but I can see the metal handcuffs from here. My breathing quickens, and the edges of my vision blur, darkening and twisting until I'm standing back in that parking lot.

"Hey." Heath's hand brushes across my arm, and I squeeze my eyes shut. When I open them again, the courtroom returns. "Hey." Heath's hand slides under mine, and I grip his fingers tightly.

"I'm okay," I breathe.

"You say the word, and I'll get you out of here, okay?"

I can only muster a nod, because then the judge is

walking out, and suddenly we're all standing. It's hard to hear anything that comes next through my own pulse thundering in my ears. One of the attorneys—the prosecutor, I'm assuming—steps up. I don't hear a word she says, that is, until the pictures.

I don't recognize the first one—a man in a convenience store—but my entire body tenses with what's coming. His body is shoved behind the checkout counter, the tiles beneath him covered in blood. Heath wraps an arm around my shoulders as the second picture flicks onto screen, another person I don't recognize. The security guard for the vineyard. His throat is slashed, his body collapsed on top of some bushes.

Heath's hand tightens on my shoulder, pulling me against his side, and I reach for his other hand, gripping his fingers so hard it must be painful.

And then the third picture appears.

All the breath leaves my lungs. I'd been told how he died, but I've never seen the photos. His picture is much different than the others. The others looked like they went quickly, like Jasper Young had caught them by surprise.

But Elijah had known. And he'd fought back. His shirt is shredded, and there are splatters of blood all over him and his surroundings. The picture is dark, but he's slumped against a tree, his eyes open. A single tear runs down my cheek, but I don't look away. Elijah deserved better than that. I can feel Heath looking at me, but I lock my jaw and keep my vision trained straight ahead.

The picture disappears as the prosecutor wraps up and returns to his table. When the defense rises, Jasper Young turns his head to the side, watching. The sight of his profile is like a knife to my stomach, and the entire room slows around me. Or maybe it speeds up. Everything becomes a blur, Heath's hand in mine the only anchor I have.

I don't know what I came here looking for. Closure, I suppose. But all I feel is sick. How long will this go on for? Days? Weeks? And even after this is over and I can put this behind me, what then?

Where do I go from there?

"Heath," I whisper.

He searches my face, his eyebrows pulled together, and nods once. A few heads turn in our direction as we slip out, but I don't care. I need to get someplace I can *breathe*. Heath wraps his arm around my shoulders, sheltering me from the looks as we head for the door, but I turn before we slip into the hallway.

Jasper Young stares back and smiles.

I INHALE the biggest breath I've taken all day the second we step out of the courthouse, then sink onto one of the concrete steps. Heath sits beside me, and I cover my face with my hands.

"I'm sorry," I gasp. "I'm sorry for making you come."

"You have nothing to apologize for."

"What happened? Is she okay?"

High heels click against the pavement around us, and I blink, at first not sure if I'm seeing Annie and Faye running toward us, or if I'm having a mental breakdown and hallucinating them.

"What are you…?"

"We thought you might need some moral support," says

Annie as she sits beside me. Faye lingers behind Heath, her arms crossed and face pinched tight with worry.

I cover my face with my hands again and let out a long, slow breath. Annie rubs small circles against my back, and I press the heels of my hands into my forehead like maybe I can force the memory of the last hour out of my head. "This was a stupid idea. I'm sorry. I just—I thought—I don't—" I pinch my lips together, ordering myself not to cry.

Heath joins on my other side and lays his hand on my thigh. "Let's get you home."

"You know, Annie and I were talking about that on the way here," says Faye. "How would you feel about getting out of town for a bit? It could be good to get away while all of this is happening. And since the new apartment's address has clearly been leaked, and we wanted to move you anyway, what about your family's lake house up north?"

"Then at least you'll be in a familiar place instead of a temporary apartment," adds Annie. "We'd prep the house ahead of time with a security system and send plenty of security with you, of course."

"Just get out of the city," says Faye. "Clear your head."

"What do you think?" asks Heath.

A shiver runs down my spine at the thought of *him* a mere wall away from me. I nod and let Heath help me to my feet. "Okay. Just please get me out of here."

CHAPTER 37
PARKER

Heath pulls up to the apartment in a car I've never seen before. When he'd insisted on driving instead of hiring a car, I hadn't thought much of it. But now looking out the window at whatever *that* is, I'm realizing maybe I should have. It's turquoise blue with a convertible top, looking much better suited for California than here. Heath's grinning when he steps out and props his black sunglasses on the top of his head. He sees me watching from the window, and his smile broadens.

I have my bags waiting by the door, as requested. A single rolling suitcase with a duffel bag on top.

I stare at the car as Heath loads my bags alongside his own in the trunk. "Is this thing...yours?"

He laughs as he slams the trunk shut and circles to the driver's side. "No. But I rented it for the week."

"And this was the only car they had left?"

"Very funny." The sunglasses return over his eyes as he checks the mirrors and waits for me to put my seat belt on, the grin never leaving his face. "We're on vacation. I thought we deserved a car that looked the part."

I snort but lean my head back, enjoying the sun soaking into my skin as he pulls away from the curb. "You better hope it doesn't rain."

"You mind if we make a pitstop?" he asks, his tone suddenly serious. "I need to take care of something really quick."

"Sure. Is everything okay?"

He sighs and runs a hand through his hair. "With Dani home now, it's great, but the hospital has been down my throat about the bills. I've been trying to keep it from Dani and my mom while I handle it, but they keep calling and sending mail. I was hoping if I went in to talk to someone there, we could work out some kind of plan so they'll stop hounding us."

"How much are the bills, Heath?" I ask quietly.

He shakes his head. "It's over two hundred grand, even after I asked them to send me a list of all the expenses and they knocked it down by about fifty thousand."

"Heath—"

"Parker, I know what you're going to say, but I can't."

"*Actually*, you don't know what I'm going to say."

"I can't take your money."

"I'm not *giving* you money," I insist. "Just let me pay your salary in advance. It'll be exactly what you would have made, not a penny more. You'll just get it now instead of later."

His fists tighten around the wheel, and a muscle in his jaw jumps.

"Please don't make this a big thing," I whisper. "I have the means to help, Heath, and I *want* to. Both for you and your family. You've already done so much for me, and this is nothing. Please, just let me help."

He doesn't say anything else until we get to the hospital, and I don't push it more. We sit in the car in silence for several minutes after he turns it off. I peek at the side of his face, trying to gauge what he's thinking. He sighs again and rubs his eyes.

"Not a penny more."

"Not a penny more," I say immediately.

When he looks up at me, an array of emotions plays across his face. Exhaustion is the clearest. But there's also some relief. This has been weighing on him for so long. And there's something else in his eyes. Something I can't place.

"I can have Faye set it up right now. It won't cover all of it, but it'll be a good start, right?"

He takes the sides of my face with both hands. I stare back, but then he leans forward and presses a kiss to my forehead. "Thank you," he murmurs. "Thank you."

His mood noticeably lifts as we pull away from the hospital. It's about a five-hour drive up to the lake house, and we stop outside the city for snacks at a gas station. We both hesitate before climbing out of the car, and I imagine he's remembering a lot of the same things I am. The fire. The smoke. The glass and blood and ringing ears.

"Wonder what the statistic is," Heath says. "Nearly getting blown up at a gas station *twice*. I feel like the odds must be low, don't you? We should be in the clear."

I let out an incredulous laugh and shake my head. "That's not funny."

"Yet, you're laughing."

I punch his arm, unable to kill the smile on my face as we climb out and head inside. Heath watches me with a bemused expression as I meander through the aisles, weighing my options.

"What are you smirking at?" I mumble.

He stands in the next aisle, a coffee and bag of plain potato chips already in hand. We're the only people in the store, and the man behind the counter is singing along to the radio like we're not even here.

"The snacks someone chooses for a road trip says a lot about a person."

I quirk an eyebrow at his choices. "And yours says…what? You lack imagination?"

He laughs and circles to join me by the candy. "You're feisty today."

"It's your chipper attitude," I say flatly. "It's getting on my nerves."

"Doesn't like to see other people happy," he muses. "That probably also says something about you."

I push his chest and reach past him for a bag of sour gummy worms. "Is this an acceptable choice?"

"Seems to match your mood," he mutters, still smiling.

The man behind the counter doesn't stop singing, even while he checks us out, and Heath shoots me a knowing look. He twirls the car keys around his finger as we head back outside, now humming the same tune the cashier had been singing, then nudges me with his elbow before I climb in.

"You want to drive?" he offers. His voice comes out light, that carefree smile in place, but his eyes search my face when he says it, a line of concern forming between his brows.

I'm not clueless. I know what he's doing. He's trying to cheer me up, to get my mind off everything else. I bite my lip to hide my smile and snatch the keys away from him. "You have no idea what you just got yourself into."

"YOU'RE GOING to get us pulled over," says Heath, though there's a laugh in his voice.

I let out a yell as my hair blows behind my shoulders. The roads are mostly empty, and even though the temperature has dipped the closer we've gotten to the coast, I refused when Heath offered to put the top up.

"So when are Faye and Annie coming up?" he asks.

I shrug. "Closer to the end of the week. They had to take care of a few things first."

Heath nods, then turns to look out the window. I bob my head along to the radio and drum my fingers on the steering wheel. With the roar of the wind rushing past and the music vibrating the car, it almost captures that same feeling I get onstage. I smile, letting it wash over me.

"The car was a good idea," I admit. "I haven't been able to drive myself in so long, I—thank you. I miss it."

"Yeah, the lack of practice shows."

"Oh, shut up."

"Parker?"

I hum and flicker my gaze between him and the road.

"It's good to see you happy."

I swallow, focusing back on the road. *Happy.* Have I not been happy lately? I've had periods of being *okay*, but maybe not as far as *happy.* And even though my immediate instinct at hearing the word is guilt—how can I be happy with Elijah gone?—I know he'd agree with Heath. He'd be relieved to see me like this again too.

"Are you tired? We can pull over and I'll drive the second half, if you want."

"Are you that worried about my driving?" I tease.

"No, I just—"

"I'm kidding. Actually, yes. I could use a nap."

I pull off at the next exit and stop at a gas station. The wind has picked up, and I shiver as I climb out of the car, then head to the trunk to pull out a sweatshirt. Heath stretches his arms overhead, his shirt hiking up enough to expose a small sliver of skin above his jeans. I quickly avert my eyes and yank the sweatshirt on.

He frowns up at the sky and the dark, gray clouds rolling in. "We should probably put the top up."

I sigh. "It was nice while it lasted." I snatch the bag of gummy worms up as I climb into the passenger seat. "At least now I can guard these. Don't think I didn't see you stealing some earlier."

He shrugs innocently as he pulls the top of the car over my head. I catch that same flash of skin again, this time very clearly making out the V of his hips.

"I'm gonna run in and grab another coffee before we go. You want one?" he calls from outside.

"Sure."

He disappears into the convenience store, and he waves at the cashier as he passes. I dig in my purse for my Chapstick as I wait, shoving aside my phone. I turned it off before we started the trip, not wanting to see whatever news alerts popped up about the trial. This is supposed to be my week to get away from it all. Following it on my phone wouldn't be any better than sitting in that courtroom again. Every time I try to sleep, I see Jasper Young catching my eyes before I left, that knowing smile on his face.

"Here you are."

I jump as Heath hands me the coffee through my window. He quirks an eyebrow but says nothing as he circles the car and climbs back in.

"You okay?" he asks as he sets his coffee in the cup holder and adjusts the seat.

"Yeah, yeah, of course." I sip the coffee. "Just ready to get back on the road."

The car hums to life, and the moment he pulls onto the highway, the first drop of rain hits the windshield.

I smile, lean my head back against the seat, and tuck my knees into my chest. "Well, this is perfect now. I love sleeping when it's raining."

He laughs and shakes his head. "I can never sleep when other people are driving. Don't trust them enough."

"I trust you," I say quietly, then close my eyes before I can see his reaction.

CHAPTER 38
PARKER

It's been years since I've been to the lake house, but everything looks the same as I remember it. Well, except for the new security system Faye had installed beside the front door before we got here. It isn't a large house, but the view by far makes up for what it lacks in size. With a modest three bedrooms and three bathrooms, the house is two floors, the main focal point being the open floor concept on the main level. The front room houses a white grand piano surrounded by floor-to-ceiling windows. It leads directly into the kitchen and dining room, where there's a massive gray-stone fireplace. The windows along the back of the house look out toward the water lapping against the dock. This is where Heath finds me after dropping our bags off in the rooms upstairs.

"This house was the first frivolous thing I ever bought with the Ryker money," I murmur, transfixed by the way the sunlight glitters off the waves. "I put my parents in a nicer house first, then put my baby brother through school and got him an apartment. We paid off all the debt, set aside retirement funds for us all, and an emergency fund. After trying to be responsible with it, especially because at that point, we had no idea if it would last, I'd felt so guilty buying this place. There was no need for it. We'd only come up a few times a year. But man." I sigh, wrapping my arms around myself. "This place has become one of my favorite places in the world."

I glance sidelong at Heath, but he just stands beside me, hands in his pockets, looking out past the dock. A slow smile creeps onto his lips.

"Wanna go for a swim?" he says.

I scoff. "That water is freezing."

"We'll just go out to the dock then."

"Sounds like a ploy to get me out there so you can push me in."

He laughs and scoops a blanket off the chair in the corner. "I wouldn't do that the very first day we're here. That would give you *far* too much time to retaliate."

The cold air bites my skin the moment we open the sliding glass door. Heath unfolds the blanket and lays it over my shoulders as we head down the dock, the wood creaking faintly under our feet. We pause at the end, staring out at the sun setting in the distance. The wind whistles through the trees surrounding the property and the water brushes gently against the dock, but other than that, it's so *still* out here. Our nearest neighbors are nearly a mile away, and even that property I'm pretty sure is a vacation home.

"It's so quiet out here," murmurs Heath.

"A nice change of pace from the city, right?"

He nods and crouches down to sit and hang his feet over the edge. I do the same on the opposite end and lean against the post, pulling the blanket up to my ears. Heath trails the tips of his fingers along the water, sending tiny ripples across the surface. He winces and pulls his hand back.

"Good call on the swimming."

"You want something hot to drink? I could go make some tea or something?" I offer.

"I can make it."

I shake my head, already pushing to my feet. "You won't know where anything is." I toss him the blanket before turning back and heading for the house. A small smile brushes my lips as I turn the kettle on and watch Heath through the window. He glances back at the house, squinting against the sun reflecting off the windows, then wraps the blanket around his shoulders. After pouring two mugs, I rifle through the linen closet near the side door and grab two towels, dropping them on the dining room table before heading back out so Heath won't see them.

He turns and smiles when he hears my footsteps. "That was fast."

"Sorry in advance," I say.

He furrows his brow. "Sorry—?"

Then I kick him into the water. The blanket falls from his shoulders and lands on the dock, and I set the two mugs down a few feet away.

He gasps as he breaks the surface.

I laugh and cover my face with my hands.

"Parker!" he shouts.

"So, uh, how's the water? Good swimming temp?"

A mischievous smile twists his mouth as he swims closer to the dock. "You better get in here."

"Hm." I pretend to consider this, glancing over the edge. "I don't know. Seems kind of cold."

Heath's teeth are full on chattering now. Then faster than

I would have imagined possible, he pulls himself back onto the side of the dock. Water drips from every inch of him, but before I have the chance to retreat, he runs at me, wrapping his arms around my waist as he throws us both into the water.

The cold doesn't register at first, just the impact. The water rushes over my head, Heath's arms around me as we sink. He must hit the bottom first, because then he's pushing off, pulling me up with him.

The air turns the numb feeling on my skin to ice, and I gasp.

"Holy shit," I breathe, lips already trembling.

"Great swimming temp," Heath says, floating on his back.

I splash water in his direction, already wading back toward the dock.

"Not so fast!" He grabs me by the waist and spins me around so we're both facing the sunset, my back pressed against his chest.

"I'm going to lose toes," I complain, turning in his arms, and then suddenly his face is very close to mine. He blinks the water from his eyelashes as his gaze travels from my eyes to my chin and back again, lingering on my mouth.

I wrap my arms around his shoulders as we tread water, his skin like ice to the touch, but warmth blazes through me at the contact, at the look in his eyes, at his breath on my skin.

And then his mouth is on mine. Liquid heat fills my veins, magnifying and glowing with each brush of his lips, gentle at first. His body tightens against me as I open my mouth to him on a sigh. He kisses me harder, deeper, his tongue mingling with mine as he twists his fingers in my hair, pulling hard enough that a delicious spark of pain shoots all the way down my spine. The fire inside of me rages higher, hotter, threatening to swallow every last ounce of my self-control. Urging me to lose myself in his skin and his mouth and the low groan he makes in the back of his throat.

But that momentum, that bottoming out of my stomach as I feel myself start to fall, jars me awake as if from a dream. I pull away, breathless, and put a hand against his chest as a barrier between us.

His arms stay securely locked around my waist, and he searches my face.

"Heath," I breathe. "I can't—"

Something like hurt flashes behind his eyes, and I shake my head, trying to find the words to make him understand.

"I'm a complicated disaster right now. You don't want anything to do with me."

He considers me for a moment, his eyes still searching, assessing. "Yes, you are," he finally says, pulling me closer until our lips nearly brush. "But yes, I do."

"Why would you want any part of this? You've seen what—"

"Why would I want any part of this?" He lets out an incredulous laugh, a hand coming up to push my hair behind my ear. He leaves his palm against my cheek, and my eyelids flutter involuntarily. His voice lowers until it nearly blends in with the gentle ripples of the water around us. "Because no matter how hard dealing with everything around you is, being with you is easy. Talking to you is easy. Laughing with you is easy. The only hard part is when I leave at the end of the day, because I miss you as soon as I close the door."

I press my lips together, unsure if the wobble in my chin is from the cold or something else. He gently strokes his thumb against my cheek, his eyes holding mine.

"And because I see you," he murmurs. "Past the names and the fronts and the excuses, I see who you are, Parker Beck, and there's nothing you can say to convince me that I should be anywhere but here. So if you want to scare me off, you're going to have to try a lot harder than that."

"I'm not trying to scare you off," I whisper. "I'm giving you an out."

He nods, his hand trailing to cup the back of my head. "Noted. And rejected."

I let out a small, pitiful laugh around the shivers rocking my body, from the cold, the relief. Because he should take the warning and walk away, for his own good.

But I don't know what I would have done if he had.

I meet his eyes again. "Can we…"

"Can we what?" he asks.

I swallow, a million different images that I don't want to think about flashing through my head. Elijah's grave, Jasper Young in that courtroom, seeing Rick's face in the paper under those terrible headlines, Erica's wedding dress ruined from the blood.

I shake my head, trying to clear it. "I need—can we take things slow? Just after everything that's happened, I…"

"You've got me as slow or as fast as you want…as long as we get the hell out of this water right now."

I nod my agreement, my teeth chattering uncontrollably now, and we scramble for the dock. He grabs my hips, hoisting me up first before climbing out after me. I grab one of the mugs, and even though it's not that hot anymore, it nearly burns my frozen fingers.

"Let's get inside." Heath grabs his mug and the blanket with one hand, his other pressing against the small of my back, then we head back to the house, making sure to reactivate the security system once we're in.

I throw him one of the towels I'd set out and nod toward the stairs. "I'm just gonna jump in the shower really quick to warm up, but then we can start making dinner, if you want. I think Faye had someone stock the pantry. And there's a shower in your room too, if you need it."

"Sounds good."

I linger at the bottom of the stairs, looking at him a moment too long as he strips off his wet shirt to throw in the laundry room, before finally forcing myself to turn.

THERE'S a roaring fire in the corner by the time I make it back downstairs, and Heath's standing in the kitchen with his back to me. I grab another blanket off the couch and wrap it around myself as I pace toward him.

"That smells good," I murmur.

He turns, smiling, and waves a wooden spoon at me. "You like stir-fry?"

"Sounds good to me. Need any help?"

"Nah, I'm almost done." He flicks the stove off and digs in the cabinets until he finds the plates.

I slip past him toward the wine pantry and pull out a bottle of red. "Should I be on guard for some kind of retaliation from the lake?"

Heath smirks and pours the stir-fry onto two plates. "If I were planning something, *why* would I tell you?"

I bump him aside with my shoulder so I can reach the wineglasses in the cabinet by his head. "Take pity on me?" I stretch onto my toes but can't reach the shelf.

"Here." He reaches over me and pulls down two glasses, his chest brushing my back. He lingers a moment as I lean into him before setting the glasses in front of me.

We settle into the two seats nearest the fire, and Heath watches me as I take my first bite, gauging my reaction.

My eyes widen. "I guess I should've known it would be good from the last time."

He chuckles and uncorks the wine.

I cover my mouth as I chew. "I never evolved much past making pasta out of a box."

"I like having someone else to cook for. It's not as much fun when it's just for me."

We meet each other's eyes, and for the first time, his smile looks kind of shy. I smile back and drop my gaze to my plate. The silence that settles around us isn't uncomfortable; it falls naturally as we finish off our meals and watch the fire.

"I think I'm just going to go to bed early," I murmur, setting my napkin on my plate.

"Okay." He waves his hand when I start picking up my dishes. "I'll get them."

"You cooked. The least I can do is help clean up."

"Parker." He lays a hand on my arm. "Just go get some sleep. You look exhausted."

I relent and wrap the blanket tighter around my shoulders as I head for the stairs. "Goodnight."

"Goodnight," he calls. "I'll be right next door...just, if you need anything."

I smile. "Thanks, Heath. I had a good day."

He smiles back, the earlier shyness gone. "Me too."

I DON'T HAVE a prayer of falling asleep. I know it the second my head hits the pillow. I can hear Heath washing up at the sink in the kitchen, and then his footsteps as he comes up the stairs and goes to the bedroom on the other side of my wall. I lie on my back, staring at the ceiling, somehow simultaneously thinking of everything and nothing at all.

I wonder what Heath's doing, if he's already fallen asleep. If he can't get his brain to turn off like me. After a few hours of tossing and turning, I sigh, sit up, and push the hair out of my face.

The blankets on the beds are heated, but the second I slip out and my bare feet touch the floor, goosebumps rise on my skin. I'd forgotten to pack pajamas, and since the last time I'd been here was in the middle of summer, the only things I could find in the dresser were matching silk shorts and a tank top. There's a silk robe hanging in the bathroom too, and I quickly wrap it around myself.

The stairs creak quietly under my feet as I head downstairs and notice the fire is barely holding on to life. Heath left a few other logs off to the side, and I push them in, waiting until they ignite. The flames flicker, casting odd shapes of light around the room. They reflect off the glossy surface of the piano, and I pause, a faint melody humming in the back of my mind.

I haven't worked on that song I'd been writing since the day in the temporary apartment, but it's been playing in the back of my mind ever since, like it was waiting for me to come back to it.

I slide onto the piano bench and gently push up the fallboard. The keys are cold to the touch, and I sigh, fingers hovering over them. I press a single note and listen to it sing through the silence, the sound crisp and clear. My eyes fall shut, and I glide my fingers over the rest of the keys, feeling my way through the song. After letting out a slow, calming breath, I start to play.

It's clumsy at first, but after a few seconds, I fall back into it, tilting my head and adjusting as I find the right notes. It's like I can hear it in my head a moment before I play it, but the song doesn't have a beginning or an end. Just a stream of consciousness, one note blending into the next. But then, as easily as I'd fallen into the flow, the notes cut off, and I open my eyes.

"That was amazing."

I jump and turn to see Heath standing by the edge of the stairs. He's shirtless, his gray sweatpants hanging low on his hips, his hair messy like he just rolled out of bed.

"I'm sorry." I close the fallboard again. "I didn't mean to wake you up."

"Oh no, don't stop." He paces over and slides onto the bench beside me. "Best thing I've woken up to in a long time." He pushes the lid up again. "Are you writing a new song?"

"Trying to. I haven't been able to write in... Well, anyway. The melody is coming along, but I don't have any lyrics for it yet. Which is weird. The lyrics usually come first."

"It sounded really good."

I smile a little. "Thanks."

"You couldn't sleep?"

I shake my head, wrapping my robe tighter around myself.

The intensity in his gaze momentarily steals my breath. He holds my eyes, then looks down at my lips. I can see how much he wants to kiss me. I can *feel* it.

But he doesn't.

He doesn't move a single muscle. And I remember what I said to him in the water. I'd asked him to take things slow. And now he's looking at me in a way that makes my whole body burn, but he's waiting for me to make the first move.

"Can I ask you something?" he murmurs.

I nod.

"Do you really think you could give it all up for good?"

I blink, surprised. That's definitely not where I thought the conversation was headed.

"I saw you up there, Parker. I've never seen you look more in your element. You are so *good* at what you do. And your fans don't just love you. They *adore* you. And then I saw that guy in court. And he's just...nothing. And I can't stand the idea of him taking away something so important to you on top of everything else."

"I would miss it," I admit. "A lot. But I just don't know if it's worth it anymore if I feel like I can't have a life outside of that. I know so many people would kill for fame, but it was never about that for me. I just wanted to play my music. That's what Ryker was for in the first place."

"Don't hate me for saying this, but it seems like your life is never going to go back to the way it was. It's out there now, and it is what it is. The only thing you're doing by retiring is giving up the one part of this life you actually like."

I don't have anything to say to that, mostly because I know he's right. But the idea of carrying on this way just feels too heavy right now to even consider. Maybe it won't someday. But for now, it's unimaginable.

But if not this...I have no idea what to do. No idea what I even *want*. Aren't you supposed to know that by twenty-four? By then people are graduating college, moving up in their careers, starting families. People have always told me I was so ahead by having my career start at eighteen, but now I just feel behind.

His fingers graze my thigh, and he hesitates before lowering his hand and stroking his thumb lightly back and forth across my skin. I don't know what it is about his touch, but it's like all the tension in my body fades to the background.

I lean forward until our noses brush, and he sucks in a sharp breath, his eyes never leaving mine. I reach up, my hand sliding from his chest to his neck, then cross the rest of the distance between us.

His mouth lands on mine, warm and strong, no trace of the earlier hesitation. He kisses me like he's trying to breathe me in, like the only oxygen he *can* breathe is between our lips. My hands tangle in his hair, and I slide across the bench as he pulls me to him, one arm tightening around my waist, the other holding the back of my head.

He pulls back an inch, his voice low as he asks, "Taking it slow?"

I'm already shaking my head before he gets the last word out. "Changed my mind." Our mouths crash back together, and his hands glide up my waist. "If that's okay with you."

He grabs my face with both hands and kisses me in response, his teeth tugging on my bottom lip. I can't get close enough to him fast enough. Our hands fly over each other in a frantic dance, until he grips my hips and pulls me onto his lap. I straddle his legs, my hair falling over my shoulders like a curtain between us as I lean into him.

His hands trail back to my waist, where he unknots the robe, then pushes it off my shoulders. I gasp as his lips trail to my jaw, then my neck, and all the way down to my chest, where he pulls my nipple into his mouth through the thin silk of my shirt. My head tilts back as a small, helpless moan comes out.

I've had plenty of time to imagine this since our phone call—the way his mouth would feel, his hands, his body against mine. But never, not once, did I imagine it could feel like *this*. My heart swells in my chest, frantically pounding against my ribs, and intoxicating heat ignites every nerve in my body until I feel like I might combust.

"Parker," he breathes, one hand tangling in my hair as he brings his mouth back to mine.

His chest is warm and hard beneath my hands, the muscles tensing as I run my fingers down to his waistband. Before I can get very far, his hands grip my thighs, and he hoists me up, our mouths never breaking the kiss. I lock my legs around his waist, but then he's laying me out on the piano.

He stands over me, the light from the fire flickering across his profile as he takes me in. I sit up to reach for him, and he presses our foreheads together, his blue eyes holding mine as his fingers skate under the hem of my shirt.

"Tell me if you want me to stop," he breathes.

I lay my hands on top of his, then grip the shirt and pull it over my head. His eyes darken, and he licks his lips.

"I don't want you to stop."

His body presses me flat against the piano, and I dig my fingernails into his shoulder blades. Every inch of my skin burns as his mouth travels the length of me, starting at the delicate skin below my ear. He takes his time, pausing at my breasts, where he gently digs in his teeth. I gasp, and then he's moving again, all the way to the sharp points of my hips. He digs his teeth in there too as his fingers hook under the waistband of my shorts.

"Lift your hips for me, superstar," he murmurs against my skin.

I do as he says, and he meets my eyes as he slowly slides the shorts down my legs, leaving me in nothing but my thin underwear. At first I think he's going to pull those off too, but then he kneels and dips his head between my legs, his mouth finding me through the fabric.

My head rolls back against the piano as he hooks one of my legs over his shoulder. He hums as he moves his mouth over me, the vibrations coaxing out another whimper. He moves slowly, methodically, like he has all the time in the world. I squirm under him, begging him to move faster, but he just pins my hips with his hands and continues his slow exploration.

My fingers grip the edge of the piano as he moves my panties to the side and inserts a finger inside of me, easing in and out before curling against my inner walls in exactly the right place. As he gradually speeds up, his body appears over me, his lips finding mine in a hungry, deep kiss. I grab his hair, holding him there as he slides another finger in.

"Fuck, I want you so badly," he growls, and my back arches, desperate to feel his skin against mine.

"Then have me," I gasp.

A laugh rumbles deep in his chest as his teeth scrape along the hollow of my throat. "You're very impatient."

"Yes," I agree, reaching for his pants. He doesn't stop me this time as I yank them down his hips and his cock springs free. He lets out a harsh exhale as I slowly stroke my hand up and down the long, hard length of him. "Shit," I breathe, mostly to myself, as I take in his size, and my mouth goes a little dry.

He must sense my hesitation because he leans back, his

eyes searching mine, and presses a gentle kiss to my mouth. "You trust me?"

I pull in a shallow breath and nod once.

"Then trust I'll have you good and ready first." He pumps his fingers and slowly curls them against my inner walls in a way that has my lips parting and head involuntarily tipping back. "That's it."

He urges me closer and closer until I'm on the knife's edge of coming, breathless and wound so tight I feel like I might snap in two, but then he backs off, his thumb slowly circling my clit. A frustrated whimper escapes me as I raise my hips, desperately seeking friction, but he pulls his fingers out, his eyes never leaving mine as he brings them to his mouth and sucks.

The look in his eyes sears into my flesh, my soul. I sit up, stroking him again, and the line of his jaw turns razor sharp as I lean down and take him into my mouth, just barely. His harsh exhale stirs the hair on my neck as I slowly drag my tongue around the tip of his cock and his muscles flex in response. But then just as quickly, he fists his hand in the back of my hair, pulling me up to seal his lips over mine.

But I need more. My body shakes with need, the slickness between my legs cooling against my thighs as I feel my pulse everywhere.

"Fuck," he breathes. "Parker, I don't have a condom."

"I have an IUD."

He stands, pulling me off the piano with him and kicks off his pants the rest of the way. He turns me so I'm facing the piano, and I grip the edges hard as he brushes my hair over my shoulder and slowly trails kisses down my spine. His hair grazes my lower back as he gets on his knees and slides my underwear the rest of the way down, lifting one foot and then the other to help me out of them. But instead of rising back up, his hands circle my ankles.

"Spread your legs."

I do as he says, my breaths coming in short, harsh gasps.

"Lean forward."

I press myself flat against the piano, and his hands skim up my thighs. His tongue slowly sweeps along the wetness rapidly gathering between my legs, but then he's standing behind me, the hard length of him pressing against my leg. He grabs me by the back of my neck and pulls me up, one hand coming around the front of my chest to hold me against him. Taking my chin with his other hand, he turns my head. His lips brush my ear as he commands, "Look at me."

I meet his eyes, and his chest rises and falls against my back perfectly in sync with my breaths. His pupils dilate as he nudges himself forward, and I arch my back.

He pushes in slowly, gauging my reaction with every inch. Even with how wet I am, a dizzying ache spreads through me as my inner walls desperately stretch to accommodate him, hot and pulsing and *addicting*. I dig my fingers into the back of his thigh, holding on, until every last inch of him is inside of me.

He holds my gaze as he starts to move, and usually, I wouldn't be able to hold the eye contact, but *fuck*, I can't look away. He leans forward and presses his mouth to mine.

"God, you feel incredible," he breathes against my mouth.

I turn, bracing my hands against the piano as his thrusts turn punishing, claiming, and it's all I can do to hold on and breathe. His chest presses against my back, his hands coming down on top of mine as he pushes deeper, and we both moan.

"Heath," I gasp as I toe the edge once again, but then he pulls out. I turn, and he grabs my legs, pushing me up to sit on the edge of the piano. He kisses me, slower this time, his hand cupping the back of my head.

"I want to see you," he says. I lock my legs around his waist, grinding my hips against him. He takes my breast in his mouth, tugging hard enough with his teeth that I gasp.

"I think," he says, pressing his lips against mine, "we should take this upstairs."

I nod and wrap my arms around his shoulders as he hoists me into his arms, his mouth never breaking from mine, not until we reach his room and fall onto the bed. I hook my legs around his waist as he drives into me as deep as he can over and over again.

"Fuck," I cry out, and he grabs my hands and pins them above my head.

"Tell me what you want," he pants against the crook of my neck.

"I can do you one better." I flip him onto his back, and he grins as I slowly lean down until every inch of our bodies is pressed together.

I grind against him slowly, teasing him like he did to me. "Parker," he gasps, his fingers digging into my hips, but he doesn't try to change my speed. I can feel his heart thudding in his chest, pounding against mine. A muscle jumps in his jaw as he fights for control, the effort of holding back written all over the sweat glistening on his skin, the veins bulging in his forearms.

I rest my forehead on his shoulder and brace my hands on the bed above his head as we move together. As much as I'd love to make him wait, I'm just as fucking desperate for it as he is.

"Heath, I want you to—"

"Like this?" He holds me flat against him and thrusts up, hard enough that it knocks the breath from me.

I gasp, nodding against his shoulder. "Oh God, just like that."

"Fuck, Parker." He fists his hand in my hair. "I'm close."

"Me too." I squeeze my eyes shut, the words fading into a moan as the pleasure knifes through me, all-consuming, demanding, every thought, sensation, memory disintegrating until there's just this, this, *this*.

I turn my head into the pillow, muffling my cries, but he pulls my head back by my hair, eliciting a sharp, delicious sting at the roots.

"Don't. I want to hear you."

A sound tears out of me—something between a scream and a sob—as I completely unravel, my fingers digging deep into his shoulders as he holds me down and finishes, one wave after another crashing into me until I'm a boneless, breathless mess. I go limp on top of him, and he lets out a shuddering breath, but his arms stay locked around me.

His hands that had been so firm and unforgiving before stroke my back softly, gently, his lips pressing against the side of my face, my neck, in just a whisper of a kiss.

When my brain finally starts functioning again, I breathe, "Oh my God."

He nods his agreement, but still, neither of us moves. Once I manage to catch my breath, I shakily untangle myself and roll onto my back. A slow, sleepy smile creeps onto his face as he looks at me, and he winds an arm behind my back.

"Come here."

I tuck against his side and prop my head on his chest as he takes my hand and gently kisses each finger one at a time.

Smiling, I trace the lines on his palm, the veins in his wrist, the winding black lines of his tattoos.

"Do these mean something?" I murmur.

He skims his fingers down the side of my ribs, sending ripples of goosebumps over my skin. "You can't laugh."

I push onto my forearms on his chest to look down at him. "Of course I won't laugh."

The barest whisper of a smile lingers on his lips as he tucks my hair behind my ear, then leaves his thumb stroking my cheek.

I pull his hand down so I can see the tattoo more clearly. It's an intricate expanse of trees, the roots reaching toward his hand, and they slowly morph into smoke as the tattoo brushes his elbow crease.

"I like it as a reminder," he says as I trail my fingers along the lines. The work is so much more detailed up close than I realized. I've never been much of a tattoo person—never wanted one myself—but this is *beautiful.*

I search his eyes. "A reminder of what?"

"That life is short. Everything ends. We're all inching toward the smoke every day, and it's easy to let it pass you by. To stop paying attention. To not care about what roots you leave behind, what beautiful things you could have appreciated while you were here." His brow furrows on the last line, the intense way his eyes are soaking me in making my skin tingle.

"And this one?" I ask, skimming my fingers down his other arm, this one less of a single cohesive image and more of a patchwork of designs. Dozens of insects and animals twisting and blending perfectly around one another.

"That one...uh...you can blame Dani for that. Lost a bet when I was eighteen—she was thirteen. She got to choose what I got. Should've seen it coming considering her phase at the time. It was my first one, actually." He points to one of the smaller designs on the inside of his wrist—a butterfly. "Decided to just keep going with the theme."

"What was the bet?"

He chuckles. "Can't even remember now."

The black lines are more faded than a lot of the others, the design simply shaded, the wings folded together. A direct contrast to the butterfly, there's a scorpion beside it on one side, a snake on the other. I smirk, imagining a younger Heath hurrying to get something more *manly* to compensate for Dani's design.

I hum, but my breath hitches as I meet his eyes again. The way his gaze is...marveling, admiring.

"You're too beautiful to be real," he whispers, his thumb dragging across my lower lip before he takes my chin in his hand and pulls my mouth back to his.

It's soft, sweet, such a stark difference to the ravenous way he'd kissed me just minutes ago. When I settle back against his side, he laces his fingers through mine and presses our hands right above his heart.

"You're staying in here tonight," he decides.

"Oh, am I?"

He tightens his hold on me. "Not up for discussion."

I smile as I drape a leg over his, nestling closer to him. "I guess. If I have to."

CHAPTER 39
PARKER

The sunlight is the first thing I see. Heath's blinds are cracked open, and a stream of it runs right into my eyes. I roll over, stretching my muscles, but the bed beside me is empty. The light in the bathroom is on, and the shower's running. Heath must already be up. I yawn and search the ground for my clothes, then remember they're downstairs by the piano.

My skin burns at the memory, and I rise from the bed on shaky legs. I find one of Heath's dress shirts and pull it on, then head downstairs, already craving coffee.

The evidence of last night is scattered all over the floor. I scoop up my clothes, finding my shorts first, then my tank top, then my robe. I pause, cocking my head. I push Heath's sweatpants aside to make sure they're not hiding under there, then look under the piano, but my underwear are nowhere to be found. But I distinctly remember him taking them off down here.

I shake my head and set the bundle of clothes on the piano stool before heading to the kitchen. The coffee maker roars to life, and I drum my fingers on the counter as I wait. The shower upstairs is still running by the time I pour myself a cup, so I meander back to the piano and sit down.

There are handprints and smudges all over the glossy surface—I'll have to remember to clean it later. Setting the coffee beside me, I push the lid up and try to remember where I left off last night. It's really just the beginning and end of the song that need work. I try a few different combinations, but nothing sticks.

"I thought I might find you down here."

Heath picks up the clothes and sets them on the piano so he can slide in next to me, his eyes lingering on his shirt on my body.

"Well," I say, turning back to the piano. "*Someone* interrupted me last time."

"Hm." He pushes the collar of his shirt aside to brush his lips across my shoulder, his warm breath ghosting along my skin and raising goosebumps in its wake. "Will you play what you have so far for me?"

I sigh and skim my fingers along the keys. "I'm struggling with the beginning." I hit a few notes, then drift into the middle section I'm happy with. I can feel him watching me as I play, and I smile a little, but then stop halfway through the song. "I just can't get that opening right."

He clears his throat and lays his hands over the keys. "What if you tried something like this?" He leans his head to the side as he plays. "Or maybe more like…" He tries another few chords.

I stare at him. "How did I not know you played?"

He shrugs and drops his arms back to his sides. "Not *well*. And it's been a while. I stopped when I was a kid."

"Didn't love it?"

"Didn't love the performing. Hated it, actually. Massive stage fright. Can't even do public speaking. I can't do crowds. That's why I find what you do so impressive. You're so *natural*. I don't know how you do it."

"The more you do it, the easier it gets. Will you play that first one for me again?"

He runs his hands over the keys, and I quickly play it back, swapping out a few notes.

He grins. "That was perfect."

I flutter my fingers in front of me like I'm grabbing something. "I need a pen and paper before I forget."

He jumps up off the bench and heads for the kitchen. He pulls a notebook and pen out of the first drawer and slides it across the counter to me, waiting silently until I've finished writing. I grin up at him as I set the pen down. He smiles back like it's a reflex, and I nod to the coffeepot behind him.

"I made coffee."

I glance at the piano as he pours himself a mug. "Have you seen my underwear? They're not with the rest of our clothes, and I can't find them anywhere."

He braces his arms on the counter so our faces are only a foot apart, and my breath hitches, a dozen moments from last night flashing through my mind. "Did you check under the piano?"

I nod.

"I'm sure they'll show up somewhere. We probably just kicked them under something last night."

"Yeah, probably," I murmur.

He runs a hand through his wet hair and sets his coffee on the counter. "What would you think about maybe going into town and doing something today? I was doing some research, and it looked like they had some cool stuff."

"Yeah, I'd like that." I nod toward the TV hanging over the fireplace. "Want to turn the news on and see what the weather will be like?"

After a brief search of the counter, he finds the remote. A news reporter flashes on screen as I venture to the coffeepot for a refill.

"You know, in all the years we've had this house, we've never really gone into town."

The music shifts behind me, and I glance at the TV in time to see the solemn face of a female newscaster as the words *breaking news* scroll across the bottom of the screen over and over again.

"Jasper Young, the alleged murderer of three people, was reported missing yesterday. Sources say he escaped from his cell before his trial and hasn't been seen since. There hasn't been any comment on why it took so long for his disappearance to be reported, but they did find his two security guards dead and locked in his cell in his place. There were signs of tampering with security footage, leading investigators to believe Young may have had help on the inside..."

The mug falls from my hands and shatters across the floor. Hot coffee splashes against my bare legs, but I barely feel it.

"Young hasn't been located, and authorities urge anyone with information to come forward..."

Heath rushes to my side, grabbing a hand towel.

"If you see this man, do not approach him. He's dangerous and likely armed..."

"Parker." Heath leans down and wipes the coffee off me, then stands up, forcing his face into my line of sight. "Parker."

I open my mouth to talk, but the words get lost.

He grabs my face with both hands. "Parker, look at me."

"I need my phone," I whisper.

"Okay. Okay. Where is it?"

"My room."

"Okay. I'll be right back." He takes off for the stairs, and I collapse against the cabinets, digging my fingers into the edges to keep me upright.

Heath returns with my phone, and I power it on with shaking hands. More than forty missed calls and messages flood the screen.

The doorbell rings. I jump, my hand tightening around the phone.

Heath runs a hand over my hair. "It's okay. Just stay here."

"Heath," I whisper, but he's already heading for the door.

If Jasper Young were here, he wouldn't ring the fucking doorbell. The logical part of my brain knows this. But it's pretty hard to hear past the screaming echoing in my head.

When Heath returns to the kitchen, two middle-aged men I don't recognize are following him.

"Faye sent over some backup security," Heath explains. "Just in case. They're going to check the surrounding area to make sure everything looks okay."

I nod, unable to speak. The two guys nod back and disappear outside as Heath fishes his phone out of his pocket.

"Shit," he mutters, his finger scrolling along the screen. Something makes him pause, and his brow furrows as he brings the phone to his ear. "Hey, Mom. Sorry, I just saw your—" The color drains from his face. He turns his back to me and paces to the front of the house.

I pull my phone back, skipping over the missed calls and finding a handful of texts from Faye, saying she and Annie are on their way, they sent more security and called the local police. Not to panic.

But panic feels like a very rational thing to do right now.

Heath steps back into the kitchen, and he opens his mouth a few times before managing to speak. "That was my mom. Apparently the yard has been full of reporters all day, and someone broke into the house. They're at the hospital."

"Oh my God," I breathe. "Are they okay? What happened?"

"I don't know. She said Dani's in surgery. She sounded pretty frantic, then a nurse cut her off saying she needed to be examined too. I don't—I don't know if—I have to—I have to get back."

"Of course. Um. Okay." I smooth my hands over my hair. "Let me get my things, and we'll go."

His expression doesn't change. I stare at him for a few seconds before it sinks in.

"You want to leave…without me."

He runs a hand down his face. "You'll have the other guys here. Faye and Annie are coming. They're sending some local police over. You have the security system. You'll be perfectly safe. And with the reporters and everything, if you come with me, you'll just—"

He stops abruptly and looks at his feet.

I fall back against the cabinets like he hit me. "I'll just make it worse."

"Parker, no, that's not what I meant."

"But that's what you were going to say." I clench my jaw to hold the tears back and nod. What hurts most of all is he's right. The reporters wouldn't be there if it weren't for me. His family wouldn't be hurt. And me showing up, they'd flock around us like moths to a flame.

But still. He wants to leave me here.

The man who tried to kill me is unaccounted for and he wants to leave me here.

"Well, you should go then. Yeah. You should go."

The look he gives me is stricken, but I don't care. "Parker…"

"Like you said." My voice shakes around the words, and I hate myself for it. "I'll be fine here."

He bites his lip and looks around the room like he's looking for something to help him. "I'm going to do a sweep of the house before I leave to make sure everything looks okay. I'll check on all the security cameras and talk to the guys outside, let them know—"

I walk past him wordlessly, heading for the stairs.

"Parker—"

"If you're going to leave, just leave, Heath," I say, my voice flat, then head into my room and lock the door behind me.

CHAPTER 40
PARKER

The sun sets, but Annie and Faye still aren't here. The police stopped by earlier to check on the house, but after finding nothing wrong, they left and told me to call if anything happened. The two new security guys whose names I don't know are downstairs.

I changed out of Heath's shirt and into some sweats as quickly as possible, feeling stupid.

I believed every word he said to me. And it's not that I don't understand or have sympathy. But he looked me in the eyes down there. He's seen what all of this has done to me. He saw how terrified I was, and he still left me here.

I trusted him. But I'd also trusted Rick and look where that got me.

If this keeps happening, maybe it's my fault. I'm the problem. Just stupid and naïve and pathetic. Throwing myself at any guy who gives me the time of day. Never doubting them as they tell me what I want to hear until they get what they want from me.

My stomach growls from neglecting it, so I venture to the kitchen. The two guards nod at me as I pass.

"We're going to do another sweep of the property," says one as I open the refrigerator. "It should only take a few minutes." I nod and watch as they head out the front. The security alarm gives a little beep as the door shuts.

My eyes land on the leftovers Heath put in the fridge, but I can't bring myself to eat them, so I swing the door shut and head for the pantry instead. There isn't much, but I manage to find a pack of ramen toward the back.

The clock ticks steadily on the wall as I wait for the water to boil. I listen for the groan of the porch as the security guys return, but it doesn't come.

Turning the porch lights on, I glance out the back windows, looking for them along the sides of the house, but I see nothing. I double-check the lock on the door, then turn the lights back off. My footsteps echo around me as I head to the front of the house to look out the window, but there's no sign of them out there either.

A chill runs down my spine, and my heart beats faster in my chest.

I shake my head at myself and walk back to the stove to add my noodles. They're fine. I'm being paranoid, which is a completely reasonable response given the situation.

Just in case, I pull one of the larger knives out of the knife block and set it beside me on the counter.

Slow footsteps creak on the front porch—a single set, not two. I freeze, my breath catching in my throat. I slide the knife off the counter, my hand trembling almost too much to hold it.

And then: a knock.

The security guys wouldn't have knocked.

I tiptoe toward the front door, careful to stay out of sight of the windows. Slowly, I bend over to peek outside.

"What the hell?" I breathe and throw the door open.

Rick stands on the other side, fist raised to knock again. His eyes go wide at the sight of me, then drop to the knife in my hand, and go even wider. "What is *that* for?"

"What are you doing here?" I demand, glancing both ways behind him and then grabbing him by the shirt and yanking him inside. "Did two guys try to stop you before you walked up?"

"Two guys? What? No."

All of the air leaves my lungs. They weren't supposed to let anyone up to the house. And there's no way they would've missed Rick's car pulling in.

"Oh my God," I breathe, a tear rolling down my cheek. "Rick, you shouldn't have come here."

"Hey." He grabs my shoulders, his expression completely stunned. "I came to apologize. For real this time—"

"Rick, we really don't have time for this right now. Do you have your phone on you?"

"I—what? Yeah. Why?"

I turn a full circle, scanning the rest of the house, and lower my voice. "Call the police. Tell them Jasper Young is here."

His eyes search mine for a split second before it *finally* clicks, and the confusion gives way to determination. He pulls the phone out, dials 911, and nods toward the stairs. "Go upstairs. Lock yourself in the bathroom."

My hand tightens around the knife, but I do as he says as he starts talking with the operator. When he sees me hesitate, he nods and mouths *go*.

I shake my head, waiting. No matter how I feel about

Rick right now, I can't have his death on my hands too. Not over this.

"Not without you."

When he hangs up the phone, he takes both of my shoulders and forces me to look at him. "Okay. We're not going to panic, right? That's not going to help."

I nod, swallowing down the tears.

"Your security guys are missing?"

Another nod.

"But you have a security system here installed? And it's activated?"

"Yes," I whisper.

"Okay." He squeezes my shoulders. "The police are on their way, and I'm right here with you. Okay? Are all the doors and windows locked?"

I blink, and a few tears squeeze themselves out. "I don't— I don't know."

"Okay, okay," he says quickly, wiping the tears from my cheeks with his thumbs. "I'm going to check upstairs. You stay right here, okay?"

"No, no, Rick." I grab his sleeve, suddenly desperate for him not to leave.

"Parker." He leans his face close to mine. "I'm going to be right back."

I force myself to nod, then shakily hand him the knife. "Take this. I'll check down here."

"Okay." He gives my shoulder one last squeeze before heading up the stairs, light on his feet.

I blow out a shaky breath, forcing myself to run through all the entrances. The front door is definitely locked. I double-checked the back door earlier. None of the windows have been opened since we got here, so they should all be locked too. The only possibility on this floor is the side door off the kitchen.

Swallowing hard, I tiptoe through the dining room and straight to the side door. The lock is latched. I exhale in relief and squint into the trees beyond, but nothing's moving out there.

"It's good to see you, Parker."

Every nerve in my body goes cold.

CHAPTER 41
HEATH

I've seen my mother afraid plenty of times. She tried to hide it from me and Dani when we were growing up, but even then, I'd seen enough of her real smiles to be able to pick out the fake ones. But even in our harder years—when we almost lost the house as I was starting middle school, or when Mom had a cancer scare right before Dani graduated high school—I've never heard her voice sound the way it did on the phone today.

It was more than the fear, the crack in her voice. Everything about it was wrong. The tone, the cadence. The desperation. Hearing it cut through me, all the way to my bones.

For a moment, that picture of Parker the night of the wedding was all I could see. But instead of Parker, it was my mom with the handprints around her throat. It was Dani with blood covering her dress.

But neither of them made it out alive like Parker had. They would end up collateral damage, just another body in the trees like her bodyguard. A footnote in the news story as the survivors' pictures took the front page.

Because the news doesn't care about people like us.

The rock in my chest expands with each mile I put between me and the lake house until it's pushing down on my lungs, my throat, my heart. I tighten my fists around the steering wheel.

With every blink, I see that look on her face when she realized I was leaving. Anger would've been better. And that certainly trickled in a few moments later. But before that, the amount of hurt that had filled her eyes...I'll never get that image out of my head.

I clear my throat and flick the AC on as high as it can go. She'll be perfectly safe with the other guards and Faye and Annie on their way. She has a whole team of people to look out for her.

Mom and Dani just have me.

My foot jerks to slam on the brakes as I blink back to the road. A sea of red taillights comes into focus, and I let out a frustrated breath through my nose. There had hardly been any traffic on the way here, but now that I need to...

A police car speeds past me in the opposite direction, its red and blue lights staining my vision.

It could be anything. It could just be—

A second surges down the road, even faster than the first, then a third, a fourth.

My heart comes to a complete stop in my chest.

No.

The cars around me are at a complete standstill, and the next exit isn't for another mile. My breaths come in hard and fast as I look around. I yank the phone out of my pocket, my hand shaking as I find the right contact.

Duncan—bless him—picks up after the first ring. "What's up, Bridgers? I thought you were—".

"I need your help. It's an emergency."

There's silence on the line for a beat, then: "What do you need?"

I empty all the air out of my lungs on an exhale, grateful but too tense to feel any relief as I look in my rearview mirror. An expanse of idling cars sits behind me now too.

"My mom and Dani, they're at the hospital. Can you and some of the guys head over, just until I can get there? Let me know if you get any updates?"

More police cars stream past, their sirens drowning out his response. My heart races faster in my chest as I take in the cars still moving on the other side of the road.

"Fuck it," I mutter, then yank my steering wheel to the side. Horns blare as I surge down the small embankment and flip around to merge.

"What the hell is going on?" Duncan demands.

"Can you do it or not?" I say through my teeth, more cars honking and swerving around me as I right myself in the fast lane and stomp on the gas.

"Of course, but—"

I hang up and toss the phone into the passenger seat. He can give me hell for that later.

Maybe I'm overreacting. I hope to God I am. And I don't care how selfish it makes me to wish it's someone else in crisis, but I do. Anyone, *anyone* but her.

I swerve in and out of the other cars, ignoring their blaring horns, and tighten my fists around the wheel. I'd only been driving for twenty or so minutes. It shouldn't take me that long to get back.

But if something has already happened, *is* happening...

I shove the thought away, not even willing to entertain it. But the one thought my brain can't stop playing on a loop is:

I left.

I left.

I left.

CHAPTER 42
PARKER

He's standing by the fireplace. I have no idea where he came from, because there is no way he was there a minute ago. I try not to let my reaction show on my face when I realize he's wearing one of the security guard's uniforms. He must have knocked him out and taken it.

God, I hope he just knocked him out.

"Quite the house here," he continues, pacing along the edge of the dining table. My eyes flick to the counter, trying to gauge my options. The knife block is too far away. If I open a drawer, he'll hear it. The water on the stove is still boiling. A wolfish grin takes over his face. "I like it. But not as much as I liked the show on the piano last night."

My heart drops into my stomach, only for my stomach to bottom out to my feet. A full-body shudder rolls through me, so visceral it's like his hands are on my skin.

He's been here the whole time. He's been here, and he's been *watching* us. Watching us talk and laugh and...

The memory is already too raw and painful to think

about after *he* left, but now it's also tainted in an entirely new way.

Feeling violated is nothing new to me. It comes with being in the public eye. Everyone feels entitled to your business, your life, no matter how personal. You become public property, a spectacle, a character. You'd think you'd get used to it over the years, but instead of building a thicker skin to it, the dehumanizing nature of it all builds and builds on itself.

But *this*?

It's not even the thought of him seeing me naked. Sex has never been something simple to me. There was only one person before Rick, and now with Heath—that's a total of three. The intimacy of it, the complete trust and openness you have to have with another person...that doesn't come easily to me. Maybe that's yet another product of living without privacy for so long.

For someone else to see me like that, with all of my walls down, someone who didn't belong there...

My throat closes up, but I clench my jaw against the heat dancing across my skin and the tears threatening to build in my chest.

Where else has he been while we were here? What else has he seen?

"A shame your boyfriend had to take off. A new one this time, isn't he? I was hoping we could've been introduced. Although, he doesn't seem that much more reliable than the last, huh?"

I can't see his hands behind the table to check if he has a weapon. Surely he must. Even if he didn't have one when he came here, he must now from the security guards.

That would mean he has a gun.

I clear my throat. The police are on their way. All I have to do is keep him talking and keep him away from me and Rick until they get here. I force my voice to stay even as I ask, "What do you want?"

"What do I want?" he muses, tilting his head to the side. He takes another step toward me, and I inch closer to the stove. "Maybe I just want to talk, Parker. I realize now I may have gone about things the wrong way last time. Jumped the gun, if you will. Let my emotions get the best of me. You see, I was so *angry*. But now that I've had time to give it some thought—and especially after you came to see me at my trial. I was touched by that, truly—I realized, if I could love Ryker Rae, maybe I could love you too. It's so hard to be betrayed by someone you love. It's hard to look past that. But that's something you and I have in common, isn't it?"

My eyes flick to the front of the house, hoping for a glimpse of police cars. But there's only darkness outside the windows. "If you want to talk, we can talk, but I don't want anyone else to get hurt."

He sighs and shakes his head. "I'm afraid I can't promise that, Parker."

My heart pounds in my chest so loud I can hardly hear anything else. I swallow hard. I need to stall, but my brain is spiraling so frantically I can't think. "I owe you an apology," I blurt.

A skeptical wall falls over his expression.

"Because you're right. I do know how bad it is when it feels like someone you loved betrayed you. And I wouldn't wish it on anyone. And if I made you feel that way, I truly am sorry. But I hope you can understand, I was just trying to protect myself. I didn't mean to hurt anyone."

He cocks his head, and his boots thud against the floor as

he takes a few steps closer. I tense, my hand twitching toward the pot.

"You're different from Ryker," he muses. "Softer."

The way he says it crawls over my skin. Like he knows a damn thing about me. A stair creaks, and I freeze, but he doesn't seem to hear it. Slowly, I glance toward the front of the house out of the corner of my eye. Rick is standing in the foyer, a baseball bat in his hands. He meets my eyes.

I snap my attention back to Jasper before he notices Rick, racking my brain for something else to distract him.

"Is there any way you can forgive me?"

The floorboards creak again. This time, Jasper's head whips around, and he spots Rick in the middle of the room.

He lets out a low growl and raises a gun.

"No!" I scream and grab the pot from the stove. The shot rings out as I throw, showering him in the boiling water. My ears are ringing from the gunshot too much to hear his screams, but his mouth opens wide and veins stand out on his neck.

But he doesn't drop the gun.

I don't think. I just move.

Grabbing the closest chair to me, I rush him and swing. It connects with his shoulder, and the gun goes flying across the room.

"You little bitch," he spits through his teeth, the skin of his face splotchy and red.

He grabs the chair and yanks it from my hands. I stumble back, looking around desperately for another weapon. Where did the gun go? I run for the kitchen, but he grabs me by the hair.

I cry out, and he tightens his hold, pulling my head back

until I'm looking at the ceiling. I swing my arms and try to stomp on his feet, but he evades my every attempt.

But then glass shatters, and he releases me.

I fall to my knees as broken glass rains down around me —a vase? Jasper Young stumbles back into the dining room table, a dazed look in his eyes.

"Come on."

I look up to see Rick as he grabs my arms, hefting me to my feet. One of his pant legs is soaked through with blood.

"Rick," I gasp.

"*Go.*" He pushes me toward the back door, but when he tries to follow, his leg gives out, and he hits the floor on his side.

I grab his arms and yank him toward the doors, my arms burning with the strain, and he still barely moves.

"Parker, just go," he rasps.

"Rick, please." The words come out like a sob. I crane my neck to see if Jasper is by the table...but he's gone. "*Rick,*" I say, my voice shaking.

We manage to get him standing again, one of his arms over my shoulders to help support his weight, and turn, taking in the rest of the room. But it's quiet. Empty.

"The gun. Where's the gun?" I whisper.

"There." He juts his chin toward the fireplace, and I hurry over, snatch it off the floor, and shove it in the waistband of my pants.

"Do you have your car keys?" I ask as I reposition his arm over my shoulder.

He nods, every muscle in his body stiff as we inch toward the back door.

I hold my breath as we step outside, my head whipping back

and forth to take in our surroundings—every corner, every shadow. But it's still out here too, no sound but the wind rustling through the trees and skating across the surface of the lake.

Rick hadn't hit him hard enough to kill him. And he wouldn't just leave. He wouldn't give up that easily.

But then where the hell is he?

My teeth chatter, and it has nothing to do with the cold. Rick tests his weight on his injured leg beside me, trying to walk on his own. I tighten my arm around his waist, shooting glances over our shoulders as we shuffle along the back of the house.

Maybe it would be better to find someplace to hide out and wait for help to get here, especially since Rick can barely move. Lock ourselves in a room. He's probably expecting us to head for the car. Hell, that's probably where *he* is. Waiting for us out front.

I hold up a hand for Rick to stop walking, then bring one finger to my lips. I point to the bushes along the side of the house, then push the gun into his hands. "Wait here," I whisper.

His hand tightens around my wrist in a bone-crushing grip. "What are you going to do?"

"I'm going to see if the coast is clear before taking you out there."

"Parker," he warns in a low voice.

"Just stay out of sight." My voice comes out a lot more confident than I feel. I wish I would have grabbed the knife or something before we left the kitchen—not that I would have been able to carry it with my both of my hands preoccupied trying to keep Rick upright. My breaths pass through my lips shallow and shaky as I head not toward the front of the house, but to the dock.

If he is waiting in the driveway, if he sees me coming around the corner, there won't be enough time to react. But there's a view from the dock that's harder to see from the front, especially with it this dark out.

The wood creaks faintly under my feet, and I wrap my arms around myself as the cold air drifting off the water raises every hair on my body. I can see Rick's hiding spot from here. He watches me with wide eyes, his back pressed against the house as he crouches low in the bushes. It's so dark you probably wouldn't even see him there if you didn't know where to look. As I near the end of the dock, my steps slow, and I crane my neck, surveying the front of the house. Still no sign of the police. Rick's car sits out front, and the porch light is on, casting a dim glow on the gravel.

He could be hiding behind the car, beneath the car, *inside* the car. Or he could be waiting on the other side of the house. Wherever he is, I can't see him from here. My body trembles as every scenario flashes through my mind, one after the other, every image more drenched in blood than the last.

I need to get back to Rick.

A flash of movement out of the corner of my eye freezes me in place, followed by the shuffling of rocks. My eyes snap back to Rick. He waves his hands, pointing at the dock, then gesturing underneath. It takes me a moment to realize what he's mouthing.

Hide.

More rocks shuffle, louder this time, getting closer.

I don't think. I just move.

As gently as I can, I ease myself off the side of the dock and into the water, then drift until I'm right below it. There's a small pocket of space, so if I lean my head back I can gasp in a breath of air. I dig my fingers into the wood of the dock, trying to anchor myself in place. Water covers my ears, muffling the sounds around me.

But what if he finds Rick first? He's in no state to defend himself.

Slowly, I brace my hands on the wood and inch closer to the house.

How much more time until the police come?

Are they even coming at all?

Maybe that's what Jasper disappeared to do. What if they were already here?

I stop that thought in its tracks, my throat tightening so much it's hard to breathe.

Something brushes my ankle, and I bite hard enough on the inside of my cheek to draw blood to hold back from screaming. *Probably just some kelp or whatever the hell is in this water.* Every muscle in my body trembles, my face, hands, and feet already going numb from the cold. I tread a little closer to the house, almost to water shallow enough for me to touch the bottom.

"It didn't have to be like this, Parker!"

I stop moving, trying to find where the voice is coming from. It's far off, echoey. Somewhere to the left.

If he's making himself known like this, does that mean he doesn't know where we are? He's trying to draw us out?

"How can you keep making the wrong choices again and again? With guy after guy? I thought you were smarter than this, Parker. I really did."

His voice is closer now, close enough that I can hear his footsteps accompanying it. He's in the grass somewhere. I peer through the slats in the wood, trying to see the shore.

"It makes me question your judgment. Your character," he

continues, his voice sounding farther away now. Is he going the other way?

Moving feels twice as difficult as usual, like my body is starting to shut down from the cold. I can't stay in this water much longer. My toes brush the ground as I drift forward.

A branch cracks, and I freeze.

Then rocks crash together somewhere up ahead, like someone is taking off at a run.

Rick.

I surge forward, coming out from beneath the dock and looking around wildly. Jasper is circling the back of the house, headed straight for Rick—or at least, where I'd left him. I can't see him in the bushes anymore.

Oh God, what if he passed out? I should've tried to bind the wound or something. He was losing so much blood...

"Leave him alone!" I scream.

Jasper doesn't even flinch at the sound of my voice. He doesn't turn.

Like he'd known where I was all along.

I scramble onto the dock, then break off into a run as soon as I get my feet under myself. My body protests every step, my muscles trying to thaw. Jasper disappears around the corner of the house, past where Rick had been hiding.

I run faster, then blink at the empty spot where Rick used to be. He must have moved while I was in the water. He went for the car, maybe?

There's no way he left me here. He wouldn't just...he wouldn't just leave...

But when I hit the side of the house, his car is still in the driveway—dark, untouched. I pivot and head for the back door. Maybe he went to hide inside?

"Rick," I hiss as I step inside, but he's not here either.

He's not dead. He's not dead. He's not dead. He has to be around here somewhere.

I gasp as a man steps around the corner—not Rick, but not Jasper Young either.

The new driver Annie and Faye hired. Did he drive them? Are they *here*?

Between the shadows cast over his eyes and the beard that monopolizes the rest of his face, I can't read his expression at all. Has he seen Jasper Young? The bodyguards' bodies? Does he have any idea what he just walked into?

"Oh thank God," I breathe, taking a step toward him. "Have you seen Rick? Are Faye and Annie here? We have to get out of here. He's..." I trail off as the driver paces closer to me, revealing the rest of his face. His eyes are narrowed, watching me like a predator watches its prey, and he cocks his head.

Every hair on my body stands at attention, my intuition screaming at me to *run*.

"Andrew Michelson" is all he says.

Is that his name?

"Right," I say, hoping my impatience doesn't come through. It's not really the most important detail right now. "We—"

"You don't even know who that is, do you?"

My mouth opens and closes, my brain forgetting how to formulate words.

He scoffs at my hesitation, turns and paces to the front door, then whips around and paces back just as fast. "You don't even care, do you?" His voice is so loud it makes me flinch. "You don't even care what damages *your* actions have caused."

I blink, my breaths shortening as I risk a step back.

"My brother *died* because of you, and you don't even know his fucking name."

His brother? I—

His brother must have been one of Jasper Young's other victims that night—the store clerk or the security guard.

Oh God.

It was him.

The copycat. The note, the explosion.

Of course he'd known everywhere I'd be, what time. He was the one driving the fucking car.

The fact that he's still blaming me when the actual person who killed his brother is *right here* would probably make me laugh if I didn't feel like vomiting.

"I wouldn't worry too much. He went pretty fast."

I gasp and stumble into the kitchen as Jasper Young steps through the back door.

A gunshot cuts through the room, and I duck instinctively behind the counter, my arms covering my head. I don't even know where the shot was aimed, who has the gun.

My eyes lock on a crumpled figure across the room. His body is limp beneath the dining room table, his blood soaking through the rug.

Rick.

No. *No.* He can't be dead. He can't be—

A door slams somewhere, then the kitchen falls silent. I search the room as best I can from this vantage point, but I can't see anyone else. I cover my mouth with my hand, trying to quiet my panting breaths.

Rick's head twitches.

Alive. Oh God, he's alive.

I crawl toward him without thinking, but as soon as I make it out of the kitchen, a hand fists in the back of my hair from behind. I cry out as they tackle me to the ground, and my head smacks against the hardwood. The hand in my hair never lets go, and it yanks me hard enough to throw me onto my back. Jasper straddles my hips and squeezes both of his hands around my throat.

My hands fumble at my sides, but there's nothing to grab.

He grins, and blood drips down his lips as he tightens his hold.

I'm not weak. I'm not helpless.

I claw at his hands, drawing blood with my fingernails, but his grip doesn't loosen. The edges of my vision blur, and I start to beat at his face with my fists. With every hit, I can feel the strength leaving me. The sounds around me ebb away, like I'm underwater.

His eyes stare back at me, triumphant.

And after all of this, after everything, *this* is how it ends?

It would mean all the precautions, all the sacrifices—Elijah dying—were for nothing.

It was all always going to come back here.

It was all for nothing.

My fingers loosen around his hands, then fall to the floor beside me. My legs stop kicking. When I close my eyes, I wonder what I'll see. Maybe Elijah will be there. Maybe he's been waiting for me all along. I cling to the small amount of comfort the thought gives me.

Blood erupts around me. The pressure leaves my throat, and then the full weight of Jasper Young slumps on top of me. I gasp for air and writhe under him, shoving and pushing until his body rolls to the side. His blood soaks into my clothes, drips down my face.

As my vision starts to clear, I see Rick lying on his side behind the table, a gun in his hands, his face white as a sheet.

He gives me a small smile, then drops the gun, and his body goes slack against the floor.

"No," I breathe, crawling to him. Blood smears beneath me on the ground. "Rick."

His eyes are closed when I reach him, and I shake his shoulders. "*Rick.*" I lean down, pressing my fingers to his throat and hovering my ear over his mouth. He has a pulse, and he's breathing.

But blood is seeping out of his leg. I yank my sweatshirt off and use the arms to tie it around his leg, right above the bullet wound, but it's soaking wet and basically useless. I press down hard to try to stop the bleeding.

"Rick, please wake up," I gasp, tears streaming down my face.

His eyes flutter open, just the smallest amount. He reaches up to touch my face, his hand covered in blood.

"I'm sorry," he whispers.

I grab his hand, holding it there. "I know. The police are on their way. Just hold on for a little bit longer, okay?"

"Parker," he whispers, then his head slumps against the floor.

"Rick? Rick?" I grab his chin between my fingers, forcing him to look at me. I lean down again, but he's not breathing this time.

Why is it taking so long for the police to get here?

I climb on top of him, positioning my hands over his chest. It's been years since I took that CPR class, but I don't know what else to do.

"You're not allowed to die," I grit out as I pump my hands against his chest, then lean down to blow into his mouth. Push down at least two inches. Two beats per second. One, two. One, two. One, two. "You're not allowed to die. You're not allowed to die. You're not allowed to die."

"How many people have to die around you? Why do you get to live and they all die?"

My hands slow on Rick's chest as the chauffeur steps through the front door. His pant leg is soaked through with blood, but he limps forward, a gun in his hand. But it's pointed at the floor, not me.

"You don't have to do this," I choke out. "No one else has to die." I glance from the gun to Rick's still face, then keep pumping his chest. If he's going to shoot me, I won't be able to get up in time to stop him anyway. And if this is the way I go—trying to save someone else's life—it's better than the alternative. "I never wanted any of this to happen," I whisper. "I never wanted any of this."

A shot rings out, and I freeze, my eyes squeezed shut and shoulders braced for the pain.

But it never comes.

A body thumps to the floor in the doorway, and red and blue lights fall over us through the front window, but I don't stop. The room blurs around me, my focus on Rick's face, the blood smeared from his lips to his collarbone. Muffled voices echo around me, and the ground shakes with footsteps. But I keep pumping out the same rhythm and trying to force air into his lungs.

"You're not allowed to die. You're not allowed to die. You're not allowed to die."

Hands circle my waist and start to pull me away.

"No!" I shriek, and it comes out more animal than human. I thrash, but the hands tighten their hold and easily lift me from Rick's body. Two paramedics kneel on either side of Rick, and I stop fighting.

They're here. They're going to help him. He's going to be okay now.

"Parker, Parker."

The voices slowly start to sharpen around me, and I turn. Faye and Annie are standing behind me, the color drained from their faces as they take in the room, then the state I'm in. I look down at myself, dripping wet and covered in blood.

The person standing beside me, the one who pulled me off Rick, comes into focus last.

Heath.

Blood runs down the front of his shirt. He's talking. His lips are moving. He reaches for me, but I lurch back.

"Don't touch me."

He's looking at the blood, they all are.

"I'm fine," I snap. "None of it's mine." I look back at Rick, then Jasper Young's body, then the driver's, and the pools of blood scattered everywhere in between.

How many people have to die around you?

Why do you get to live and they all die?

I can't stay in here for another minute. "None of it's ever mine," I add quietly, then turn and head for the door.

I breathe out a sigh as I hit the fresh air, but the relief is short-lived. I collapse onto the porch step, watching as the lights from the police cars stain the yard red and blue. When I look down at my shaking hands, they're covered in blood. But no matter how much I wipe them on my pants, it doesn't come off. So I do the only thing I can do: let my head fall against my chest and cry.

AN EXCERPT FROM PARKER'S JOURNAL

I'm so afraid
of being truly alone

the feeling has followed me
through the years
and crowded rooms

but it's a shadow
of the real thing

the opening act

and when they're gone

when they're buried
and mourned
and spoken about
in past tense

what will that shadow become?

I'm scared of trying to live through this grief
without you

CHAPTER 43
PARKER

I think a paramedic is the first to approach me. He doesn't say much, and when I don't respond to his questions, he wraps a silver blanket around my shoulders, then retreats into the house. I'll have to pull it together and talk to them eventually. Probably give them a statement. But truthfully, I have no idea how he got into the house. How long he's been here. If the security cameras caught any of what happened. And the more I think about it, the more my skin crawls. The more I feel like I'm going to throw up.

He's been here the whole time. Watching.

And the driver...he's been around all this time, so why wait until now? If he wanted to ensure I died, he had a million opportunities to do it. Had he been waiting, watching, trying to decide if I deserved it?

If he showed up tonight, I must not have passed whatever test he'd come up with.

They take Rick out on a gurney and put him in an ambulance. But he's not covered in a sheet, and they aren't too

KATIE WISMER

frantic or hurried, so that must be a good sign. The police linger after they take him away, poking around inside and probably dealing with the bodies. Maybe they're searching the property for the missing security guards.

I scrub my face with my hands and pull the blanket tighter around myself as the porch groans under someone's weight. They sink onto the step beside me, and I don't have to look up to know it's Heath.

"Parker." His voice cracks around my name, and a wave of exhaustion crashes into me.

"Why are you here?" I ask, my voice coming out hollow.

"Parker." He shifts his body toward me, but I don't look at him. "I realized what a bad call I made after I left and turned around, but they had the road blocked off and I couldn't get through. Parker, I—" He blows out a shaky breath, his voice dropping to barely more than a whisper. "You have to understand, my dad's been gone as long as I can remember. It's always just been me, my mom, and my sister. I've always been the only person to look out for them. So when I thought they were..." I see him wrap his arms around his knees and hang his head out of the corner of my eye. "I'm sorry it took me too long to realize you needed me too. I know it doesn't make it right, but I tried to fix it. I tried to get back."

"Your sister?"

He swallows and doesn't respond at first. "I called and had some friends go stay with them until I could get there."

I press my lips together and nod.

"Parker, you have to understand, I *never* would've left if I hadn't thought you were safe—"

"Please just stop talking." I press the heels of my hands into my eyes, and see Jasper Young crouched over me, his

342

hands around my throat. Then I see Heath after he pulled me off Rick. The blood all over him—he must have been the one to shoot the driver. He saved my life.

And yet, it's still not enough.

The pulsing ache in my throat returns.

"Please look at me," he whispers. "You have every right to be mad—"

"I'm not mad." I push to my feet, and he stands. Sighing, I force my eyes away from the house to look at him. His entire face is pinched together, stricken. I shake my head and wrap the blanket tighter around myself. "I understand why you did it. And I don't have any right to be mad that you were protecting your family, right? I could never expect you to choose me over them."

"No, I—"

"But understanding why you did it doesn't change how it felt, Heath. And it *hurt*. You looked me in the eyes and you saw how terrified I was, and you left me here."

He reaches for me, but I pull away and take a step back, shaking my head. Tears roll down his cheeks, and I clench my jaw so I don't cry too.

"So now all I see when I look at you," I say through my teeth, "is another person I can't trust to be there if I need it. All I see is someone who left."

"Parker—"

"And you know what? Maybe it's not fair. Maybe it's too much to ask, but I deserve more than that. I deserve, just for once, to have someone choose me over everything else."

He opens his mouth. Closes it again.

"So you? You can go home, Heath. You already got what you came here for, right? You got the money. You got in my bed. And now you can go."

His face falls, and he lets out a harsh breath. "Parker—"

The front door creaks open as a man in a police uniform steps out. "Are you ready to answer a few questions, ma'am?"

I meet Heath's eyes one last time, then step around him. "Yes. I am."

CHAPTER 44
PARKER

"Please stop crying," I murmur, but the words come out like a croak. The doctors said shock or adrenaline can keep you from feeling the full extent of your injuries in the moment, which is probably why the pain didn't register until midway through answering the police's questions.

But with all things considered, a concussion, a bruised windpipe, and some burst blood vessels in my eyes, I feel like I got off easy.

"I'm sorry, I'm sorry." Annie sniffles and excuses herself into the hall. To be fair, the angry red splotches around my eyes *are* pretty scary to look at. I'm sure the bruises circling my neck aren't much better.

But not any worse than after the wedding had been.

"I'm going to go check on her," Faye says quietly, leaving me with Mom, Dad, and Nick.

Some security guys I don't know are standing outside my door. And it takes me a moment to realize I'm looking for a face I won't find.

KATIE WISMER

"I'm really gunning for that record list with hospital visits," I say.

No one laughs.

Mom takes the seat beside my bed and smooths her hand over my hair. Dad clears his throat and turns away, probably trying to keep me from seeing the tears in his eyes.

"Have they given you any updates?" I ask.

Dad crosses his arms over his chest as he faces us again. "Both were declared dead at the scene. They found some of *his* belongings in the cellar, so they think he was there for at least a few days. The security company is going over the footage and any alerts they might have missed in the system."

I swallow hard, trying to keep my expression neutral, and nod. This should be good news. Gone. They're both gone and can't hurt me anymore.

But no part of me feels like celebrating.

"And Rick?" I ask.

"He's stable." Mom pets my hair, her other hand finding mine in the sheets. "They think he'll make a full recovery. Said you may have saved his life."

"That's good," I whisper and nod a few too many times. "That's good."

"Oh, sweetheart." Mom gently wraps me in her arms, careful of all my obvious cuts and bruises.

"I said *get out* of my way. If you want to carry me out of here, then fine. But I am getting in there first."

My head snaps up, for a second convinced I'm hearing things.

But no, that is most definitely Erica standing in the hall, waving her finger in the faces of the security guards. She's in matching silk pajamas, bunny slippers, and has her hair in rollers. I guess it is close to four in the morning now.

"Let her through," I rasp.

The men step aside, and she rushes into the room, tears already streaming down her cheeks by the time she reaches my side.

"We'll give you two some space," Mom murmurs as the rest of them step out.

"Rica?" I whisper.

"I'm so sorry." She sobs as she pulls me into a hug, hard enough that it hurts, but I don't care. "I'm so sorry, Parker. I'm so sorry. I'm so sorry."

"Shh." I rub her back. "It's okay."

"No, it's not." She sniffles and pulls back, her eyes widening as she takes in all the injuries. "I've been so selfish and stupid. You've been going through all of this, and I haven't been here for you at all." She meets my eyes again. "You're my best friend."

The tears break free and run down my cheeks, the ache that had been sitting squarely in my chest since everything that went down at the wedding finally releasing. "I've missed you so much."

She holds out her hands like she wants to hug me again, but then takes in my bruises and opts to pull up a chair instead. "Are you okay? How are you feeling? Are you in pain?"

"I'm okay." I force a smile and squeeze her hand.

Her eyes dart to the hall at the security guys standing there, then back to me. "And that psycho? Did they—is he?"

I nod. "He's dead."

She squeezes my hand tighter. "Tell me you at least got in a few good hits first."

I let out a startled laugh and lean my head against her shoulder. "Yeah. Yeah, I did."

CHAPTER 45
ḤEATH

"The watching me sleep thing is getting creepy, Cliff."

"And constantly worrying about you is getting old, so I guess we're both out of luck."

Dani squints an eye open and tucks herself deeper into the blankets. She moved out of Mom's house a few years before the accident, taking all her recent stuff with her, so the bed is back to the green and pink comforter she had when we were kids. It's dizzying, seeing her among her old belongings but fully grown now.

Shimmying a pill from the orange bottle, I sit beside her and drop it into her waiting palm, then hand her a bottle of water.

"How are you feeling?"

She winces as she swallows, then takes a deep breath through her nose.

She got lucky.

That's what the doctors said.

The chaos had started with the paparazzi, but after

pictures of them swarming the house ended up on social media, it caught on like wildfire. Then dozens—maybe even hundreds—of overzealous Ryker Rae fans were added to the mix, thinking Parker was in the house.

Things got out of hand.

That's what the news stations said.

As if a dented car roof from people standing on it, Mom's entire garden being uprooted from people trampling it, and a broken window in the back of the house was just a tiny accident.

Dani was in the room when the window shattered, barely able to move with her casts. She'd fallen in surprise, landing on her ribs that were already fractured in the accident, puncturing her lung.

She was already out of surgery and stable by the time I made it to the hospital.

I wasn't there in time to help her.

And I wasn't there in time for Parker either.

So then what the hell had I been doing? Sitting in my goddamn car, not helping anyone at all.

Sure, I'd taken the driver out as he stood over Parker with a gun, but she looked like she'd been through hell and back already by that point, her clothes soaking wet and covered in blood, her skin cut and bruised from getting strangled.

If her ex hadn't shown up—

I inhale a sharp breath. I can't let myself go there.

He was there for her, and I wasn't.

"You should call her."

I blink, Dani's voice snapping me back to the room. Clearing my throat, I take the water bottle from her and set it on the nightstand.

"Heath…"

"She blocked my number. She doesn't want to hear from me."

Dani scoffs. "So that's it? You call once and give up?"

"Of course not." I wince as my voice comes out like a growl, then push to my feet. "They already moved her out of the apartment. I tried her parents; they blocked my calls. I tried her manager. Her publicist. Every goddamn person I could think of, and no one will tell me where she is. No one will answer my calls at all anymore." I pace to the end of the room and run a hand through my hair, pulling at the roots. "You didn't see her face, Dani."

"So try harder."

I let out an incredulous laugh. "What else would you have me do?"

She shrugs, her eyebrows sky-high, not at all sympathetic. "You fucked up. So yeah, she's upset. She's hurt. She's mad. And you need to man up and fix it. You thought it was going to be easy? If this girl means to you what I *know* she does, then you need to figure it the fuck out. Otherwise, you're no better than that ex who sold her to the press. You're no better than John." Her voice wavers around his name, but her glare doesn't. "You're no better than Dad."

"That's not fair. It's not the same."

"Isn't it?"

I grind the heels of my hands into my eyes.

"I've never seen you like this about a girl. And now you're just going to let her get away?" Dani demands. "She's not worth trying harder for?"

"Of course she is, but I—"

You looked me in the eyes and you saw how terrified I was, and you left me here.

So now all I see when I look at you is another person I can't trust to be there if I need it. All I see is someone who left.

I deserve more than that. I deserve, just for once, to have someone choose me over everything else.

And she does. She deserves that and so much more.

More than me.

I left.

I left.

I left.

It'll feel like ripping my own heart out of my chest, but maybe the right thing to do is to let her go. Maybe it's selfish to keep trying if there's someone better out there for her.

"Shut the fuck up."

A pillow strikes me square in the side of the face, and I fall back a step. Dani glares at me from the bed, steam practically spilling out of her ears.

"I didn't say anything!"

She points a finger at me. "I can see what you're thinking, and it's bullshit and we both know it. You're a lot of things, Cliff, but I never thought you were a coward. You know, I'm sure that's what Dad told himself, right? That we'd be better off without him."

I flinch. Because she's right. That's probably exactly what he did.

It's only been a week without her, but it feels like years. Years without her laugh, her smile, her awful dance moves when she lets herself get lost in the music, the little sounds she makes when she's trying to build up the courage to do something. Without the way she sticks her tongue out to concentrate when we're playing cards, the peace in her face as she pores over the piano, how her hand fits so perfectly in mine, the weight of her head on my chest as she fell asleep, her smile as she threw her head back, the wind in her hair as she sped down the road like a maniac.

I grit my teeth, my eyes burning.

Like the truly pathetic idiot I've become, I've started listening to her music just to hear her voice again. I've been checking those awful tabloid sites to see if there's been any sign of her, any update on how she's doing.

But there's been nothing. Just complete and total radio silence.

"I can't lose her, Dani," I whisper.

She meets my eyes, the look on her face not unkind, but showing no pity. "Then don't."

AN EXCERPT FROM PARKER'S JOURNAL

I'm unsure how to be

and if no one's listening
maybe that's not a reason
for discouragement

but rather

a permission slip
to loosen the reins
unfilter the gaze

to stand in this space

without worrying about
what it looks like
from the outside

CHAPTER 46
PARKER
THREE MONTHS LATER

"Good, Parker. Now strike hard!"

I hook my foot around my partner's knees, sweeping his legs out from under him while jabbing my shoulder into his chest. He hits the ground on his back, the air making an audible whoosh as it leaves his lungs. He lies there for a second, staring at the ceiling, then tries to roll over, though the thick layer of padding surrounding his body gets in the way and he ends up looking like a turtle stuck on its shell. I reach down to help him up, and he fist bumps me.

"Nicely done."

We step off the mat so the next pair can spar, both breathless and sweaty. I help him with the Velcro on the back of his pads as our instructor claps for the next two to begin.

"You didn't let me win, right?" I ask as his gear falls to the floor.

Jeremy smirks and reaches for his water bottle on the ground. "As much as my pride would like to say yes, that was all you. I didn't stand a chance."

I glance at my watch and curse under my breath. "I've gotta get going. My class is all the way across campus."

He grabs my backpack from the ground and hands it to me. "A couple of us are gonna hit the weight room at eight tonight. You in?"

I grin, sliding the pack over my shoulders. "Definitely. Meet you guys there?"

I can hear the echoes of the self-defense class as I slip out of the workout studio and hunch my shoulders against the icy rush of air. I'm still getting used to Utah's weather. Although New York got *cold* this time of year, I always knew what to expect. Here, it's different every day.

I wind my sweaty hair into a ponytail as I walk, the campus mostly empty since classes won't let out for another few minutes. Usually, I wouldn't have to leave early, but our seminar is in one of the bigger lecture halls clear across campus today after a water leak in our room.

A few girls skip down from a dormitory on my right and nod as they pass, heading for the mess hall behind me. The movement is entirely casual and friendly, no recognition in their eyes or double takes when they see me.

There were some of those when I first got here, but the spectacle has worn off much faster than I could have hoped for.

The sun glints off the mountains in the distance, and I smile. There are times when I miss the city, when I miss being close to family. Sometimes I even miss parts I'd hated so much from my old life. But every time I see those mountains, this unexplainable sense of calm washes over me, and I know I'm exactly where I'm supposed to be.

I hum under my breath the melody I've been working on for the past few weeks. It's easier now, somehow, without the silent pressure hanging over me—the constant need to be working on the next album, the label execs always wanting updates.

This one might very well never end up on an album.

It might never be heard by anyone but me.

I wrestle my phone from my backpack and punch the few lines I've been mulling over into the notes app.

I slap Band-Aids over
missing limbs
and smile
say
I'll grow from this

the leaves have browned
the snow did fall

we do not speak
it's ~~unbearable~~
survivable

The lecture hall is quiet when I slip inside, just a few students scattered among the seats. I find a spot in the middle row and pull out a notebook and pen.

There's a piano onstage along with the podium—maybe Dr. Gaillot is going to play for us. This class is on the history of classical music, but apparently Dr. Gaillot was a big deal back in her day. Not that she told us that. A freshman internet-stalked her and came into class with an article about her. We've been begging her to play for us ever since.

"Hey, Parker." Andrea, one of the only seniors in the class, slides into the seat on my right. At first, I'd thought being a twenty-five-year-old freshman would earn me weird looks, that my time for going to college had passed and I wouldn't get the same experience out of it now. But no one here seems to care. Andrea started school a few years after high school too, so she's nearly twenty-four. "Did you hear about that slam poetry reading this weekend? They're having an open mic night."

I flip to a blank page in my notebook and quirk an eyebrow. "You going?"

"Only if I can find someone to go with me. Everyone else said it sounded lame."

I smirk. "So this is where I come in."

She bats her unfairly long eyelashes at me. "I will supply you with as many drinks as you want."

I laugh. "Sold."

She pumps her fist in the air. Other students trickle in and fill the space around us until every seat is taken. Since this is a prerequisite for a few different majors, it's my biggest class. Big enough that I don't recognize half the faces in here.

The chatter in the room dies down as Dr. Gaillot steps onstage, her clogs making hollow thumps against the wood. She shuffles in, her back perpetually bent with age, her gray hair always styled in a bun. On the first day, she reminded me of a sweet old grandmother.

That image was quickly squashed.

Today, however, she seems to be in a good mood. Her wrinkled lips are pressed in a smile that looks almost secretive, like she has something up the sleeves of her bright red cardigan.

She scans the room, then pauses on me. I freeze under the

scrutiny, but her smile deepens the lines of her face, and she lays her hands on the podium.

"We have a guest today," she says.

I furrow my brow. She can't be talking about me. I know there are a million faces in this room, and she probably doesn't know half our names, but based on how many times she's scolded me in her office over my not-so-impressive essay skills, she must at least remember my face.

Her gaze drifts to the red curtains surrounding the stage, and a figure steps out.

A jolt of electricity surges through my body. I can't see his face, but I don't need to. Heath's head is down, his hair longer and shaggier than the last time I saw it—long enough that he has the top half pulled back in a bun. He's in a black suit, and he blows the air out of his cheeks as he lifts his head and takes in the crowd in front of him. His eyes widen like a deer caught in headlights, and a blush creeps up the side of his neck.

The entire room feels off-kilter. It's been months since I've seen him. Not since that night at the lake house. And after I blocked his calls and packed up my life to come here, I decided cutting him out with the rest of that life was for the best. It was the only way I'd be able to leave it behind completely.

As much as I've been trying to convince myself I haven't been thinking about him, wondering about him, I have. I haven't let myself act on it, thinking it would fade with time. That he would fade. But the memories are as raw and fresh as they were three months ago. Like him showing up here burned away whatever progress I'd made.

I wait for his gaze to find me, but it doesn't. He turns to the piano, slides onto the bench, and pushes up the lid.

Oh my God. Is he going to play?

He clears his throat and hovers his fingers over the keys. Voices buzz as people lean their heads together, whispering. Probably trying to figure out who he is. If he's someone important.

The first note hits my chest like a bullet, then he falls into the song effortlessly, like he's the one who wrote it. And in a way, he is.

It's the song I'd been trying to write but abandoned after everything happened. I couldn't bear to play it anymore. It was too intertwined with those months of my life, with *him*.

His fingers fill in the gaps I left behind, finding the perfect notes I could never place. Tears prick the corners of my eyes, but I clench my jaw, forcing them down.

I shove my notebook in my bag. I can't stay here. I can't listen to this.

But then he opens his mouth and starts to sing.

she was a
freefall
uncalled
for
wakeup call

I cover my mouth with my hand as a few nervous giggles rise from the crowd. His voice breaks and wavers around the words, so fundamentally *bad*, but he pushes on.

she had the
right mind
right timing
but I know

359

that she won't
pick up
look up
when I call

I grab my bag from the floor and throw it over my shoulder. Heads turn in my direction, but I shuffle through the aisle, pointedly not looking at the stage, and head for the exit. Blood roars in my ears as I shove the doors open and step outside, gasping in the fresh air. My hands are trembling, my heart pounding in my chest.

How did he even find me here? And why would Dr. Gaillot agree to this?

"Parker."

His voice breaks through the haze in my mind, violently pulling my surroundings into focus. But I don't stop. I walk faster.

"Parker." I can hear him jogging to catch up with me, but I tighten my grip on my backpack straps and keep my gaze trained straight ahead.

I feel him before I see him, his presence falling over me like a second skin. He comes in front of me, forcing me to stop.

He looks...exhausted. Dark circles line his eyes, his hair overgrown and disheveled. Stubble marks his jaw. When it becomes clear I'm not going to say anything, he clears his throat.

"I would've been here sooner if I'd known where to find you. Faye and Annie refused to tell me. I drove up to your parents' place, and they wouldn't tell me either."

I don't let my surprise show on my face. No one said anything to me about this.

I cross my arms over my chest. "Then how did you?"

He cracks a small smile. "Your brother caved."

"Fucking Nick." Since when did he become a goddamn romantic anyway? "What are you doing here?"

"I've missed you." His words are barely audible, but I feel the weight of them in my bones. Or maybe that's the resonance of my own feelings trying to voice their agreement after all these months of suppressing them. Because of course I've missed him. Leaving hadn't been easy. But it was what needed to be done, cutting ties with him included.

"I've missed you every single day," he continues. "And I know I don't deserve your forgiveness, but I'm asking for it."

I shake my head and turn to the side, facing the mountains as I draw in a deep breath.

I've gone over that night a million times, trying to put myself in his shoes. No matter how much I can understand where he was coming from, it doesn't make it hurt any less.

No amount of missing him makes it hurt any less either.

"You should go home, Heath."

He steps into my line of sight, forcing me to look at him. "I *am* home."

His eyes are pleading, earnest, but instead of softening my resolve, it reignites that fire in my chest. As if it's that simple. As if it's that easy. A quick "sorry" and it's like it never happened.

"What do you want me to say, Heath? How did you expect me to react to you showing up here?"

"Parker, I know—"

"No, you don't. You don't know." I take a step back from him, then another. "This wasn't a fight. This wasn't a misunderstanding. And some grand romantic gesture isn't going to be enough." I throw my hands up, my voice cracking on the last word. Quieter, I add, "I want it to be, but it's not, Heath."

He shoves his hands into his pockets. "I know. And I'm not asking for your forgiveness today, Parker. I—" He winces, his face pinching together like he's debating his next words. "I have an apartment in town and a construction gig for the next few months. So I'm not...I'm not going anywhere. We can be friends, if that's what you need. Or you can hate me, and I'll keep making a fool of myself trying to win you back, but my point is, if you're happy here, if this is where you want to be, then this is where I need to be too. I'm prepared to wait as long as it takes for you to trust me again —hell, I'm prepared to beg, Parker. I will get down on my knees right now."

He bends like he's actually going to do it, and I sigh, glancing at the people who've stopped on the surrounding paths to gawk at us, and grab his sleeve. "Stop, stop."

But the intensity of his face doesn't falter. "I mean it, Parker."

The rest of his words sink in. *Apartment. In town for months.* "I—what about New York? What about Dani, your mom?"

He nods, acknowledging this, and rubs a hand down his face. "They'll be okay. I'll always do everything I can to help them, but you were right. I should've let myself have my own life too. I just wish it didn't take losing you to figure it out. And I'm—" He breaks off, a small smile rising on his lips. "All I'm asking for is a trial period. Let me prove to you that I'm the man for the job. And if you still hate me after that, I'll be on my way."

A small, startled laugh breaks out of my chest. That day in the elevator feels more like a dream than a memory. I can't even imagine what my life would've looked like if I hadn't agreed. If I hadn't given him a second chance.

The smile eases from his face, and his eyebrows draw together. "I made the wrong call. I know that. But you have to understand, I've never had anyone in my life I cared about as much as my family, until now. Never given myself the chance to. I didn't even know that I could. But I can't stand the idea of you hurt or unhappy. And I can't stand the idea of you not being in my life. Parker...I'm—I'm in love with you." His hand brushes my arm, and I take a step away.

"Don't." I throw my hands up, needing a barrier between us, not at all moved by his words. Not at all losing my resolve. Not breaking. Not—not—

I'm in love with you.

I haven't let myself think anything close to those words in our months apart. But as soon as he says them, they land home in my chest.

Because that's it. I didn't want to acknowledge it, but that's exactly why this hurts so much.

"It's not that I don't want to forgive you, Heath," I whisper. "But I don't know how to."

"I know. But I swear I will spend the rest of my life trying to make it up to you."

I swipe at my face with the back of my hand, annoyed at the tears determined to break free right now. Heath cups my other cheek before I have the chance, wiping the tear away with his thumb. I let my eyes fall shut at the warmth of his hand, and he slowly steps closer, then pulls me against his chest. I don't hug him back, but I don't move away.

Because I don't know what the right answer is. Is it dumb to forgive people and give them the opportunity to hurt you again, or is it worse to never let anyone in at all? To be too afraid to trust anyone? To be safe and secure but always alone?

All I know is I *have* been happier here. For the first time in a long time, life has started to make sense again. I've looked forward to getting out of bed, to seeing where this path takes me instead of feeling trapped at a dead end. Curious about how things will work out instead of terrified of not knowing where I'll end up.

But I've also spent nights curled in my bed, alone, remembering his hand in mine. The sound of his laugh. The understanding in his eyes. How nothing has ever felt more aligned in my life than kissing him.

If it had been Nick—or Mom or Dad or Erica—would I have made the same call? If they'd had no one else to look out for them but me, if I felt responsible for them, if I'd honestly thought he'd be safe if I left him behind...

I take a step out of his arms, needing space, needing air. If he's touching me, I can't think. I can't breathe.

I take another step back, and he searches my face, and his expression—so open and pleading and broken—cracks the last of the resolve in my chest.

"You can have two weeks," I whisper.

He sucks in a sharp breath, and after a moment, he stands up straighter, folds his arms in front of his body, and gives me a single professional nod. "Two weeks."

We hold each other's eyes, a million unspoken words passing between us. He wets his lips, and I know if we stand here for much longer, he's going to try to kiss me. And as much as my body is begging for my mind to shut up and let him, I break the eye contact and murmur, "That song was really bad."

A deep laugh rumbles in his chest, and it shatters the

layer of tension between us. He shakes his head. "God, I know. Is it sad that was the best I could do?"

"The music was good."

"Of course it was. You wrote it." He eases something out of the inside pocket of his suit, a stack of papers bound with twine, and twists it around in his hands. "If you thought the lyrics were bad..."

He holds the papers out to me.

"What's this?"

He rubs a hand along the back of his neck. "When I couldn't get any calls through to you, I...I started writing letters. But I didn't have anywhere to send them. So."

I run my thumb over the folded edges of the papers and press my lips together, fighting a smile. "You wrote me love letters?"

"Is that cheesy?"

The smile breaks through. "I guess I'll know once I read them."

He smirks as he pulls me against his side, wrapping an arm over my shoulders. The embrace is casual, *friendly*. The kind with zero implications, zero expectations. And it finally lets the rest of my muscles relax. "God, just please don't read them in front of me. And maybe burn them when you're done. *So.* You wanna show me around?"

I let myself lean into him, my eyes momentarily falling shut at his warmth, his scent. "Only if you can manage not to embarrass me again."

"I'll have you know, after you left, they asked for an encore."

"We might need to teach you the difference between people laughing with you and people laughing at you."

"They can laugh all they want as long as it worked."

I arch an eyebrow as I peer up at him. "You're still on probation."

He shrugs as we start down the path, the sun setting behind the mountains in front of us. "Fine by me. Worked out pretty well last time."

AN EXCERPT FROM PARKER'S JOURNAL

don't you realize
holding on
is the hardest part?
once you let go
and let yourself fall
the rest is just
gravity

EPILOGUE
PARKER – TWO MONTHS LATER

A knock pounds against the door, barely audible over the music vibrating the room. "You're on in five!"

I blow out a breath, and when that's not calming enough, I shake my hands out at my sides and jump up and down a few times. But the energy thrumming through me, coating my skin, and raising every hair on my body, it's not nerves. And it's not dread.

Just familiar, warm excitement.

Applause fills the small space as the first band wraps up, and I cast one last glance in the bathroom mirror. The makeup is dewy, glowy, with deep brown lipstick and feathery fake lashes.

But my hair is blond, straight, and mine.

"You ready, superstar?"

Heath stands behind me, rolling up the sleeves of his white button-down. I think that's the third time I've watched him redo them.

"It's not too late to back out," I say.

He straightens and runs a hand through his hair. "Why would I do that?"

"So you're not nervous?"

He flashes a fake, pained smile as he props the door open. "Nah."

The crowd quiets as we take the small platform meant to be a stage, a few dozen people packed into the tiny bar. I grin at Erica, Dani, Nick, and my parents in the front row as I head for the mic and Heath takes the piano. The rest of the crowd is mostly comprised of my classmates with a professor or two thrown in there and some random townies.

The spotlight warms my skin as I pull the mic from its stand and whip the cord to the side. "How's everybody doing tonight?"

Erica lets out a "whoop!" while the rest of the room claps.

"Now, I don't know if you know this. But this is my very first time back onstage in over six months."

The applause thickens, more shouts adding in.

I do a little bow. "Thank you. Thank you. I'm so excited to be doing this here with you all. And I hope you don't mind that I roped a friend into helping me tonight."

I gesture to Heath at the piano, who ducks his head as he waves, and Erica lets out a loud, suggestive whistle.

"Now, in honor of such a special occasion, I thought we'd go back to my roots and start off with a throwback, if that's all right with you."

More applause, though it's mostly coming from my family in the front row. It sounds so different in such a small room compared to a stadium. But in here, it's not a blurry mass blocked out by the lights. Now, I can see each seat, each individual face.

Before, it felt like a dream. An illusion.

This feels so much more personal. Real.

I meet Heath's eyes before I smirk and raise the mic. "This first song is called 'Lie for Me.'"

I'M STILL BUZZING LONG after we leave the stage. It wasn't a full set—just three songs—and I'm already itching to get back up there. To sing until my voice gives out. To see how much of my old choreography I remember. To try out some of the new things I've been writing. It's not until I perform something live for the first time that I truly know if I like it, if it sticks with people.

And somehow, I didn't think about *him.* Not even once. I didn't spend the night searching every corner of the room, bracing myself for the worst. The bar had a few officers on standby, just in case, but it wasn't until I passed them on the way out that I even remembered they were there.

Maybe it's the antianxiety meds I started a few months ago, or the regular therapy appointments, or maybe it's just the time and distance from it all. But for the first time in a long time, I have this certainty that everything is going to be okay.

"You were *so* amazing up there," Dani gushes, hooking an arm through mine, Erica on my other side. "You really command every eye in the room. I don't think I looked at Heath once."

"That's not the insult you think it is," Heath says behind us.

"Not everything is about you, Cliff," says Dani, though she falls back to walk beside him. He swats her hand away as she tries to ruffle his hair.

I'm just glad the two of them have managed to stay close through all of this. Heath and his mom are talking again, but I can tell it's not like it was before. I hate that it's because of me, but at the same time, selfishly, I'm glad she didn't come tonight. I haven't seen or spoken to her since that night at her house, and although our paths will probably cross again eventually, that would have drastically changed the mood of the evening.

"It really was amazing." Erica squeezes my hand. "How did it feel?"

"Honestly? Like I never stopped. Hey, thank you guys so much for coming. You really didn't have to."

"Are you kidding?" says Erica. "I wouldn't have missed this for the world."

Our steps slow as we reach their rentals parked along the street across from the bar.

"So proud of you, bug." Dad smothers me in a hug the moment Erica lets me go, kissing the top of my head.

"I think that was my favorite performance we've seen from you," Mom agrees. "You were always so amazing as Ryker, but..." She trails off and gives me a watery smile, not bothering to hide her tears.

"Oh, please don't do that." I hug her before she can start crying in earnest and share a look over her shoulder with Nick. "I'll see you guys tomorrow for brunch?"

"If you can pull yourself away from your adoring fans," says Dad.

I roll my eyes, waving as everyone departs for their cars. I do a double take as Nick gives Dani a wave goodbye, looking kind of shy. Is he *blushing*?

Heath notices my attention and pulls me away before I

can tease him. "You don't think that's weird?" I hiss under my breath. "Your sister and my brother?"

Heath shrugs as we wander back through campus toward my dorm. His car is in the opposite direction, but he walks me home, the same way he has every day for the past two months he's been here. "It's a crush. And they live on opposite sides of the country. He'll get over it."

Flurries of snow twist through the air, though it's barely sticking to the ground and will be gone by morning. My breath puffs up in a cloud as I tilt my head back, relishing the sensation as the flakes melt on my face, the two mojitos I had warming me from the inside out.

"Didn't you at least have a *little* fun?" I ask.

A shudder rolls through him and he shakes his head.

I laugh and nudge his shoulder with mine. "That was only your second time onstage! And honestly, Dr. Galliot's class doesn't really count. You just need more practice."

"That's a nice thought, Parker, really, but I think I'll just leave the performing to you."

I say nothing, though *he'd* been the one set on getting up there with me tonight, not the other way around. So he can complain all he wants, but no one forced him into it.

But I know the real reason he did, even if he won't say it. He was worried about me performing for the first time again, and he suffered through the show just so I wouldn't have to be onstage alone.

"How was it?" he asks, a softer quality to his voice now. "Being up there as Parker?"

"Honestly? I didn't really notice. Did it seem different? Me performing as myself instead of Ryker?"

He shakes his head and tucks his hands in his jacket pockets. "You're a natural either way."

I snort and push him lightly in the chest. "Kiss ass."

He ignores that and gives me a sideways glance. "You didn't play any of your new stuff though."

I purse my lips, and I can picture the stack of journals staring accusingly from the corner in my room. All filled with new material but hidden away for only my eyes to see. "Don't think I'm quite ready for that yet. But I have another three years here to work up to it. Oh, sorry." I swipe at his coat, trying to get the glitter off. "Tell me this isn't what you were planning to wear to your interview tomorrow."

He shrugs. "Chefs are always eccentric, right? They'll probably think it was intentional. Well...here we are."

He props a shoulder beside the dormitory's entrance and crosses his ankles as I fish my key card out of my purse.

"I'll be at that interview for lunch, and I work until six, but I'll be around tomorrow night if you still need help studying for that stats test."

I groan. "Don't remind me. I'm pretending that class doesn't exist."

"How's that working out for you?"

The door beeps as it unlocks, and he grabs the handle to hold it open. This has become a familiar stance for us. The moment after he walks me home, just to the building, never to my room.

He smiles, just a soft curl of his lips on the one side. "You were great up there tonight. Never doubted you for a second."

"Wish I could say the same."

He clutches a hand to his chest like I've wounded him, then slips a finger beneath the bright pink wristband to rip it off. He holds it out to me but pulls back an inch before I can take it. "Don't throw it away."

"What are you—"

"For your scrapbook," he explains. "I think this night is worthy of a feature."

I fold my smile between my teeth as I take the wristband and tuck it safely in my purse. I started dabbling in an old scrapbook a few months ago, though I'm rusty, to say the least. But it's nice sometimes. To have something I can do with my hands when I'm trying to quiet my mind.

I almost forgot I'd mentioned it to Heath. It would have only been once, briefly. An insignificant comment that would have been all too easy to forget.

"Thank you, Heath," I murmur. "For walking me home, for doing this with me tonight, and just...for everything."

The amusement in his expression softens, his eyes holding mine. "Anytime, superstar. Goodnight."

"Goodnight," I echo. The heat washes over me as I cross the threshold, and I watch Heath through the glass door as he heads back the way we came, hands in his pockets.

It's been two months since he showed up here. Five since everything at the lake house. And despite the careful distance I've kept between us, true to his word, he hasn't left, and he hasn't pushed me. And now that his construction gig is wrapping up next month, he's looking for a more permanent position.

A part of me thought the healing would be linear. The hurt would fade until it disappeared. But instead, it's morphed into fear. Fear of crossing this line again. That now there's been too much build up. Too much time. Too much anticipation.

This friendship might be punctuated with words unsaid and suppressed temptations, but it's nice, in its own way. The easy laughs. How safe I feel when I'm with him. It feels fragile, unstable, like leaning too far to one side might have the entire structure tumbling to the ground. It's not exactly what I want with him, but it's better than nothing, right?

But those sound like excuses, even to me. A desperate attempt to keep him in my life without ever actually having to put my heart back on the line.

He said he'll wait, but I can't honestly expect him to hang around like this forever. It wouldn't be fair to him. But the thought of him moving on, of him giving up on me, of him falling for someone else...

I open the door before I can talk myself out of it. "Heath?"

He stops walking and hesitates before turning. The yellow streetlamp glows against the side of his face, small flurries of snow cutting through the pocket of light. "Yeah?"

I prop the door open a little wider, and his eyes track the movement. "Would you like to come in?"

The breeze kicks up, rustling his hair. He presses his lips together and shakes his head. "Parker, I...I wouldn't trust myself to keep my hands to myself if I did."

"Well then it's a good thing I don't want you to."

His eyes snap to my face, searching it. The moment lasts a lifetime. The snow falls harder between us, but the cold doesn't register. He takes a step closer, then another, never breaking my gaze.

A tremor works through me, and I can't put a name to it. Anticipation? Nerves? Fear? It only grows stronger as he crosses the last of the distance between us, joining me in the doorway. The air pulses, like lines of electricity connect us.

Slowly, he raises a hand to my cheek, pushing my hair behind my ear.

I swallow hard, my body shaking as he studies my face, his jaw working and his forehead creased.

"Are you sure?" he asks, his voice rough.

Unable to bear the tension any longer, I rise onto my toes and press my lips to his. His mouth opens for me instantly, his other hand coming to my waist as he kisses me slowly, softly.

His hair is damp beneath my fingers from the snow, and he tightens his arms, lifting me a few inches off the floor as he carries me the rest of the way inside.

"We can still take this slow," he murmurs.

"Oh, there's plenty more groveling left to do," I say, my lips curling into a smile against his as we back our way into the elevator. "But I think you can take tonight off."

"That's very generous of you."

I pull away to hit the button for the fifth floor, but Heath moves with me, his hands weaving into my hair, his hips pressing into mine as he backs me against the wall. The elevator lurches as it starts its ascent, and Heath's body cages me in, overwhelming every one of my senses with his scent, his touch, his taste, the low groan in the back of his throat, the piercing blue of his eyes as he gazes down at me.

"I won't let you down, Parker," he whispers. "I promise." He holds my face between both hands like something precious, breakable, looking at me almost in reverence as he slowly brings his lips back to mine, the kiss a slow, deliberate exploration of my mouth that sinks into me bone deep.

He drifts to my jaw, my neck, his hands gliding along my curves. My body responds to his touch of its own volition, arching into him, heat already pulsing between my legs with need like it remembers the last time even better than my mind does.

I let out a shaky laugh as his breath ghosts across my skin. "There's a security camera in here."

He hums, acknowledging this, then hits the emergency stop button with his fist and lowers to his knees.

"Heath!" I gasp as the alarm shrills overhead.

"Lift your foot for me." His hands slip up my skirt and tug my underwear down.

"Heath—"

"*Foot.*"

"You trapping me in an elevator again?" Bracing my hands on the wall for support, I do as he says. The moment he slips them off, he rises to his feet, locates the security camera in the corner, and reaches up to hang my panties over the lens. When he turns back to me, his smile has twisted into a devilish grin.

"Now, where were we?"

READ HEATH'S LETTERS

Download for free by signing up for my newsletter here:
https://dl.bookfunnel.com/ta179bq7wh

Which Katie Wismer book should you read next?
Try *The Anti-Relationship Year*—a standalone college friends
to lovers romance...and maybe learn more about that United
Fates singer Grey...